Praise for *12 Hours to Say I Love You*

'Beautifully tend...
Tom Allen

'This drowns in love'
Siobhán McSweeney

'Relatable. Funny. Glorious'
Deborah Frances-White

'Hilarious and heartbreaking'
Sara Pascoe

'Captivating. I loved it'
Rebecca Hall

'Witty, tender and compulsively readable'
Diana Gabaldon

'Wonderfully romantic'
Keira Knightley

'Such a brilliant, poignant story'
Isabelle Broom

'This novel will make you swoon'
Sunday Telegraph

'Tender and life-affirming'
Culturefly

'Smart, moving . . . A cleverly conceptual love story'
Metro

'Heartbreaking yet life-affirming'
Heat

'Such a beautiful love story'
My Weekly

Olivia Poulet and Laurence Dobiesz are writers and actors based in London. Married for six years, they have written together for radio and screen. *#blessed*, a comedy drama love story, was written by them for radio, and broadcast on BBC Radio 4.

12 Hours to Say I Love You

Olivia Poulet   Laurence Dobiesz

REVIEW

First published in 2022 by Headline Review
An imprint of HEADLINE PUBLISHING GROUP

First published in paperback in 2022 by Headline Review

Cataloguing in Publication Data is available from the British Library

Paperback ISBN 978 1 4722 7118 1

Typeset in 12.15/14.40pt Garamond MT Std by Jouve (UK), Milton Keynes

Printed and bound in Great Britain by Clays Ltd, Elcograf S.p.A.

HEADLINE PUBLISHING GROUP
An Hachette UK Company
Carmelite House
50 Victoria Embankment
London EC4Y 0DZ

www.headline.co.uk
www.hachette.co.uk

For our fathers, Peter and Roger, for believing in us.
And our mothers, Katie and Rebecca, for helping
us believe in ourselves.

Prologue

May 1997

Pippa

Bet Claire Danes didn't have to deal with any of this. Bet Leo was the consummate pro. Seamless connection in the casting, respect and deep admiration from the film studio and effortless communication with Luhrmann. The two will have demonstrated supreme support and onscreen kinship from day one.

Not like Jonty Ronson, who smoked a loaded skunk spliff on the way to the dress rehearsal, pulled a cataclysmic whitey and hadn't even learned his lines till yesterday. Jonty Ronson, whose flirty attention had led me to believe that he only had eyes for his Juliet, but who quickly became a plague on both the households, promptly marking his territory by snogging the Nurse, then fondling Lady Capulet's bounteous buttocks, and now trying it on with Lady Montague as she carries out her extensive (and exposing) physical warm-up. How am I supposed to move my audience to tears when my Romeo is too busy nuzzling his mother stage-left to run lines with me?

Deep breath, Pippa. And release. I shall not be dragged down by a lack of professionalism in others. I will give my all. I will sail over any troubling impediments thrust in my path. I will rise up like a phoenix from the dust. This is my big chance. This is the night I put any doubt aside and prove to my parents that I, Pippa Lyons, their only kith and kin, am destined to be a great actress. After all, it's not every day that a fifteen-year-old gets the lead role in the centenary play, is it?

And it's certainly not every day that the show is taking place in the local boys' school that my dad just happens to be the headmaster of. If there could ever be more reason for me to dazzle, I couldn't conceive of it. And boys playing *boys*!? Now there's a novel concept. Up until now, I've cornered the market in those roles: from Mr Bumble, to John Proctor, to Worzel Gummidge (okay, maybe the latter wasn't my finest hour), usually sporting a supremely itchy false beard and gamely kissing my own thumbs during any girl-on-girl embrace. But this is different. This time we have the full gamut of the sexes covered! This time I'm in a costume that actually fits! This time thumbs are to be replaced by human lips! And *this* time I'm playing the *lead*! And not just any lead – *Juliet*!

I spot Tania on the other side of the stage. She is as jittery as I am, hopping from foot to foot, fiddling with her cravat and occasionally throwing nervy punches into the air. Tania Marley. My partner in crime. My stubborn, excitable, ferociously loyal best friend from day one of junior school, when the deal was indelibly sealed over a swapped friendship bracelet and a shared passion for Garbage Pail Kids. The only girl from All Hallows Girls School who had insisted she play a boy's role despite the availability of the real McCoy.

'Sod that,' she had announced to our director (teacher) on the first day of rehearsals. 'We all know Mercutio's the most interesting part in this play, and *I'm* going to play him.'

And as usual, what Tania wants, Tania gets.

She looks up and sees me in the wings, her face breaking into a twinkly grin. She looks barely recognisable. Her unruly hair is scraped back into a slick bun, and heavily pencilled eyebrows make her face look even more angular than usual. She is wearing a black satin jumpsuit and gold cowboy boots and I already know her punchy and avant-garde Mercutio is going to bring the house down. With perfect synchronicity we raise our left arms and do our four-fingered BFFFE (Best Friends For Freakin' Eternity) greeting. It falls somewhere between the Girl Guides salute, the thing they do in *Star Trek* and an unfortunate touch of Heil Hitler. And with that we return to our own private panic chambers.

I begin circling my arms furiously, loosening my pelvis and humming sliding scales till my cheeks feel zingy. Next, I chew a ball of imaginary chewing gum in my mouth – a ball that grows bigger and bigger and bigger until I'm gurning like a madman, but no matter; as Dame Penny says in *Behind the Scenes*, 'an extensive warm-up is *essential* for Shakespeare'.

'Ten minutes, please, ladies and gentlemen!'

I glare at Mr Carter, who takes no notice.

'TEN MINUTES!'

He has no idea how penetrating his voice is. The whole audience will have heard that. They're probably laughing at it – we've probably lost them before we've even started. I peer through the shonkily erected curtain – a waft of lavender moth spray hits my nostrils – and out into the stalls (of our gym). Holy shit. It's Wembley Stadium out there. I am confronted by at least two hundred chatty, inebriated parents, drinking wine from beige plastic cups and consulting their programmes (pieces of A4 paper) with indulgent looks. My pumping heart catapults into my mouth. As if this packed house isn't bad enough, I suddenly see *them*.

Mum and Dad, side by side – on the FRONT ROW!

Mum is wearing more make-up than Lily Savage, a fuchsia-pink silk shirt with an oversized ruffle at the front, and as for her haircut, well, I can barely bring myself to look. It has been freshly cropped into a severe Rachel cut, along with half of Woking, most of the girls in my year, and me. I begged her not to do it. I implored. I went down on my knees. 'Get any style, Mum, any cut, any colour, just please, *please* don't get the exact same one as me!' But she just grinned and said, 'Pippa Lyons, you baffle me. Imitation is the highest form of flattering your trendy-wendy daughter, as someone famous and interesting once said! Anyway, your father thinks I look chic. So there!' She keeps swooshing her hair from side to side like she's the model in the Pantene advert (albeit a *very* old version), and I can see the poor couple in the row behind being savagely whipped across the face but being too English to say anything. Centre stage, as always. Even at *my* play. Quite an achievement.

She's giggling with Tania's mum, Sylvie, doing that cringey, hand-wavy thing she does when she's telling a story. Sylvie is lapping it up. It's so embarrassing. Anyone would think Mum was fourteen, not forty-six. Suddenly she lets out a colossal snort and a projectile spray of white wine squirts from her left nostril. Sylvie hiccups with delight as Mum pulls her red hankie from her coat pocket and blows her nose. They both find the whole thing deliciously entertaining.

No, no, no, Mum! Oh open up, ground, and swallow me, I beg you. What must people think? Why can't she just behave? Honestly. It's like she's never been to a *proper* theatre before.

Dad is slouched, almost out of view, reading the *Evening Standard*, or pretending to at least – surely it's impossible for him to concentrate with Mum carrying on like a hoodlum beside him? I can't say I blame him. I would want to hide too. Why does she have to be *so* embarrassing? I will never under-stand how my father, the sanest, calmest, wisest man in the universe, ended up with *this*. I mean, I love her, don't get me wrong, but she is volcanic. Everything she touches seems to erupt. Nothing is ever calm or simple. Everything becomes a drama.

4

I scan the sea of parents, just in case anyone else has an excitable untrained puppy for a parent. Nope – no one else's mum is behaving like they've been let loose in a sweetshop and are high on E numbers. God, why can't she be quiet and sophisticated like Alicia Koha's mum? Just look at her. Perfectly behaved. Seven rows back, legs neatly crossed, muted M&S colours, nostrils free of Chardonnay, carefully studying her programme (piece of A4 paper).

I retreat, letting the lavender curtain swish back into place. Thanks, Mum. How am I meant to focus now? How am I going to 'free myself from the shackles of the day-to-day and immerse myself in the universe of another'? Help me, Dame Penny. Surely you've a chapter on 'How to Block Out Mortifying Mothers in the Audience' somewhere in your book?

Right. Run my lines. That will get me in the zone. I close my eyes, breathe deeply and begin.

How now! Who calls?

Then comes Lady Capulet's line. Yep, another terrorising matriarch. God, poor old Juliet, she must have shared my chagrin. Wonder if her mum got a Rachel cut the very same moment— No, Pippa! Focus.

Madam, I am here. What is your will?

And then she says . . . Oh good God. What does she say? Think! Think!

Nothing.

My head feels thick. A rain cloud has taken refuge inside my brain, leaving no space for anything else. Clear it. Clear it.

Madam, I am here. I am . . . But they're gone. All of them! Every single one of the Bard's beautiful words. This can't be happening.

I hear the scraping of a chair and the tapping of a glass. Slowly the chatter peters out as a hush of anticipation descends. My father's steady voice emanates from behind the curtain. I peep out again.

'Good evening, ladies and gentlemen, friends, pupils, fellow St Vincent's staff. How lovely to see so many of you gathered here tonight for our centenary performance. Welcoming the staff, parents and pupils from All Hallows Girls to St Vincent's tonight is a real honour for me. A proper premiere!'

Someone claps and a student whoops.

'So. I won't give too much away about this little-known text you are going to witness tonight.'

A ripple of appreciative, knowing, parent laughter.

'Let's keep it as a nice surprise, shall we? What I will say, however, is that the hard work and commitment that has gone into this production, by pupils and teachers alike, is a testament to our magnificent schools and their passionate approach to the arts. Thank you all for your support, and enjoy the play.'

A burst of applause. I see Dad making to sit down, but then . . .

'Oh, and one last thing, for those of you who have glanced at the programme on your chair and may have noticed the surname of tonight's leading lady, I want to clarify that I had nothing whatsoever to do with the All Hallows casting in this production.'

More adulatory murmurs. A tidal wave of pride washes over me.

'And if anyone needs another drink or a visit to the toilet, now's your moment. The show will begin in five minutes.'

I swiftly draw my head back behind the curtain. How can he be so calm? Shit, shit, shit. We're about to start any minute and my heart is threatening to burst through my chest like that guy in *Alien*. Is this a heart attack? Is this what it's like to die? I can't remember the lines and now I'm never going to get my chance to show everyone what I can do. I squeeze my eyes shut, praying for a miracle.

'Hey, Pippa.'

I open my eyes, my heart still throbbing in my throat. A small, shadowy figure creeps up behind me. Is this what Death looks like? Come, sweet Death. Take me. You are welcome.

'Just wanted to wish you luck.'

His voice is vaguely familiar, but I can't place him. Maybe he's a stagehand? A stagehand wearing a cape? Well, stranger things with drama folk.

'Thanks. You too, er . . .'

'Steve. Gallagher. I'm playing Second Watchman.'

Second what?

'We've got a scene, well, a *bit* together. You know, at the end?'

Nope.

'I say, "Here's Romeo's man", move the Nurse's bench to the back and then I leave.'

No idea who I'm talking to.

'Oh yes! Of course. That bit at the end.'

Rehearsals, up till now, have been consumed by Jonty – furtive glances and meaningful accidental brushes of the arm. All other scenes and cast members have merged into one.

'Well, nice to meet – *see* you. Break a leg.'

I turn away. But he doesn't leave.

'I just wanted to say, you're amazing in this.'

I can hear he's blushing, even though it's too dark to see his face.

'And I always cry when you die.'

Wow. Bit weird?

7

'Five minutes, ladies and gentlemen of the company! FIVE MINUTES!'

Steve winces. 'He's so loud. Hope the audience can't hear.' He starts to fiddle with the string on his cape, wrapping it around his thumb like a threadbare bandage. The next bit comes out fast, his words tumbling over each other in their haste to be free.

'You just do this thing, this funny little thing with your mouth. And it makes me cry. Don't know why.'

We look at each other for a moment. It's different, not like with Jonty or the other boys. It's never easy being with them. I always feel the need to impress with a laddish joke or seduce with a flirty put-down, and invariably end up feeling mortified.

'Anyway, sorry. You need to prepare. I'll leave you to it.'

He begins to back away into the shadows.

'No! Stay.'

My fervour takes us both by surprise. And there's more.

'I can't remember any of my lines. Not a single one. They've all gone. I'm going to ruin this for everyone.'

The breath catches in the base of my lungs. Trapped like a caged bird. It's like the stitch I get in netball, only worse. More intense. Christ. Maybe this is a panic attack.

As he turns back to me, a shard of light catches his dark eyes. They are disarmingly gentle, and for one moment my manically pounding heart slows down; it's like he has opened a valve in me and the adrenaline is draining out of my feet like water. I look at him, willing him to save me. Suddenly he reaches under his cape and fumbles for something.

'Rescue Remedy. Four drops on the back of your tongue.'

He's holding out a small bottle. I take it from him, unconvinced.

8

'Mum got it for me. For my nerves. Not a natural performer, if you know what I mean. Not like you.'

'What am I meant to . . .'

'Here, let me show you. Stick your tongue out.'

I do as I'm told.

'Head back a bit.'

I tilt my neck. He unscrews the cap and carefully administers four drops of liquid from the small pipette onto my outstretched tongue. This should be embarrassing, but it isn't. It's strangely intimate.

''astes 'ike 'andy.'

Steve laughs. It's a rich sound.

'Yeah, it does. I think it basically *is* brandy, to be honest.'

How on earth did he understand me?

We stand in silence for a moment, the Rescue Remedy gently warming my chest. I don't know if it's the alcohol or his sweet unprompted kindness that is causing the change in me, but I feel my nerves subsiding.

'We can run lines if it would help?'

'But you don't know my scenes. Do you?'

He looks down at his feet for a second – school loafers doubling as Elizabethan boots.

'I've sat in on a few rehearsals. Maybe your first bit with Romeo? Act 1 Scene 5?'

How does that scene start? With me or Romeo? My mind, though calm, is still blank. Steve clears his throat.

'If I profane with my unworthiest hand this holy shrine, the gentle sin is this . . .'

He really *does* know the lines.

'My lips, two blushing pilgrims, ready stand,' he goes on, 'to smooth that rough touch with a tender kiss.'

And before I have time to think, my response bubbles out of me, almost like a natural thought.

9

'Good pilgrim, you do wrong your hand too much, which mannerly devotion shows in this; for saints have hands that pilgrims, hands do touch . . .'

I find myself holding my palm up as I do in the scene. He slowly does the same.

'And palm to palm is holy palmers' kiss.'

Our palms are pressed flat against one another's now. They feel warm . . .

'Beginners, ladies and gentlemen of the company. BEGINNERS!'

We are jolted back into reality with a thud. The house lights are dimmed, the audience finally falls silent, and we find ourselves plunged into expectant darkness. My stand-in Romeo's hand falls away from mine.

And as if by magic, out they come. Emerging from their cocoons to test their wings. Butterflies – the good kind. Fluttering up through my belly, a rush of energy like a fountain, and I know I've found her, I've found Juliet! This is it. My moment to shine. I've got it back together and am ready to blow their tiny minds. Waves of excitement displace the clots of terror that have been blocking my veins, and adrenaline courses freely through my body. I glance behind me, but the Second Watchman is nowhere to be seen, retreated into the shadows from whence he came. I'll thank him for the rescue stuff later. What was his name again? Never mind. This is *my* time.

I look out through a gap in the drapes, and can see Dad smiling proudly from his seat. I step out towards the bright lights, and into the unknown.

2 March 2019

00:39

He can't remember the last time he saw her so still. It was a joke between them, her inability to stop wriggling. His jack-in-the-box. Countless times he'd stopped a jiggling knee by laying his palm on it or stilled her tapping fingers with his own. Even her eyebrows had a life of their own, reacting to the world's mysteries like expressive windscreen wipers on a clip-art car.

What he wouldn't do now to see her fidget beneath the paper-thin hospital gown drowning her tiny frame. A shrug of a shoulder, a wrinkling of her nose, a point of her toe. Anything. But she is stony still. Her feet like carved alabaster, looking pale and somehow smaller than usual. The green crêpe of the robe barely masks the outline of her breasts, the swell of her stomach, the dip of her pelvis. As he watches her chest rise and fall, he feels an overwhelming urge to cover her with his jacket to keep her warm – an instinct from a thousand and one nights on the sofa, when the wriggling finally stopped, her head lolling dead on his shoulder, which told him she was asleep; his cue to pull the Scottish wool blanket over her and flick over to the football highlights.

A nurse brushes past him. She is focused and diligent. He moves aside to give her room, whispering a barely audible 'sorry' in her direction. She shoots him a quick, kindly look over her shoulder, a look that says, 'What have you got to be sorry for? I'm sorry for *you*.'

She's joined by another, younger nurse, a trainee, who falters for a second when she sees the state of the patient lying in front of her. She becomes aware of the man standing in the corner but avoids making eye contact, afraid that the pain he is radiating will burn her.

He watches the nurses inspect then reattach the half-empty drip, moving in practised synchronicity, keeping time with the rhythmic accompaniment playing from the machines. *Whir, beep, click. Whir, beep, click.* When they are finished, they glide away in tight formation, leaving a space for him to move into. But he doesn't make his move at first. He can't. He is trapped in the middle of a dance and he hasn't been taught the steps.

Slowly he edges closer to the bed, focusing on his wife's mouth – one part of her that, despite the cold plastic dummy forcing her teeth apart, seems almost unaltered. That freckle on her top lip, which she insisted was a beauty spot; that tiny scar on her chin cleft from the roller-skating disco at Alexandra Palace. If he were to shut his eyes tightly enough, he could transport that mouth to a thousand happy, hopeful places. He tries to ignore the blue and yellow hard collar that has been fitted around her neck (he remembers someone saying something about immobilising the spine, but it's all a blur). Instead, his eyes drift up to hers, and the sight of them forces out an involuntary moan.

Sockets black and green, crystal blood round her nostrils. Her forehead dark with bruising, hair plastered with more caked blood. His breath catches, fluttering somewhere between his chest and his throat, and he is forced to grip the rail surrounding the bed, desperately trying to remain upright.

'Mr Gallagher?'

He turns. A shape emerges from behind the black spots that have filled his peripheral vision. Polished shoes, white coat, clipboard. He tries to muster a response, but has momentarily forgotten how to form words.

'Steven?'

He blinks, thinks, then nods his head.

'I'm Mr Bramin, consultant trauma surgeon. You're the next of kin, is that right? The husband?'

Steve appears to register the question, but in truth it has sailed past him. His focus has instead landed on the man's face. His left ear lobe, to be precise.

Is that an earring?

'Your wife has suffered what we call a traumatic brain injury, where the brain has been shaken around inside the skull. Her condition is serious. As well as the head trauma, she has also sustained injuries to her pelvis, arms and chest. The CT scan revealed an epidural haematoma.'

Should a doctor – a qualified, life-saving doctor – be wearing an ear-ring? Earring says casual. Earring says youth. Earring says—

'We've removed a blood clot from her brain, and she's now sedated – placed into what's known as an induced coma. This will hopefully help relieve some of the pressure. We're going to keep her in intensive care, and our ICU nurses will monitor her closely. She is in very good hands. Her pulse, blood pressure, breathing and oxygen levels will be looked at regularly, as well as how much liquid she is taking in and how much urine she is passing. Then we can alter or adjust her medication accordingly. The next twelve hours are going to be critical. That's where you come in.'

Through the haze, a small opening. A muted flash of a lighthouse in a storm. A task. Steve understands tasks. Something to do, something practical. He forces his attention from Mr Bramin's ear.

'I can't make any promises, but we have seen some amazing recoveries when loved ones have kept talking to patients. Perhaps that could help your wife, too.'

'Pippa. Her name is Pippa.' Steve doesn't recognise his

own voice. It's the first time he's spoken out loud since he entered the building.

'Very good. Pippa.'

Bramin unhooks another clipboard from the end of the bed and scans the pages. He scribbles something, the sound of the scratching nib forming a new strain in the room's orchestra. Steve is still clinging tightly to the bed frame, as if he were on the deck of a sinking ship, the thin rail keeping him from falling overboard into the crashing waves.

Bramin replaces the clipboard and tucks the biro safely into his top pocket in one fluid movement. Steve feels a flutter of anxiety. Did he depress the nib? There wasn't a click. If he didn't, he will soon have a sprawling ink stain on his white coat. Ink is notoriously hard to get out in the wash. Steve knows this from when Pippa was flamboyantly telling him a story with an unsheathed ballpoint in her flailing hands. Should he say something?

'Does this all make sense to you, Mr Gallagher? Any questions?'

Whir, beep, click, breath. Whir, beep, click, breath.

'I don't know what to say to her.' Steve's voice is muffled, like he is deep underground.

'You'll think of something. Is there anyone you'd like to call? Family? A friend?'

'My phone-a-friend? I don't know. I could sure use a lifeline right now.'

Someone like the real Steve, the Steve who makes badly timed jokes, has finally entered the ward. Mr Bramin simply looks at him.

'Talk to her, Mr Gallagher. Exercise her brain. I believe she's listening.'

The doctor's pager vibrates. He looks down at it, then

gives the attendant nurses a cursory nod and sweeps out into the corridor.

The room falls quiet, but for the beeping and Pippa's small, supported breaths. Tentatively Steve takes her hand in his. It feels warmer than he expected.

Perhaps she is still in there.

He runs his index finger over her engagement ring, his grandmother's ring, an action as familiar as breathing, righting the small diamonds so they sit up, catching the light. But this time it feels different – almost like the moment he first slid it onto her finger seven years ago.

'What happened, Pip?'

Whir, beep, click, breath.

'Where the hell were you going?'

Whir, beep, click, breath.

He senses the fog closing in once more, and the lighthouse's beam vanishes into the mist. The room starts to spin. His legs buckle, and he sinks into the leather-wrapped foam of the chair beside the bed. He clutches her bruised hand to his chest. But it isn't Pippa's hand – it's limp, and punctured with a butterfly needle, unable to squeeze his back.

'Don't leave me, Pippa.' His voice is shaking now. 'Don't you dare leave me!'

He feels heat around his ribs, behind his eyes. A painful lump rises in his throat. A tear gathers and rolls off his lower eyelash, landing with a tiny *plink* on the bed rail. Just as he nears the point of collapse, something happens. A light touch on his shoulder. A human connection.

'There now. Deep breaths.'

The voice of the young nurse is kind and soothing. Steve does as he is told and breathes as slowly and as deeply as he can.

'You need to be strong now. For your wife.'

He wipes away a tear with the back of his sleeve. Nods.

'Just keep talking.'

'But how?' he says, his eyes wide and afraid. 'What about? Where do I begin?'

'Just begin at the beginning. Tell her you love her. Tell her *why* you love her.'

And with that, she leaves, the door swinging shut behind her.

'*Why* I love you? Bloody hell, we could be here all night. But as it happens . . .'

He gently brushes a strand of hair from her forehead and leans in, bringing his mouth close to her ear.

'Right then, Mrs Gallagher. If you're sitting comfortably . . .'

Whir, beep, click, breath.

'Shall we begin?'

November 2007

Steve

With my canvas kitbag weighing heavy on my shoulder, I turned right out of Embankment Tube and climbed the steps of the footbridge. A familiar walk, it was the way I always crossed the Thames, though I'm sure there are more expedient routes available to a smart commuter. It was the journey I happened to make when I arrived at Waterloo aged sixteen, on my first solo visit to London, destined for a point-less and regrettably expensive Christmas shopping trip to Oxford Street. ('Why didn't you just go to Bentalls in the town centre?' Mum was always right.)

Today I didn't mind jostling through the throng of suits hurrying home from their office jobs. I was glad to feel the sharp end of my Nikon D200 press against my hip when they bumped up against me. Poor sods, I thought. Some of us have just got lucky.

Today I didn't stop halfway over the bridge to admire the late November sun setting in the windows of the queuing red buses, the dome of St Paul's creeping up behind them. (Though I did get a little thrill to think what a great photo this could make, especially if I were skilled enough to cap-ture the blurred bodies of the rat-racers in the foreground.) Today I didn't care, because I had a job! An actual paid job, doing what I loved. Yes, it was only the launch of a spread-able butter, but still, the feeling was magic. I floated over the river, skipped down the Festival Hall steps and strolled along the South Bank, bouncing past the booksellers and skateboarders.

The only concern I had was Oscar, who had agreed to be my assistant for the event. He wasn't what you'd call reliable, dependable or, indeed, able, but he was my best friend, and I hoped his support might make me feel like less of a charlatan. Perhaps he was *valuable* (even if having him there meant I had to split my fee). I rested my bag on a bench and gave him a call.

'Stevie G!' he answered, as he always did. 'What you up to?'

'The job, Oscar,' I said. 'It's today. It's *now*.'

'I know.'

'Do you?'

'Sure, man.'

During our eight years of friendship, Oscar hadn't once sounded rushed or ruffled. If he was lying to me and had forgotten, I wouldn't have known.

'And you know it's the Tate Modern, yeah?' I said. 'Not Tate Britain.'

There was a pause.

'Modern, yeah. With the Warhols, right? Lovely stuff.'

'Right,' I said, as I veered off the Thames path towards the great brick monolith. 'Well I'm arriving now.'

'See you in a bit!' Oscar said, and hung up.

I had left plenty of time to get there, but suddenly the sky was darkening, so I picked up the pace, crossing a tree-lined square that was beginning to fill with nine-to-fivers necking plastic pints. I'd have to set up without him. A shame, really, but this was Oscar – what did I expect? I was hardly bouncing now, more goose-stepping, as the hard soles of my new black brogues slapped the concrete, weighed down by a great swinging sack filled with pretty much all the equipment I owned, about a quarter of which I really needed for the gig, but which I'd stuffed in because I wanted to look like I knew what I was doing.

''Ello, 'ello,' came a voice I knew. It was Oscar, who was leaning against one of the skinny silver birches.

'You're here?' I said, puffing slightly.

'Arrived early, man. Made some tricks under the arches.'

It was only then that I saw he was wearing baggy jeans, with a skateboard by his feet – feet that were clad in a pair of battered Vans.

'You better change your shoes,' I said.

'But I don't have anything else.'

'You're kidding? We can't go in like this!'

'Sure we can. It's an arty-farty crowd, they'll love it.'

'It looks like I'm a father who's brought his son to work.'

'What's wrong with that? My old man showing me the ropes.' Oscar could see I wasn't amused, and grew more serious. 'Here's an idea. I'll pull my socks over them, like we used to do to get into the Slug and Lettuce.'

'Your socks are white.'

'So they are. Shit.'

Oscar's eyes flickered to a group of smartly dressed women tottering towards the gallery. The launch party guests were arriving and I needed to be inside twenty minutes ago.

'Stevie, I can't help but feel a bit responsible,' he said. 'So tell you what – I'll waive my fee.'

'That's generous, mate.'

'Hey,' he said, kicking up his board. 'You got this.' He rolled it onto the path, jumped on and skated away. It was hard to stay mad at Oscar.

I followed the women to a side entrance, where a doorman was lifting a red velvet rope to admit them. He saw me, and drew himself up to his considerable height.

'Yes?'

He had perfected the doorman's thousand-yard stare, and as if in Pavlovian response to those Slug and Lettuce days, when Oscar and I had been turned away on many a Friday night by similar man-mountains, I started to perspire.

'I'm here for the launch. Val booked me.'

'Name?'

'Steve – Steven. Gallagher. The photographer?'

He frowned, then put his finger up to an earpiece that was sitting uncomfortably in the cauliflower floret stuck to the side of his head.

Take a breath, Steve, I told myself. Chill out. This is going to be fun. You're living the dream, remember? You're here now, and—

'Late, are we?' said Val, the event manager. 'Not a great start.'

'Yeah, sorry – the guy on the door . . .' I said, daring to blame the doorman now he was out of earshot. Val was having none of it.

'Thought we had an assistant?'

'We did. I did. Yes,' I stuttered. 'But he's ill. Sorry.'

'I don't care,' she snapped back. 'As long as we get all the shots.'

She'd been so nice on the phone when she booked me, but now she was frogmarching me through back of house like I'd been caught shoplifting. She pushed me through a set of double doors into a kitchen, where harried chefs were stuffing mini Yorkshire puddings with slices of roast beef and squirts of horseradish, then through another door into a dark, crowded cube.

The heat of two hundred bodies hit me. My eyes adjusted to the pinky-purple haze to reveal a mass of guests, all shouting into each other's ears to be heard above the din. I didn't know if it was the music or my heart that I could feel pumping, but I was worried. *Where's the light?* How was I meant to capture a decent photograph in here? It was more like a nightclub than an art gallery. I looked around for somewhere to drop my bag.

'Is there an office, or a cloakroom perhaps?'

I could only hear snatches of Val's answer, but I got the gist: '. . . *so* busy . . . limited space . . . *very* important guests . . .'

She stopped short and lassoed the arm of a woman I vaguely recognised from the tabloids. One of the VIGs.

'Can we . . . here with the lovely Kerry?' All smiles now as she plonked the tipsy bleached blonde in front of me. Kerry's eyes were glassy. She needed to visit the St John Ambulance for a nice cup of tea and a digestive.

'Erm . . .' I hadn't even turned my camera on, let alone taken a test shot, but Val was waiting impatiently, so I pulled it out and took three snaps (to avoid blinking eyelids) before Kerry staggered back to the bar.

'Did we get a good shot?'

I knew we hadn't, but I glanced perfunctorily at the screen on the back of my Nikon, trying not to wince too visibly when I saw the full extent of the horror: an unfocused swirl of bodies with Kerry's uplit magenta face in the centre. A bit like Munch's *The Scream*, though this would never hang in any gallery. I couldn't even sell it to the *Daily Mail*.

'Looks great,' I lied.

'Over there, Keith and . . . get them next to the branding. Chop chop!' Val clapped her hands, then waved me towards a couple who were propping up the trestle table bar.

'Can I just fix the flash on? The light's a bit . . .'

But she was already there, throwing her arms wide at the celebs, air-kissing them, before beckoning me to join. I put on a smile and walked over as slowly as I could, trying to give myself an extra second to blindly fumble out the flash and click it into place on top of the camera. Stumpy, dishevelled Keith stood beside a trendy-looking girl with a sheer black fringe. Behind them, on a stretched canvas, were the words *Edibility and Spreadability* with a pair of red lips erotically welcoming a very buttery slice of bread. I quickly set the camera to auto, said a little prayer, then *snap snap snap* and they were off, leaving behind a row of drained champagne flutes on the white cloth.

'. . . just leave you to it? Make sure you . . . speeches in an hour.' And with that, Val disappeared.

Now, how awful are these shots?

I looked at the display, zooming in on Keith's face, and was pleasantly surprised at how passable the image was – average, even! I scrolled across to inspect the branding behind him. It was a little bit overexposed, sure, but I could fix that later with a bit of—

My heart stopped and the room fell silent around me. I was paralysed by a cluster of pixels staring back at me from the tiny screen. Specks of colour that seemed to represent a tied-up bunch of red hair, that familiar jawline, lips parted in concentration, all sitting between those slightly jutting shoulders . . .

I lowered the camera and the crowded party began to swing again, the photograph coming back to life in front of me. But she was gone. Like a birdwatcher who had let a rare sighting escape him, I followed her direction of flight. *There!* A swish of ponytail, ducking between cuffs and cocktail dresses, trying to slip out of my grasp. Back on the scent, I drove forward, but was slowed by a bottleneck at the canapé hotspot where the bar and the entrance to the kitchen met. Ahead, the ponytail was destined for the exit. *Think fast, Steve.*

'Excuse me,' I called out. I wasn't exactly sure what I was going to say next (I fear it was 'Coming through!'), but to my great relief, I didn't have to say anything. As the guests turned to face me and spotted my camera, they fell obediently into position, pouting, awaiting the flash. I obliged – *snap snap* – before moving on. The sea parted as other guests felt me coming, robotically posturing with an arm round their partner's waist, dropping a bony hip. I snapped gratefully – only once now, and only in their general direction – until I was free and heading for the door.

The skipping in my heart dropped down to my belly as I peered into a narrow, dimly lit anteroom. On my right, a bored-looking guy, installed as guardian of a rail of designer coats, looked up at me for a second before deciding I was no one important and returning to his phone. And there ahead, only yards away, was Pippa. Even with her back to me, and after all these years, I knew it was her. Something unmistakable in the way she was arched over, awkward yet elegant, like a ballet dancer limbering up at the barre. One hand was rubbing a shoeless heel through her tights, the other grasped a fold of the black curtain that lined the walls of the make-shift cloakroom.

I cast a shifty glance at the coat guardian, but he was still buried in his phone.

Here goes. I cleared my throat.

'Need a plaster?'

Hero. Always prepared. Now I was glad I packed for all eventualities.

She turned sharply, losing her balance. As she staggered towards me, I knew I had to catch her. In one move, I let the bag slip from my shoulder with a cracking thud – *there goes a grand's worth of uninsured accessories* – before lurching forward and taking her gallantly in my arms. As we found ourselves in a tangled embrace, I noticed that her hair was glowing a shade redder under the light.

'Whoa! Shit, sorry,' she said, looking up at me.

'No, my fault. I made you jump.'

We fixed on each other's eyes – hard not to when you're three inches apart – and immediately I became worried that I'd held onto her a beat too long, so attempted to stand us both up. This required a reverse lunge, a manoeuvre that would surely be challenging enough under my weight alone, but with Pippa in my arms . . . I strained to make it feel quick and effortless, and a very non-gallant squeak was emitted. Pippa laughed. I had to earn back some cred, so I flipped open a side pouch on my bag and pulled out the green plastic Compeed box. She laughed again.

'Oh, you actually do have some,' she said, impressed (I think).

'Take any one you like,' I offered.

As she peeled the plaster away from its wrapping, I tried not to stare at the uniform she was wearing – a tight black top with our buttery employer's cringeworthy slogan emblazoned across her chest. I'd imagined bumping into her again so many times, trialled the conversations we might have over and over in my head; but now that she was here, I was tongue-tied, petrified of the silence opening up between us.

Say something. Anything.

'Well, fancy meeting you here.'

Anything but that, you idiot.

I couldn't read Pippa's expression. Her lips wore a smile but her eyes weren't so sure.

'Both of us . . . here.'

'I'm sorry,' she said. 'Do we know each other?'

'It's me,' I said. *'Steve.'*

Still no flicker of recognition.

This was definitely not one of the reunion scenarios I'd envisaged. There was nothing else for it. I had to adopt my best Kenneth Branagh voice and find my light . . .

'Here's Romeo's man.'

And there it was. I could almost see the tsunami of memories – tumbling, crashing snapshots that flickered behind her eyes like a fast-paced résumé at the start of a second series. The nervous first rehearsal. The bus rides home with Pippa holding court on the back row. The cheap hot chocolate I surprised her with as she stood shivering, underdressed for the fireworks.

'Steven Gallagher. My God. It's been—'

'Ten years. I know. Time flies.'

'What are you doing here? Are you a waiter too?' She clocked my camera. 'A photographer. How cool are you?'

I said a prayer, asking the pink light to spare my blushes.

'Sure,' I said. 'You must remember me at St Vincent's? Coolest kid on campus.'

'Of course I remember you,' she smiled. 'It's just you look so . . . grown up.'

'Thank you?'

'Sorry. I meant that as a compliment.'

'I'll take it.'

Now it was her turn to blush.

'Don't suppose you've got a fag in that Mary Poppins bag of yours?' she said. 'My break's about to start.'

'Absolutely,' I said, though I'd never smoked in my life. 'I'm gagging for a smokeroo . . . er, fag.'

'Amazing. Can I . . .'

'Er, I left them inside, on the . . . side. I'll just go and get them.'

I re-entered the fray, having completely forgotten what I was meant to be doing at this party. The roar in the dark gallery filled my ears. Everyone talking, no one listening. A silver-haired couple, glamorous and flushed with boozy excitement, turned towards me, flashing white teeth. For a moment I thought they were just pleased to see me. Then I realised that they were posing – tilting their champagne flutes ten degrees and waiting expectantly for me to take their photograph. I duly snapped them, three times, as if on auto-pilot. A waitress squeezed between the couple, holding aloft a vast tray of canapés whilst self-consciously covering her chest with her free arm.

Edibility . . . Spreadability. That's why I'm here!

I cast my eyes around the room, from table to table, searching for an unattended pack. Nothing. *Damn that smoking ban! No one's at it any more.*

'How are we getting on?' Val was upon me, bouncing impatiently on her toes like she needed the toilet.

Would it be unprofessional to ask her if she smokes? The look in her eyes said yes, but I allowed myself a little sniff at the air as she spoke, just to be sure.

'I need one of Dale,' she said. 'He's just arrived.'

'Sure thing,' I said. 'Which one is he?'

'You're kidding, right?'

'Of course. Ha!'

She didn't appreciate my cheeky joke, probably because she knew it wasn't one.

I set forth to find this Dale, while actually trying to find a pack of Marlboro Lights. The launch had been one Easter egg hunt after another, but I didn't mind – the prize at the end was worth it. (*She's not a prize, Steve. And she won't be waiting for you much longer if you don't come back with a ciggie soon.*)

'Dale?' I said feebly to every man I passed who might suit the name. 'Dale? Dale?' But no one was answering to it.

If there was a crowd gathered round someone here, I thought, hanging on their every word or trying to get a selfie, then I could pick out the celebrity. I should have done my homework – should have watched more daytime TV at uni.

'He's just arrived,' Val had said, so he should be near the entrance.

Sure enough, a tall, tanned man *was* lingering at the threshold, looking around for the safety of someone he knew. He took a glass of champagne from a waiter whose arms were trembling under the weight of a heavily colonised tray.

'Dale?'

'That's me.' He brightened, dialling up the charm.

'Thank God it's you,' I said. 'Can I get a photo?'

Snap snap snap. And then, without thinking, 'Got a cigarette, Dale?'

He looked at me, stunned.

So unprofessional.

'It's for a girl,' I said. 'From school. I mean, not a schoolgirl, obviously . . .'

Balls. Time to put my camera on eBay. I'll never work again.

Dale put a hand on his hip and leaned backwards like the Laughing Policeman. I was off the hook. Even better, when he'd recovered from his peals of laughter, he pulled a box of twenty from his inside pocket.

'Help yourself,' he said.

My heart was thrumming, legs prickling under my thermal long johns. I was fifteen again, fireworks above my head and in my belly. I'd escaped my sister and her boyfriend (reluctant chaperones, happy to lose me as they snogged in front of the bonfire), my white Reeboks ruined from the wet sludge of the out-of-season cricket pitch, returning from the clubhouse to a crowd of cool kids with two plastic cups of hot chocolate.

Back in the cloakroom, a couple of waitresses had snuck in a tray of canapés, which they were sharing with the protector of the cloak rail, wolfing them down in a huddle, staying vigilant in case Val wandered in to catch them in the act. But Pippa wasn't there. Had she given up on me?

'Excuse me,' I said. 'Do you know Pippa?'

A waitress nodded, her mouth full.

'Do you know where she went?'

She shrugged.

'Do you know where you can smoke? On your break?'

She rolled her eyes, then, chewing deliberately on the last morsel of Peking duck pancake, flicked her head towards the emergency exit.

I let myself out onto a freezing fire escape, where the music and chatter from the launch party gave way to shouting and clanging from the busy kitchen, which poured through an open window. A pair of chequered trousers swung out over the ledge. They belonged to an agitated chef, who didn't waste any time lighting up a cigarette and inhaling deeply.

'Steve!' Pippa called out. 'Up here!'

She was sitting at the top of the iron staircase, hugging her legs. I clambered up, still towing my ridiculous bag. The handrail had turned to ice, making my fingers ache.

'Ta-da! Two of my cigarettes and – bonus – two hoisin wraps.'

She thanked me through chattering teeth.

'Hang on,' I said, and I pulled an *Evening Standard* from my bag and spread it out like a picnic blanket. I shared out our duck wrap dinner, which we clinked together in a mini toast, then she produced a bright green lighter from inside the waistband of her skirt and lit a cigarette, savouring the first drag like the angry chef had done. It looked tempting – almost. She turned the flame to me.

'Oh,' I stuttered. 'No. I've just had . . . I've had *loads* already.'

'I'm the same,' said Pippa. 'It's the only thing that gets me through these soul-destroying catering jobs.'

'That and meeting nice people?'

'Yeah, right. The staff are all miserable and the guests are all like, "so, are you Edible and Spreadable, too, darling?"' I didn't point out that by *nice people*, I meant me. 'The view up here is kind of amazing, though,' she said.

I hadn't even noticed the view, but it really was. The lights reflected on the Thames were truly dazzling from this height. As if someone had turned the city on to high definition. The sky was crystal clear, and pinprick stars were appearing all around us.

'So,' I said, 'what do you do?'

What a terrible question. I sounded like Prince Charles addressing a line-up on a royal visit.

Pippa shrank slightly. 'I'm *trying* to be an actress,' she said, as if this required an apology.

'But that's great! I hoped you would be.'

'Really?'

'You were so good – *are* still good, I'm sure.'

'You don't have to say that.'

'I mean it. I used to watch you in awe from the wings. The rest of us were acting in a school play, but you were . . .' I felt my mouth turning dry. 'How you spoke the words and made it all sound so, you know, real?'

Pippa smiled through the haze of smoke escaping from her nose.

'Ignore me,' I said. 'I'm talking rubbish.'

'No. I like how you speak your words, too.'

We sat like that for a moment, listening to the sirens and the crackle of her cigarette, which was diminishing too quickly for my liking.

'I never thanked you, did I?' she said. 'For being so kind to me that night. And so calm. Or for your magic rescue potion.'

'You can thank me now.'

Pippa took a final drag, stubbed out the cigarette and flicked it over the edge. I feared that meant our picnic was over.

'Thank you, Steve.'

We looked at each other, and suddenly we were back in the wings at St Vincent's. It might have been the cold, but my palms began to tingle. The five-minute fag break stretched before us and behind us, as if we had all the time in the world. Did she feel the same?

'Your turn now,' she said. 'Photography! Exciting.'

'It is. I think. This is only my . . . tenth or eleventh job, to be fair.'

'Wow. You're busy.'

I shrugged nonchalantly.

'Shame you don't do headshots.'

It is *a shame I don't do headshots!* a voice cried in my ear. *I could do headshots. Why don't I do headshots?*

'I do, as it goes,' I said. Another little lie.

'Really?' asked Pippa.

'Well, I'm trying to break into that field. Just need a guinea pig.'

'I could be your guinea pig! You could do me a freebie? Boost your portfolio.'

I had to swallow so hard on my excitement, it made me hiccup.

'You're on,' I said.

'Next Wednesday?' she suggested.

I pretended to consult my extremely busy mental diary.

'Yep. Wednesday could work, actually.'

'Cool. Well. See you then.'

We were facing each other now, inches apart, our icy breath mingling. Neither of us seemed to want to move.

*

When I stepped back inside, the launch had hit its riotous peak. This time I was swept up by the music and clamour. Lifting my lens to the room, I captured the drunken joy in the guests' faces and was reminded why I loved this; why I was risking being poor, risking the sharp cut of my mum's disparagement. I was a snap-happy pap, at the top of his game. I even joined in with the dancing for a second, something I hadn't done since my sister June's wedding. Maybe it was inadvisable to high-five Dale, but it was my party now and the smiles and laughter were all for me!

So I lied about being a more experienced photographer to impress her. That was okay, right? At least I didn't stare at her chest – dear me, no mean feat. And the headshot thing? Just another white lie. *Better get practising. Better clean the flat. Wednesday, Wednesday, Wednesday.*

Pippa appeared from behind the bar carrying a bottle of champagne wrapped in a white cloth. Would bubbles be too much on a first headshot date? *Slow down, cowboy.* She looked across at me and raised it to her mouth, taking a joke swig. It was full, so a spurt of liquid fizzed from the neck. She couldn't hide a flash of panic, her eyes bright with laughter but her mouth crooked with guilt. I raised my camera and snapped her, and she shot me a chastising glare before moving off.

This is going to be fun, I thought. And I didn't mean the shoot on Wednesday; I meant the rest of our life together. I knew deep down I was being hugely optimistic – that she wasn't interested in me, not like that – but I allowed myself to get carried away by the excitement. Anything was possible with this girl, and any doubts or fears had lifted. I looked down at the photo. It was the best thing I'd ever captured: candid, fun and beautiful. Pippa in a nutshell.

Yes, she's out of my league. Yes, I'm an amateur, with the camera as well as women. But I don't care, because I got a date!

2 March 2019

01:39

It would be slanderous to the coffee bean to allow this insipid liquid to share its name. More like the juice that gathers in gutters after an April shower. Whatever it is, Steve's hands are shaking so much that most of it is now spreading across his crotch. Still, he can't let go of the plastic cup; it is a lifebuoy keeping him afloat.

Something in the repetitive action of drinking is soothing. Lift, tilt, sip, repeat. Lift, tilt, sip, repeat. Cause and effect. Anything that gives a modicum of order in this hurricane. He pulls a handkerchief from his jacket pocket to wipe himself down, and is paralysed by six tiny embroidered words in a corner of the cotton square: *One Year On, My Only One.*

The memory floods over him in technicolour. A twilight walk. A 'Pippa Picca-Nicca' of cheese and Marmite sandwiches squashed into an old ice cream tub, a slightly burnt sponge cake and warm Prosecco slugged from the bottle. The canary yellow of her new sandals. A light package placed lovingly in his hands. 'Happy anniversary, my darling.' Their smiles colliding as she pressed her Vaselined lips against his.

Steve stares at the swirling letters.

My Only One.

My Only One.

He stands, steadies himself, then leans over his wife, trying again to focus solely on her lips, perfect and unbroken.

'Let's clean you up a bit, darling.'

He licks the hankie to moisten it, then gently, tentatively, as if she is made of fine glass, dabs at her blood-streaked forehead. It's so dry, almost ironed on, that barely a fleck dislodges.

'There. Better. Beautiful.'

He slips the precious handkerchief back into his coffee-stained jeans and looks around the room.

What next?

He can think of nothing to do or say to help save her, not really. The bare walls of the ICU feel like they are closing in, slowly but persistently, focusing their blankness on him and threatening to expose his presence here as entirely futile. Somewhere nearby, a clock is ticking. He hasn't heard it before, but it gets louder and louder, the second hand moving in unison with a vein sending blood rushing past his temples. The bass drum of the pump as her chest rises. The creak of air as it swiftly falls.

He could leave her for a moment. Go outside into the corridor to quieten the noises that are crowding his thoughts. Movement. A change of scene. That would be positive.

No. Too far away.

If he leaves her now, even for a minute, it could allow whatever did this to her, whatever wicked spirit or masked intruder made invisible by the dark of the night, to slip under the door and snatch her away from him.

No. Not on my watch.

'I'm here, Pip. I'm not going anywhere. I won't let anything hurt you.'

He speaks the words out loud to cut through the noise, but when he hears them, they lack weight. Words that used to have meaning, that would never fail to stir something in Pippa, are now as flimsy as a moth's wing.

Too little, too late. How can this be? He swore to protect her. To lay down his life for her. To keep her from harm.

Now look at her.

Lifeless, but for the bellows-like ventilator. A husk. A shadow. Bloodied, bruised, broken. His vibrant, energetic, infuriating soulmate. His lover and friend and champion, holding on by a mere whisper, dangling on a silken thread between light and endless dark.

With clenched fists and eyes shut tight, he shakes his head violently, as if trying to refresh her image in his mind's eye. A picture from the past. Her smile when she kissed him goodbye. Her giggle when she found that cartoon sketch he did of her folded into the tooth mug. Her yelps when she stubbed her toe on the hoover and hopped around the hallway.

Anything but this.

He tries words again, some normal conversation this time – if they have no weight, try something light for size.

'The shoot went really well, I think. Never can tell a hundred per cent, but I can't wait to show you the pictures. Got a few I'm really proud of. The client seemed happy, so fingers crossed . . .'

So pointless, so trivial. He ploughs on.

'Best of all, the main woman had a nine-week-old puppy she carried around in a Chanel handbag. You'd have loved it.'

Whir, beep, click, breath.

'Guess what breed it was?'

Whir, beep, click, breath.

'A Shit-Poo! I kid you not.'

He attempts a smile. It feels alien on his lips.

'She tried to tell me it was a *Shy*-Poo, but I wasn't having any of it. A Shih Tzu and a poodle does not a Shy-Poo make.'

Whir, beep, click, breath.

'Definitely a Shit-Poo, am I right?'

'My fella has a collie–poodle cross.' A sing-song voice from the end of the bed.

Steve turns round sharply to find a nurse unclipping Pippa's notes. A slim, stubbled man in a blue mob cap.

'I mean, everyone's at it now, aren't they? A dog's not a dog without a bit of poodle thrown in,' he chuckles, moving round the bed to inspect Pippa's monitors. 'I wanted to say Poo-Coll, but apparently they're Collie-Poos. Less fitting if you ask me, which of course he wasn't. I'm Craig, by the way. You'll be seeing a lot of me. Just checking your lovely wife's vitals.'

As he leans close to Pippa's head, he sees her for the first time, and his joviality dissolves, replaced by a single-minded focus. His voice drops in register.

'Hello, Pippa. I'm just going to check your oxygen levels and see where we're at.'

He turns the screen towards him and begins jotting down notes on the clipboard. Steve scrutinises his face for a hint, but Craig's expression barely alters.

'How's she doing? Any change?'

Craig writes quickly, avoiding Steve's eyes.

'I'm just going to have a quick word with the doctor about something.'

'But can you—'

'I'll be right back.'

He leaves, and Steve is alone with Pippa again. The room should be quiet now, but the white noise is sudden and earsplitting. His heart throws itself against his ribs like a caged tiger. The walls constrict again, squeezing the breath from his lungs.

He clamps his eyes shut, battling the flight impulse with every fibre of his being. Finally he slides his camera bag from under the chair.

'I brought you something.'

He pulls out a small, squashed lump, swaddled in a wad of kitchen towel.

'Granted, they don't look very appetising now, but I swear they're the best brownies. I wrestled the last two off a waitress and got her to wrap them for you. The guests were like gannets. I saw one bloke filling his briefcase. Fudgey, with a crunch on top. Just as you like them.'

Whir, beep, click, breath.

'I'll just pop them here. You can have one when you wake up.'

He places the brownies on the bedside cabinet, empty but for a wisp of plasticky paper, torn off some sterile packaging.

'And if *that's* not a reason to come back to us, I don't know what is!'

Whir, beep, click, breath.

Looking down into the open bag, he reaches in perfunctorily, removing a *Time Out* and his wallet. He places them beside the brownies, not intending to read, but wanting to introduce a semblance of homeliness, perhaps. He picks up the wallet, slips a finger behind a rarely used loyalty card and pulls out a small black and white photo. A tattered cutting, about the size of a passport picture, from a contact sheet of headshots he took over a decade ago. His favourite photo of Pippa – head thrown back, cheeks pushing her eyes into a squint, a lock of cascading red hair falling across her cheek. A split second of pure, invincible, youthful joy, fossilised in his wallet.

He runs his finger over her face.

'I know you're still in there. Come back, my darling. Come back to me.'

November 2007

Steve

Half asleep, I reached for the water beside my bed, carefully transporting it to my lips so as not to spill its precious contents, and chugged the half-filled pint glass in one. It was not enough to quench the scorched desert that was my mouth. The dastardly red eyes of my digital clock told me it was 6.20 a.m. I couldn't snooze now. I might as well get up.

Nursing a fresh glass, I sat on the loo long enough to read a year-old *Empire* magazine cover to cover (a bellyful of butterflies, beer and north-west London's cheapest pizza had made for a rude awakening).

On my way to the kitchen, I passed a shadow in the shape of Hugo, my Spanish housemate. We respectfully ignored each other. Hugo was so elusive that sometimes I thought he might only exist in my imagination. I would often hear him arriving home in the wee hours, only to set off again before I was out of bed. I didn't know if it was the party or the work end of the candle he was burning hardest, but he looked like the walking dead.

I shuffled along the worn carpet in my beloved slippers, shivering, willing the sun to rise and warm the place up a bit. The central heating had never been turned on – I wasn't sure if it even worked – and this was not the day to test it. The flat sat above a carpet shop (I'd asked the landlord a couple of times if he could replace ours with something less sticky; even offered to go downstairs and try to haggle a discount from my buddies in the shop, but he never returned my calls). If the boiler were to explode, the fire would quickly spread downstairs, Carpet Planet would become an inferno and Kilburn High Road would be known as the new Pudding Lane. For the time being we'd make do with jumpers and lower gas bills, which suited us fine.

Oscar lay sparked out on the tiny sofa in the kitchen. His body was all bent out of shape, limbs at right angles. I put the kettle on to make a cup of tea, as quietly as I could, though there was no danger of being heard above his rasping snores. He could sleep anywhere, could Oscar, free of any anxiety, oblivious to the stresses and pressures of the real world. I envied him. He looked so . . . asleep.

It was a dark, chilly morning – the start of a cold snap, the weather report said – which only served to make the flat look more uninviting. My head had begun to pound. *How am I so hung-over?* I was reminded how by a dozen lager cans lying crumpled by the bin. 'I'm not drinking,' I'd told Oscar before he arrived. 'I need to be on it in the morning.' But one with dinner inevitably led to two, and two times three is six beers each.

I put the offending beers in the recycling (ripping apart the plastic loops to avoid strangling any seagulls) and began digging around the freezer to try and find some bread for toast. If I didn't eat something soon, I might pass out. On the top shelf there was a Tupperware box of Mum's shepherd's pie alongside half a choc ice; the second shelf had fish fingers and bits of broken pitta bread; and on the third shelf, nothing. I inspected the choc ice; it looked fine, no green bits, so I ate it and was glad of the sugary hit.

A few hundred kilojoules were then spent trying to figure out the optimal layout of some carefully chosen props that I'd bought to dress the kitchen table. A scented candle (vanilla and cinnamon – festive yet classy, I thought), some chocolate brownie bites arranged on our one unchipped plate, and a book on New York street photography the size of a breeze block. I found that if I put the candle in the middle it looked too much like a dinner date. If the plate of brownies was in the middle they were too far away to reach, but if they were at the edge it looked like they'd been sitting there, forgotten, for a few days. The book was best suited to the middle of the table, but if she picked it up it would uncover an ugly patch where the varnish had flaked away over the years (not helped by me picking at it while listening to particularly nerve-racking episodes of *The Archers*, a detail I intended to share with no one, ever). Eventually I settled on the 'cluster' configuration: all three items scattered nonchalantly more or less in the centre.

I lit the candle, to help get the ambience established, then stood back and admired my work.

Not bad.

A patch of light appeared on one arm of the battered sofa, the sun finally poking its head round the corner of the snooker hall over the road, brightening the room in warmer golden shades. But the result was the same – it was still a shithole.

'Got to sort this place out,' I said, hoping the message might drift into Oscar's dreams and rouse the Sleeping Beauty of the Settee.

Pippa would be coming up the stairs soon, expecting to find herself in a professional headshot photographer's apartment-cum-studio, not the set of *Withnail and I*. What if she was early? What if her Tube skipped some stops, went full-on Bakerloo Line Express?

'You ready for your date then?' Oscar yawned, one eye on me, the other stuck shut.

'It's not a date,' I said. 'If it was a date, I wouldn't have asked you to be here.'

He put himself back together like a crash dummy, forcing his neck and spine into place with clicks that went right through me.

'Why am I here again? Oh yeah, to be your manservant.'

'It's called a job, mate.'

'A *job*, you say?' He adopted a hybrid French–Polish accent. 'I 'ave never 'eard of dis vord, *job*.'

To his credit, he'd leapt at the chance, keen to make up for the Tate Modern debacle. (I didn't tell him I was actually pleased he didn't make it past security in the end. If he'd been working with me that night, would I have chased Pippa down? Would we have had our moment on the fire escape? Would I now have reason to rope him in to pose as my assistant for the day, hoping this might put Pippa at ease and help support the narrative that I was the very employable headshot photographer I wasn't?) I'd attempted a briefing last night, before the second beer was opened, telling him that he'd be expected to fetch coffee, hold reflectors and change batteries – all of which went in one ear and out the other, all of which I knew I'd end up doing myself. In fact, Oscar might be the last person you'd want to call on for help with something like this. But who else to ask? I could probably count my close, trusted friends on one finger.

My sister June, I suppose, was a possible candidate; she wasn't working at the moment. But I knew what she'd say: *What are you playing at, Steve? You're lying to this poor girl, trying to get into her pants. I thought you were better than that.* And then I'd have Mum on the phone: *What's this our June told me? You had a girl round your flat? Why haven't I met her?* Then there was Lola, of course. She'd come and play the assistant superbly, I had no doubt. But it would break her heart.

Oscar was up now, and sniffing round the table, nostrils twitching, like a hog at the foot of a truffle oak.

'Euch!' he retched when his snout fell on the candle. 'That is nasty.'

'It isn't.'

'Where did you get it, pound shop?'

'No.' I reached across and cradled the candle in both hands, defending my purchase. 'It's meant to be deluxe.'

'It's giving me a headache.'

'I'll blow it out, then.'

I did so, and the scent intensified. It *was* bad, like someone had sprayed cheap air freshener in a hot car to mask the smell of cigarettes. Oscar pulled up the neck of his sweatshirt to cover his mouth.

'You should have got something light and citrusy. Something with fig, or lime leaf.'

'How do you know so much about it?'

'I enjoy an occasional candlelit bath, if you must know. Particularly if I'm listening to the cricket. I could spend a whole Test match in the tub.'

I'd bet money that Oscar had spent an entire week in the bath. He was the most leisurely man on earth. Every day a Sunday. But not today!

'She's going to be here soon, so listen up,' I said, taking up a commanding position in the doorway, blocking his escape route. 'We're going to establish some *rules* and some *roles*.'

'I'm not getting paid enough for this,' Oscar sighed. 'Actually, nothing at all.'

'Technically I've already paid you with a large Meat Fiesta.'

'Fair.'

'First thing to remember,' I continued. 'This isn't a date; it's a portrait session.'

Oscar put up his hand like he was in class. 'Thought you said it was headshots?'

'Same thing.' I ploughed on. 'This isn't the kitchen, it's the meet-and-greet area.' I could see that he was about to crack up, but I didn't give him the chance. 'The bathroom is for hair and make-up, and my bedroom is the, er . . .'

'Yeah?'

I cleared my throat. 'Where the—'

'Magic happens?' he beamed, his head dancing from side to side like a nodding toy.

'No! It's my studio, okay? So please don't refer to it as my bedroom or my *boudoir* or anything else. Now shut up and come with me. We're going to flip my bed over.'

'Eh?'

I had managed to convince the guys at Carpet Planet to lend me some offcuts of lino, which, when patched together with gaffer tape and hung from my bookshelf with bulldog clips, made a pretty good backdrop. But the just-larger-than-single bed took up most of the floor, and as much as I'd have secretly liked the shoot to take place between the sheets, it was probably wise to free up some space.

'I'd keep it where it is if I were you,' Oscar said. He sprawled across it and started taking imaginary photos, writhing around like Austin Powers. 'Yeah, baby. Show me what you got!'

'Please get off my bed or I'm going to have to fire you.'

I stripped the bed, and stuffed the knackered old duvet into my wardrobe, Oscar giggling all the while. The ludicrousness of the charade wasn't lost on me, but he was starting to get on my nerves. On three, we lifted the rickety bed frame onto its side, revealing a rectangle of thick, dark dust on the carpet, peppered with odd socks and about £1.50 in loose change.

'What are we doing?' I said, my chest tightening. 'This is never going to work.'

'Relax, mate.'

'I'm going to call her. Take a rain check until I can afford to rent a proper studio.'

Oscar looked at me. He dropped his silly grin, becoming sensible all of a sudden. 'You're going to be fine. Let me hoover this up.'

I was grateful to see my old friend, the lesser-spotted Reliable Oscar, standing before me when I needed him.

'Thanks,' I said. 'I'm going to have a shower. You've used a hoover before?'

'Ha ha,' he said, deadpan. 'Yeah, baby.'

Scrubbed, tubbed and finally fed, we sat in the meet-and-greet area, awaiting my client. So much for her being early.

'If she's not here by eleven,' said Oscar, circling the kitchen table, 'I'm starting on the brownies.'

'Fair enough.' I sighed and checked the clock again. 'Feels like I've thrown a party and no one's going to turn up.'

'Some party.' He prodded at the plate, clearly deciding which brownie he was going to eat first. 'Are you sure you didn't make her up?'

I was so certain that Pippa wasn't going to materialise that I didn't recognise the doorbell as my own.

'I'll get it!' Oscar was down the stairs in a flash, like a stir-crazed puppy bounding to greet the postman.

Here we go, then. I couldn't believe she'd actually come. Pippa Lyons in my flat! There were murmurs of greeting, then the front door clicked shut. *No turning back now.*

'I didn't know he had an assistant.' Her voice floated up the stairs.

'You were lucky to get a slot,' said Oscar. 'He's booked up for months.'

My toes wiggled with excitement in my slippers. *Slippers!* I was still wearing my slippers. *Love you, slippers, but this is not*

43

your time. I kicked them off into a corner. I could have floated up into the air as Pippa appeared on the landing, her red hair curly and loose, her cheeks slightly flushed from the cold, followed by . . . one, two – no – *three* of her friends.

'Here they all are!' Oscar announced.

There they all are.

'Sorry I didn't warn you,' said Pippa with a guilty grin.

She politely introduced her entourage. There was Gus, a lithe blonde Jarvis Cocker-like, who was eyeing up the flat with a look of disdain; Jen, who was short, shy and hiding behind thick glasses and a beanie; and then a face from back in the day that I could never forget – Tania Marley, another exotic, slightly terrifying All Hallows girl, whom a large number of boys from my school took as their main subject. She was even taller now, a dark mannequin in a beige trench coat.

'You remember Steve,' said Pippa.

'No, should I?'

Pippa glared at her. You could almost hear the nudges and winks.

'Oh yes.' Tania raised a perfectly plucked eyebrow. 'Steve from school. School Steve.'

Pippa laughed nervously, and I copied her, Beavis to her Butt-Head.

'I know it's cheeky,' she went on, 'but the guys are desperate for new headshots and I thought, this sounds like a job for Steve!'

It sounded like a nightmare for Steve. It sounded like the photographer formerly known as Steven Gallagher's first and last job before he was found crying in a naked heap outside Snappy Snaps.

But she was here and she was all I could see.

'It would be good for your portfolio, right?' she added,

giving my elbow a little squeeze, which sent pubescent chills multiplying up my arm.

All I could say was 'It's fine. It's great. Wonderful, really.' And I meant it.

We remained in a loose circle on the landing, me looking stupidly at Pippa, everyone looking at me looking stupid. This is where I'd have liked my assistant to butt in and give me a push, remind me of the job at hand, but he was enjoying watching me make a fool of myself too much. Instead, it was Tania who got things moving.

'Let's do it, then. You can be first up, okay, Gus?' she said, not expecting an answer. 'We need a touch-up.'

Oscar looked at me quizzically. I could see the endless smutty ripostes lining up in a disorderly queue in his brain, desperate to be aired, and prayed that he'd keep a lid on them before it all got a bit *Carry On Photographer*.

Tania slid a glittery gold pouch the same size as her handbag from her handbag. Jen followed suit, unzipping her backpack and removing a make-up bag, hers the size of a pencil case. But Pippa didn't copy her friends.

'I don't think I want any more face on,' she said.

Tania looked at her as if she was mad. 'Are you sure? These photos are meant to get you noticed, Pips.'

Pippa was unmoved. I sensed that she'd had similar conversations with Tania before. 'Going for the natural look.'

'There's natural and then there's see-through,' said Tania, waving a diva's finger. She turned to me. 'What do you think, Steve?'

'I think she looks perfect,' I answered without hesitation. *Can't believe I just said that. I've blown my cover, surely.*

'There's a mirror for hair and make-up in the bathroom,' I said, trying to sound more businesslike. 'It's just down the hall. Oscar, could you show Gus to the studio, please?'

Tania shrugged, said, 'You're the professional,' and turned on her heel.

Gus looked from me to Pippa, then back to me again. A protective look, or a jealous one? I couldn't tell.

'He's the best in the business,' said Oscar with a sparkle, before gesturing to Gus that he should follow him upstairs.

The entourage dispersed, leaving me and Pippa alone – for the moment, at least. We drifted silently into the kitchen, *I think she looks perfect* hanging in the air. I wanted to apologise, to assure her that this whole headshot act wasn't a ploy to get closer to her. But it was, wasn't it? Who was I kidding?

She scanned the kitchen – the sofa, the candle, the brownies.

What is she thinking? Is she embarrassed? Scared?

'Brownies?'

She was facing away from me, and I couldn't tell from her voice if that was a good 'brownies' or a bad 'brownies'.

'Oh,' I said. 'I've always got them in.'

She turned, and she was smiling. *Thank God.*

'My fave! How did you know?'

'Help yourself. They're for you – *all*,' I quickly added. 'For all of you.'

Her hand hovered over the plate, but then she balled up her fist, pulled it away.

'Better wait till after,' she said. 'Not the best look for a portrait, chocolate in the teeth.'

'Not unless you want to be cast as a Victorian peasant.'

She laughed and I was in heaven.

I wanted desperately to keep her there, keep her laughing, keep her for myself. I scrabbled around in my head, looking for a zinger follow-up to the peasant gag, but nothing was forthcoming.

''Scuse me, Stevie, er, boss, er, chief.' It was almost a relief when Oscar peered in. 'Gus is ready for his close-up.'

Gus's session was mercifully short. The first forty-odd shots were a write-off – I couldn't get the flash to fire at all. Gus and Oscar waited in opposite corners of the room, Oscar looking out of the window whistling the theme to *Cagney & Lacey* (daydreaming about being back on his sofa watching daytime TV). Eventually Gus suggested sardonically that I plug the flash in, which I laughed off until I realised he was right. Then silence reigned again, but for the click of the shutter and my assistant's tuneless whistle.

Gus stared into the lens, cold, hard, unblinking – presumably hoping to force casting directors to give him a job through sheer hatred.

'Shall we try something else?' I suggested. 'Maybe a little . . . happy?'

He grimaced back, as if happiness were anathema to him.

'Well then,' I said, after only a minute and a half of shooting. 'I think we're done.'

I was sure he would kick off, demand his (no) money's worth, but he seemed completely satisfied with his one-look wonder.

Jen was next, so transformed that she was almost unrecognisable but for the dreamcatcher earrings. Her eyes were ringed in smoky black like a panda's, the sides of her face so heavily shaded that she now had four cheekbones. She was chaperoned by Tania, and it was evident from Tania's expertly conceived visage that she had practised her own look on Jen first, like my sisters painting their dolls' faces when they were little ('Saturday Salon', they called it). I'd have liked Jen to wipe some of it off, but how could I put that to her without seeming rude? Instead, I asked Oscar to bring the light down a bit, an attempt to temper the harshness of the make-up. Rather than turning the brightness dial on my very basic knock-off studio light, however, he brought the whole lamp down so that now only Jen's red Converse were lit. That was the moment Pippa entered. She looked down at Jen's shoes, which were glowing like ruby slippers, and must have thought I was insane.

'Like that?' Oscar asked hopelessly.

Tania's was the longest, most trying session, and not just for me. Even a crew of five, crammed into my tiny bedroom, couldn't deliver the high production values that she demanded of her shoot. Oscar held her Evian bottle, Jen powdered her forehead, Gus and Pippa told her she looked fabulous, while I tried to find an angle that avoided capturing an attendant's elbow. At one stage we were taking turns fanning her with books to create a wind-machine effect. You could see her thinking, *Because I'm worth it*, hair blowing in the booky breeze.

Pippa was left till last, which should have meant I was warmed up, ready to make her photos the best of the bunch. But she had drawn the short straw. There was an end-of-term feeling in the room now, with everyone sitting on the floor, spent from the effort put into Tania's extended session. They gave little or no attention to Pippa, who was shyer in front of the camera than I'd expected.

'I have no idea what face I should be pulling,' she apologised. 'So you'll have to tell me where to look.'

'Just be natural,' I offered unhelpfully. *Be natural. Just what you want to hear when you feel uncomfortable.*

Tania and Gus threw in some even more unhelpful direction – 'Think *sexy*', 'Think of England!' – before rolling around in hysterics. I tried to ignore them and focus on Pippa, but I was tired now, and could feel myself growing tetchy. I'd have liked to send them all downstairs, but didn't want to be accused of sounding like a teacher.

'Quiet on set!' I attempted to quip, but could hear the irritation in my voice.

Oscar had seen my patience pushed to the limit before. It never ended in a De Niro in *Goodfellas* explosion of violence or anything like that; more a surrendering, a shut-down. Like sitting under the dining table in protest when I lost at Monopoly. He may have recognised this, taking it as his cue to escape and fetch us some coffee but failing to take the rest of the class with him.

Pippa didn't seem to mind the heckling. She'd known how to deal with Tania's diva display earlier and she was able to chuckle along with them now. They were her friends, after all. But I hated to think they were taking advantage of her. She looked as amazing through the lens as she did through my eyes, of course, but I knew the pictures would disappoint in the end. I wanted them to be everything. I wanted *me* to be everything for her. That was too much to ask. I'd built the day up and was now surrendering to the idea that it was a failure.

Three hours, two multipacks of Duracell and a thousand exposures later, we were back in the kitchen, and I felt like I'd gone ten rounds with Ricky Hatton. My first and last time photographing actors, I promised myself.

Oscar had well and truly left his assistant persona in the studio, and was firing off his repertoire of anecdotes to entertain our guests. The One with the Escaped Donkey. The One Where He Makes It Into the Local Paper. The One Where He Crashes His Dad's Car. It was like a weekend omnibus of *Friends*. He directed most of it to Tania, who remained resolutely unimpressed, while Jen tittered gleefully.

49

Gus stood to one side talking on his mobile, his Kurt Cobain hair draped over his eyes, hand covering the microphone in secrecy. Scoring drugs? Was that an actor's life?

Pippa looked over to me and mouthed, 'You okay?' to which I gave a thumbs-up. I had no chat left in me (if I'd ever had any), so I disappeared into my camera, reviewing the images in the display screen in the hope of finding some wheat in the chaff.

Oscar moved on to The One with Jude Law's Credit Card – which was a goodie, I had to admit, especially in present company. Pippa followed the story, enthralled, along with the rest. While Oscar had their attention, I secretly raised the camera, capturing the moment with a couple of candid snaps. At the story's climax, where Oscar turns the credit card over to reveal its owner's name, he was cut off by Gus, who ended his call, announcing to the room, 'I've got a casting.'

Tania's head swivelled. Jen let out a small yelp. Pippa punched the air and yelled, 'Gus, that's brilliant news! What's it for?'

'It's a recall, actually. For a Ryanair ad.'

'A *recall*?' The word seemed to hold great wonder for Jen.

'I never knew you had an audition in the first place,' said Tania.

'I didn't think you'd be interested,' replied Gus, a little petulantly.

'Oh gorgeous Gus. Of course we care.' Pippa took both his hands in hers. 'You're going to smash it.'

This news seemed to remind the troupe that the world outside was waiting for them, and they gathered their coats and bags. Fame, fortune and budget airline auditions awaited. Gus looked very happy with himself and, without thanking me for giving up my day for free, sauntered off with a smile creeping over his face. Funny how he couldn't move the corners of his mouth northwards during the photos. Oscar offered a crooked arm each to Tania and Jen, like a toddler performing 'I'm a Little Teapot', and led them out into the hall, leaving me alone with Pippa for a precious few seconds.

'Thanks for putting up with us,' she said, pulling on her gloves. 'You must be shattered.'

'Not at all! I enjoyed it.'

'When can we see them?'

'Ah. Well, I can show you the proofs in a few days. In person or by post.'

'In person would be nice.'

'Yes. I agree.'

'Great,' she said, as she picked up the remaining brownie from the table. 'For the journey home. Do you mind?'

'Of course not. Want a sandwich bag or some foil or . . .'

But she had already popped it into her coat pocket, rubbing the crumbs off her stripy woollen mittens.

'We're having a party at ours next weekend for Tania's birthday. Nineties fancy dress! Lots of booze, some sort of food, I guess.'

'Oh. Nice,' I said, not understanding that this was an invitation.

'Wanna come?' she asked.

Fancy and *dress*. Two words I'd buried deep in my subconscious since my thirteenth birthday, even managing to avoid engaging with them throughout university.

'Just try and stop me.'

We were standing in the kitchen doorway when a sprig of mistletoe hanging invisibly over us seemed to move her to peck my left cheek. It sizzled, delighted. I was almost jealous of it.

'For the chocolate,' she said, as if to excuse the kiss.

'Any time,' I stuttered. 'There's plenty more chocolate in the, er, cupboard.'

'So you'll be there?'

'Yeah, baby, yeah!'

Idiot.

Pippa didn't notice me squirm; she was already running down the stairs to catch up with the others. From the window on the landing I saw her wave over her shoulder to Oscar. Then she looked up at me, and called through cupped mittens, 'Bring a bottle!'

December 2007

Pippa

A lesser-known fact about me. I *hate* fancy dress. Every single thing about it makes my skin crawl. Strange, I know, seeing as I have chosen to earn my living donning the garb of others, and prancing around demanding attention for it. But there it is. I think it's something to do with the competitiveness of dressing up, the whole super-casual *What, this old thing? Just found it in a charity shop.* Oh come on! We all know for a fact you've spent weeks trawling the high street for the best-fitting nun's habit so you can strut in looking more like Kate Moss than Mother Teresa.

But Tania insisted, and the universe obliged. As per. I think that should be the name of her autobiography – *And the Universe Obliged.* Besides, it's her twenty-fifth, and she took me to see Adele for mine so she's kind of got me over a barrel.

I can't remember who first floated the notion of us coming as the Spice Girls, but from the moment it was mooted it became a cast-iron decision in the drama house. Tania's decision.

'Five group members. Five outfits. Five residents in 309 Egerton Road. I mean, no-brainer, right? This is the money.'

Sure, one of those residents was of the boy variety, but Tania was not going to let that minor glitch deter her. Besides, Gussy Atkins has better legs than any of us and was too laid-back (lazy) to think up an alternative. Tania naturally took on the role of choreographer, director and curator, bagging the much-coveted Posh Spice role before you could blink.

'We all agree it's vital I get to look *actually* hot on the night, don't we? You know – not just *funny* hot, but *hot* hot. 'Cos at the end of the day, it's my party and *technically* most people will be looking at me.' How Tania gets away with saying things like this and still being adored by almost everyone she meets is a bona fide mystery.

Sweet, plump Jen Hale got saddled with Sporty, which we all agreed was pretty harsh, but someone had to draw the short straw. Jen was one of those unfortunate girls who seemed to have missed the stop for Youth and ended up on the direct train to that far-off town of Middle Age. She wore shapeless frocks and open-toed sandals, and try as we might, she refused to make friends with the under-arm razor. I mean, don't get me wrong, none of us fancied the Reebok tracksuit slash au naturel look (not when there was gonna be a lot of coveted totty turning up), but poor Jen was definitely the least equipped of us all to carry it off. She looked less Sporty Spice and more soon-to-be-retired netball teacher. The slightly pulling-under-the-crotch tracky bottoms and her thick horn-rimmed glasses did nothing to aid her cause, but we all rallied round as good girlfriends should, and to give her credit, she was as good-natured about it as a saint.

'Jen, seriously, if Mel C was standing right there, I wouldn't know which one was which,' Tania enthused. 'It's like a Mel mirage.'

'Do you really think?'

'Absolutely! It's like you're her twin.'

'That's sweet. I was wondering if, just this once, I should try a little make-up?' ventured Jen.

'No way. Sorry. Mel *never* wears make-up. It's just not

Sporty,' explained Tania patiently. 'And if we're all going to look *exactly* right, I'm afraid that means you can't either.'

Jen looked briefly downcast. Tania ploughed on.

'Listen, Jen, if Posh never wore make-up, I *totally* wouldn't either. It just so happens that she wears loads of it, so I'm just doing what she does. We're all kind of suffering for our art.'

This made absolutely no sense, but once again, Tania got away with this ludicrous non sequitur.

Jen pushed no further. I was quietly impressed by the self-restraint.

'Look at Nish! Now that's a Scary Spice and a half.'

Nisha Rain, law student, school friend and only non-actory resident, was standing hands on hips, leopard skin catsuit ripped nonchalantly to the belly button and overt PVC bra on display.

'Amazing. One thought,' Tania continued. 'I'm thinking maybe you could backcomb your hair? I've got some heavy-duty spray. If that's cool with you?'

She handed over the spray without waiting for a response.

'And look at Pips! Totally rocking the red hair!'

Tania had asked (ordered) that I dye my hair 'Colorista Copper' – 'Your natural ginge just isn't quite ginge enough, babe.' Two hours and three sachets later, my hair was the colour of Irn-Bru and the tips of my ears looked like a child had been let loose on them with orange felt tips. I was wrapped in a Poundland polyester Union Jack flag fashioned into a tight halter-neck dress and Tania's red leather high heels and red pop socks doubling as PVC boots.

Tan studied me like a sculptor surveying her work.

'Not bad at all. Geri's definitely got bigger knockers than you, but we can always pad you out a bit.'

Ah. Best friends. Aren't they swell?

Last but not least came Baby Spice. Aka the only boy in

our household – Gus. The long blonde wig fitted him like a glove, and when we put it into the iconic high pigtails, it looked as though no other hairdo would ever suffice. God, he was annoyingly attractive. The pink wedge trainers, minute pink mini skirt and lace scoop-neck crop top set it off perfectly. A slick of brown mascara, a smudge of rosy lip gloss and he was ready to take on Wembley. Without doubt, he looked the hottest of all of us.

Tania was not impressed.

The bass notes from a maxed-out hi-fi speaker pulse through the frayed carpet, vibrating into my calves. Our lounge is a freakish sea of half-cut drama students and their waif-and-stray London pals, rolling joints, downing cans of unpronounceable Polish lager and singing show tunes in the round (clichéd, but sadly true).

I check the clock on the DVD player. Christ, it's only ten to nine. Feels like midnight. I'm stuck in Cactus Corner (imaginatively named after Jen's collection of hazardous pot plants, which have taken up residence here). Stu 'Call me Bronson, everyone else does' is lounging on the wall beside me. Dressed as Rambo, he is swigging from a hip flask of Buckfast and has been talking at me for the last fifteen minutes. Stu – sorry, Bronson – and personal space have clearly never been friends. A pungent stench of Hugo Boss oozes from his bare chest, and his tongue is ever so slightly too big for his mouth, causing him to mangle his consonants and spray spit particles into my eyes on a regular basis.

He has three huge love bites. The glowing violet-tinged bruises look like stepping stones paving the way from his torso to his chin, and he's making no attempt to conceal them. Maybe he sees them as some kind of badge of honour? Well, I'm not going to be his next conquest. His eyes linger shamelessly on my conically padded breasts. Admittedly they are distracting, as Tania has wildly overdone the cotton wool stuffed down each bra cup, but it would be nice if he bothered to make actual eye contact every now and then. For a while I tried to lip-read what he's been saying from his massive drooly mouth, but now I've given up. He is clearly so delighted by his own narrative, so swept up in the bravado of his supreme existence, that the entertainment of others comes very low down his priorities. A delusion that, I'm ashamed to say, I am currently fuelling by laughing at suitable intervals (mainly when his mouth stops moving) and nodding in animated agreement. I'm so bloody English sometimes, I hate myself. He's convinced he has me sucked in. I guess I *am* sucked in, just unwillingly. *Give me strength*, I mumble to myself, a bit too loudly. But he doesn't even notice, just drones on and on and on.

Shit. My toes are already killing me in Tan's scarlet skyscrapers. I feel like one of those Chinese women in the book I'm reading. *Wild Swans*. The bones in their feet broken and bound as youngsters to keep them from growing to full size. Tiny feet were a status symbol apparently. The most desirable brides possessed ten-centimetre-long feet, known as 'golden lotuses'. Don't know why I'm so obsessed with this fact, but for some reason I can't stop thinking about it. I decide not to share it with Bronson. Can't imagine Chinese culture would pique his interest much. Besides, no time between his snatched breaths to fit so many words in anyway.

Wow. He really does go on.

Occasionally he makes lame excuses to touch my face.

Think you've got a bit of crisp just there.

He brushes my cheek with his rough hand. Now he is rubbing his thumb across my mouth.

Is that a lipstick smudge on your top lip?

57

It is now. His fingers smell of cigarettes and steak. I swig the last dregs from my fourth – or is it fifth? – Watermelon Bacardi Breezer and make a bid for freedom.

'Sorry. I really need to check on the birthday girl.'

Snippets of his sleazy response as I scurry away.

'No. Don't go . . . just getting to know . . . somewhere more pri . . .'

But, thank God, I'm gone, squeezing past a couple who are clashing teeth over the punch bowl, then wriggling into the jungle of sweaty bodies. I clock Nisha, who is drinking Campari and soda with an achingly cool group of musos. They are clearly intoxicated by her. She speaks rarely, but when she does, her words suck up attention like a black hole.

A bong made out of an empty 7 Up bottle is being passed around the circle. The lanky one who knows Amy Winehouse looks at me and holds out the smoking plastic contraption. Almost a challenge.

Now, weed doesn't suit me. It makes me sick, paranoid, depressed, possessed, insecure – you get the picture. But hey, it's a party, right?

'Inhale, hold your breath and count to ten.'

I do as I'm told. Leaning forward, I take the damp bottle opening between my lips and breathe in deeply.

One, two . . . The sickly smoke is crackling in my saliva like popping candy. *Three, four* . . . whistling past my tonsils and burning through the fibres of my lungs. *Five, six* . . . My eyes are welling up. Is that smoke coming out of my ears? A flash of Gus on the sofa having his pigtails fondled by a tipsy shaven-headed Britney Spears. *Seven* . . . The world is grinding to a halt, the cacophonous party chatter stretching out like chewing gum. *Eight, nine* . . . The musos' faces merge into one, a beautiful-ugly gargoyle. A snort of laughter rises through my legs, a fleeting thought that my pulsing heart could burst through my chest and leave me drenched in blood. Then, just as suddenly, a feeling of supreme calm descends. For a single moment as I scan the room, everyone looks happy. Or do they? Perhaps I am everyone? And the happiness is in me? Or everyone is . . . Wait. Stop. My head hurts. Too many words. *And ten*.

I exhale. More of a splutter. The musos clap and laugh. I doff my imaginary cap, attempt a jaunty bow and sway off. I've got this! No problem. 'You all right Pippa?' I think I hear Nisha's voice. 'You look a bit—' I hold my hand up to stop her. No. Everything is absolutely perfect. I feel terrific. I feel . . . Oh shit. I'm wading through treacle. My hands are not my own. Crashing wave of nausea. I steady myself against the strategically placed wall. Thank you kindly, Mr Wall. Right, get it together, Lyons. You're cool with this. You can take your gear. But the sickness is rising in my belly. Thin, salty water filling my mouth like a sprinkler. No, no, no. I suppress the sensation with my whole being. As I do so, the warm bath of slow motion I climbed into drains sharply away and the party mania crashes back in front of me. Full tempo. More deafening and intense than before.

I try and look up. I see Tania in the kitchen. She is perched on the draining board, pouting for a photo. Unsure if she has seen me, I close one eye and wave unsteadily. She smiles and blows me a kiss. I am *not* going to be sick. My pulse is getting louder in my ears, like the volume being turned up on a car stereo. Shit. I'm on a roundabout, spinning faster and faster. But I am a hundred per cent, totally, definitely *not* going to be sick.

I retch over the toilet bowl, my body juddering again and again under the force of the expulsion. Will it never end? My forehead is damp and prickling with sweat, and I rest it against the toilet seat. Ah, cool porcelain, you are a wonder.

Why have I never acknowledged your beauty before? Clinging to it like a long-lost lover, I try to coax my legs back into action. Whoa, this standing-up thing is harder than I remembered. I catch a glimpse of my reflection in the mirror. My eyes widen.

Jesus God, Pippa.

I raise my left hand slowly, hoping that the ashen girl looking back at me will keep hers firmly by her side. Alas, this stranger lifts hers in sync. Get it together, girl. I grab the uncapped toothpaste and squeeze a string of it onto my tongue. I swill it around in my mouth, watching my pale reflection, and spit it out. A white frothy smear tracks its steady path down the drain like a snail trail and I stare at it, spent.

Okay. A smear more red lipstick on my cheeks and mouth, a shake-out of my bright orange hair – good as new. Well, good as nearly new with the batteries missing, anyway. Ding-ding, round two. Or ding-dong, was that the doorbell? I hover at the top of the stairs, eyeing the front door, convinced that one of the milling guests will open it, but no one seems in the least bothered about the repeatedly ringing bell.

I head carefully down the stairs.

I barely recognise him at first – which is weird, because his concession to fancy dress is minimal to say the least. He is wearing an oversized England football shirt and holding a family bag of Walkers cheese and onion crisps.

'Gary Lineker?' I say.

'Bingo. Sorry I'm late. Took me *ages* to get this costume together.'

I smile. Feels weirdly alien on my lips. Steve frowns.

'You okay, Pippa? You look . . .'

'Fine. I'm fine.'

He's unconvinced.

'Hang on.'

He takes off his backpack and rummages inside, then holds out a Dime bar and a bottle of cava.

'According to Oscar, eating chocolate before drinking reduces hangover symptoms by half.'

He looks at me.

'Might be too late, though.'

'You could say that.'

'I did have two bars, but I ate one because I've been out here so long.'

'You haven't, have you?'

'No, it's fine. Not really that long at all. I mean, twenty-five minutes – is that long?'

He dives into his bag again and hands me a box of something.

'And if the chocolate thing turns out to be bollocks, those'll do the trick.'

I look down. A multi box of Alka-Seltzer. It makes me laugh. Which makes him laugh. I may be drunk, but I am struck by how nice it is to see that silly, hopeful face in the shadows.

'Come on in then, Gaz. Madness awaits.'

'Why, thanking you. Loving the flag, by the way. Geri always was my favourite.'

I raise an eyebrow. *Come on. We all know Geri is no one's favourite.*

I shut the door behind him, and now we are standing face to face in the hall.

'Hello, by the way.'

'Oh yes. Hi.'

I lean in to kiss him on the cheek. He leans too, but turns his face the same way and an awkward part-lips part-cheekbone collision takes place. We pretend it hasn't happened.

'Right. I've not had a drink for at least . . .' I check my watch, 'ooh, fourteen minutes. My body is going into shock. Let's find booze.'

Grabbing his hand, I pull him into the throng. And then the strangest thing happens. As we are crossing the room together, hand in hand, I suddenly see things through his eyes. I can't explain it any other way. The weed has worn off, so it's not that. But it's like we are momentarily linked, his hand providing me with a direct conduit into his mind. I notice things afresh, as though I'm showing a tourist around my home town: the naked gang reading Rilke poetry in the corner; the lonely face of the anorexic girl who has started growing face fur to keep her warm; a make-up-less Jen sidling off to bed carrying a discreet mug of Horlicks and a battered copy of *Middlemarch*; the cross-dressed limbo taking place under a tape measure in the kitchen; the spin-the-bottle in the garden, where an attempt at a six-way snog is under way; Tania's terrified tabby Gordon Brown (so called because of his sad eyes) cowering behind the lava lamp.

Drama students, reprobates, actors, loners, sinners. Christ, what must he think of us? We are the underbelly, the left-overs of society, the bruises on an apple that you cut away before eating. Desperate to be loved. Desperate to be seen. Desperate to be acknowledged. An incomprehensible gaggle of folk who shouldn't be unleashed on kind-eyed photographers who still believe in Father Christmas. I lean into him to be heard over the din. As I do, I smell the soap on his skin, and an unfamiliar ripple of deep calm passes through me.

'You don't have to stay. This is . . . this is . . .'

'Your average Saturday night?'

He is smiling. Which makes me grin back. He looks alive, more confident than I remember him. He scans the room, drinking in the plethora of sights. A new world is opening up before him and I can see the photos he is taking in his mind's eye. Snapshots from Pandora's box of eccentric misfits.

Suddenly someone grabs me by the waist.

'You missed me, sexy?'

Rambo is back. He slaps my arse and drags me off into a wild conga round the room. My fingers slip from Steve's hand. I clutch wildly at his football shirt, but it's too late. The crowd closes in around me and he dissolves into the void. A strange chill in my bones like someone has ripped off my duvet cover. I try to disentangle myself, but Rambo has latched his octopus arms around me. More people join the snaking line, and now I am sandwiched between him and Cleopatra, on a speeding train that I have no hope of getting off. 'Mamma Mia' blares out from the hi-fi and the flat erupts. Drinks are sprayed across the carpet, voices become shrieks, bodies are heaved onto shoulders, the party boiling over.

I'm being nudged from the line by Rambo's hips, which are grinding perilously close to my buttocks. He half congas, half shoves me up the corridor and, before I can react, pushes me into our small bathroom under the stairs. He is leaning heavily against the door. A greasy smile. His face orbits towards me and suddenly that drooling mouth is sucking mine like a leech. I wriggle from his grasp.

'What's up?'

'No. Not happening. I don't want this.'

'Come on, sexy. Don't be a killjoy. S'only a bit of fun.'

His hand reaches out and, uninvited, traces the curve of my breasts (cotton wool cones) through my dress. I want to kick him in the shin but my legs won't respond. Shit. How annoying. I'm scared.

'God, you've got amazing—'

A knock at the door startles him. He places a hand against the handle.

'We're busy.'

Another knock. He swings round, angrily and opens the door a smidge.

'What do you want?'

And then, Steve's voice.

'Pippa in there?'

Rambo's back straightens.

'And you are?'

The muscles in his shoulders flex, his hands forming fists.

'Surely that's obvious. Costume as good as this one!'

But Rambo doesn't crack a smile. I'm feeling scared for Steve now. He's not a fighter. He's Gary Lineker – he never got a red card his whole career. He peers in through the gap.

'There you are. Everything all right in there, love?'

Love? What is he doing?

'Listen, darling. Just to say, I think we should get back to the dogs. Can't leave them more than four hours, can we? And we've got the oven man coming early, don't forget. I've called us a taxi. Meet you out front.'

Rambo drops his arms. He looks back at me, confused.

'Didn't tell me you had a fella.'

'Didn't tell me you were an arsehole.'

He smiles. He thinks I'm being cute. His wet lips orbit in once more.

An intense rush of rage, and I shove him. Hard. He falls clumsily against the toilet.

'Whoa. Chill pill, babe.'

'You're a dick. Has anyone ever told you that? And your tongue is too big for your mouth.' And I'm out of there, slamming the bathroom door behind me.

I pick my way over drunken bodies blocking the corridor. The house looks like a crash dummy test centre, bodies scattering any available floor space. I glance into my tiny bedroom, which is being used as a love den. Ignoring the calls from inebriated actor pals inviting me for 'one last shot', I grab my bag from the banister and fling myself out of the front door. Only when I feel the slap of cold air on my cheeks do I allow myself to breathe again. I lean back against the porch and close my eyes, willing my rocketing heartbeat to steady.

'Hey. Are you all right?'

I open my eyes and he is there, his face close to mine – so concerned, so caring. I nod.

'You're shaking.'

He's right. My teeth are jangling in my skull like beans in a maraca.

'Here.'

He takes off his jacket and places it gently over my shoulders. The knot in my stomach gradually loosens.

'Thanks.'

I look up at him. Then . . .

'We have dogs?'

'Yeah. Sorry about that. I didn't know where you'd gone; someone said you were in the loo. With a guy. Which kind of felt off, but I didn't want to judge, so I . . .' He peters off.

'Oven man coming. Nice touch.'

He laughs. 'The devil is in the detail.'

Without thinking, I am standing on my painful mummified toes and kissing him gently on the cheek. We stay there for a moment as though posing for a non-existent photographer. Finally I step away.

'Thank you. Seriously. Don't know what I would have done if you hadn't . . .'

The sentence hangs in the air, unfinished. He gently squeezes my hand. As he does so, something warm like hot wax floods through my chest and I have an overwhelming impulse to grab his T-shirt and kiss him on the mouth – but then I remember the projectile whitey I've just pulled and decide against it. The moon has passed behind a cloud so I can't really make out his expression, but I can hear that we are smiling at one another.

Maybe fancy dress parties aren't so bad after all.

2 March 2019

02:39

'You should take a seat, Mr Gallagher. There's going to be a lot to take in.'

Steve shakes his head. He would rather stand. He knows he must be upright to hear this. If he allows himself to weaken, permits his knees to bend beneath him, he may never stand again.

'Very well,' Bramin continues. 'Your wife's condition is still critical. Her intercranial pressure is stable, which is good, but she has sustained some profound injuries. Our X-ray showed broken ribs, so we will be monitoring her for significant haemothoraces, bleeding in the chest cavity, though we'd rather not have to operate again. She's likely to be on this ventilator for some time.'

Whir, beep, click, breath.

Steve blinks hard.

Must focus. Must stay vertical.

But the floor supporting him has begun to feel thin, the foundations hollow – bouncy almost, like he's balancing on cling film stretched over a dish of leftovers. At any moment, a mischievous sprite might rip it from under his feet, sending him plummeting down an abandoned well from which he will never climb out. Steve remembers a raucous Gallagher garden party, and his nine-year-old, magic-obsessed brother repeatedly attempting to whip a napkin out from under the lemonade without spilling a drop.

'Mr Gallagher?'

He tries to ignore the voice calling him back to reality. He clings hard to the memory, desperate to stay in that place of safety, love and family. A time when things were simple. But the image is collapsing underfoot, like quicksand, the past giving way to the present, and then to the future.

'Steven? Are you all right?'

Steve blinks and tries to focus on Mr Bramin's face. He nods. The doctor continues.

'As I said before, we still cannot predict the full extent of the damage to Pippa's brain. She suffered considerable trauma on impact.'

Bramin's mouth is moving, but the sentences are scattered, words skimming past Steve's ears like pebbles on a lake.

'The operation has certainly reduced the pressure in her skull, but we cannot give you any exact information on her recovery. We will be doing another MRI later to help prognosticate, as her EKG does show a degree of brain activity but we cannot pretend it's an exact science, even at that stage.'

A foreign film without subtitles. Steve listens harder, willing a sentence to penetrate.

'I am aware that this is a huge amount for you to take in. I wish I had more optimistic news. What I will say is that people can be stronger than we realise.'

Steve is staring at the freckles across the bridge of Pippa's nose. Her solar system, he called them. He can hear the explosion of laughter when she looked in the mirror to find he had drunkenly joined the dots with a biro while she was asleep.

The doctor is encouraged by Steve's smile, though it wasn't for him.

'I believe that it's best for loved ones to be in possession of all of the facts. I don't like to sugar-coat things and I cannot comfort you with vain hope. These are critical hours. But I have been a doctor for almost twenty years, and so often we have seen that the spirit and fight in a patient can make all the difference.'

He pauses.

'Is there anything you would like to ask me, at this stage? Anything at all.'

Steve looks up, finally tearing his eyes from his wife's face.

'When are you going to give me the bad news?'

Mr Bramin remains impassive. He double-pumps some sanitiser from the bottle at the end of the bed and swiftly rubs his hands together.

'I will be back to check on her soon.'

He heads to the door, then turns back to face Steve.

'Keep talking to her, Mr Gallagher. Remind her what she's got to come back for.'

Steve watches him leave, then instinctively reaches for his phone, hoping – and dreading – to have heard from Diana. But there are no new calls or messages on the screen, just him and Pippa silhouetted against a San Francisco sunset.

Why would she have called back? She'll be in bed, oblivious.

He received the sickening voicemail just after midnight. An unknown number, then a stranger's voice, earnest and quiet. He quite calmly called a cab, and from inside the cab he called Diana. But her phone just rang and rang and rang. What did he expect? She was often asleep by ten. Part of him was grateful she hadn't picked up, and he cut off without leaving a message.

Now he unlocks the phone, and his thumb hovers over her name. Is there any point in calling again? What if the worst happens and she isn't able to make it in time to say goodbye? Even entertaining the idea makes Steve shudder, but he knows he must keep trying to get through. He thumbs the screen, then turns his body away from the bed, as if to protect Pippa from the vacant ringing of her sleeping mother's phone. At last Diana's voice greets him: 'Hello, this is Diana. Please leave a message and I'll call you back after doing what I'm doing. Bye now! Chris, which button do I press?'

This time he knows what he must do.

'Diana, it's Steven – Steve.'

His voice is hoarse, and he can feel the phone trembling against the tip of his ear.

'Um, can you call me, please? Right away. I'm at the hospital, and . . . Pippa – she's been in an accident. I'm so sorry. Please call. And don't worry. But do call me. Please.'

He hangs up and places the phone on the far side of the over-bed table, as far away as he can get it. He didn't expect the call to leave him so shaken. He urgently wants to hold Pippa close now. Did Mr Bramin say he could touch her? He can't remember. Perhaps he should ask someone.

From the hall, a woman laughs. Then another cries out, apparently in delight. Both noises seem so unlikely to Steve that he is momentarily distracted from his wife. He focuses on the voices, tuning in to snippets of conversation from the reception desk down the hall.

'Did you win?'

'Fifty quid!'

Another yelp of joy.

'Get out!'

'Double my wages.'

'Ha! That's true.'

The sound of palms meeting in a high-five.

'You getting the bus home?'

'Taxi. Treat myself.'

'Do it. Why not. Rich lady now!'

'Night.'

'Night, love.'

There is no more laughter from the corridor, just the faint *pfft* of doors swinging shut around the hospital, condemning unlucky souls to the late shift.

Steve permits himself to land his middle finger gently on Pippa's forehead. He traces the constellation of freckles, half of which are hidden under the gauze of dried blood, the routes between them bumpier now, but he knows their tracks perfectly from years of study.

'Look at that, Pip. A perfect Orion's Belt.'

June 2008

It was my brother Mickey who planted the seed. Apart from telling Oscar, who knew all my secrets, I'd been keeping my feelings close to my chest for the last six months. But on one of my too infrequent trips to visit Mickey and Pat in Brighton, I drank a whole bottle of wine and started blathering about my long-unrequited devotion for a friend called Pippa.

'Cook for her,' Mickey suggested. 'They say the way to a man's heart is through his stomach, but I'm sure it's the other way round.'

'What,' said Pat, 'the way to the stomach is through the heart?'

'Don't be foolish,' Mickey cuffed him on the back of the head. 'Women like to eat too, I mean. And they're extremely impressed if a guy knows his way around the kitchen.'

'How would you know?'

'I cooked for boys *and* girls before we met, remember?'

'Yes, yes,' said Pat, opening another bottle. 'We've all heard about your little knocking shop in Camberwell.'

'But I can't cook,' I said.

'We can teach you,' said Pat. Mickey looked at him aghast. 'Well, *he* can.'

'The only meal Pat ever makes is turkey burgers off the George Foreman.'

It was Pat's turn to smack Mickey now, which quickly turned into a playful sparring session.

There followed a lot of drunken talk about flavour pairing and techniques and cuisine, but I'm not sure if we ate any actual food at all that night.

Initially my vision was to create a simple, classic French menu. Being someone who feels more comfortable with a plan, I went to the internet café to print off some recipes. When I read them properly, however, I learned that classic does not mean simple. Where would I find morels on Kilburn High Road? How could so many ingredients be required to make a jus? And how so many *pans*? I'd have to rob a John Lewis to come close to being kitchen-ready.

I shared my concerns with Oscar, who offered to lend me his 'legendary wok'. The idea that Oscar was now into cooking – an activity that requires time and effort – was a stunning revelation. It was inconceivable that he even owned a wok, let alone that it had reached legendary status. But according to him, it had unlocked the secrets of the Orient and had people eating from the palm of his hand.

'Maybe buy some bowls?' I suggested.

'Honestly, Stevie, this wok has changed my life.'

'You make it sound like you've inherited a samurai sword enriched with power from victories of stir-fries past.'

'Do you want to borrow it or not?'

'Yes, I do.'

A wok-based dinner seemed less intimidating than French – I'd certainly eaten more crispy duck than *à l'orange*. This change of direction also meant that I could simplify my shopping options down to one: the Chinese supermarket.

Expecting to make a big haul, I had emptied my camping backpack and taken it along as I stepped into the unknown, beyond the valley of silver fish piled up outside in polystyrene crates of melting ice. How had I never ventured in here before? I'd been missing out! It was a cornucopia of treasures. I picked out a bag of king prawns from the freezer, for a statement starter. Next to the prawns was a chicken that looked just like a chicken, in that it still had its head and feet. I held it aloft, and all of a sudden didn't trust myself to cook with meat.

'What do you have that's like meat, but not meat?' I asked the girl at the till, who had been watching me in amusement.

'Bean curd,' she said, and pointed me towards a shelf stacked with twenty types of tofu.

When I asked, 'How do you cook it?' she shrugged. Guess I'd have to be led by my instincts – and Oscar's magic wok.

I reached the till having managed to fill two baskets for a fraction of the price I'd have paid anywhere else. Two extremely heavy baskets of mostly canned, but – most importantly – *authentic* ingredients. So authentic that some of the labels weren't even translated into English. I hadn't gone mad and thrown just anything in; I'd hedged my bets by investing in a wild array of exotic produce. Some pickled stuff, some dried stuff, some stuff that I thought was rice, some stuff with a cartoon lobster on the packet, a magnum bottle of sweet chilli sauce, and some kind of seaweed crisps that had been wonderfully translated as 'sea wee wees', which I picked out just to make Pippa laugh.

I arrived home strapped to a hulking backpack, looking like I'd just returned from the gap year I never had.

'Arthur?' I called out. There was no answer, but that didn't mean he wasn't in. Like Hugo, my previous flatmate, Arthur was some kind of night creature. A vampire, maybe? Probably the ideal flatmate, to be honest. We got on quite well when he moved in, even went to the pub to watch the football – 'He might become your second friend,' Oscar had joked – but I hadn't seen him since. Anyway, this was not the night to rekindle our short-lived bromance. I planned to woo Pippa with the most romantic meal she'd ever eaten, then come clean about my feelings. If I played it right, we'd soon be feeding each other across the table in the tiny kitchen-diner-living-room. A ghoulish sub-letter sitting between us could really kill the mood. I didn't have his mobile number, so earlier in the day I'd fed a handwritten note under his door, explaining that I'd be cooking for a friend, a girl, that evening, hoping that he would work out what that meant.

I'd set aside the whole day to prepare. Just as well, because the process of clearing space on the kitchen surfaces was about to take me the best part of an hour. When I say 'surfaces', I mean a miniature garden table Mum and Dad were throwing out, the washing machine, and a square foot of countertop smeared with black grease. Looking closer, I found a couple of rusted wheel nuts. Arthur must have been fixing a bike part in here. *Not cool.*

'I'm just leaving your bits outside your room, Arthur,' I said from the hall. The nuts should serve as a passive-aggressive reminder not to use the kitchen as a workshop. Was that a greenish light spilling under the door? I thought about having a look in, but decided it was best to leave his lair undisturbed.

I emptied my backpack onto the table and stared blankly at the pile of jars and shrink-wrapped foil pouches, herby green tendrils poking through gaps in the rubble. It was like an edible mound of landfill with every food group represented. What was I making again? I tried to organise ingredients into starter, main and dessert, but the menu I'd devised on the walk back had dropped out of my head. I thought about calling Mickey for directions but decided against it – his ideas would be too advanced for a chef of my abilities. This was my race; I had to rip the armbands off. Pippa wasn't due for a couple of hours yet.

I laid a stained plastic chopping board on top of the washing machine, put the bunch of coriander on it, then rested the blade of the big knife on top of that. Holding the knife with both hands, I rocked it over the coriander like I'd seen on TV, expecting it to turn into a small heap of fine flakes. Instead, most of it went behind the machine and onto the floor.

'Oh, you absolute—' I cursed the air, jabbing the knife at nothing.

I had my head under the sink, reaching for the dustpan and brush, when the doorbell rang. A delivery? I hadn't ordered anything. I decided to let it go, I was too busy. Deliveries were often left in Carpet Planet anyway. One of the benefits of living above a shop.

The bell went again. I'd better go down, I thought.

'Sorry I'm so early.'

It was Pippa. She wore leggings and a hoodie, and had an overnight bag clutched between her thighs.

'It's great you're early,' I lied.

I took the bag from her and she pecked my cheek in return.

'Have you come from the gym?' I asked. She didn't have flushed cheeks or small beads of sweat dotted along her hairline, the usual marks of a workout.

'I need to work on an audition scene – do you mind?'

'That's great news! What's it for?'

'A play.' She sighed. 'Well, more of a workshop. Unpaid.'

Pippa always sighed when talking about auditions, as did all her friends if they had one looming. It was as if the idea of having to interview for a job was tiresome, a trick designed to catch them out. If they didn't have any auditions, however, they were livid, let down by the cruel and merciless world of showbiz. Either way, I had learned that auditions were an affront to an actor.

'The company are very *movementy*,' she said, with great meaning. 'So I might need to physicalise it.'

I wasn't quite sure what this meant, but the idea of Pippa Lyons physicalising anything in my flat stirred me. I prayed again that Arthur had got my message, and leaned in to listen at his door as we passed it, but heard nothing. No news is good news? I crossed my fingers.

'I've got some proper clothes in the bag,' she said, before putting on a posh accent. 'To *dress for supper*.'

I wanted to get into the kitchen ahead of her, to put myself between her and the chaos within, but I was too slow.

'You've started already,' she said, surveying the mess I'd made.

'At sunrise,' I joked, though that wasn't far off.

'And you're cooking . . . just for me?' She cast a doubtful eye around the room, but there was no party of dinner guests hiding behind the sofa.

'For us both,' I said. 'Three courses.'

'Three?'

'Maybe four.'

'Lucky me!' she clapped her hands together and performed a spontaneous pirouette, which travelled her the whole length of the kitchen.

'You know,' she said conspiratorially. 'A couple of the guys said . . .' She trailed off, leaving the thought dangling above the limescale-caked kettle.

'What?'

'Doesn't matter,' she shook her head and took the gym bag from me. 'You carry on cooking up a storm.' Then she poked me in the ribs and danced out.

I swept any coriander that wasn't on the floor into a large bowl, while upstairs Pippa began a very vocal warm-up (or was it a very physical vocal warm-up?). It sounded like she was jumping off my bed and crashing into the wardrobe.

'Are you okay?' I called up.

'*Caw!*'

Another thump.

'Are you hurt?'

'*Cawl!*'

'What?'

'*Call off! Call off the search!*' came the reply, and then more snatches of her audition script, followed by more thuds. If this level of noise didn't rouse Arthur, then there was no danger of him waking.

I emptied the bag of frozen prawns into a colander and ran the cold tap over them. I'd seen my mum do this a few times, but didn't really understand the science behind it. It seemed like a waste of water – couldn't I just use the microwave? As I stared into the sink at the little balls of ice, which uncurled as they thawed, turning from grey to blue, I found myself wondering how I'd open up to Pippa about my feelings. What would I say? *I love you* was too strong. *Care about you*? Sounded ominous.

'Pippa,' I began, speaking softly to a raw king prawn, 'I want to tell you something. I've wanted to say this ever since you stepped through that entrance to the music block and into—'

'What's cooking, chef?'

Pippa was standing in the doorway. I hadn't heard her come back down. How long had she been there?

'Oh, erm, hello.' I gathered myself, patting my hands dry on a tea towel. 'Have you finished doing your audition thing?'

'God, no,' she said. 'I haven't even finished warming up yet.'

'Sounded very thorough.'

'Ugh, bloody auditions,' she exclaimed, throwing a bare

foot onto the top edge of the washing machine in an athletic glute stretch that sent a lime tumbling. 'I've had *so many* lately.'

'That's good, isn't it?'

'But I haven't *got* any of them.' She swapped to stretch the other leg, and knocked another lime onto the floor. 'Oops. Sorry.'

'That's okay, I bought about fifty.'

'Anyway, enough about that. What are we having?' she asked, looking around.

'I'm still developing the menu.'

'*Oh là là*, Steve!'

'But for a snack, I've got some nice crisps.'

I opened a bag of the fanciest crisps I'd found on my travels, and poured some into a bowl from a height (I was saving the sea wee wees for later).

'Mm, sweet chilli! My favourite,' Pippa said beaming, and skipped out into the hall with them.

Music to my ears.

There was something of a theme to my menu. To start, I would be serving a salad of king prawns with Chinese leaf lettuce, coriander, cucumber, lime, and a sort of Marie Rose dressing made from mayonnaise and sweet chilli sauce. For the main, I would be utilising Oscar's legendary wok and stir-frying rice, an assortment of veg, and tofu marinated in . . . sweet chilli sauce. If I'd learned anything from my forays into cooking as a student, it was this: a smothering of the sticky stuff and your dish is saved. Sweet chilli sauce pizza? Yum. Sweet chilli tuna wrap. Sorted. Sweet chilli baked bean and sausage stew? Transformed. I considered giving the meal the title *An Ode to Sweet Chilli*, as if to own it as a decision rather than highlight its shortcomings.

'*C-c-c-caw! Cawl! Call off the search!*' Pippa continued to warm up in the hall, occasionally stopping to crunch on a well-earned snack.

'I hope you're not allergic to anything?' I called out, though I was pretty sure we'd covered allergies in one of our many rambling bedtime phone conversations, after which I'd fall asleep with Pippa's voice resonating in my skull, one side of my brain gently braised with radiation.

'I'll eat anything you make for me,' she said, appearing in the proscenium of the doorway and lowering her voice in a sultry way that mocked me to the core.

'Crustaceans?' I flirted back, immediately lamenting my choice of words.

'Anything,' she said. 'Just not coriander.'

I thought she was joking and had spotted the coriander that was still scattered everywhere but the ceiling, but as she lunged out into the hallway, resuming her audition cries, I realised she wasn't. Starter was off. The salad was already sitting in a bowl with shredded coriander leaves clinging to every morsel.

I can't just do a plate of prawns, I panicked. It was meant to be a statement starter.

I opened the fridge, hoping to find half a lettuce in there. What I saw first, dangling over the middle shelf like a melted Dali clock, was a response from Arthur, written on the other side of my note. How had I missed him again? He must be a shape-shifter.

I go abseiling this night. Good luck dinner man. Hope she is your girlfriend at the end. Don't look in blue bag.

There was a blue plastic bag on the top shelf. Without thinking, I pulled it open and peered in. Something – *meat?* – was tightly wrapped in paper and yet more plastic. Against my better judgement, I gave it a sniff, then quickly wrapped it back up again.

Behind me, a saucepan had started to rattle as the water boiled, sending bubbles rolling onto the hob plate with a hiss. I took the lid off the pan, and a cloud of steam wafted into my face, followed by a pond-like smell that took me back to a memory I couldn't place. I lifted out some of the small beige grains I'd thought were rice, and the memory came to life: the fishing bait my dad would force me and my brother to hook onto the end of his rod during long, boring Sundays by the river.

My main course, spiced tofu fried rice, was crossed off the menu.

I was going to have to improvise with what I had left. *How hard can that be? I watch* MasterChef. *Give me an onion and I'll give you . . . something oniony.*

'How long do you take?' I asked the block of tofu that I'd smothered in chilli sauce. I poked it with my little finger, which slid right through, a sensation I wasn't expecting and didn't enjoy. 'You're not like chicken at all!'

I can't serve it raw, can I? I'll chuck it in the wok with some carrot, bean sprouts and spring onion, and see what happens.

What happened was the tofu turned to mush. And the more I stirred, the mushier it became.

'Call off the search! The children of the sun are found!'

I clattered through the cupboards that contained dried goods. The first resembled someone's larder from about 1944: custard powder, a tin of soup and a jar of Bovril. Noodles would have been a good idea, but that was about the one Asian foodstuff I hadn't bought. Spaghetti could deputise just as well – *same thing, right?* I reached to the back of the next cupboard. No spag, but there was a bag of penne. That would have to do. We were taking a sharp left at the world buffet and going Asian–Italian fusion. With a bit of war spirit, I'd make do and mend my menu.

'Lay down your scabbard and rest. Rest, sir!'

I put the pasta water on and tried a mouthful of the mush.

It wasn't that bad – a bit sweet, a bit chilli. Not a lot of depth, though. It was definitely depth I was after, considering I was going to toss the lot into plain old pasta.

'*La-la-laay down your scabbard. Sca-sca-sca-scabbard.*'

I began to open some of the mysterious pouches. Water chestnuts? In you go. Tamarind? Just a splodge of that. Miso paste? That should give it some oomph. But how much oomph? Luckily the miso had some guidance printed on the sachet.

Pippa must have heard a lull in my clanking, and became still herself. 'Let me know if you need any help,' she said, her voice somehow compressed. 'But not, like, *hand* help, just verbal. I'm in a downward-facing dog.'

'Actually, I am a bit confused,' I said.

'About downward dog?'

'Well, yes. But I also have a quantity query.'

'Go on.'

'When it says add a tablespoon, does it mean—'

'A heaped spoonful,' Pippa cut in.

'Not a level spoonful?'

'No. A tablespoon is not a tablespoon,' she said authoritatively. 'It's more than you think.'

I studied the piece of cutlery in my hand.

'So this tablespoon . . .'

'Is a dessertspoon, I bet.'

'Ah,' I said, none the wiser.

'Glad I could be of assistance. *Call off the search! The children of the sun are found. They lay in their beds on the scorchèd ground.*'

I ladled four heaped dessertspoons of miso paste into the mix before liberally sprinkling on soy sauce.

'*Lay down your scabbard and rest.*'

'I'm nearly ready to serve,' I said.

'Okay, I'll get changed,' Pippa called back.

I owned two matching plates that were vaguely presentable.

Mickey had left them behind the one time he and Pat came round for dinner, knowing that mine wouldn't be suitable, even for a takeaway curry. I'd washed one up, but the other was nowhere to be found.

'Are we eating in the kitchen?' Pippa said, halfway up the stairs.

'Afraid so,' I called back.

'*Do not be afraid, for I love you.*'

'And I love you,' I replied, unable to stop myself. My head was in a cupboard, so the words reverberated around my ears in stereo. I waited to see if Pippa had heard. I hoped not – this was not the way I wished to serve up my feelings.

'What did you say?' she asked, only feet away.

I could smell the wok beginning to smoke and knew that dinner was off the menu. Like a metal drum heaped with salvage, it was destined to be incinerated. Something also told me that now was the time to tell her, when I was frazzled by all the cooking and had nothing to lose. I pulled my head out of the cupboard and got to my feet.

'We have to talk,' I began, trusting my mouth to find the right words.

'Oh?' Pippa said, looking to the bomb site behind me for a clue as to where this was going.

'Yeah, there's a thing I—'

In the hall, a phone began to ring. Her eyes shifted towards it.

'The thing is,' I carried on, but so did her mobile.

'It'll stop in a sec,' she said. It did stop, but the moment I drew breath, it started again. 'Hold that thought.'

I blew out my cheeks and shook out my wrists like an Olympian about to go for gold.

'I'd better get this,' said Pippa from the hall. 'Unknown number, but they've called three times.'

'Sure, go ahead.'

I heard her take a breath, readying herself like I had just done. As she spoke, I rifled through a drawer spilling over with fossilised batteries and long-expired warranties, looking for a takeaway menu for the Chinese.

'Oh my God!' Pippa cried out.

'What is it?'

She re-entered looking like she'd seen a ghost.

'Good news?' I asked.

'Oh my God,' she said again. Then she started to weep.

'Bad news?'

'I got one,' she managed to say. 'I got a job.'

'Fantastic, Pip!' I said. 'Let's crack open the bubbly to celebrate, though it might still be a bit warm. Did I say I'd bought bubbly? Was going to be a surprise.'

But Pippa wasn't listening. She was texting someone – *everyone* – at twice the speed of sound.

'What job, by the way?' I said as I popped the cork and poured the Asti.

Pippa took one of the mismatched glasses and looked at me with glistening dilated pupils, as though she'd been possessed by a very happy devil.

'I'm going to Broadway, baby.'

February 2009

Pippa

The linen-suited man across the aisle is gawping at her, jaw hanging slack like a drunkard, as she sashays towards my seat. He cannot quite believe his eyes.

Dolores ('Always Here to Help') flashes me a dazzlingly white, migraine-inducing smile. A smile that smacks of the blinding lights and giddy heights of America.

'What can I get you, ma'am?'

I survey the selection.

'Erm, one Kit Kat, please. And a small white wine.'

'Certainly.'

As she leans over her stacked trolley, a cloying scent of hairspray and nauseatingly sweet perfume explodes into the air. She crouches down, rummaging through the second shelf. Her tight pencil skirt leaves nothing to the imagination, cupping her spin-classed buttocks, and showing off a washboard-flat stomach to spectacular effect. Linen Suit Man is now practically drooling, his eyes popping out on stalks. I imagine the queues of frequent flyers who must have asked her on dates over the years. She's definitely one for the fantasy league. The frazzled mum of twins in the window seat glances down at her own rounded, spongy belly and pulls her beige cardigan around her with apologetic resignation. Finally Dolores snaps back up, placing the items on my tray table. A Southern drawl glides from her lips.

'That's nine pounds eighty-five, please. Or would you prefer to pay in dollars?'

Now what is it about flying and airports that make you think it's entirely reasonable to spend the best part of a tenner on a small chocolate-covered wafer biscuit and a minute bottle of fermented grape juice?

'Pounds, please.'

I hand over my wildly overused bank card with what I hope is a nonchalant flourish, and watch as the French-manicured fingernails tap, tap, tap against the card machine, like hail on a pane of glass. *Please work, card, please work, card, please work, card.* Seconds pass. The machine mulls over my digits, contemplating its decision. Is it my imagination or is everyone looking at me, judging me? Dolores' flawless foundation, those painstakingly applied fake lashes that flick out like ski slopes, the heavily drawn kohl brows, those candyfloss-pink lips settle in a patient mask. I have an overwhelming urge to tell her how well she would fit in at Madame Tussauds, but realise this would mean nothing to her so bite my tongue.

Next to me, obese banker Tony ('I always book an extra seat in coach – extra *body* luggage!') – who, after four gin and tonics and three Advil at take-off, promptly passed out on my shoulder, his bowling-ball head lolling unashamedly, a stream of sleepy spittle snail-trailing its way down my cardigan – suddenly wakes. He must have a sixth sense for the proximity of food, as he is now sitting up right, eyes bright, alert as a meerkat.

Finally, after what feels like hours, the machine takes pity on me and beeps in compliance. *Transaction complete.* Dolores too blinks back into life, handing me my bashed-up card with a twinkly 'Have a nice day' and another flash of her pearly whites.

As Tony places his trolley-emptying order, I turn to my Kit Kat. Well, well, hello, old friend. I slip off that reassuring red paper sleeve, familiar from childhood packed lunches, and run my fingernail down the thin tin foil valley between the sticks. I snap one off and nibble at the chocolate around the wafer, a habit that always drives my mother to distraction. A strange calm descends with the distinctive taste of home, and I scroll through the in-flight movies. Thrillers? Too stressful. Foreign Language? Too much commitment. Comedies? Seen them all. Action? Too many plane crashes. Tragic Romances? Too close to the bone. Classics? Hmm, possible. I stare at the iconic posters, New York in all its glory – *Taxi Driver, Manhattan, Breakfast at Tiffany's* – and suddenly, without warning, I'm back there, snippets of the last ten months fragmenting like a kaleidoscope.

I'm cycling through the East Village. I'm sauntering through the flea markets of Williamsburg. I'm smelling the freshly baked pretzels on the corner of Times Square. I'm back for my sixth solo visit to MoMA. I'm devouring a stack of fluffy blueberry pancakes like I haven't eaten for a week. I'm seeing the steam curl up from the traffic grids. I'm watching with bated breath as the luminously handsome new president addresses the nation from a battered TV in a chrome diner. If I was a sponge, New York City was my overflowing bathtub.

I had never travelled alone before – well, unless the odd weekend at Granny Delma's in Dorset counts (I know, it doesn't). All my life, New York was the place that other people went to. The city that other people lived in. Cool people, metropolitan people, trendy people, successful people, excessive people, indulgent people, fabulous people. And now *me* people. If that's a thing.

*

It was a balmy Tuesday evening when I got the call. Steve had insisted on cooking me dinner at his place, which was so sweet. And much needed, truth be told. I had been surviving off pot noodles and Shreddies, as my bank balance was not the healthiest, so the offer of a home-cooked meal was too good to refuse. I had ignored Gus and Tania's oh-so-mature taunts – 'He *lurves* you! He wants to *marry* you! You'll have Stevie *babies*!' Everything always had to be about sex with them. Why couldn't they understand we were just friends? Really, really great friends. Yes, we hung out together a lot, and yes, there may have been that tiny moment at Tania's party when something *could* have happened, but I was drunk and it didn't and now it was purely platonic. And we were both so down with that.

I had ignored the call a few times before I finally answered. I hated picking up to an unknown number, but this caller seemed oddly persistent.

'Hello, Pippa Lyons speaking.' (Gus always ribbed me for my phone-answering. '*They* rang *you*, Pip! They know who they're calling!')

A man's voice. Suave. Confident.

'Hello, Pippa, it's Simon.'

Simon. Simon. Who the fuck is Simon?

A creaking silence as I rattled through my mental address book. I didn't know any Simons.

'Your agent?'

Shit. That Simon.

'Simon! How lovely! Hey. How are things! So good to hear from you.'

Simon was the head honcho at my agency. Hence my never speaking to him. I dealt with the assistant's assistant's assistant. At best. Simon was saved for the bigwigs. For the

money-makers. For the free-gift receivers. Why was he calling me? I swallowed, panic rising.

'Simon. Hi! You've just caught me actually. I've been at the
dentist.'

No Pippa. Your oral hygiene is of no import to him.

'On the high street. My local one.'

Pippa, for God's sake. STOP.

'And I treated myself to the hygienist. I've got very high
levels of plaque apparently.'

A pause.

'Great, well I'll make it quick, Pippa.'

THANK YOU for making it quick, Simon.

'I just wanted to let you know that an offer's come through.
All quite last-minute. It's Broadway. A transfer of *The Importance of Being Earnest*. Need an understudy asap. It's an American
production and apparently some of the accents need work.
So you are kind of a BOGOF deal, if you will.' A snort; he's
clearly chuffed with this analogy. 'Pay for an understudy, get
an accent coach lobbed in for free. Job done! Travelling
Tuesday night. Money not great. Economy-class flight and
moderate accommodation included. Let me know by close
of play? Cheers.' And with that, he was gone.

I held the phone out from my ear and sank down onto the
floor, winded.

Had he just said what I thought he had said? Me. Pippa
Lyons. A job. A *play*. A *real* play. A *paid* play. With real-life
working actors! Oh, to be able to tell my eight-year-old self
that every prayer, every eyelash blown, every penny thrown,
every birthday cake cut with eyes squeezed shut, willing my
wish to come true, would one day lead to this. Sure, there was
every chance I would spend the next eight months in my
dressing room doing cryptic crosswords I could never finish,

learning lines I would never speak and being called 'babes' by the entire company as no one ever quite mastered understudies' names, but none of this fazed me. I was off to New York and I couldn't wait to tell Steve!

Three days and some majorly stressful packing and admin later, I found myself in the queue at JFK arrivals, passport in hand and an ink stamp hovering above my visa. This was it. I was about to live my dream.

The first morning of rehearsals passed in a whirlwind of jogging bottoms, swigs from NutriBullets beakers, hyperbolic introductions, trust games and air kisses. I was an interloper – that afterthought guest who had gatecrashed a very exclusive party where everyone but her had taken an ecstasy tab and was coming up at the *exact* same moment. Now, I'm notoriously tactile, but the amount of kissing and touching and stroking and back-slapping and knee-perching that went on terrified even me.

As I searched for a vacant stool in the ferociously lit studio, I heard 'Hey there!' and a striking brunette with a sharp bob and a black silk halter-neck dress sashayed over. 'I'm Sandy and I'm giving my Gwendolyn.' She held out her hand and I took it gratefully. Shit. My palm was wet with sweat. We both pretended not to have noticed.

'Oh hey there! (*'hey there?'*) I'm Pippa, from London, and I'm understudying Cecily.' I felt her wrist go limp as she slowly withdrew her slender hand and surreptitiously wiped it down on her silky thigh.

'That's so cute.' Her hazel eyes began skimming the room frantically, like a cornered animal. She might as well have flashed a sign saying *Beware! Beware! Understudy alert! The deadly strain of actor's flu that* no one *wants to catch!* She suddenly spotted an 'old friend' over my left shoulder and with a 'Great to meet' was gone.

I headed into my corner, pretending to check for something extremely important in my knapsack. Knapsack! Good Christ. What was I thinking? Nobody here had a knapsack! *This isn't 1985, Pippa! You're not one of the Goonies!* My clothes were all wrong. No one else was in jeans. Even my hair felt shameful. I knew I shouldn't have cut that fringe. And as for my *stupid* script binder that Dad had bought me with my initials on, could anything make me look more of a try-hard? I mean, it was so sweet of him, but *no one* under sixty uses a script binder.

I flicked through my notebook, pretending to read illuminating character research notes from the (patently empty) pages. *Swallow me up, floor, spirit me away.* I surreptitiously tapped my heels together three times – you never know – but nothing. I was still in the windowless box studio off Lafayette Street, lit as though for terrorist interrogation, with a group of actors who all knew one another and were entirely aware of my fraudulent credentials. I would never fit in here. I needed to get home to London and PG Tips and parents and mature Cheddar and Marmite. That was where I belonged. Who was I trying to kid? This was all a big, huge, ginormous, soul-destroying mistake . . .

Fast forward ninety-three hours and I'm underground, sitting in a secret, exclusive Lower East Side cocktail bar, surrounded by some of my *favourite people in the world*! This is the *best* job I've ever had. This is the best job I *will* ever have! This is simply the best job *full stop*! And these people are the most genuine, funny, loving souls I've *ever* encountered.

How had I survived before I knew this company? I must have been a husk of the woman I now was. Each one filled me with strength, courage and confidence. I was beautiful because of them. Magical Anita, gregarious Jack, body-popping Scarlett. Yes, I was on my fourth margarita but it was nothing to do with that. These actors completed me. I was standing on the table re-enacting a death scene from a cockney soap they'd never heard of to riotous applause. Goodbye, timid Pippa from day one. Who was that mousy, frightened outsider? Hello, hilarious Pipsy, the plucky Brit with 'such an adorable voice! Get her to say Crunchy Nut Cornflakes!' As the fourth margarita kicked in, and I was thinking this euphoric world couldn't possibly get any more heady, Kurt Sparks Jr sat down next to me and slipped his perfect arm round my waist.

What the actual . . .

Kurtis Sparks. Twenty-seven. Teeth straight white tombstones. Breath sweeter than honeysuckle. Funny, charming and discombobulatingly handsome. The maypole around which we all danced. He was something of a celebrity, having just finished a long-running teen vampire series in which he sucked the necks of unwilling (willing), wan (skinny and beautiful) girls. Surprisingly, neither the designer baseball cap pulled low over his eyes nor the *hugely* expensive shades he wore day and night concealed his much-lauded identity.

He was recognised *everywhere*. In cafés, in parks, on sidewalks (okay, so the lingo is infectious). By giggling, wriggling, hip-wiggling girls and lusty, busty, menopausal women alike. A mere flick of his sandy hair and the ladies (and 90 per cent of the gents) turned to butter. He walked among us like Moses, parting the rehearsal room waves. He was, quite simply, a god among men. And now, right now, this very nanosecond, this Adonis had his supremely moisturised hand resting in the curve of my back. Holy shit. Hold your stomach in, Pippa. Elongate your spine. Act preoccupied. Men like that, don't they? Send off your sex pheromones. Is that even a thing? Don't wriggle. Don't fart. Don't burp. Don't do anything that could scare him off.

I became David Attenborough, spotting a rare leopard on safari: *As night falls, the pack becomes frisky, but leader Kurt is focused. He has spotted something. A potential mate? Or unsuspecting prey to sate his voracious hunger? Just watch how the noble animal steels himself in the darkness. A king amongst the undergrowth, his stealth is both unnoticed and heralded. As we have seen, Kurt is volatile. Sometimes basking in the sunlight, confident, fearless. Other times hiding in the shadows, preening, readying himself for battle. One false move and it could all be . . .*

I mean, come on. Surely, that hand said ownership? That hand was saying, loud and clear, 'she's mine'. And it was. Four days in, and I fell victim to LMS – or, in layman's terms, Leading Man Syndrome. (Christ, what was I thinking? Oh, that's right – I wasn't.) Kurt Sparks Jr and Pippa Lyons became a thing. The cutest cast couple around. The cheeky little Brit and the chisel-cheeked heart-throb. We were touted and flouted and rooftop-shouted. Move over, Brangelina! There's a new power coupling in town. Make room for Pipurt! (Less of a ring to it, granted.) This understudy had become the most over-studied creature in the room.

'Have you met Pipsy and Kurt? Oh my God. They are soooo cute.'

The weeks rolled on. The show went up, to mixed notices. Okay, let's go with shocking, but who cares? I barely even thought about the play any more. This wasn't about the job. This was about Kurt. Me and Kurt. Kurt and me. What will my parents think? What will my friends think? I mean, he is so handsome it's criminal. Mind-boggling. And he wants *me*? I am his spaniel. I must not screw this up. Of *course* I want to take your signed photos to the post office, Kurt. And why wouldn't I mind being the back you lean on to do the signing? Oh yes! Please let me test you on your lines. It doesn't matter that my own are a little shaky. Lost your water bottle? Have mine! You're the lead! You need it. Accent coaching? Sure thing. Whenever you want. Day, night, moonlight. My time is your time. I massaged his shoulders and his ego.

But as the months passed, like a spoilt child tiring of a new toy, I watched as my novelty value waned. No longer would he show me off at parties; no longer would he even *talk* to me at parties. Our nightly kiss in the wings at 'beginners' became a weekly peck and then dropped off altogether. My jokes became less funny. My accent less cute. He even began wincing at my pronunciation, as though my words gave him toothache. He stopped blessing me when I sneezed or holding my hand when we crossed the road. And the more I persisted, the more he resisted, until finally, during the nightly full company onstage warm-up, he turned to me and announced, 'I need to re-find Kurt.' Apparently Kurt had 'gotten lost', and his performance as Algernon had suffered, as he was always 'too much of a giver'. It was time for him to sit with himself and have 'focused me time'. He air-kissed my cheek, pulled his cap down low and swaggered off into the wings.

I felt winded. Shell-shocked, I looked around at the others for clarification. Had that just happened? Had I just been dumped from the greatest height, without so much as a backwards glance? The shifty expressions of my teammates suggested that yes indeed, I had. And there it was. The end of Understudy Pippa and Movie Star Kurt. Any fantasies of being Mrs Kurt Sparks Jr and spawning mini baseball-cap-wearing narcissists dissolved like aspirin. But there was more. This hugely public dumping clearly wasn't considered brutal enough by the powers that be. The very next morning, the play folded. Just like that. No explanation. No dwindling audiences. No period of adjustment. Just here today, gone tomorrow. Our stage manager, Morag, announced over the tannoy that these would be our final three shows. (There was meant to be another three months.) No one had warned me that one bad notice can bring a show down on Broadway. But that was the American way.

I guess I must have dropped off, because I'm woken by the pilot informing us that we're approaching a patch of elongated turbulence and that the fasten-seat-belt sign has been switched on and will remain on for the foreseeable. I fumble with my belt fastening, trapped as it is between my thin blanket and the hook of my jeans. Turbulence never worries me. If anything, I get a kind of thrill out of it – perhaps a throwback to my addiction to funfair rides as a child, that sweet rush of adrenaline as the roller coaster hurtles down into nothingness. I reach down under my seat and pull my eye mask out of my backpack. Hooking the elastic over my head, I adjust my travel pillow. Just as the darkness is lulling me back to sleep—

Crack! A noise like nothing I have ever heard. The food and drink trolley leaps off the ground like it's possessed and crashes against the roof of the plane. My seat belt strains against my pelvis and I lurch out of my seat. It feels as though I'm being sucked out of my own skin. The cabin lights snap off. Shock gives way to terrified screams as the passengers realise that something truly terrible is happening. The once anodyne airline staff are now grey, clinging to our armrests in a bid to stay upright. It's all happening so fast and yet so terrifyingly slowly. It feels as though I'm watching through someone else's eyes.

We are dropping out of the sky.

Then suddenly there's a voice. A steady voice that seems

to break through the cacophony. A voice that speaks straight into my soul. And it isn't God. It isn't the pilot. It's Tony the banker. His gin and tonics, his dribbling pools of saliva, his overindulgence all slide away as he turns to me, his dimpled face, once so corpulent and jocular, suddenly dignified and courageous. Our gazes lock.

'Look at me. I've got you. Keep your eyes on mine.'

And for a moment, I do as I'm told. There's a freckle by his left eye that looks like a tiny map of Italy. His crow's feet sit nestled amongst the folds of his cheeks. But then I hear her. The screams of the young mother across the aisle as she clutches her twins to her chest. Primal. Gut-wrenching. The death-defying bellows of motherhood.

I whip round to see tray tables, cutlery, bread rolls and plastic coffee cups suspended in the air. From ahead, the sound of crystal and china crashing. First class is no protection against disaster. Whichever side of the red cloth curtains you're seated on this flight, whatever your class, bank balance, creed or colour, we are all in the same position right now. We're all together facing the end of our world. Parents are gripping their offspring. Husbands and wives are embracing for the last time. Two elderly gentlemen press their foreheads together as they quietly cement a lifetime of love. A young woman is crossing herself in prayer. Tony's plump fingers knit through mine and he squeezes hard.

'Think of someone you love. Do it. Nothing else matters. Think of that person and hold them in your heart.'

I do as I'm told. I close my eyes.

And just like that, as my existence is about to be snuffed out, there you are. You and me, Steve. Side by side on a riverbank. Hands and feet touching like a human paper chain. Above us a canopy of stars and dreams. Below us rich soil made of the flesh and bones of previous young lovers. And

I know as clear as day that if I see another dawn or breathe another sunrise, it has to be with you by my side. If I get to kiss another pair of lips or wake swaddled in another pair of arms, they have to be yours. Nothing else matters as long as you are by my side, pressed palm to palm forever.

I don't know how far we plummet, or why the plane finally rights itself. Maybe it's minutes, maybe only seconds. It feels like days. All I know is that precisely thirty-seven minutes later, we land at Heathrow airport to an onboard party the likes of which I have never seen before or since.

There are no words you can say to someone who has held your hand during the most petrifying moment of your life. And so Tony and I part in silence, strangers once more as the sea of passengers swallows him up. But I will never forget him. I drag my two huge cases from the baggage carousel, commandeer an enormous, unwieldy trolley from a distracted tourist and push my precarious tower of luggage to the front of the taxi queue. Excuse me, good people of Heathrow, I am in something of a rush! No time to lose here! This is the beginning of the rest of my life. Queues are for those who do not have to sail into the arms of their tomorrow.

Steve's address comes back to me like it was yesterday. I can see the place so clearly. That blue varnished door in dire need of a repaint. The cracked stoop with heavy moss sprouting in the corners. Those council bins overflowing with other people's greasy junk food wrappers. Oh. How beautiful it sounds. Like musical notes. Maybe this perfect haven is to be my new home. I have never felt so calm, so resolved, so sure of anything in my life. Even the wind seems to be blowing me in the right direction. A taxi pulls up and somehow we fit all of my bags into the boot and back seat.

'Flat 1, 116 Kilburn High Road. Quick as you can.' I feel like I am in my own romantic comedy. I should be saying 'Kilburn! And don't spare the horses!' This is the moment I will tell our kids about.

The moment Mummy knew Daddy was her prince.

We carve our way through the city, and I feel I am seeing it all again for the first time. Back streets, shop windows, impressive buildings, red buses – London opens before me like a pop-up book. I press my nose against the cold window pane.

Wait for me. I'm coming, Steven Gallagher. I'm coming.

Finally we pull up outside a Turkish mini mart. And there it is. Right next door. His flat. So this is what it feels like to come home. I tip the driver as he helps me unload my luggage. My heart is thumping. Steve is going to see me and he is going to know instantly why I am here. He is going to open his arms and I am going to nestle there for hours. Neither of us will need to say anything. We will both simply know. I walk to the door slowly, letting my finger linger on the buzzer. Number One. How apt. As I press it, I feel as though I am seeking access to the rest of my life.

A moment, and then a burst of footsteps. I am too excited to breathe. The door opens, and there . . .

. . . is a tall, slim brunette in stylish Sweaty Betty exercise clothes and immaculate make-up.

My mouth goes dry. I feel as though I have been punched. Is this the wrong address after all? Where is he? And who is . . .

Oh Christ. No. No.

After this, everything happens in double time. I check the girl's finger for an engagement ring. None. Thank God. But I glance past her into the hallway and I can see several photos of Steve with his arms around this woman. Blood rushes to my head.

Sweaty Betty smiles. Fuck. Nice as well as beautiful.

This is not what the path to destiny looks like in the movies.

'Hi.'

'Er, is Steve Gallagher in, please?'

Why the hell am I using his surname?

'Sorry, he's still at work. Who should I say came round?'

'Oh, erm . . .'

Think, Pippa. Think.

'Estate agent. Property valuation?'

'Oh. We're just renting.'

We. She is his *we*.

I'm too late. The ground begins to spin. I'm struggling to stay upright. She reaches out and touches my arm.

'Are you okay there? You look a bit pale.'

Her hand. My arm. Steve's house. I swallow hard.

'No. It's fine. I'm fine. Don't worry, I'll call him some other time. Thanks anyway. It was nothing.'

It was nothing.

It is nothing.

I'm nothing.

I stagger back into the street, my face burning. I feel like I've been dragged out of a blazing building and my heart and soul are blistering.

I think of the beautiful girl standing in the doorway. I think of her flawless skin and slender waist. I think of her home, *their* home, and I realise that I am never destined to be the heroine. She's the girl who bagged the lead part. The one who will make the headlines, snatch the reviews, kiss the leading man. It seems that yet again, I am destined to be the understudy. The one watching silently from the wings, prepped and ready to leap, but never quite making it onstage.

2 March 2019

03:39

'Diana. It's me, again. Just wanted to call and keep you updated. Not that there's much to, erm . . .'

Steve clears his throat and takes a sip of water. It's luke-warm and tastes metallic. He has a strange and unwelcome flash of the old rusty pipes bringing water into the hospital, and puts the cup down.

'She's doing as well as can be expected. They don't seem to be able to tell me much more at the moment, but she's being looked after brilliantly. I'm next to her as we speak. And I reckon she can hear me.'

He falters. Saying it out loud only brings the reality into horrible focus. Does he really believe that? He takes a deep breath to steady the quiver in his voice.

'So. You have my number, don't you? This is my mobile. It should show up on your phone. Can't believe I don't have your landline after all these years. Crazy, really. Anyway. I'm so sorry, you'll be asleep now and then you're going to wake up to all these messages and . . . I'm sorry. Call me, okay? Well . . .'

Well what?

Well . . . I'm terrified?

Well . . . help me?

Well . . . don't leave me here on my own?

Well . . . if anything happens to your daughter, my life, *your* life, is over?

Any of the above would cover it.

He lets the sentence hang, eyes squeezed shut, clutching

the phone to his ear. He doesn't want to cut off, terrified to break the frail connection with someone so familiar, someone so . . . *Pippa*. This woman who, despite having an unparalleled ability to drive him to distraction, is the only tether he has to the living, breathing Pippa, who has momentarily left the building. He needs to see Diana, to hear her voice, to watch her bustle around the room like she is late for a vitally important appointment. He needs to be close to the genes of his wife, the life force that gave Pippa her first breath. Maybe she will be able to bring her back to him.

'Well, take care, Diana. Speak soon.'

And then . . .

'Love you.'

He drops his mobile in his lap. His head follows, and is caught in his hands, where it rests until his palms turn slippery with tears.

Poor Diana. What will this do to her?

Snapshots of his mother-in-law. The moment she sees his missed calls, the moment she hears the messages, the moment she's confronted with the sight of the battered frame of her only child. He is winded by guilt and shame.

He alone has failed her.

A wave of exhaustion steamrollers him, like he has been running up a mountain. His limbs are leaden, the weight of three Steves sits on his chest like a totem pole. The clock ticks tirelessly on, oblivious to its cruel nagging insistence.

He still cannot bring himself to call his own parents. He knows that the sound of his mother's voice would prove too much. One word of comfort or alarm or support would be his undoing, and his delicate armour would collapse, cascading around him like autumn leaves.

No. Kindness is not his friend right now. Kindness, as they say, could kill him.

Not his family then, but someone. Someone who will listen. Someone who will pick up at this ungodly hour. So he rings the only person in his life who might still be up, as late Friday night becomes early Saturday morning.

'Guten Morgen,' answers Oscar, above a low throb of electronic music.

Steve is taken aback to hear his friend's voice. He'll be gaming, or have his decks out, he thinks, warmed by the charming, childish normality of it, though he cannot find a suitable reply.

'What you doing up, man?' Oscar waits, but Steve doesn't speak. The PlayStation is paused, the TV muted. There is silence but for Steve's heavy breathing.

'Have you bum-dialled me, Stevie? I hope I'm not about to hear you and Pippa at it.'

'I'm here,' says Steve, though it's an effort.

He can hear another spring dying inside Oscar's weather-beaten sofa, as his friend sits up sharply.

'Everything okay?'

'No. No, I'm afraid not.' Steve can only speak slowly, each word lubricating the next. 'Pippa crashed her car. I was working. They rang and . . . and now I'm here. I'm here with her.'

'I'm coming there now,' says Oscar.

'No! You can't.' The thought of another person he loves behind the wheel tonight fills Steve with horror.

'I absolutely can.'

'But you've been drinking?'

'Nu-uh. Dry January.'

'But it's—'

'March, yes. To make up for a heavy Jan. And Feb.'

Steve shakes his head, and a half-smile brightens his face for a brief moment. An exasperated smile, typically reserved for his best mate. It almost feels normal, except that when he looks over at Pippa, she isn't rolling her eyes, pretending not to laugh at their infuriating repartee. The emptiness of her response wipes Steve's smile clean away.

'I just don't want you to drive. Okay?'

'I get it, man,' Oscar says. 'So. How bad is it?'

'Looks bad.'

'And how are you feeling?'

'I don't know,' Steve says. 'Terrible. Confused. Really fucking scared.'

He feels a fresh emotion, agitation or anger, amassing under the surface of his skin. It forces him out of his seat. He doesn't know why, but it feels good to unload on his friend.

'What does it matter what I feel?' he continues, his voice raised for the first time since he arrived at the ICU. 'I don't matter!'

He begins to pace the room, his breath becoming short.

'You'll stay strong for her,' says Oscar, firmly. 'I know you will.' He listens carefully, like a safe-cracker awaiting the click of a pin sliding into place. Soon Steve's breathing steadies. 'I love you, man. I love you both.'

'We love you too,' says Steve, and he looks to Pippa again, her lifeless body plunged into soft focus as his eyes fill with tears.

'Sure you don't want me there?' Oscar says. 'I can skate over.'

'No, it's too far.'

'Fastest mode of transport. Seriously, it is. Which hospital?'

'We're out in the sticks,' says Steve. 'Buckinghamshire.'

'Ah. That is a trek. What you doing out there?'

'Working.'

'Oh yeah, you said. Wait, was Pippa working with you?'

'No.'

'Then why—'

'I don't know, Oscar,' says Steve, returning to Pippa's bed-side. 'I've got a lot of questions.'

'Of course you do, man. Of course you do. Well, I'm here for you. Phone's on vibrate. Anything I can do.'

'Actually, can you let Tania know?'

'Sure.'

'And Gus, maybe . . .' Steve trails off. He finds himself going through the same thought process that was required to decide who should make the cut when inviting Pippa's dear-est friends to stay in a Cotswold cottage for her thirtieth. He feels sick at the thought of having to inform them all about her accident, the sickness relieved slightly by the memory of Pippa's face lighting up when surprised by her waiting friends.

'You hang in there, Stevie G,' says Oscar. Steve thinks he hears an infinitesimal sniff. 'And tell your missus not to go anywhere. We got a lot of living to do.'

They hang up, and Steve sits back down in the still-warm chair. He allows himself to be comforted, just a little, by his friend's optimism. He takes his wife's hand, inanimate and stiff, and, closing his eyes, wills every positive vibration from his fingers into hers.

He could almost drift off to sleep, but there is a thunk, a shake, then a squeak, as lift doors slide open and a stretcher trolley clatters out into the empty corridor. It's followed by the blood-curdling sound of a woman bellowing in pain.

Through the narrow pane of glass in the door, Steve catches the face of a man, not much older than himself, run-ning beside the trolley. Eyes frantic, like he has woken up to find himself in the middle of a war zone. An elderly woman's hand is clasped tightly in his and tears are streaming down his bloodless face.

'Stay with me, Mum. Stay with me.' Steve can't hear the words above the din, but can see them on the man's lips.

But the woman's grip is loosening, her fingers sliding from his. Her primal cries have softened to a whimper, her fight draining away like water. A battle between life and death is being waged, the tug of war between the corporeal world and the spirit one. And death is winning the fight. Steve has a fleeting image of a painting he once saw: a man clinging to the feet of an angel who was threatening to take flight.

Just as swiftly as they arrived, they are gone. Around the corner and into a parallel universe. Steve's thoughts stay with the man with terror in his eyes for a moment longer, then he turns back to his wife.

He has his own angel to cling onto.

'You are not going anywhere, Pippa. It's not time. This can't be the end of our story. I've got so many more chapters planned.'

He gulps at air, trying to suppress a sharp bubble of emotion. He bites his lip, hard, willing the pain to keep his tears at bay.

'Our beginning was only yesterday, wasn't it?'

October 2009

Steve

It had become my daily routine. I'd sit in a coffee shop on the high road that served the cheapest coffee and the freest Wi-Fi, and try to look busy. The corner seat, which I'd kept very warm for a couple of months, was now worn with an imprint of my bum. The place was run by a Turkish couple, whose two young children would burst in every morning at 8.45, running between the tables and playing hide-and-seek behind the counter before being taken to school. Invariably they would stop and stare at me for a while, trying to figure out what my deal was, and if I was here to stay.

'What are you doing, mister?' they often asked, to which their mum would reply: 'Leave the man alone, he's working!'

I felt validated by her assessment, as if a morning spent there did count as work.

I'd reply to one or two emails, while nursing the cold dregs of a white filter, until the battery on my laptop ran out and I had to face the fact that no money would be earned today. Then back to the flat for a sandwich, where Lola would already have mended some curtains, spoken to both of our mothers, and started up a small business selling vintage lunch boxes.

She wasn't living with me, not officially anyway. When her landlord decided to sell up and turf her and her housemates out with a couple of weeks' notice, we agreed that it made sense for her to stay at mine for a while. I couldn't exactly let her sleep on the street. But soon her clothes found their way from an open suitcase on the floor to a chair, then into a chest of drawers. Her post was redirected, she took on her share of the rent and stopped actively seeking out a new flat share.

'It's lovely to see you settled,' said Mum.

It *was* lovely. For her. Mum had always made it clear that she thought Lola, the daughter of her close friend Maggie, was the one for me. Quiet but quietly brilliant Lola. Lola of Irish descent. Lola who would have waited 'like Patience on a monument'.

'You'll want to start looking for a ring soon,' was her next thought.

'Steady on, Mum, it's a bit early for that.'

'Not at all. June and Siobhan were engaged by now. Mickey chose his man in his twenties.'

'What about Charlotte? She's thirty-nine.'

'Yes dear, but she's a doctor.'

I didn't mind the idea of being settled, I just hadn't thought it would be with Lola. But when Pippa went away, I had to move on; and there she was, waiting on my doorstep with pipe and slippers in hand. (A metaphorical pipe; she wouldn't touch tobacco. Or drugs. Or drink. Or wheat. Or caffeine. My vices weren't exactly hardcore, but her clean living made me look dirty.) She was so proactive, so capable, that I felt inadequate beside her. I only had one string to my bow, and that string had worn very thin from lack of practice. Photography jobs were scarce, which I blamed on the proliferation of cheap digital cameras rather than on my inability to network.

'Everyone's a photographer these days,' I'd moan. 'People just use their iPhones.'

'You've got to get yourself out there,' Lola advised me. 'If not in real life, then at least virtually.'

But I refused to engage with social media, and was suspicious of Facebook especially – the idea of promoting oneself, as an individual or as a professional, made me cringe. I did have three LinkedIn profiles, but had forgotten the password to each of them.

'You'll be deleting your accounts in a couple of years,' I'd said, digging my heels in. 'Embarrassed by all the pictures and the poking.'

'Maybe find some other work, then?' Lola suggested. It didn't make sense to her that I kept struggling through, pursuing a career in which there was limited opportunity. 'I'll help you write a winning CV and you could take it round some printing shops, see if they need any part-time staff?'

'I guess.'

'Or you could retrain. Accounting? At least that's steady.'

'What about photography?'

'You can still take photographs. It's good to have a little hobby.'

Lola's advice was feasible, practical – I probably should have listened – but it wasn't what I wanted to hear. I was quite fond of inertia.

'I hear you're about to retrain as an accountant?' Mum would say when we next spoke. 'What a sensible idea.'

A day later, some brochures for the Open University were spread suggestively on my bedside table.

Maybe I should just propose. Sell the cameras, buy a ring, everyone's happy.

I paid for my coffee and ambled the hundred yards home, stopping outside the entrance to Carpet Planet. Looking at the bell on the panel of the peeling door that led to the flat above, I tried to imagine myself taking a Sharpie, and lovingly tagging it with mine and Lola's initials, but the letters just wouldn't sit happily together. All I could see in my mind's eye was *Steve and Pippa, Pippa and Steve, S&P.*

The last time I saw her, over a year ago, I had agreed to

help Pippa clear the bedroom she was about to vacate. In fact, I had suggested it. Any excuse to spend more time with her before she left.

'Thanks for doing this,' she said from the other side of her bed as she sorted clothes into two piles – one 'keep', the other 'cull'.

'My pleasure,' I said, trying to match up pairs of her socks, an activity that felt silly and sweet and heartbreaking. 'It's kind of therapeutic.'

'Aw, you're a good mate.' When she called me *mate*, it cut me to the quick. 'How am I going to cope without my bestie?' *Bestie*, a twist of the knife.

'You'll make new friends soon enough,' I said, unscrunching a yellow and pink striped sock then reuniting it with its sibling.

'But who's going to listen to my audition nightmares? Or be my chief line tester?'

'Some American probably,' I said, more jealously than I'd intended, but Pippa didn't notice.

'Oh yeah,' she said, 'my American boy.'

Her eyes filled with the bright lights of Broadway, and I watched as she skipped between yellow cabs, arm in arm with her new sweetheart.

'Why are girls' socks so much smaller than men's?' I said, trying to get her back into the room. 'Our feet aren't that different.'

'You've got hairy ankles,' she said, still daydreaming.

'Maybe I'll come to the airport, see you off?'

That brought her round.

'Yes, do,' she said, though it lacked conviction. 'Mum and Dad will be there, obviously. They'll have a monopoly on cuddles, I'm afraid. And Tania's coming, I think. And Jen. And Gus, actually. But do come!'

I decided against going, and left it to Mr and Mrs Lyons and Pippa's several other besties to form the farewell party.

An email arrived two days later. It was titled: *Miss you!* I read and reread the subject line a few times before I felt ready to open the message.

She misses me, I thought. She's been thinking about me for two days solid.

Subconsciously I started clearing the next few weeks in my diary, and began to picture what July in New York with Pippa looked like, as we walked arm in arm down Broadway before I dropped her at the stage door with a bunch of roses and a lingering kiss.

Then I opened the email, and read the first line:

Hi peeps, sorry I haven't emailed before. It's been a full-on but full-of-fun first couple nights here!

I couldn't read any more.

From then on, the group mail-outs arrived twice a week, and I found myself unable to reply to a single one. I had nothing to offer that could match her furiously detailed stories of long rehearsal days in an 'oven of a studio', and even longer nights out in Greenwich and the Lower East Side and Williamsburg with her new cast of adoring friends. The closer it got to opening night, the more sporadic her emails became, eventually petering out completely. In her final message, which hinted at a whirlwind 'showmance' with a co-star, she signed off: *Add me on Facebook to follow my updates!*

I hesitantly created an account using the pseudonym 'Geve Stallagher', and put her name into the search bar. Apart from an advert for missold PPI that kept repeating on TV (in which a woolly-jumpered Pippa glanced down at a bank statement before staring directly into camera to exhale the words: 'I'm owed!'), I only saw her face once while she was away, in the tiny thumbnail that headed her account.

I zoomed in to get a better look: she was in Times Square, looking so at home and so happy she could have been on the edge of tears. The picture was cropped just wide enough to reveal another face tilting towards her own. A square, clean-shaven jaw housing straight white teeth. A baseball cap. A tanned bicep nestled around her neck like a travel pillow.

Geve Stallagher's account was deleted with immediate effect. Therein lies only pain, I thought. Don't go therein. I knew that it was time to tear these feelings from my heart; much better than hanging on in the vain hope that someone I might never meet again reciprocated my distant affection.

I could have sworn I'd seen her a few months ago, hurriedly wheeling the suitcases I'd helped to pack away from the flat. It didn't make any sense, unless she'd curtailed her trip – but why would she be paying me a visit? I checked my voicemail for missed messages and my junk folder for lost emails, found none, and dismissed it as a mirage. But ever since, she'd pop up everywhere: on the cover of magazines, busking on the street, scanning my shopping at the checkout, there was Pippa.

I was still standing at the threshold to the flat, *my* flat, keys in hand, when the door next to mine opened.

'Hi, Steve,' said my neighbour from the flat above the minimart, whose name I'd forgotten so long ago that now it would be rude to ask. I wondered if it might be Alan, but that was because I'd let him borrow a set of Allen keys from me last summer.

'Oh, hey . . . man,' I said.

He stood to one side and watched me for a moment.

'How are ya? Busy?'

'Erm, no,' I said. 'I just remembered.'

'Yeah?'

'Yeah.'

He waited a beat longer to see if I was going to make any more sense, but I wasn't, so he swung his door shut and stepped around me.

'See ya.'

'See ya.'

I might have remained there all day, a post-modern sculpture (*Lost Man Staring at Keys*), if my legs hadn't made the decision for me. They wheeled me away from the door and kept walking, past Brondesbury, past Maida Vale, until the road signs began to give directions for Central London. By the time I reached Edgware Road, I realised that I'd walked two miles whilst breathing almost pure exhaust fumes, so I went down to the Tube, opting to fill my lungs with the stuffy, blackened air of the Underground rather than the filthy smog of one of the most polluted stretches of road in Europe.

I decided to go catch a film, let my mind escape for a while. The multiplex in Piccadilly would be showing everything – I could see *Fantastic Mr Fox* at a screening that wasn't filled with kids. Solo cinema dates in the middle of the day, whatever the movie, never failed to fill me with peace. A simple but powerful pleasure, the cinema draws me in the same way people are drawn to the sea – or, if you're my mum and dad, pulled into a church whenever they pass one. A chance to sit alone and become intimate with something bigger than yourself.

It was five stops on the Bakerloo line to Piccadilly Circus, and she boarded the train at every station. It would hardly take a degree in psychology to work out why I was having these visions, but today I just couldn't shake her off. There she was on a poster for package holidays to Cyprus; there she was looking at a map on the platform; there she was reminding the crowd to mind the gap. As I made my way to the exit, there she was coming down the other side of the escalator. This Pippa's hair was different – shorter, straighter, and more blonde than strawberry. Shouldn't stare, I told myself, but I couldn't take my eyes off her. She wore high-waisted trousers and had a suit jacket slung over one arm. I reasoned that she had come into town on her lunch break and was now heading back to work in the City.

As we glided inexorably towards each other, the woman was alerted to my attention by that instinct that tells you someone is watching you. Her focus adjusted from the middle distance to my gawping face. She looked into my eyes, recognising them, and I saw that it was her – it was Pippa.

In a moment, we were so close we could have reached out and touched; grabbed hold of one another across the polished aluminium, unable to let go, sending a cascade of bodies and Pret wraps and Hamleys bags down the corrugated metal steps.

'I can't believe you're here. Is it really you?' I wanted to say.

Instead, all I managed to do was wave. A small, meek wave, which she returned, her arm pulled close to her chest like it had been temporarily shortened. Then the escalator pulled us in opposite directions, and our waves morphed into ludicrous hand signals, as we hurriedly tried to communicate without words.

'Can you stop to chat?' Pippa seemed to mouth.

'Yes, shall we meet at the top?' I mouthed back.

'I'm going down. Shall I stay down?' she might have said. Our gestures were becoming more and more wild, a kind of mosquito-swatting semaphore.

Then she disappeared. I waited at the summit for a few moments before deciding that Pippa would be doing the same thing at the bottom, but as soon as I stepped onto the escalator again, she was sailing back towards me. Her face laughed first, and then I heard her. The thrum of the station, and of London beyond, was hushed; there was only her voice. It hit me like a wave just how much I'd missed her, how long those months without her had been, how staid, how samey. There was nothing and no one like her, and nothing and no one who made me feel like this.

The ticket hall was too busy for a catch-up after so long, so I followed her through the barriers and out onto the street before we spoke.

'How are you, mister?' she said. Then, before I could think of an answer: 'Can I hug you?'

'Um, yes,' I said. 'That would be acceptable.'

She giggled as we hugged, though both giggle and hug were short-lived.

'So.'

'So.'

'How was New York?' I said.

'Oh. *So* amazing,' Pippa gushed, though she didn't sound like herself. Had she picked up a transatlantic twang, or was she lying?

'And the play?'

'The play was *amazing*,' she said. 'At least I thought so. Sadly, the critics didn't, and we closed early.'

'Pip, I'm so sorry.'

'I'm over it,' she said. 'Just never mention it again.'

'We can talk about something else,' I said. 'Your hair!'

She cupped her hands to her cheeks, as if discovering in that moment that her locks had been sawn in half. She belonged on a 1960s French record cover.

'Nice?' she said.

'It's so different.'

'But nice?'

'Yes!' I said. 'It's very nice hair. I nearly didn't recognise you.'

'Well,' she said, dropping her voice and glancing over her shoulder, 'I am in disguise.'

'Oh, really?' I was so giddy in her company that I went along with her act like a child listening to a party entertainer. 'As what?'

She took a deep breath, like an inverted sigh.

'As . . . *woman, late twenties to early thirties, works for a financial firm but not too high-powered, lets her trousers do the walking and her hair do the talking.*' She planted her feet in a power pose. 'Are you convinced?'

'A hundred per cent. In fact,' I dropped my voice now, 'I heard your hair say something just then. Thought I was going mad.'

She laughed a little, then threw a bitter glare down Shaftesbury Avenue. 'Another day, another shitty commercial casting.'

'I suppose congratulations are in order,' I said.

'What?'

'You've moved into the "late twenties" casting bracket.'

Pippa jabbed at me playfully with her hip.

'Don't even start. Can you believe we're twenty-seven?'

'I'm twenty-eight,' I said.

'Christ. We are officially *old*.'

We had started walking, finding our way back towards the easy swing of friendship one step at a time. Pippa shot another glower towards Soho and the scene of her latest audition, before turning right onto Wardour Street, into Chinatown.

'Twenty-seven and I'm back living with my parents,' she said. 'Well, Dad.'

'Where's your mum?' I asked.

'Living in a flat down the road. Still sees him most days,

but it turns out she had a string of boyfriends while I was in NY. In her *shag pad*.'

'Wow, that's . . . pretty cool?'

'It's disgusting,' Pippa spat.

We stopped in front of a congregation of tourists waiting to have their photos taken with a cheaply costumed Mickey Mouse and an even cheaper block of foam that was meant to be SpongeBob SquarePants.

'Twenty-seven,' she repeated. 'Living with my dad and *single*. What about you?'

I felt her looking at me, but couldn't bring myself to meet her eyes.

'Twenty-eight, unemployable,' I said, watching the costumed characters, who seemed to be jostling for the attention of the tourists. 'Still living in that funny flat—'

'With whom?' Pippa asked immediately.

'With—'

Because of their gaping smiles, it wasn't obvious that the cartoons were fighting until SpongeBob threw a right hook at Mickey. The punch-up quickly escalated into a brawl when Goofy and Hello Kitty joined in, and I was grateful for an excuse to move away from danger – and from the topic of conversation.

'If commercials aren't filling you with joy,' I said, as we pressed through the crowds in Leicester Square, 'you could always do a bit of dressing up.'

'Do you think so?'

'You'd be great.'

'Oh thank you, Steve! I've always wanted to play Mickey.' We stopped at a zebra crossing, and she became thoughtful. 'Actually,' she said, 'I have always wanted to punch Hello Kitty.'

'It would have made a great photo, the fight,' I said as we

meandered in the direction of Covent Garden. 'Shame I don't have my camera.'

'You should always keep it with you,' Pippa said. 'I would if I had a gift like yours.'

'Yeah, sure,' I said, assuming she was taking the piss out of me in retaliation.

'I'm serious, Steve. It's your weapon. You never know when you might see something that moves you.'

I looked at her, and could see she was in earnest. Suddenly my career advice felt ill-judged and cruel.

'Like cartoon fisticuffs?' I said, but she didn't respond.

We walked a little further, Pippa slowing down as we passed a theatre.

'I guess I've not been feeling that inspired recently,' I said. 'It's become a bit of a slog.'

'That's a shame,' she said, lingering to read the reviews displayed beside the entrance.

'It is. But it's also fine, you know. I'm not that creative, really. Not like you or—'

'Oh come off it,' she said, stopping me in my tracks. 'Stop doing yourself down! Of course you're creative. You're creative and cool and sexy—'

'Sexy?' I said, a teenage trill in my voice, as if it were breaking.

'No, not . . .' She shook her head, and I could almost see the straightened strands of her new hairdo beginning to curl up. 'I don't mean you; I mean it's a sexy job.'

We fell silent, and turned to look at the press shots for the play that were plastered outside the building.

'That's a terrible photo,' I said at last.

'It's terrible *casting*,' said Pippa, jabbing a finger at the actress who was centre stage. 'Look at the face she's pulling.'

'The depth of field is completely off.'

'She's a reality TV star; what's she doing in a Chekhov?'

'It's very amateur.'

I felt Pippa's arm, warm against my own, as our bodies grew less rigid.

'Imagine if you were the photographer,' she began.

'And you were the lead,' I replied.

'It could happen.'

'It *should*.'

We stared dreamily at the glass, our faces reflected back at us; a window into another life. Then – though it may have been my imagination – I thought I heard Pippa quietly say: 'Our time will come.'

We continued on, saying little, until we were circling Aldwych and walking back on ourselves. Pippa came to a stop in front of another theatre, where *Dirty Dancing* was playing.

'Poor Patrick,' she said. 'I can't believe he's gone.'

'Did you know him?'

'Sadly not. Felt like I did.'

A few passers-by were stopping to look at the cards, the bunches of flowers, the candles that had filled with rainwater – a faded shrine to Swayze.

'Did he die here?' I asked.

'No,' said Pippa. 'He was in the film. This is a tribute.'

'I know he's in the film,' I said. 'My sisters loved it.'

'Bet you did too.'

'Never seen it.'

'What?' She was aghast.

'Whenever they put the video on, it was time to get out the Scalextric.'

'I can't believe you've never seen it,' she said. 'It's a classic.'

'A *classic*, huh?'

'Yes, Steven. It doesn't have to be *Citizen Kane* to be a classic.'

'I haven't seen that either.'

'Well you should.' With that, she clicked her heels and set off down the Strand.

I am useless at reading signals, but I'd been paying attention to Pippa for years and could tell that something between us had shifted. It didn't feel awkward as such, but rather like we had just been arguing about something we were unable to articulate.

In cutting ties with her news feed from New York, I had successfully stopped myself from sharing the experience of her triumphant Broadway debut. I'd suppressed images of her living her dream, never allowing myself to imagine her on stage, lapping up the applause or signing autographs. But I'd also prevented myself hearing from her when the pendulum had swung the other way and sent her crashing back to London. I shouldn't have buried my head. I should have been there for her.

'I'm sorry I didn't send you a first-night bouquet or anything.'

'Don't be sorry, Steve. I wasn't expecting it.'

'I didn't think it would be . . . appropriate, you know?'

'Absolutely fine. Anyway, postage to the US is ridiculous.'

We were walking more briskly now, towards Charing Cross.

'I think I should have at least sent a card, though.'

'Or an email,' Pippa said, not unkindly, but it made me feel terrible. I'd let her down – even if my radio silence was for my own sanity.

'I'm a bad person,' I said.

'You're not, Steve!' She rounded on me. As before, I didn't know if I was being chastised or flattered. 'You're better than most. You're a good mate.'

That word again. A bit better than *bestie*, but still such an unwelcome classification. This time it didn't just sound wrong to *my* ears; it made Pippa purse her lips, as if it had an unpleasant aftertaste.

As we passed the National Portrait Gallery, a girl ran across our path, almost tripping us up and sending herself tumbling.

'Sorry!' she said, breathless, picking up a tote bag covered in a rainbow of Dali moustaches. Her hands were speckled with paint, her black hair tied up with a pencil, and she had a distinct air of the girlfriend I had left at home. She smiled at us, then skipped over the road.

'How's your friend?' said Pippa.

'Oscar?'

'No, your girl friend. The one with the bob.'

Did she know about Lola? I'd certainly never mentioned her to Pippa. I stayed silent for a few seconds, hoping the question might drift away, far above Nelson's Column, but it wouldn't.

'You mean Lola?' I finally said.

'That's right.'

'She's fine. Why do you ask?'

'Well, you and her are . . . aren't you?'

I couldn't read her expression. If I had to guess, it was somewhere between nonplussed and amused.

'I mean, yeah. Sort of,' I said. 'It's not serious. How do you know?'

'Just . . . people,' said Pippa. 'Someone's Facebook, I think.'

There'd been such fluency to our relationship when we were young, free and single; but as we walked down the steps of Trafalgar Square, coming to a halt outside a small entrance to Charing Cross Tube, I felt it slipping away. If this catch-up were a workshop for our friendship, we would not be mounting a full production.

'I thought I saw you,' I said. 'A few times, but one time in particular, outside the flat.'

'Really?' said Pippa, her eyes fixed on one of the fountains. 'That's strange.'

There was a sadness in her demeanour that I'd never seen before. I yearned to put my arm around her, to protect her. But I was afraid to. It would be wrong, wouldn't it? She wasn't mine, and this was exactly the sort of confusion of desires I'd been trying to stamp out.

'Shall we make a wish?' she said.

It was time to say goodbye for good, to extinguish the flames by plunging them deep into the green water. Our chance had flown when she had. I was twenty-eight now; my bed had been made.

So why these butterflies in my tummy?

We stood side by side, inches from the curved stone edge of the fountain. I took out some change, two ten-pence pieces, and dropped one in her palm. She caressed it in both hands and shut her eyes. I followed suit.

'Don't tell me or it won't come true,' I heard her say.

A tiny drop of water was blown onto my cheek from the spray, followed by a jolt of electricity as the back of her hand brushed mine. An accident, I assumed, and shifted slightly, out of politeness. Then I felt her fingers searching for my own – unmistakable, deliberate, determined – and suddenly we were holding hands. Holding tight. Ready to jump.

November 2009

Steve's deep voice is vibrating through the thin walls of the bathroom next door. I can feel its resonance in my spine and it's making my stomach do flip-flops. I wouldn't say it's tuneful exactly, more that kind of speaky singing that David Tomlinson does as Mr Banks in Mary Poppins, but it's his tune and that's good enough for me.

'*Na na something or other . . . Pap, pap, paparazzi. Who would have na na na . . . something something, da de do da—*'

He never knows all the lyrics to a song. Especially when he's nervous. Or excited. It's a sort of tic. A 60 per cent approximation delivered with 100 per cent commitment. And I love it. It's adorable. He's adorable.

'*I'm your big admiring something, I'll follow you to something, do da, papa-paparazzi!*'

The last month has whipped by like a hurricane, knocking us off our feet, sucking us into its swirling vortex and plunging us into unknown but intoxicating waters. Winds of change nipping at our heels as we both leapt in with only instinct as our guide. Since a chance reunion on an oily clanking escalator, it has been unstoppable.

It being us.

Us.

Wow, what a beautiful word. I never knew two letters could give off such a sweet, sweet scent. Like toast and cut grass and Christmas morning all rolled into one.

That bewilderingly calm certainty that filled me as the plane plummeted from the sky, the rush of conviction that I was destined to be with him, grows with every second we spend together. How could I have been so blind? This gift has been right under my nose, ripe for the unwrapping, and yet I swatted it away like an irritating wasp.

It feels like every decision we've made, every journey we've taken, every hand we've held, every door we've slammed, every single fragmented particle of our lives has led us to this. This tiny, exact, precious moment in time. And as we stood by Trafalgar Square fountain that fateful day, fingers locked tightly together, there was no need for words. We watched the tossed coins of a hopeful child soaring through the air. We watched as they splashed into the cloudy water then sank to the tiles below, the ripples oscillating like sonar rays. We watched his eyes squeezed shut as he made his solemn wish. And as we watched, everything became clear. Schooldays. Chance meetings. Sliding doors. Other people's hearts. Unstoppable tides. Two people being pulled together by an invisible magnetic force.

The feeling was bigger than us.

And we both knew we couldn't let it pass us by.

And now here I am. Here we are. Really, truly here.

Ready, at last.

'Baby, there's no different, something or other, super starry, papa-paparazzi!'

So perhaps it may sound unspontaneous, unromantic even, but we had planned tonight. Meticulously. We were done with chaos and spontaneity and leaving things to chance. We both wanted our first time to be calm perfection. It had so nearly happened last week. Music, a bottle of wine, a strategic knot in his shoulder, a massage, some frenzied snogging, clothes cast off . . . but then a stoned Oscar crashing through the front door with a giggling lady friend, a banjo, two cans of baked beans and an insatiable bout of the munchies kind of killed the mood.

'I'll follow you to something nicey, papa-paparazzi'

The tap is running full blast as he fills the sink, and if I close my eyes, I can see him clearly. The threadbare Celtic towel tied around his waist like a sarong. His dark hair slicked back from his face like a fifties film star, his broad chest still damp from the shower. Right about now he is frothing the foam around his beautiful jaw, unsheathing the wooden-handled razor his mother bought him last Christmas and dragging it carefully over his face. His imperfect perfect face. Bottom to top. Bottom to top. Rinse the blade and repeat.

It's as though I'm watching him in a mirror. Through the walls of my mind I feel I can be anywhere that he is.

Not in a creepy way, mind you. In a magic way. In a perfect way.

In a *love* way.

Oh shit it. There's that bloody word again.

I haven't said it to him, and yet it's always there, hovering. Like a child spoiling for attention as the grown-ups try to talk, jumping up and down in my head, knocking on my skull with its tiny fist. *Over here! Look at me! Listen to me! Don't ignore me! Hey! I'll just shout louder if you turn the other way! Oi!* All right all right all right! Stop shouting, I can't concentrate. See, I'm looking at you. You have my undivided attention. Just give me a bit of time to think. I don't want you to scare him. I haven't told him about you yet.

Love.

Christ. Even hearing people saying it out loud in movies makes me feel anxious. I want to yell at the screen: 'No, Cameron, take it back! How *could* you, Goldie? Protect yourself, Meryl! Run, Meg, before it's too late!'

And yet this time, it's *me*. Me. On this bed. The leading role in my own movie. And I'm not scared. In fact, I'm smiling like a maniac. This is it, and instead of pegging it, I am a sitting duck, a willing victim, my young heart open and exposed.

They never tell you that falling in love reduces you to a walking marshmallow. Worse than that – a *toasted* marshmallow. Scorched on the outside, melted goo in the centre. That your body, mind and soul, once beacons of potent strength and womanly rationale, dissolve like soluble aspirin. You become incapable of sustaining thoughts. They seem to muddle and puddle around your feet like butter melting in the midday sun. Your single purpose in life is to fit yourself into your loved one's pocket. To be their scarf when they are cold. To bring them sunflowers when they hurt. To raise them higher when they succeed . . .

So. My seduction position is top notch. I have settled on a nonchalant semi-clad recline as my perfect pre-coital pose. *Oh hey there. What? This cleavage? These perfectly waxed legs? This scantily covered crotch? Comes natural. This is just how I roll.* I have bought new lingerie for the occasion. And it wasn't cheap. In fact it was a mind-numbingly horrifying expense, the most I've ever spent on garments that are designed to spend the majority of their working lives covered up. But it's only going to be our first time once. Old, saggy, greying undies are simply not an option.

Whilst the flickering candlelight is definitely adding to the erotic *je ne sais quoi* of proceedings, I'm aware that my shivering is becoming more and more pronounced as the minutes tick by. Despite holding my languid pose as committedly as a life model, the room temperature has suddenly dropped to Slush Puppy cold and my teeth are knocking together like rattled pennies in a piggy bank. I reach out and test the radiator. Glacial. Shit, looks like his boiler is still buggered. My plan for 'sensual goddess in an erotic foreign movie' vibe is rapidly dissipating. Instead I'm channelling more 'unpaid extra in a student porno'. The head-to-toe goosebumps are reminiscent of a defrosted battery chicken.

Not good.

New plan required.

How about being *under* the duvet when he comes back in and peeling it back erotically to reveal the treasures that lie beneath?

Yes. That's a far better idea.

'You warm enough in there, Pip?' he calls through the wall. 'I think I'm gonna bring the electric heater in.'

How the *hell* does he do that? Knows what I need before I've even asked for it? Another belly flip. I have landed a perfect, clever, loving, funny, psychic, generous, sexy, silly boyfriend. I am smiling so much I'm scared my cheeks may crack. What did I do to deserve—

Suddenly, without warning, Lola pops into my head.

Oh shit. No way. You're not welcome here. This is private! Between me and Steve. Please. Get out.

But you won't. Instead, you just tilt your head and look at me. A sad, quizzical expression on your prettier-than-mine face.

Why are you in my bed, Pippa? I don't understand.

The same effortlessly fresh face I saw in the doorway. Heart-shaped. Symmetrical. Soft-skinned. Hazel-eyed. That patient, warm smile of a genuinely decent person.

You're on my side. Can you get out, please?

The same face I saw in those framed pictures in the hallway.

I don't really understand why you did this to me, Pippa.

Those framed pictures that told of my missed months.

Are you listening to me, Pippa?

Those framed pictures that stopped my heart when I real-ised I might have lost the most important thing in my life.

'Cos I'm not going anywhere.

Those framed pictures that I found stuffed into the bot-tom of his wardrobe when I was looking for some warm socks last week.

Not for a long, long time.

Those framed pictures that I still haven't asked him about.

I mean, it's nothing. Not really. He obviously can't bring himself to throw them away just yet. And that makes sense. I wouldn't want him to. She steps closer to me, a gentle smile playing around the corners of her lips.

Wonder why he didn't tell you he was keeping my pictures, Pippa?

'Cos you were a huge part of his life, Lola. Of his family's life. You always will be. (Don't rise to it, Pippa. She isn't real.)

But it's kind of odd, isn't it? I mean, I wouldn't like it if he was keeping photos of you.

Yes, well, we have a totally trusting relationship. There is *nothing* for me to be worried about.

But then he didn't have pictures of you. He never even talked about you. I never—

'You okay in there, Pip?'

I shut my eyes and shake my head, as though trying to dis-lodge water from my ear canal after swimming. Get out, Lola. Out, out, out.

After a few moments, I open my eyes cautiously and scour the room. It *looks* empty. She's not in the corner. Not by the door. Not on his chest of drawers. Could she be . . . gone?

'Pip? You okay?'

I peer over the edge of the mattress and snatch up the duvet, convinced I will catch her unawares if I move fast enough. Nope, not under the bed. Well that's a relief. I didn't like my chances of coaxing her out from under there. Maybe she really has left the building. For now, anyway. I begin to breathe again. Thank God. Nothing quite kills the vibe like an imaginary ex-girlfriend in the room critiquing your every move.

'I'm fine, baby. But hurry up,' I add, somewhat pathetically.

I try to focus on something else.

Wow. His bedroom really is impeccably tidy. Everything is in its rightful place. He says mess makes him anxious. Well, my bedroom must bring him out in hives. Shit. That reminds me, I really must deal with my explosive floordrobe before he comes over next. Oh, and my ever-expanding collection of free magazines (who can resist a free magazine?) could do with a culling.

He *mustn't* know he's dating a whirlwind of chaos.

Not now.

Not ever.

Well, not *yet*, anyway.

It's funny. I still don't know where he keeps all his *stuff*. I mean, where are the shells and pebbles he's collected from seaside strolls? Where are the hand-drawn cards from young cousins that consume you with guilt every time you attempt to throw them away? Where are the piles of random tat from impulsive charity shop sprees? Where are the half-filled note-books with detailed to-do lists?

Maybe boys just don't have any.

Okay. I think maybe I'm starting to thaw under the covers, and momentarily consider resuming my casual lingerie pose. I point my toe out from beneath the duvet to test the current temperature. Bloody hell! No chance. Still Baltic.

The scented candle flickering on his bedside table (stool) looks new and smells of lavender and freshly laundered clothes. I don't recognise the make, but it sounds expensive. I can see him choosing it.

He's in a shop, standing in a long aisle of identical silver tinned candles, utterly flummoxed by the never-ending array of fragrances. Scanning row after row of twee perplexing names, hoping for a revelation – Night Jasmine, Green Tea and Fig, Citron Pressé, Festive Inferno. He toys with asking the friendly-looking shop assistant for advice, before bottling it, grabbing the nearest one and darting to the till. 'That'll be nineteen ninety-nine, please, sir. Would you like to pay by cash or card?' His eyes widen, horrified at the daylight robbery going on under his nose. He considers putting the candle back, cancelling the transaction and fleeing the store. But taking a deep breath, wanting everything to be perfect, he hands over his card . . .

'Ta-da!'

The bedroom door swings open and he's back, electric fan heater hooked over one hand, bottle of Prosecco gripped in the other. He nudges the door shut expertly with his bum.

'Sorry I took so long. Bloody water wouldn't heat up. Shaving in cold water is a total—'

But I have slithered from under the duvet as planned and am now lying fully exposed. Steve falls silent.

I feel unbearably vulnerable as he takes me in. He is stock still, rooted to the spot. Oh God. What was I thinking?

'Jesus Christ, Pippa.'

He hates it. I knew red was too much. I never wear lacy underwear. Too slutty. Too dominatrix. Too much.

Panicking, I scrabble frantically to pull the covers back up.

'Don't you dare.'

His voice sounds different. Gravelly, constricted, as though he is struggling to speak. He walks towards me and sits down slowly on the bed. I can see his pupils dilating into black pools, like an oil spill.

And then he just gazes. He gazes and he gazes. It feels as though he is learning every inch of me by heart.

'You look – *insane.*'

A sudden heat rises in my loins and I can feel my face flushing as I see the immediate effect I am having on his body. It is ferociously visible under his towel and I am aware of the blood rushing through me.

Suddenly all I can think about is his touch. When will he touch me? His hands. His fingers. His mouth. His—

'You are so beautiful, Pippa.'

I can feel my heart beating in my head. Christ. Please touch me. Please, please touch me.

But he doesn't.

He simply holds the duvet up and looks down at me.

'They're new. M and S. I was going to get white, but red was on offer.'

Come on, Pippa, we've been through this. Less is more.

But he barely hears. It's as though he is watching me from behind a glass.

Finally he reaches out and allows his finger to brush across my toes.

I gasp. Electricity flooding my body.

Watching me, a half-smile playing at the corner of his mouth, he runs his hand over my feet, my calves, my shins.

Now we are staring at each other. Intense. And for once, neither of us starts to laugh.

So this is it. This is really about to happen.

I rise up on my elbow and tilt my face towards him. We are nose to nose. His eyes are sparkling, his skin soft from shaving balm.

And then we are kissing. Kissing hungrily as if we want to devour each other. I lose any sense of space, time or place as the whole world contracts. There are only two people. Me and him. Jesus. I thought that was just a cliché. A line in trashy novels when the writer can't be bothered to think of anything more original. But here I am. Here *we* are. Living clichés.

My red lingerie doesn't last long. He claws at the bra fastening and slings it onto the floor. I wriggle out of my pants and we laugh as they get twisted around my ankles. I pull frantically at the knot in his towel. Until at last, at long, long last, there is nothing keeping us apart. Nothing between us. No distance, no fabric, nothing. Just skin on skin.

A hunger in his eyes that I have never seen before. A mist of desire descending upon us, rampaging through our bodies like a forest fire. Out of control. A heat that takes my breath away.

Suddenly he pulls back, looking into my eyes intensely.

'You sure you're ready, Pip? I don't want you to do any—'

Ready?

I grab his face between my hands.

Ready?

I run my fingers through his wet hair and my nails down his back. His imperfect perfect back.

Ready?

I tease my tongue across his mouth and kiss the tiny mole on his top lip.

Ready?

The heat in my groin is pulsating.

Fuck. I think I'm gonna die if you don't come inside me soon.

I take his hand and put it between my legs.

'Yeah, I'm ready.'

He smiles. A condom materialises from somewhere and is ripped open.

And then it's happening. Me. Steve. This. Here. Now.

I close my eyes and feel like this is the meaning of everything. He is inside me and I feel like I am holding the answers to all the secrets of the universe. Big Bang. Dark matter. The Pyramids.

Sex with Steve is the eighth wonder of the world. And it's mine. It's all mine.

I catch my breath as he goes deeper inside me. I feel like I'm floating. Like the tide is coming in. The waves are getting closer and closer to shore. Let this go on and on. I never knew it could be—

'Oh God, oh God, oh fuck. Christ, Pippa!'

He lets out a sharp cry and judders with ecstasy, and I feel the full weight of his body flop heavily against mine.

He pants jaggedly as he tries to catch his breath.

A moment passes.

He is burying his face in my shoulder. His voice is stifled, mortified.

'Shit. I'm sorry.'

When he speaks again, his voice sounds younger, almost like it did at school.

'It's just I've thought about that moment for over ten years. It will be better next time. Promise.'

He sounds so tragic, so guilty, so disappointed that I almost laugh.

'Don't be silly. It was perfect.'

'You don't have to say that.'

'I know I don't. But it was.'

He finally lifts his flushed face and looks at me.

'Really?'

'Yes, really.' And then – because I can't help myself – 'Anyway, you know me, short attention span. Anything longer than three minutes and I lose focus.'

He laughs and the panic dissolves from his eyes.

'What did I do to deserve you, Pippa Lyons?'

He winds my hair behind my ear. I lean into him like a cat being scratched.

And the words so nearly slip out. Every fibre in my being wants to say them, to shout them, to sing them from the rooftops.

I'm the one who has won the lottery here! I love you, Steven Gallagher! I love you! I love everything you are and everything you will be and everything you have been. I love you.

But instead . . .

'Ten-minute power nap and we can give that another bash. What d'you reckon?'

'You're on.' He kisses me gently on the lips and I roll over. He wraps himself around me, and for a moment, just for a moment, I try to clear my mind of anything but the present. I can feel his heart beating against my back. Rhythmic. Perfect. His breath warm against the nape of my neck. And the smell of him. That smell I've known for so long. The smell of my past. The smell of my future.

It's beginning to rain outside, spitting against the window pane. The universe is conspiring to heighten this perfect moment.

There is nowhere else except here. No one else except us. Nothing else except this.

And as if reading my mind once more, he mumbles into my back, 'We fit.'

I smile and close my eyes, his arm weighing heavier around my waist as he drifts off.

I want to be here forever. The two of us. *Stop, time! Be my friend. Halt your galloping pace, you fiery footed steed. Let me remain here always. I am home at last.*

Safe, secure.

Loved.

2 March 2019

04:39

Sixty-seven, sixty-eight . . .

What possessed him to have that second cup of coffee?

Sixty-nine, seventy . . .

Steve stops counting the small craters of flaked paint on the ceiling for a moment, and notices that his left index finger has started to twitch of its own accord. He had hoped that the repetition of counting might quieten his fluttering heart, but it's still throwing itself against his ribs like a hyperactive child on a space hopper.

Seventy-one, seventy-two . . .

'If we get through this,' he says out loud, 'I'm coming back to repaint this room, free of charge.'

As he turns his attention back to the count, a tremor runs through his body, hitting a dead end at the tip of his lower eyelid.

'*When*,' he corrects himself. '*When* we get through this.'

He rubs his lower back with a grunt of discomfort. His muscles are seizing up like hardening clay, rebelling against being static for so long.

Where has everyone gone? Mr Bramin said he would be back soon. And Nurse Craig promised to keep an eye on Pippa. Not a soul for almost an hour. The room wears that eerie silence of an abandoned classroom after the home-time bell.

He looks up at the clock. Again. It has become a habit. Part of his ritual. There is something reassuring about the concrete certainty that it will have moved on – that something in this room of stasis will have definitely changed since the last time he looked at it.

And sure enough, before his very eyes, 04:47 becomes 04:48. Something about the new time seems pertinent, but he can't for the life of him remember what. Something Pippa said? Or something he read?

A creeping, unknown fear launches him out of the chair. Just a short stroll, from one side of the room to the other. Movement feels good; he needed to move.

'Helps dispel the demons,' he says, inventing affirmations as he retraces the four-metre journey in the opposite direction. 'Activates the limbs. Stillness is a breeding ground for panic. Change the focus. Change begets change.'

Whir, beep, click, breath.

On one hand, Steve is grateful for the rhythmic ensemble keeping his wife alive, keeping the breath pumping through her body. On the other, he is terrified that as the voices of this mechanical pre-dawn chorus grow in confidence, they are exerting more and more control over her.

Whir, beep, click, breath.

His caffeinated finger taps against his thigh as he paces, dancing along to the life-support music like a jazz-lover tapping the side of their whisky glass.

Whir, beep, click, breath.

What is that song?

It sounds so familiar, it might be one of theirs. Or is it just that the sound of the room has embedded itself so deeply in Steve's psyche that it's already been filed in the hippocampus as a memory? The lyric-less earworm goes round and round his head, words appearing then disappearing like headlights on a bend.

He grips the nape of his neck and tries to squeeze the knot of tension that has gathered there. The pain shoots down his back and makes him cry out.

'Pip, I think your old husband may be losing the plot somewhat.'

He tries to laugh, but finds it sticks in his throat and chokes him. This isn't funny. Will anything ever be funny again?

'Too much bad coffee.'

He's had enough of hospital coffee. Enough of polystyrene cups. Enough of hospitals.

'Why are we here again, Pip?'

He glances at his phone and then realises he is checking for a message from her. Because there is *always* a message from Pippa. Always. Even when she is only in the next room or at the other end of the house.

Ping! A video of an old man who has learned to rollerblade with his aged wife.

Ping! I love you, husband of mine.

Ping! A rescue dog finding its 'Forever Home'.

Ping! A quote from the book she is reading on the toilet.

Exuberant messages, bombarding him hourly with Pippa-ness.

And now, nothing.

He finds himself at the foot of the bed, jittery as a clubber on a come-down. He realises that despite being in this room for what feels like decades, he somehow hasn't looked at her from this angle before. It's like observing a familiar painting from a new perspective. Her name is scrawled in red marker on the clipboard hooked over the bed rail, as if labelling artwork.

'Pippa Gallagher.' He reads the words out loud, allowing them to roll around his mouth like toffee. She used to be a Lyons, but now she is a Gallagher. Part of him, part of his family. And she could be gone by morning.

Steve and Pippa are coming tonight.

Pippa and Steve gave us this!

Have you asked Pip and Stevie?

How are Pippa and Steve?

An order of words that might be rendered meaningless to future generations. Two names that will never be spoken side by side, for fear of the pain they will cause.

This *can't* happen. He won't let it. He must keep these words alive forever. He will shout them at strangers and teach them to children. He will call them out of windows and holler them in parks. He will never let them be silenced.

He drifts over to the window. The rain outside is showing no signs of abating. Sheets of it, torrential, like movie rain, unrealistic in its density. Through the slatted blinds he spots a young couple loitering at a bus stop. Nineteen? Twenty at a push. The girl is holding a large polystyrene tray of chips, lifted close to her chest for warmth. The boy is draping his coat over her head, a temporary shelter. They are huddled together, smiling, tipsy. In love. Undeniably a team. A bus pulls up, its wipers sending off vast streams of water with each clunking swipe. They hop on, share a joke with the driver and collapse onto the back seat. The girl shakes the rain off herself like a puppy. The boy laughs and wipes the drips from his brow. Just as the night bus pulls away, Steve watches her feed him a chip. He eats it hungrily and kisses her on the nose.

On the nose.

Steve crouches beside the bed, his legs still too jumpy to allow him to sit. He whispers the words in her ear.

'Steve and Pippa. Pippa and Steve. Steve and Pippa. Pippa and Steve. Steve and Pippa . . .'

December 2009

'Looks like swine flu is on the way out,' said Pippa, reading aloud from a free newspaper.

'That's good,' I said.

'Glad I didn't get it. Mind you, Mum made me promise not to eat pork during the pandemic.'

'Is that how you get infected?'

'Probably not. Better to be safe than sorry, though.'

We were sitting on the top deck of the 32 bus; Pippa the narrator, me her captive audience, fascinated by what the next engrossing page of the *Metro* might hold.

'But we've been eating bacon sandwiches,' I said, recalling every hung-over Saturday breakfast of the last two months. 'We had one this morning.'

Pippa thought about this for a moment, weighing up her mum's science against her own.

'Bacon's cured, though. And smoked. Bacon doesn't count.'

Before Pippa, it would never have occurred to me to venture upstairs, unless the bus was very busy or there was a stinky mad person on the bottom deck. But ever since our virgin double-decker ride as a couple (the 29 to Camden Town), when we'd hurried up the stairs, making a beeline for the front two seats as if it were the first London bus we'd ever set foot on, it was just what we did.

Pippa turned the page to a feature entitled 'Christmas in

Bruges: A Winter Wonderland', a double-page spread full of smiling model couples walking hand in hand along frosty canalsides. She sighed, both dreamily and jealously. 'Looks so lovely.' Then she turned to face me, biting her lower lip like she had an idea that was a bit naughty. 'Shall we go?'

Isn't it too soon to go away? I thought. Can we afford it? What are the guidelines here? I was with Lola for almost a year – we even lived together – but we never went abroad. It just seemed like such a statement. Were Pippa and I ready for a statement? As for money, we had none (Pippa had touted me around town as a headshot photographer, but I was still charging mate's rates. She was working a hundred shifts a week in jobs that barely paid for her Travelcard).

'Hmm?' Her eyes twinkled with the prospect of jumping into one of the paper's pictures with me.

Things were starting to feel dangerously close to one of those spontaneous decisions that people go on about – I could already smell the Glühwein – so I tried to get a look at the prices listed in the advertorial, just to make sure we weren't about to be ripped off. But the bus was swaying, Pippa was jiggling with anticipation, and I remembered why I never rode the top deck. Dizzy with motion sickness and the tantalising dream of walking hand in hand along that canal, I agreed.

We jumped into our overdrafts with abandon, the holiday spirit taking over. Pippa picked out a new winter wardrobe for me, from woolly head to thermal toe. By the time the cashier was bagging up, I was ready for a mini break to the Arctic. I hoped it would be properly cold in Belgium so I'd feel the benefit. December in London thus far had been so mild that I got a sweat on if I wore more than one layer.

In the week before our departure, our excitement levels

spilled over into an obsession. Whenever we met – for dinner, coffee, a walk – we'd talk about it, wishing ourselves there.

'We'll be drinking coffee in Bruges soon.'

'Imagine! We're going to be in a park in Bruges.'

'I wonder if the water is hard or soft in Bruges?'

With every goodnight kiss, call or text, we'd count the sleeps till our getaway. When there were only two sleeps to go, we each laid out a suitcase and began to pack over Skype. I was apprehensive about sharing this ritual with Pippa. In my childhood, the process of packing, even for the shortest of trips, was a harrowing experience. The Gallagher family would tear itself apart, fighting over clothes, hiding passports, Mum and Dad yelling at each other to take control of the situation. The first half of our summer holidays would be spent in recovery, trying to heal the wounds sustained during the ordeal. But with Pippa, it was stress-free – *fun*, even. She paraded a shortlist of outfits that I had to choose from, scoring each one with a mark out of ten (the lowest score I gave was 9.4, which was politic, I thought, but also true). This, it turns out, was the secret to successful packing: do it seven miles apart, in different boroughs.

Winning outfits picked and packed, cases set to be zipped, we were ready for bed, just not alone. I threw my passport and my toothbrush into my luggage and took two buses to Pippa's waiting arms. Then it was just one more sleep.

On the train to Brussels, we breakfasted off flip-down tables on croissants and a mini bottle of champagne. The wine tasted tangy, mixing with the toothpaste still in my mouth. Pippa's head landed softly on my shoulder and we watched the sun rise over Kent out of the window. This couldn't get any more romantic, I thought.

Somewhat less romantically, I had started to make a mental note of our spending so far (didn't want us to get carried away on day one), when Pippa whispered in my ear.

'Shall we join the mile-low club?'

Perhaps it was because I was doing a quick conversion from euros to pounds in my head that I thought she meant we should sign up to the Eurostar loyalty scheme, to which I was agreeable.

'Good idea,' I said. 'We can start saving points to spend on a Paris trip.'

She laughed, though I wasn't sure why, throwing her head back in glee.

'So . . .?' She slid her hand up my thigh, her voice lowered. She had that look in her eye, lids heavy with desire. The look that made my pelvis a pinball machine. 'The *under-the-sea* club,' she murmured.

And then she was gone, sauntering down the carriage as if nothing remotely out of the ordinary was going on. I followed her, stopping at passing places between tables, allowing passengers returning from the buffet car to squeeze past. I could really feel those bubbles now, bursting in my head with a tinkle, like Christmas tree light bulbs blowing. I couldn't decide if this was a brilliant idea or a terrible one. Pippa started to giggle as we snuck into the vestibule between carriages and sidled up, James Bond style, to the first WC.

'I'll go in first, you keep watch,' I whispered.

I pushed on the door, but it was locked. The one opposite said *Vacant*, but wouldn't open either. I tried pulling it, fumbling with the handle, but couldn't work it out.

'You must slide the door open,' came a female voice – not Pippa's, but French.

I spun around to find myself face to face with a train guard in a peaked hat and neck scarf.

'Oh. *Bonjour*,' I said shakily, attempting to sound nonchalant, but my acting was so appalling it made Pippa corpse loudly.

The guard smiled back patiently, then continued through the next set of hissing doors. Had she guessed what was going on here? Maybe it's a very French way to travel. Or was she about to inform the police? It would be such a shame to get thrown off at the next stop.

'Maybe we shouldn't,' I said.

'Don't be such a wuss!' Pippa said, then pulled me into the cubicle, locking the door.

'I want to at least make it past Ashford International,' I said, unintentionally making Pippa howl.

I stopped her with a kiss, and the giggling subsided. It was just us now, lip-locked, the world falling away. Pippa started to undo my belt.

A voice drifted in from the other side of the door, where a man had stopped to talk business.

'I'm on my way to Brussels. Meeting at the European office.'

I hoped he would move on; his presence made me anxious. Just think yourself back home, I told myself, in the privacy of your own bed. But the blood was only rushing to my cheeks now. Pippa dropped her hands and stepped back, as far as she could in the confines of the tiny toilet.

'Don't worry,' she said, looking at the floor. 'It was a silly idea.'

I couldn't tell if she was offended or just disappointed. I tucked myself in, muttering some excuse about the guard and the businessman.

Pippa headed back to our seats first; I gave it a few beats – and a splash of water on my face – before following her, returning to our carriage much more sober than I'd left. A walk of shame with none of the risqué, promiscuous glamour, just all of the shame.

Pippa was reading when I arrived.

'I'll get my mojo back, don't worry,' I said, a cut-price Casanova.

'You'd better,' she said, taking my hand and squeezing it gently in consolation.

'Oh, it'll be a different story in Bruges all right,' I reassured her. 'A very different story indeed.'

'Are you sure this is the right hotel?' said Pippa as we lugged our cases up a creaking winding staircase. We were unimpressed by the state of the lobby, the reception and the breakfast room, none of which looked anything like the photos we had spent weeks studying.

'The building must be very old, I think. Two hundred years probably?' I said, pausing for breath. 'Might have originally accommodated tiny olden-times monks who only had few belongings and didn't have to—'

'Tiny monks? You feeling okay, love?'

'I don't know, I'm very hot.'

The heat was rising with us, and by the fourth storey, the summit, it was stifling. We let ourselves into Room 43. It could have been beautiful: a former attic, with exposed beams crossing the sloped ceiling, the bed and side tables set into the eaves, a Velux window looking out to the sky. However, it had been recently decorated in pink and lilac, the colours made more lurid by the fact that you could still smell the paint.

Pippa swung her case onto the bed and started to unpack. I had to cool down; the room was hotter than hell. I'm not self-conscious about much, but I simply cannot deal with my own perspiration. When I get a sweat on, there's not a lot I can do to stop it (God knows, I've tried everything), and the threat of more sweat just exacerbates my condition. So far, in our relationship as friends and more-than-friends, I'd somehow managed to spare Pippa and cover it up in time. No one wants a clammy boyfriend, do they?

The window was set far too high up in the roof for a human being to reach, so I had to locate the valve on a radiator that had been installed in the Middle Ages – a rusty metal wheel that burned my hand when I tried to turn it. Finally I pulled off my coat, gilet, jumper and shirt, leaving just my thermal vest. When my head emerged from the penultimate layer of clothing, I saw that Pippa had scattered the entire contents of her suitcase on the floor. Expecting her to start putting everything away, I opened the wardrobe door, which she ignored. Instead, she sat on the bed and began to read from a slim guide to Bruges that had been left there by its previous occupant.

'Is that you unpacked, or . . .?' I said, half to myself, half towards Pippa's cloth heap.

'Yes, Steve. That's me done. Okay?' She shot me a challenging look, the kind I shouldn't have messed with.

'Okay,' I said, unzipping my case. 'Well I'm going to use this drawer here.'

She sighed, exasperated, and took herself to the bathroom, which wasn't quite a room, rather a screened-off area in the corner. There was no free-standing bath, as we had hoped.

'This is *not* the bathroom from the photos,' she remarked.

I tested the bed, which felt pleasingly springy and new. Falling back onto it and spreading myself out, I could see Pippa's left foot past the edge of the concertinaed plastic screen, knickers and tights wrinkled around her ankle.

'I can seeee you . . .'

'What? Go away! Stop looking!' She whipped the screen across, so fast it almost came down entirely.

'Now I can't see you.'

I picked up the Bruges guide, which folded out to a handy map.

'Hey, there's a *frites* museum here!'

'Steve . . .'

'Sounds fun, huh?'

'Sorry, but I can't go with you there, listening.'

'It's okay, I won't listen.'

'Aaagh!' she yelled. A sound previously reserved for her mother and her agent.

'I guess it's you who can't perform this time.' I couldn't help myself. 'In the toilet.'

Then a sound I hadn't heard before. .

'GET OUT!'

I nearly fell off the bed.

'Sorry, Pip! I didn't . . .'

'Just go, will you?'

I waited outside, tail between my legs, like I'd been sent out of class. It was obvious I'd overstepped a line. We were too close for comfort and I couldn't take a hint.

How long do I give her? Five minutes? Ten? I knew I could spend a good half-hour on the throne, in quiet contemplation, often getting up to find my legs were dead. Lola would be in and out in the blink of an eye (and never seemed to use up any loo roll). Were all girls the same? I had no idea. I'll leave it another three minutes, I thought, then check in with her.

I was startled by a sudden creak of ancient floorboards as a Scandinavian couple came puffing up the stairs. They stopped beside me and nodded hello, taking out a key to Room 42. This is ridiculous, I thought. I couldn't stand there indefinitely, hovering by their door in a thermal vest – they'd start to worry that I was about to break into their room with an axe. As quietly as I could, I opened our door just wide enough to reach round and whip my coat from the hook. Then I went downstairs and set out for a stroll around the block.

I had been worried that travelling abroad together might be too much of a gesture, but now I was starting to fear it might be too much of a test. It was new territory for both of us. For the first time, we were truly alone, with nowhere to run or hide, our relationship exposed.

I wandered down a side street that was pockmarked with dustbins, extractor fans and greasy kitchen windows. A couple, in their late teens, were sat on the kerb staring into the road. They wore matching white shirts and aprons, and didn't seem to notice that the hems of their aprons were drawing up grey water from the gutter. The young man got to his feet, brushed himself down, then walked past me, his face like thunder. The girl watched him leave, sobbing gently. Then her mascara-streaked eyes met mine, and she sniffed, smiling politely, before the tears resumed. I should have said something to console her, but I was useless at that sort of thing. The street was a dead-end, so I just turned away and followed in the footsteps of the lover who had taken flight.

Suddenly I felt Lola's presence, as if she were keeping an eye on me from the whispering alleyways. I had tried not to think too much about her, and how I'd ended things almost as abruptly as they had started. But occasionally I'd come across a hairband, or a mug she'd left behind in the flat, and in an instant I'd be saddled with the old Catholic guilt.

That fateful afternoon, returning home from Trafalgar Square, I hadn't even unbuttoned my coat before the words spilled out of me.

'I'm so sorry, Lo, but this can't go on. It's not you, it's—'

It's Pippa? How honest did I want to be?

'It's me. All me.'

Mum assured me that Lola was devastated, but I thought she took the break-up well. Her face barely registered the shock, so I thought she must have felt the same as me: that we respected each other – always had and always would. That that was all we had. Not love, not desire, but mutual respect.

'Our mums will be disappointed,' I said. 'But you can't stay in a relationship just to please your mother, can you?'

She didn't reply. That's probably when I should have stopped talking, too.

'Because we were doing this for them a bit, weren't we?'

'You might have been, Steve.'

It didn't take her long to pack, it doesn't when your belongings are so meticulously ordered. I had the strange sensation that a lodger was moving out.

'It's good to see you take control of your own fate,' she said finally.

We hugged, only lightly, and when I looked into her eyes they were resolutely dry.

'Really. I wish you the best.'

And that's how it ended. On civil terms, like the termination of a contract between two firms that respected each other, but would be going their separate ways.

After a couple of wrong turns, I lost my bearings, but found them again with the help of my new trusty pocket guide. When I finally returned to the hotel, Pippa was waiting at the top of the entrance steps. Red lips pursed beneath a fur hat, one heel cocked up against a stone pillar. I'd have forgiven her anything.

'Where have you been?' she said.

'Just having a look round.'

'You were ages.'

'Did you miss me?'

She cocked her head. Yeah, she'd missed me.

'You look a million euros, by the way,' I said.

She turned her face away, but not fast enough to hide the delighted smile curling up her top lip.

'Shall we have a drink here, with the large selection of Trappist beers?' I was pointing at the map, on which I'd circled a number of cafés and bars that we'd read about during weeks of research. 'Or this place, with the interesting history?'

'We're here now, Steve,' said Pippa. 'Can't we just see where we end up?'

'Yeah, sure,' I said, with a spontaneous shrug of the shoulders. 'We could even begin here,' and I steered her towards Tripadvisor's No.1 Most Romantic Café in Bruges, and the first port of call on my mental itinerary.

We sat at a rattan bistro table, looking out onto the square, and ordered a couple of beers. The Markt was bustling with tourists, some shopping for presents at Christmas-themed stalls, some warming themselves with mulled wine and messy trays of twice-cooked *frites*. A chorus of bells began to peal from the Belfry, drawing everyone's gaze towards the tower. The whole city was enchanting, a grown-up's Disneyland.

'Look at these!' said Pippa, delighted, as our beers arrived in wide tulip glasses that were almost too beautiful to drink from. 'We should steal them and take them home as mementos.'

'Pippa, you're intent on us breaking the law,' I said.

'What do you mean?'

'The . . . sex plan? On the train?'

'That's not illegal,' she said, trying to work out how to take a sip of beer without dipping her nose in the foamy head.

'I think you'll find it is. Even under international waters.'

'You can't get arrested for having sex. Do you think they'll mind if I ask for a straw?'

The great thing about drinking small amounts of good beer, Continental-style, is that you remain your best half-cut self for longer. Even after six or seven glasses, it doesn't make you sleepy or lairy or sicky, but a pleasant, holiday sort of drunk. Once we had acquired a taste for the foam, we went from bar to bar, beer to beer, drinking 8 per cent proof ales from glasses that were chunky and squat like the jolly monks who smiled at us from the tin posters adorning the walls; and fruity, complex wheat beers in tall, curvy Jessica Rabbit glasses.

It could have been the perfect evening, were it not for the Leapers, a middle-aged English couple who kept leaping out at us from every corner. Wide, wobbly people, as jolly as the monks, with tans left over from a Caribbean cruise, they looked like they'd bounce back up if you pushed them over (I was tempted).

'You again!' Jim would joke.

'We can't get away from them!' Jane would riposte.

It was amusing at first, but by the fourth leaping, I started to wonder if they were following us.

'They seem nice enough to me,' said Pippa, as we queued at one of the many *frites* vans.

'Maybe. There's just one thing I can't stand when I'm abroad—'

'Breaking the law?'

'Yes, that. But also hearing other English people. Two *frites*, please.'

'How ironic.'

'I know, I know. It's just a bugbear.'

'A *bête noire*?'

'Exactly. Keep that up, *s'il vous plaît*.'

The array of condiments set out before us was staggering: a myriad of ketchups and mayonnaises for every taste. Pippa was very decisive about hers. 'It *has* to be Dijon mayo and plain ketchup,' she informed the bandanna-wearing vendor standing behind the fryer, as if he were wrong to stock anything else. I went slightly off-piste, choosing a Thai curry mayonnaise that was nowhere near as delicious as my taste buds had imagined. Pippa smirked, very pleased with herself to be winning at chips, as I tried to dig underneath the mound of sauce for one unadulterated by the spicy sludge.

'I'd have taken your wife's advice, son,' came a voice from behind. 'Gawd knows I get in trouble when I don't.'

'Jim, stop that!' said Jane, tickled pink by her husband's ribaldry.

'Oh, I'm not his wife.'

'We're not married.'

'Ah,' said Jim. 'Not yet, anyway.'

'He wishes,' Pippa said, giving me a gentle dig in the ribs.

Both Jim and Jane exploded into gales of laughter, their already ruddy cheeks turning puce. Pippa looked at me, bemused but also gratified by their reaction. It took them a full minute to recover.

'*He wishes*,' said Jane, wiping away a tear. 'That's a good one.'

'You should be on the stage,' said Jim.

That was enough to win Pippa over, and soon we were sitting on a row of stools at a busy after-hours place, the Leapers treating us to round after round. We spent the rest of the night propping up the bar with them; Pippa, Jane and Jim putting the world to rights, me reading the drinks menu until I'd learned it by heart. They were nice enough, a well-meaning couple enjoying their retirement, but I didn't want to share Pippa tonight, and I hated feeling beholden to them.

The interminable double date finally ended when it was

decided that Jim had had one too many, having leaned back off his stool only to be caught by a heroic barman. As we said our goodbyes, they became very sincere, impressing on Pippa that she was 'a brilliant, talented actress, destined for great things'. (I mean, she is, but *how would they know?*)

Jim turned my way, addressing me for about the second time that evening.

'Young man,' he said.

Hate that.

'You look after this young lady.'

Hate that even more.

Don't patronise me, old man, I thought.

'Thank you, Jim. I will,' I said.

Back in our room, we collapsed fully dressed in each other's arms on our bouncy bed.

The next morning was a write-off. Our heads were throbbing, it was tipping it down outside and our room had turned from sauna to steam room, damp permeating our clothes and bedding. There was certainly a rain check on any amorous activities. Was the world conspiring against us ever having sexual relations again?

We couldn't face the outside world, so we ordered in pizza, which arrived with a knock at the door, followed by the delivery guy's thumping footsteps as he scarpered down the epic staircase to avoid any complaint. The box was so soggy with rain that it took both of us to gather it up from the landing. We ate the damp pizza on the damp bed, watching a documentary about sheep farming on a Flemish news channel.

'When in Bruges,' Pippa smiled as she scooped up a slice with both hands.

The rain finally stopped, and we emerged from our hotel – and our hangovers – onto the wet cobbles. Our last supper had been carefully chosen. A solidly 4.5-star restaurant, our 'treat' meal, where we would dine extravagantly without worrying about the cost (though it did offer a good-value set menu).

We were invited into De Kruisbes by a waistcoated maître d', hair worn in a tight bun, who apologised that our table wasn't ready and offered us a complimentary cocktail. Pippa's eyes lit up as we were led to the bar, where she ordered two vodka martinis 'with the twisty bit of lemon'. The martinis were placed on small black napkins and slid across the thick glass towards us. There's something especially delicious about an unexpected free drink, and these were no exception: frosty, slightly bitter and satisfyingly strong. We tried to look cool and sip them slowly, as if we often started a meal like this, but it was all too new and exhilarating. The holiday we'd dreamed of was finally opening up before us, and we ordered two more.

When summoned, we followed the maître d' as she snaked her way through the dining room. She stopped beside the freshly laid table, proudly gesturing towards it with a swish of her arm. As we took our seats, we heard a familiar voice, a devastating flashback to last night's outing.

'Well if it isn't young Pippa and her gentleman caller!'

The Leapers were sitting three feet away, napkins sprouting from their necks, about to tuck into a Chateaubriand. They were holding cutlery with jumbo carved wooden handles that made them look like oversized Borrowers.

'What are the chances?' cried Jane.

'Pretty flipping high, it turns out,' I grumbled to Pippa.

'You okay with this?' she asked me, under her breath. 'We could sit somewhere else, but that might be a bit—'

'On it,' I said, already looking around for a free table in the crowded restaurant. Bingo! A couple sitting by the window, finishing their coffee, credit card coming out.

I turned back round to speak to the maître d', but Jim had already captured her, the sneak, and was pointing towards us.

'He's asking to push our tables together!' I hissed.

The tables weren't moved, however. Instead, the sommelier came over with a bottle of wine, which he opened with such care that it had to be expensive. He then gave Jim and Jane a courteous bob of the head, and they responded by raising their glasses to us. Pippa's eyes welled up in gratitude. The wine was beyond delicious (not just because it was free), the act beyond generous, and the whole bloody thing now made it impossible to feel aggrieved.

The Leapers allowed us to enjoy our starter in relative peace, but soon their chairs were edging closer and closer to us, like a game of grandmother's footsteps, until they were in our ears, regaling us with tales from their travels, from Guadeloupe to Budapest. At each stop there was a version of the same slightly xenophobic joke, which involved Jim finding a foreign word funny.

'Tell them about the taxi driver in Sifnos, Jim.'

'Well. His name was Simos . . .'

'Yeah? Yeah?' Jane egged him on as if this wasn't the hundredth time she'd relived the story.

'And he was from Sifnos!'

'Ha!' she burst out. '*Simos* from *Sifnos*! Brilliant!'

Pippa laughed along with her. I couldn't understand what she saw in them, and told her as much.

'Why are you being such a grump?' she said. 'I think it's wonderful how they still make each other laugh.'

'But you don't find him funny, surely?'

'I find him *endearing*.'

'His jokes are terrible, Pip.'

'They're no worse than yours.'

'That's just cruel.'

'I mean, they're no *better* than yours. They're just as bad. Or as good.'

I picked up the wine, filled my glass, then put the bottle back down without topping up Pippa's. She sat back in her chair and folded her arms in response. We remained like that, neither looking at the other, until the waiter came to clear our unfinished plates. He propped up a small chalkboard on the table.

'For dessert?'

I saw Pippa's eyes flicker to the menu, and was in no doubt that she was about to order the brownie. '*Non, merci*,' she said.

I was shocked to the core. 'Pip?' I exclaimed, forgetting that we were in the middle of an argument.

'I'm not hungry.'

'Monsieur?' The waiter turned to me. 'It is included.'

Every cell of my digestive system, from tongue to lower intestine, was screaming out for dessert. *What's it gonna be, Steve? Something chocolatey or fruity? Crunchy or creamy? Mmm. Pick anything! We trust you, Steve!* Not wanting to be the one to back down from this battle of wills, however, I declined.

'Just the bill, please.'

Perplexed, the waiter tucked the chalkboard under his arm and took away our plates. As he passed the Leapers, Jane called over: 'I hope you ordered the warm brownie with salty caramel and home-made vanilla ice cream?'

Pippa turned pale. '*Excusez-moi?*'

The waiter turned back, eyebrow raised. Pippa leaned across the table.

'Couldn't live with myself if I missed out on a brownie.'

'And a warm one, at that,' I said.

'Oh great God,' she dribbled.

'Madame?'

'Brownie, please.'

'Make that *deux*,' I added. 'With extra salty caramel.'

We said what I hoped would be a final farewell to the Leapers, and retraced the cobbles back to our lodgings, the moonlight glinting on the thin layer of ice that had settled after dark.

Alarms set for 6.30, we were woken at 4 a.m. by a mini earthquake from next door: our Scandi neighbours were the second couple to take it upon themselves to put the kibosh on any romantic notions we might have had this weekend. As we drifted in and out of sleep, interrupted by their acrobatic cries, the only saving grace was that we had no grasp of what they were screaming. It was really very selfish sex. Isn't there a code of behaviour to prevent such noise pollution? It should be printed under the fire procedures you find on the back of hotel doors.

'Should we say something?' I asked, bleary-eyed.

'I really don't think they'll hear us,' Pippa replied, burying her head beneath the pillow.

The train home was quiet enough that we were able to sit opposite each other at a table, with all four seats to ourselves.

'Just going to the loo,' I said.

'Mm-hmm,' she replied.

I sat in the cubicle, watching shapeless Belgian roofs flash by through the frosted glass, and wondered how we had become a couple that said *mm-hmm*. I thought about the Leapers, on the next leg of their midlife gap year. Would they be giving each other the silent treatment? I doubted it. What would Jim do?

I took out my phone and texted Pippa.

Very lonely in this here toilet

I could see my message had been delivered, but there was no reply.

Never too late to join the club?? 1st on left

A couple of minutes went by, then my phone pinged.

You still there? Pippa texted.

Yes! I wrote back.

Been knocking! First loo on the left?

I spun round and realised that I was now facing the opposite direction from our seats.

Other left sorry

Seconds later, there was a gentle knock at my door.

2 March 2019

05:39

Whir, beep, click, breath.

For a glorious split second, Steve has no idea where he is or what he's doing here. He had been teetering on the brink of sleep for a while and must have finally nodded off.

Whir, beep, click, breath.

That noise. What is it?

Whir, beep, click, breath.

He lifts his head and his eyes are dragged into focus. He sits bolt upright and the waking world comes alive with a thunderclap. Pippa is there beside him. Where she belongs. Looking as peaceful as a child. Early dawn light peers through the aquamarine window blinds, picking out golden strands of her hair. Maybe there has been a mistake? Maybe she is just sleeping after all?

'Morning,' comes the cheerful voice of a woman from the other side of the door, but it isn't meant for him.

'Morning, my love. You're in early,' replies another.

'Swapped with Anna.'

He could not have been asleep for more than a few minutes, but during this time the hospital has swung into life. The chatter of voices, bright and well rested. The drone of a hoover commencing its morning chores. And outside, the low growl of thickening traffic.

He reaches for his phone, a reflex developed over the last few hours, checking the home screen for missed calls. Still nothing. He checks the time. Diana will be waking up soon. He is hit by a wave of nausea at the thought of her listening to his messages. He must call again soon; better she hears it in person.

Scrolling through his texts, he comes across a message from an unknown number:

Super Savings Saturday! Buy any pizza and get a second HALF PRICE. Go on. Treat yourself!

The text, and the texter, riles him. They should know better. It reminds him of Pippa's elation whenever she finds a deal for a sneaky weekend treat, as if the email or voucher were arranged especially for her.

When will they do that again? When will he be able to come home and surprise her with extra-crispy fish and extra-vinegary chips? He shouldn't have accepted the job last night. He should have stayed in and eaten sneaky pizza on the sofa that has morphed into a third person in their relationship. He'd cancel every job, let go of every ambition, if it meant she'd wake up soon – anything, just to sit and eat and grow old and fat with her.

'I've been thinking,' he says, his eyes on an inch of her elbow that isn't draped in tubing. 'We still haven't ordered from the new Chinese.'

Whir, beep, click, breath.

'I mean, the old one that's changed its name. With the good reviews. It can be our next sofa date. Deal?'

Whir, beep, click, breath.

Steve's belly groans. He rubs it absent-mindedly, suddenly realising that no food has passed his lips for almost twelve hours. He reaches into his pocket and pulls out a two-pound coin.

'Hope the machine gives change.' He stands up. 'Two minutes, darling. Just going to grab some crisps or something.'

Crisps. A word that never fails to stir his wife from lethargy. *Crisps.* A word, a suggestion, to displace the tension of a pointless quarrel. *Crisps.* A word that always brings a smile to the lips of the woman he loves.

But not this time.

This time the magic word has no effect, simply bouncing around the walls like a pinball.

Steve hasn't left the room, has barely strayed more than a couple of metres from Pippa's side, for the last five hours. As he emerges, the world outside seems strange, as if he were stepping out of one bad dream into another. Harsh strip lights reflecting off the newly polished floor beckon him down the impossibly long corridor, at the end of which the vending machine looms large, sandwiched between the men's toilet and a short row of blue plastic seats. He surveys the contents of the machine from A1 to F9. A voice in his head vaguely wonders when it became the norm to charge a pound a pop for a bag of ready salted. He stands there for some time, until the rumbling in his stomach tightens back into a double knot. Maybe he isn't hungry after all. Maybe he should return to his wife.

He turns around and is surprised to find that someone is standing behind him, waiting: the man he saw two hours ago, the man with the dying mother, the man with terror in his eyes.

'Sorry,' Steve says, shuffling aside to allow the man a free run at the machine. 'Didn't hear you.'

'S'okay,' the man mumbles in reply before stepping forward and scanning the selection in front of him.

He frowns, then shakes his head, and Steve finds he is able to read his thoughts.

How can I stand here trying to choose between a chocolate bar and a packet of sweets when I should be in there praying that her next breath is not her last?

He feels a kinship with the stranger, a bond created by the

shared experience of a hitherto unimaginable emotion that twins hope with grief.

'What you in for?' he asks.

The man regards him with a wary side-eye.

'Sorry, wrong words.' Steve backs away, regretting that he tried to make contact. 'Long night. Gotta get back to Pippa.'

He turns, then hears the man clear his throat.

'Who's Pippa?'

He turns back and sees the man properly for the first time. He must be in his early forties, and looks as tired as Steve feels. The cuffs and sleeves of his jumper are streaked with blood.

'She's my wife.'

'I'm sorry.' The man shakes his head again, this time in commiseration. 'I'm here for my mum. She had a bad fall, hit her head.'

'Lucky you were there.'

'I'm always there. I'm her carer,' he says, wringing his hands. 'I rang 999 straight away. I wanted to bring her in myself, but they said to wait for the ambulance.'

Steve notices that his hands are faintly orange – coloured by nicotine, perhaps, but more likely he was unable to fully wash the bloodstains from them.

'I'm sure you did the right thing.'

'And your wife?' the man asks. 'Pippa?'

'She was . . . in an accident. A car accident. I wasn't there,' says Steve, wishing more than ever that he had been. Wishing that he could trade places with her.

'Christ, I'm sorry. That's—'

But a fanfare of feet interrupts them as the doors at the other end of the corridor swish open. Mr Bramin enters, followed by a nurse and junior doctor. The private conversation has been brought to an abrupt close, with both men turning their focus on Bramin in fearful anticipation.

'Mr Redmond?' says the doctor, holding up a folder. 'I have the results from your mother's CT scan. Shall we?'

The man, Redmond, takes a deep breath. 'Okay,' he says, before turning to Steve. 'Good luck.'

'You too.'

'And Mr Gallagher,' says Mr Bramin, 'I'll be along to check Pippa's bloods shortly, and to discuss our next steps.'

Steve nods back in thanks, but he feels a long way from grateful.

He watches as the two men disappear down the corridor and through the double doors. A draught carries Pippa's song into the corridor, faint but siren-like, calling him back to her.

Whir, beep, click, breath.

If this is going to be it, it can't be here. He'd like to carry her out, lay her down in the back of his car and take her home.

Somewhere safe.

Somewhere she loves.

Somewhere that is anywhere but here.

Christmas Day 2009

Steve

Pippa's childhood home was round the corner from my old school, in a cul-de-sac I never knew existed, populated by quaint terraced cottages. If there were only snow, it would have been like walking into a scene from a festive biscuit tin.

If you'd told fifteen-year-old Steve that in the last days of the first decade of the new millennium he would be spending Christmas at his headmaster's home, arriving on the arm of Mr Lyons' daughter as her official, going-steady boyfriend, he'd have bitten your mittens off.

I'd met Pippa's parents before, out for dinner and at a play-reading above a pub, but staying at the family home was a far scarier prospect. And yet here I was, on the threshold with a bag of presents and an £8.99 bottle of wine.

'Darlings!' Pippa's mum, Diana, pulled us inside before we could speak. She kissed me on each cheek – the kind of kiss I used to receive from great-aunts, where I could feel the lipstick cracking on my skin afterwards – then squeezed her daughter tight and held her at arm's length, checking her over. I knew this move. My mum would use it on my eldest sister, Charlotte, on her return home from university. It was usually followed by a comment about how tired she was looking. Char hated it. I knew Pippa hated it too. But on this occasion, it wasn't a challenge or a judgement, just a gesture full of love.

Diana looked from Pippa to me to Pippa again. 'You're

both wonderful.' It was the most relaxed I'd seen her. The gin and tonic sitting on a ledge in the narrow hallway might have had something to do with it. The ice inside the glass had nearly melted, and the lime wedge had started to wither. I reckon she'd topped up the drink two or three times already.

Pippa ran to her dad, who lifted her off her feet with a hug of surprising strength. She shrieked in delight and I found that I was jealous (if you can be jealous of such a thing without having some kind of Oedipus-in-law issue). I hadn't picked Pippa up enough; I must try it, though I should probably ask her permission first.

'Steven, my lad.' He turned to me, comically making half a move to pick me up too. My core stabilisers engaged in readiness, but thankfully it only resulted in a firm handshake.

'Mr Lyons.' I couldn't bring myself to call him Chris yet. 'We brought this.' I held up the bottle. I know nothing about wine, but this had been reduced from £12 (above average, but below showy) and had a lovely label. It seemed just right for the occasion.

'Ah, you've brought a bottle of . . .' He studied the label briefly. I thought he might have been admiring the calligraphy, as I had done. 'Red. Very kind.'

As Diana led us into the living room, I saw Mr Lyons slide the bottle to the back of a bureau, behind a mug of pens and a stack of notebooks. I couldn't tell if this meant it wasn't fit for consumption or whether he was saving it for another time.

We spent the evening drinking G&Ts, while Pippa flitted around the living room, perching on the sofa, then a chair, then rifling through old photo albums, all the while filling her parents in on her latest audition horror stories.

I sat in a comfy battered armchair, politely nibbling from a bowl of nuts – occasionally feeding one to the dog – until they were all gone. I was expecting dinner, but none materialised, and by the time I'd had two nightcap Scotches, I was woozy. I don't remember saying goodnight or being shown upstairs to the guest room (I had secretly hoped we'd be staying in Pippa's old bedroom, a place of mystic wonder in my pubescent imagination, but it had recently been converted into a study).

'Is this the traditional Lyons Christmas Eve?' I asked Pippa as I sank into bed.

'What, lots of booze?'

'Mm-hmm . . .' I was already falling asleep.

'I guess so.'

That night I dreamed I was back home, where Mum would have served up her traditional whole salmon with potato salad.

In the morning, I was woken by Pippa poking me in the back with her knee, or perhaps her elbow.

'What are you doing?' I said, confused and groggy. My confusion was compounded when I opened my eyes to see that her half of the bed was empty. 'Where are you?'

I turned over to find myself face to face with Hardy, the family's ten-year-old Labrador, who was communicating with his wet snout. Once he was satisfied I was awake, he shook out a little sneeze, as if to say: 'Don't forget, this is still my house you're in.' On his way out, he sniffed at my chinos, which were lying in a heap on the floor, and cast me a withering look over his drooped shoulders.

I took the hint, put on my trousers, splashed my face with water and went downstairs. I could hear a soft but rapid shuffle of slippers, followed by the swish of dressing gown cords, as father, mother then daughter whizzed past. They had fallen into an old Christmas routine, each carrying out their historical tasks without the need for discussion or fanfare. It was the furthest cry imaginable from the anarchy that would be raging at my folks' place at that moment, which I could almost hear fifteen miles away.

'Would anyone like a cuppa?' I asked, attempting to join in.

'We've had ours,' answered Pippa's mum, carrying a roll of wrapping paper and scissors. 'But do help yourself.'

I spent much of the morning hovering between the kitchen and the dining room, as the Lyonses glided in and out with candles, cutlery, crackers. Fearing that I was becoming a bit of a passenger in proceedings, I kept asking what I could do, but every job on offer was completed before I had a chance to start.

'Can I trim the Brussels, Diana?'

'Already in the pot, love.'

'Pippa, let me help with something!'

'Erm . . . you could walk the dog?'

'Hardy's been to the park, dear. Just got him clean.'

'You could cut a sprig of holly from the garden, Steven.'

'Be glad to. Where do you keep the, er . . .'

'Secateurs? If you go into the garden, there's a small shed. It might be padlocked, though. You know what, I'll just do it myself.'

I soon gave up and sat at the table, out of everyone's way. Better to let them do their thing, I thought. Mr Lyons waltzed past humming, playing catch with a netted bag of chestnuts. He stopped short, feigning surprise at my being there with a sort of single double-take.

'Steven. You've made yourself comfortable, I see.'

But sir! I very nearly said in protest.

'You relax, we'll be joining you shortly.'

As he regrouped with the cooks in the kitchen, I sensed he

was mentally writing my end-of-year report: *A rather quiet Michaelmas term. Pippa prepped the sprouts, Diana made the bread sauce, Mr Lyons basted the turkey and made gravy – even Hardy hoovered up some of the trimmings – and all the while Gallagher watched. Could do better.*

He was a popular headmaster, I remembered, though I didn't have much personal interaction with him at school. There was no cause for me to be called into his office, as I never stood out amongst the thousand other boys as a high achiever or sports star or Saturday detention stalwart. But I did remember this persona he had when I encountered him in corridors or at assembly, an act to get pupils onside: the benevolent chieftain, not taking this whole headmaster thing too seriously, always ready with a joke but leaving you in no doubt he was in charge.

Turns out it wasn't an act. He kept me on a psychological leash all morning, announcing over a glass of champagne and smoked trout that 'I might tell you later about some strange goings-on with Steven here when he was in Year Ten . . .'

'What do you mean?' Pippa pleaded with him to spill the beans, but he zipped up his lips and kept us all on tenterhooks.

What *did* he mean? What was I up to back in Year Ten, apart from avoiding GCSE revision with *Goldeneye* multi-player sessions? Suddenly there were dark holes in the recesses of my adolescent memory. *Strange goings-on* made me sound like a right weirdo. I was fifteen! Doing things fifteen-year-olds did! Perhaps he was bluffing? Or perhaps he had been told something by Herr Rondell, my German teacher, who always had it in for me (well, frankly, there was something *nicht richtig* about him).

Dead on 3.15, the radio was flicked over from the Queen's

speech to carols, and Pippa's mum entered carrying the turkey. I raised my hands to clap it in, not because it looked so impressive (which it did – perfectly golden, wearing a Caesar's crown of plaited bacon), but because that was what happened in my family on Christmas Day; a Pavlovian response to twenty-eight years of celebrating the wonder that a bird big enough to feed all of us could fit in the oven and come out edible and on time. But there was no applause from the Lyonses; just a silent recognition that the centrepiece of the precisely laid table had arrived. Silent precision was the order of the day.

'Do you like Brussels, Steven?' asked Diana as she handed me the bowl of Pippa's perfectly prepped sprouts, unrecognisable from the boiled balls of methane that I usually passed on at home. Bright green, buttery and 'topped with crumbled bacon and chestnut', Diana informed me, accidentally doing an impression of Nigella Lawson.

'If I didn't before, I think I do now,' I said. 'They look delicious.'

I'd never say it to Mum, but the Lyonses' Christmas dinner topped the Gallaghers' on nearly all fronts. The potatoes were crisp, the turkey moist, and those Brussels . . . I was *almost* a convert. The only thing I missed from home was Siobhan's bread sauce, which, if I'm honest, we all know comes from a sachet.

The tranquil sound of a family just enjoying their food in each other's company was also a new concept to me. No TV, no tantrums, no tearing away from a half-finished plate to answer the phone to a boyfriend or girlfriend.

The past few months had been far from tranquil. Being Pippa's boyfriend, she'd warned me early on, meant loud conversations with loud people in loud places. It meant being pulled out of my comfort zone, in unexpected directions. And I'd gone along with it willingly: she was a roller coaster and I'd spent too long on the teacups. But it was different here, in the Lyonses' cottage. This was where her quiet side lived. If Pippa the actress was wild, Pippa the friend a party animal and Pippa the girlfriend emotional, Pippa the daughter was homely and content. Pippa's her *father's* daughter, certainly.

She and Diana, however, were forever locked in a cold war that threatened to escalate given the slightest provocation. I'd seen her get so worked up by her mother that she'd come off the phone to her primed for an argument with me. But today, it seemed, their backs were down, swords sheathed, and all was comfort and joy.

It was strange to see my old headmaster in a paper hat. Something about it looked so wrong, almost unconvincingly festive, like those staged photos they publish in the papers around Christmas of the prime minister playing charades with his family, or the Queen hanging a bauble from a twelve-foot pine in her front room. I can never quite believe that they're pulling crackers and reading bad jokes about snowmen like the rest of us. Even here, in the flesh, Mr Lyons' pink crêpe crown looked as if it might be Photoshopped.

It was even stranger to see Pippa's parents so obviously in love, despite the fact that according to Pippa, they were most definitely not an item any more. She assured me that they had split up years ago, that Diana lived in a flat down the road, and that legally, romantically and (as far as she knew) physically, they were not a couple. Watching them cuddled up on the sofa the previous evening, they didn't look like your average separated parents, getting together at Christmas to play happy holidays for the sake of the children, with painted smiles that would fade come Boxing Day. The walls of the cottage were covered in photos, not only of their beloved only daughter, but also of the pair of them as long-haired young lovers and wide-eyed newly-weds. They told of a love story spanning months of intense courtship, two decades of successful marriage, and then, apparently, several more years of even more successful divorce.

'But they just seem so . . . *together*,' I'd whispered to Pippa last night as we brushed our teeth at a small sink in the corner of our room.

'I know. Especially at Christmas and birthdays and things. She'll be here till New Year.'

'Why doesn't she move back in?'

'I don't know! That's not how they want it. And before you ask – no, it's not an open relationship.'

Pippa may not have been bothered by her parents' post-modernism, but it was the sort of 'unconventional' that made me feel very Catholic indeed. I thought about how I might explain the arrangement to my own parents. A divorce of convenience? It wasn't something Mum would approve of.

'Looks like Steven enjoyed that,' noted Diana, as I scraped up the last of my gravy.

'Growing boy,' said Mr Lyons, and I felt slightly ashamed.

I had tried my best to keep pace with everyone else, but I could have cleared my plate twice over before Pippa and her parents had finished theirs, and had my eye on a very crispy potato that had gone untouched. Being from a large family, I was used to having to wolf down my dinner as fast as I could if I hoped to score any seconds. 'You chews, you lose,' Dad would joke.

'Oh no, I forgot!' Diana exclaimed. Another course? Some pigs in blankets getting burned in the oven? 'I meant to ask if you say grace at your house, Steve?'

'Occasionally,' I replied. 'Mostly for my aunt Niamh's benefit, if she's over.'

'We could all benefit from more spirituality at this time of year,' said Diana. 'Here, have another spud.'

Hallelujah. I raised my plate like Oliver Twist, praying that Diana would pick out that crispy specimen I'd been ogling. That was when Mr Lyons dropped the bombshell.

'In our family, we like to sing a song at Christmas lunch.'

Diana looked at him with uncertainty. 'Do we?'

'Yes!' said Pippa, and I knew what was coming next. 'And as our guest, Steve has to go first.' She had tried to get me to sing on several occasions – pushing me forward when another actor friend of hers brought out a karaoke machine at a party, or urging me to be heard above my usual mumble during 'Happy Birthday'.

'I've got to warn you, I'm—'

'Tone deaf.' She finished my sentence.

'No such thing,' said Mr Lyons dismissively.

'That's what I said!'

Pippa and her father turned their chairs towards me, settling into their seats, and I noticed for the first time just how similar they were: those protruding neck muscles, the same proud ears and curious eyebrows.

I sucked in my guts and went for an easy one.

'*Weee – wish you a merry Christmas,*' I could see Pippa wincing slightly at the noise I made, '*we wish you a merry Christmas, we wish you a merry Christmas . . .*' I was expecting someone to join in, but they just watched; intrigued, I think, as to whether I might find the melody. I didn't. '*And a happy new year.*'

I finished with a flourish of my hand, then reached for my wine glass. But Mr Lyons wanted more.

'Yes? Good tidings we bring . . .'

'*Good tidings we bring, to you and your kin,*' I carried on half-heartedly. '*We wish you a merry Christmas and a happy new year.*'

'Aw,' said Pippa, clearly glad that it was over.

But Mr Lyons still wasn't satisfied. 'Now bring us some figgy pudding?'

I thought I'd picked the shortest one! I stumbled through another verse, but again Mr Lyons prompted me: 'For we all like figgy pudding . . .'

'You're making it up now!' I complained.

'No I'm not. Go on, or there'll be no figgy pudding for you.'

Pippa threw her head back with laughter.

Sod it, I thought. I stood up, thrust out my arms and sang operatically: '*For we all like figgy pudding, we all like figgy pudding, we all like figgy pudding . . .*' I looked to Mr Lyons for the last line, but this one was beyond even him, so I finished with: '*And a happy new year!*' to rapturous applause.

'That was great!' Pippa put her arms around me and kissed my nose, before adding quietly, 'But you don't have to sing any more.'

During the hiatus between turkey and pudding, when you could almost hear our tummy muscles stretching tight, trying to make a bit more room, Pippa turned to her father and said, 'You still have to tell us about Steve's strange goings-on, Dad.'

'What? Oh, that.' He winked at me before adding, 'Yes, very strange indeed. Maybe I'll tell you later.'

I was sure he was bluffing, and was tipsy enough that I almost wanted to know what he'd invent if pressed further.

'Should we play a game after lunch?' I suggested, attempting to turn the spotlight away from me for a bit.

'The book game!' Pippa clapped her hands together and left the table, making for the bookcase.

'Are you sure?' Mr Lyons said, with some consternation, as if there were some history to this game that made it more dangerous than it sounded.

'The book game, really?' Diana said, returning from the kitchen.

But Pippa wasn't listening. She was too busy seizing books from the shelves, piling them up in the crook of her arm as if she were robbing a library.

So after Christmas pudding with brandy butter and cream – and a cheeky mince pie – we settled around the coffee table, which was now covered in piles of books. Pippa held court.

'Right. You all know how to play—'

'I don't.'

'Steve! I can't believe you don't know it.'

'We usually play charades.'

'It's the best game ever. These are the rules.'

I had to pick a book and read out what was on the back cover. Next I would secretly write down the first sentence of the book, while the rest would attempt their own version of what that sentence might be. Then we'd take it in turns to guess at the correct version, trying to call each other's bluff.

'Try not to pick a book you know,' Pippa concluded.

'Shouldn't be a problem for me,' I said, because I didn't recognise a single one. I picked up a thick history book about the Romanian revolution and began to read the blurb on the back.

'Really, Steve. That one?'

'Let him read, Pippa,' Diana snapped.

'But it's not a good one to start with.'

'You picked them! Anyway, it's up to him.'

I read on. Now Pippa and her mother looked just the same: their scowls, the way they held their pens, arched over their strips of paper in poses of intense concentration. Mr Lyons seemed to be thinking the same as he watched his girls, smiling with pride and amusement.

The paper strips were passed to me, I wrote down the actual first line, then read them all out. Mr and Mrs Lyons won the first round with strikingly similar sentences involving a dictator, the Iron Curtain and some very specific dates that were probably bang on.

'That was amazing – almost telepathic!' I said.

'Almost like *cheating*,' said Pippa, shooting her mother a cold look.

In the next round, Mr Lyons read out our made-up first lines for an Alan Bennett diary. I was fooled by Diana's effort, in which she'd written about 'whispy whispers' or something similar. This didn't please Pippa.

'Why did you pick her one, Steve? It was so obvious!'

'Sorry.' I laughed uncomfortably.

Pippa clearly hated losing at this game, or losing to her mum; possibly both. She couldn't even bring herself to enjoy her dad's disturbingly good impression of the author. Diana read next, from the back of a biography on Shakespeare. While we were scribbling our sentences, she said: 'Of course, Pippa ought to win this round.'

'Oh for God's sake,' said Pippa, throwing down her pen.

'What? I picked one that you can get.'

That was it. In a flurry of movement, Pippa jumped up, swearing at her mum, and a pile of books went flying across the table, knocking over an open bottle of port. Hardy ran in, disturbed by the sudden commotion, and, unsure how best to help, stiffly clambered onto the space vacated by Pippa on the sofa.

'Every year,' said Mr Lyons, as he rescued the bottle, leaving behind a ruby pool that was being soaked up by a paperback. 'I'll go get a J Cloth. Hardy, off! Off!'

Upstairs, a door slammed.

'What did I do?' said Diana, and sank back into the sofa, innocently sipping her wine.

*

I was relieved that the Lyonses' chocolate-box Christmas was as susceptible to the same pressures and torments suffered by everyone else. Anyway, it wouldn't be as much fun if it was perfect. Not that Pippa was very receptive to this argument.

'Can you let me in, Pip?' I asked quietly from the other side of the bathroom door.

Eventually I heard the brass lock slide open, and entered to find her sitting cross-legged, making a sort of star shape on the floor out of cotton buds.

'This looks . . . fun.'

'Hmm,' she grunted in ironic agreement.

'Don't be upset.'

She looked at me. 'I'm not upset. I'm embarrassed.'

'I'm sorry,' came Diana's voice from the doorway. I thought for a moment that Pippa was going to slam it shut again, but she didn't. 'I love you,' Diana added.

Then Pippa was up, arms wrapped around Diana in a koala hug, a cheek pressed to her mother's chest. It looked like there should be tears, but none followed, just a deep, contented sigh. I saw toddler, teenage and twenty-seven-year-old Pippa in that embrace, and wisely said no to the impulse to join them in an awkward three-way tableau.

Downstairs, Mr Lyons was sitting in the middle of the sofa, focusing on the TV remote. Hardy was resting against his master's feet, which were now in leather slippers. Any remnants of the crime scene had vanished: the table was clear, clean, and the books had been tidied away – for another year, at least. Afternoon had become evening – a bit late, I thought, for *Bedknobs and Broomsticks* to be on the telly. Pippa and Diana settled either side of Mr Lyons, then all three began to sing along with the film's opening number. They knew every line. It was then that I realised this was another

Lyons tradition. The film wasn't playing on television, but from a DVD, spinning its way towards the end of another year.

Not wanting to be left out of the love-in, Hardy sidled up to me, nudged at my knee, then heaved himself onto my lap.

'Hardy . . .' I said, expecting to hear Mr Lyons shout: 'Off!'

But the three Lyonses just looked over and chuckled at the sight of their guest buried under the dog, who was draped over me like a smelly old blanket, while Angela Lansbury sang us all to sleep.

Boxing Day 2009

Pippa

The stench of adrenaline and exhaustion clings around the school gates. It's mid June, but the clouds are heavy, and as we enter the yard, the heavens open. Miss Bernard would call this 'pathetic fallacy'. I call it a pathetic pain in the arse, as I haven't brought a coat.

So here we are, on the edge of Armageddon. Peering into purgatory. Feeling the heat of the Holy Inferno of Babylon (I might have made that one up). Or, in layman's terms, history A level. Have any facts actually sunk in? Have the long late nights spent cramming paid off? Will this be my Agincourt (25 October 1415) or my Ypres (definitely 1914, but which month?)?

Through the driving rain, the examination hall rises up over the brow of the hill like a Disney villain. I see the snake of All Hallows' girls in frog-coloured uniforms hopping nervously from foot to foot – an expansive, twitching centipede. My arm, as ever, is linked with that of Tania, who is uncharacteristically silent. I think she may be regretting those Hooch-fuelled gatherings on the common in place of her revision. Beside us, Nisha looks calm. Nisha always looks calm. Hey, wait a minute, is she still completely dry? That's impossible. Epic rain is soaking my thin white shirt and rivulets of water are streaming down my face. And then I see it. Somehow she is repelling the water, deflecting all of its drenching fury onto me! What the hell? It's as though she is exuding a magnetic field. I watch in awe. The power of Nisha vs Nature.

I'm reminded of my dad, borrowing half a potato from a Little Chef that time the wipers stopped on the M4.

'See this, Squeak,' he said as he rubbed it over the windscreen. 'Wet side down.'

Together we watched, transfixed, as the rain beat a new path around the outside of the glass, dispersing entirely and leaving the centre of the windscreen clear. I asked if it was magic.

'Not magic. Starch. Works miracles.'

Well, Nisha must be made of starch, as she is still dry as a bone. I look at her immaculate plait hanging long and shiny down her straight back. A plait that tells of an efficient, stress-free morning. A soldier prepared for the battle ahead. The Rock of Gibraltar on a stormy night. I feel like a kid who has found herself on the front line – jittery, inept and unable to tell one end of a rifle from the other. My fingers clasp my see-through pencil case containing my only weapons – a new Parker pen and a double-ended ink eraser. Who did Ferdinand make that final treaty with? And why did Henry bump off all those wives? Did the Italian wars begin in 1494? Or was it 1493? Where did Wolsey—

'Another drop, Pippa? Go on. It's Christmas!'

The room snaps sharply into focus, and I'm in the middle of another test altogether. I am seated at a long oak table, laden with an eclectic spread of festive leftovers. Doilies are strewn beneath glass bowls of tinned fruit salad, mini Toblerones, and hard-boiled eggs, 'reduced to clear' pâtés, chutneys and miniature jars of condiments that bear the logos of the hotels they were stolen from. It looks like the front cover of one of Mum's seventies cookbooks. Around the table sit more people than I ever believed could constitute a single family. Yesterday we were tucked up in the bosom of my tiny clan for Christmas lunch. Today it is the turn of the Gallaghers.

'Erm . . .' I tilt my glass, still half full, but when in Rome . . . 'Sure. Why not.'

I smile and hold it out. The man behind the bottle twinkles back at me. His eyes are some of the kindest I've seen.

'Ah, good girl. Our Stevie told us you liked a drink.'

Before I have a chance to vehemently dispute the indisputable, my glass is topped up. Or should I say, filled up. To the brim. My mother's voice suddenly pops into my head. 'Never more than a third full, Pippa. The space in the glass is designed to hold aromas.' Not a good time, Mum.

'That'll put hairs on your chest.'

He has a strong Irish brogue that makes every sentence sound like a compliment, and is wearing a bright red Christmas jumper with a rapping sunglassed Santa on the front holding a ghetto blaster to his ear. The slogan reads: *Christmas with all my Ho, Ho, Ho's!* He clearly has no idea what it means and is therefore sporting it with no irony whatsoever. His naïvety is endearing and makes me warm to him instantly. Maybe one day I'll know him well enough to tell him that his handsome rugged face would be much improved with the removal of the retro tache.

'Thanks, Mr Gallagher.'

'You are so welcome, pet. And call me Frankie – everyone else does. Really delighted you could make it.' He squeezes my arm with his work-worn hands before spotting something concerning across the room.

'Oi! Juney!' It's his daughter, attempting to lift three enormous boxes single-handedly, whilst carrying a plate of Scotch eggs. 'Bend your knees when you pick up heavy boxes! Come here to me . . .' and with that he's off to assist. I watch him hurrying to his daughter's aid and am struck by his likeness to Steve.

I navigate the enormous bowl of liquid to my lips, dripping some on my new 'meeting the family' dress from H&M, and swig gratefully. But the generous servings of (slightly warm) Freixenet are not helping the task in hand. My faculties are becoming woolly under its giddying influence and my poor brain, a once well-oiled, razor-sharp piece of kit, is creaking under the pressure. It feels a long time since the beery benders of drama school, when pints followed by Jägerbomb chasers couldn't dull my busy synapses. These days, just a few glasses and my brain shuts up shop, like a granny after her third sherry, kipping in front of *Bargain Hunt*.

Well, wake up, brain! Afternoon telly is over! It's time for *Mastermind*, and my specialist subject: the Gallaghers.

I look around, trying to take them all in. They seem to be multiplying like amoeba under a microscope. And the noise! The decibel level at the Gallagher Family Circus is about to blow the big top roof off. Children demanding chocolate, mothers needing attention, fathers relating anecdotes, dogs squabbling over turkey trimmings – and that's before the chorus kicks in.

Twelve glasses filling
Eleven plates a-breaking
Ten doors a-slamming
Nine knives a-scraping
Eight mince pies burning
Seven smoke alarms beeping
Six crackers cracking
Five sib-a-lings (I'm especially pleased with that one – even got the rhythm right. Yowzers, I'm definitely a bit pissed.)
Four screaming kids
Three smashed mugs
Two unopened gifts
And a Pippa meeting Steve's family.

That is most excellent. Must remember to sing it to him later.

Shit. My bowl of bubbles is nearly empty. Again. How did that happen? I know I'm drinking too fast, but I can't seem to help it. I must be more nervous than I realised. I'm scrabbling for mnemonics or rhymes or visual aids or *any* bloody tricks that I can dredge up, to help me retain twelve names and eleven faces (identical twins – I'm not *that* drunk).

There are two small children sitting on my lap. At least I've got their names down: Sammy (Snoopy Shirt Sammy) and Ruby Mae (Red-Cheeked Ruby). I say 'sitting' – currently Sammy is trampling on my thighs, his light-up trainers flashing as with one tiny hand he grips my right ear, attempting to forcibly remove a sparkly earring that has caught his eye. With the other, he makes a beeline for my nose, determinedly poking his felt-tip-stained fingers up my left nostril. I feel like Gulliver being tied down by the tiny Lilliputians. Ruby Mae, meanwhile, is facing me, legs clamped round my waist like an orang-utan. Unabashed, she stares down my top at my cleavage and announces with quiet authority, 'Your booties are a big bit bigger than Mummy's.'

I blush. She looks up at me, a tiny frown whispering across her brow, clearly bemused why this should elicit any kind of reaction. Her hazel eyes are intent and curious. As she stares, she is completely still for the first time, and I get my first proper look at her heart-shaped face. She is like one of those children from a Victorian picture book. Smooth skin, untouched by the trials of daily life. A sieving of tiny freckles scattering her retroussé nose. For a moment I feel my heart swell with love for this pocket-sized angel. I want to protect her from the unfair agonies of this planet. To keep her safe and away from harm. A little gem too precious for human consumption. And just as the maternal warmth spreads across my heart, another warmth spreads across my lap, trickling down my tights and into my shoes. Ruby Mae beams. A proud smile. 'I just made wee wee in my big-girl pants.'

And with that, they both abseil off me, using the top of my dress as a safety rope. I look down to see that a large pool of water is now gathered under my seat. How can such a small human contain so much liquid?

Quick as a flash, Ruby is hoicked into the air by a wildly apologetic June.

'So sorry, Pippa.'

A tea towel is thrust at me. Steve appears with a roll of kitchen paper and begins wiping the floor.

'Ruby Mae! What did Mummy tell you? We tell Mummy when we need wee wees.'

Ruby Mae's bottom lip begins to wobble. I insist that it couldn't matter less, 'happens all the time . . . kids are forever pissing on my lap . . . didn't even notice', and smile as I pat the urine from my legs.

'There. All gone!'

It isn't. I'm drenched. It's getting cold. And it's starting to sting. I catch Steve's eye as he wipes up around my feet. Why does he look so delighted?

He whispers, 'She's right, though. You do have the best 'booties' here.'

I blush and flick him with the pissy tea towel.

Two more top-ups and a heaped plate of 'Mum's Coronation Turkey Surprise' later (the surprise being the pickled beetroot grated over it and the controversial addition of dry-roasted peanuts to the mix), and I think I might just be getting somewhere. Maybe, just maybe, I am starting to grasp the sprawling tentacles of Steve's family tree.

Right. Story so far.

On my right, we have my Steven. Youngest child and not allowed to forget it. Photographer and professional gentleman. In the words of his mother, 'Practically perfect in every way.' No pressure there, then.

On his lap sits Tom: three years old, obsessed with tractors. The chocolate down his dungarees and the matted bird's nest on his head tells of a day of epic adventures. Tom – or Tiny Tim, as the family helpfully call him – is the youngest child of (Strident) Siobhan, elder of the identical twin girls by seven minutes. No, wait, was it nine minutes? Wouldn't do to go getting that wrong; she is *very* particular about it. They are bang in the middle of the Gallagher clan. Hang on, though, maybe Tom belongs to the other twin, (Jittery) June. But no, June owns pee-down-my-legs Ruby Mae and Snotty Sammy, who is currently eating only red food and going through a biting phase (my bleeding ankle is testament to this).

Siobhan is brash, loud and initially scared the life out of me. Her auburn hair is cropped short and her face is entirely make-up-free. She eats and drinks with a ferocity that suggests every meal might be her last. Her speech is littered with words like focus, acumen, achievement and strategy; anyone would think she worked in the City.

'I started Kidz Just Wanna Have Fun two years ago. Party bags. Varying price brackets. The strategy was sound. Annual turnover of forty-eight K gross. Who knew balloons, bubbles and Chupa Chups could be so lucrative?'

The timid man in the *Star Trek* sweatshirt with the unfortunate comb-over explodes with laughter. It would appear that this is the best joke ever. This is (Dismal) Davey, or Kipper to the family (I haven't asked why and don't intend to; got enough on my plate.). Six years Siobhan's junior and utterly blinded by her light, he gazes at her as she speaks (shouts) with a devotion bordering on cultish. It seems his sole purpose in life is to stroke, bolster and inflate his already inflated wife.

Across the room sits Charlotte, eldest of the Gallagher children. She has Steve's eyes, and I like her at once. She is perched almost apologetically on the counter top, her long thin legs crossed over each other, stapling Christmas cards to a length of red ribbon to hang around the doorway. (Mrs

Gallagher – Kathleen – was a few chairs short, so decided that Charlotte could 'hop herself up there. She's the only one of them that won't damage my counter! She's light as a feather. Feel her! Like hugging a Twiglet.') Charlotte is a GP. I know that for sure because she pointed out the psoriasis on my forehead. This would usually make me want to run a mile, but she did so with such concern and sweetness that I welcomed it. She recommended me a brilliant seaweed ointment that she uses herself.

'My colleagues are forever prescribing steroids, but honestly, this is the best stuff. I'll get you some.' She is, somehow, currently single. 'Don't ask. String of wrong 'uns, Pip.' I like how she started calling me Pip straight away, as my family and old friends do.

Finally, out on the frosty back step squats (Muscly) Mickey, the love child of Colin Farrell and Penelope Cruz. If I didn't know better, I'd think Kathleen had accidentally copped off with a Spaniard after one too many fish bowls on a girls' holiday to Marbella. Beside him stands (Perfect) Pat, his boyfriend of seven years. He's from Manchester and is a special needs teacher at the local school. They're one of those couples that make you believe in love. It just feels like the stars have aligned to bring them together, and perhaps it's the booze, but as I watch them laughing in the twilight, I come over all teary.

'Now then, light of my son's life. It's sofa time.'

Mrs Gallagher is beaming at me and patting the empty seat beside her. Oh God, it's happening. The moment Steve warned me about. The parent stamp. Steve glances over from the washing-up, mortified.

'Mum. Leave it. Let her lunch go down.'

'Ah, don't you "leave it" with me, little Stevie. I'm allowed to be excited to finally meet the love of your life.'

'Mum! Seriously.'

Mrs Gallagher chuckles – 'Don't worry, I'll behave' – then turns her turquoise eyes on me.

I cross the room and perch beside her.

'There you are.'

'Here I am!'

You can do better than that, Pippa. Come on! Parents usually love you.

'So wonderful to meet you all, Mrs Gal— sorry, Kathleen. Steve's told me so much about the family.'

For a second I feel like I'm being X-rayed, like she can see through my skin, my bones, my muscle and deep into the inner ventricles of my heart. She smiles and begins pawing at me like a monkey cleaning her young. Any minute now she's going to check behind my ears for ticks. Suddenly she cups my face with her small hands – 'Pretty as a picture' – then runs them through my hair and lets out a coo of pleasure. 'Ah! What a lovely thick mane. And *auburn*. Stevie, why didn't you tell your ma she was one of us?' She drops her voice for effect but can still be heard by the whole room. 'Both of you having the red genes . . . there's every chance of a little—'

'*Mum!*' Steve's face is puce.

'Such a prude, my son,' she giggles. 'Oh, your eyelashes! And I'm so glad to see you don't pluck your brows. Au naturel is so much prettier than this drawn-on look that's doing the rounds at the moment. Our Stevie tells me you're an actress. That's so exciting. Tell me all about it.'

Maybe it's the booze, maybe it's her disproportionate excitement, but I'm so close to telling her the truth: *No, it's not exciting. It's ninety-eight per cent torture. It's scrabbling around trying to make ends meet, waiting for the phone to ring, getting drunk on Mondays, and knowing that there's no one but yourself to blame for every disappointment.*

184

But instead I beam and say, 'Yes. It's great. I'm loving it! Feel so lucky.'

Kathleen looks over at Steve, who has retreated to the dishes again, then leans in and whispers earnestly, 'Now that he's not listening, I wanted you to know: even though our Lola was such a *huge* part of the family, and yes, of course it was a terrible shock when she moved out – I can't pretend Frank and I didn't think an engagement was on the cards – but you *mustn't* feel threatened in any way.'

Whoa. Mic drop.

I didn't. I hadn't. But I sure as hell do now.

An engagement?

Kathleen rattles on gaily, oblivious to the translucent hue my face has taken on.

'Dear me, the Kerrs didn't know what hit them. I've known that woman for well over thirty years and I've never seen her in such a state. Bless her. No one saw it coming. All convinced that that was our youngest done and dusted! Just goes to show, doesn't it?'

Words. Lost. For.

'Lola moved back home for a while, you see. Needed a bit of Mum's TLC.'

Steve, help me. I try to send him a message across the room. *Come. Over. Here. Now. Save me.*

But our telepathic lovers' link is clearly down, out of range, as he laughs at a cracker joke read out by one of the kids. If he had been listening, he'd have surely thrown a plate at his mother by now. Beside me, though, Kathleen shows no signs of abating.

'Bless her dear little heart, she seems much better now, though. Just needed some time to get over the shock, I guess. And it was a shock! For all of us. But when I had lunch with her the other day . . .'

Did she just say *lunch*?

'. . . she seemed far more the ticket. More like the little Lol we all know and love.'

She finally pauses for breath and turns to me.

'You look a little peaky, love. Still hungry, perhaps? We've got Frank's trifle to come yet.' She leans in conspiratorially and lowers her voice. (Does this mean she *is* capable of tact?) 'He still hasn't worked out his custard-to-cream ratio after all these years, but bless the old goat for trying.'

She looks fondly at her husband, who is crawling across the kitchen floor, Ruby Mae astride him, whooping with joy and demanding that 'Horsey go faster!'

I allow my focus to rest there, praying that Kathleen will suddenly remember some forgotten vol-au-vents burning in the oven.

She doesn't.

'And look at our wee Stevie. Pretending to be washing up over there, but I can tell his ears are burning. Bless his heart. Desperate to come and be with his girl. It's lovely. We all know he's out and out cream crackers about you.'

For God's sake, Pippa, speak! Say something. Make it clear that you are absolutely FINE about Lola. It couldn't matter LESS that Steve has LIVED with her, LOVED her, DESIRED her for most of his adult life. No. In fact, it's COOL! You are TOTALLY confident that he is over her. COMPLETELY. Right?

I try various responses on for size and none of them seem to make it past my collarbone. I feel like one of those performers roaming the Royal Mile in Edinburgh whose trick is to sound like they have a tiny version of themselves trapped inside their mouths. The tiny Pippa ensnared in my chest, who has been hammering against my ribcage, desperate to escape, is about to make a break for it when the front door is flung open.

'Ta-da!'

There stands Oscar, sporting a newly cultivated bushy beard, a shrunk-in-the-wash reindeer jumper and a sack of presents slung over one shoulder. A hipster Father Christmas. He is carrying a crate of cheap beers under one arm and his skateboard is balanced precariously on top.

'Hi, honeys! I'm home!'

And just like that, my time under the spotlight snaps to black as Kathleen leaps from the sofa to embrace 'our Oscar'.

Oh Oscar. You beautiful idiot. I have never been so happy to see your daft face.

Like ants around a rotting mango, the Gallaghers mob him and clamber on him and embrace and tickle him until he all but disappears under their weight. When he emerges, unburdened of his beers, Ruby Mae is slung under his arm like a rolled-up carpet and Sammy is attached koala-like to his calf. He calls out, 'I better be in time for Frankie's trifle. 'Cos we all know that's the only reason I'm here.'

The crowd erupts into a frenzy of activity, as everyone wants to be the person to get Oscar his bowl of Frank's famous trifle. Bedraggled, Steve extricates himself from the scrum and joins me on the sofa.

'For once, I'm pleased to see that plonker,' he whispers with a fond smile.

I snuggle into his arms.

'God, that's better. I've wanted to do this all day. You all right?'

'Fine, yeah. All good.'

He scans my face for clues. 'You sure? I saw you got mummed. Couldn't get over here in time.'

'Nothing I couldn't handle.'

He laces his fingers through mine and strokes my palm with his slightly rough thumb. Strange how quickly this makes me feel like I could fall asleep on his shoulder. Some kind of magic spell.

'She loves getting involved. What did she say?'

'Oh, nothing much.' Too bright. Way too bright.

He narrows his eyes.

'Really?'

'Totally really.'

Totally really? Why didn't I just tell him what she said about Lola? I want to so badly. I need him to reassure me that everything is okay, that Lola was just a fling, that it wasn't my fault they broke up, that I am the love of his life and nothing can tear us apart and that one day his family will love me as much as they clearly love her. But instead . . .

'We mainly talked trifle. Oh, with a side of *Midsomer Murders.*'

He laughs. 'Yeah, she hasn't stopped banging on that her son is dating a girl from the telly! Glad she didn't say anything dopey.'

He kisses me lightly on the lips. His beautiful eyes stare into mine, and for a second the Gallagher army seems to disappear. His voice drops to a gravelly whisper.

'Pippa Lyons . . .'

'What?'

'Did I ever tell you . . .'

I lean in and close my eyes. Almost nose to nose now, I can feel his breath on my cheeks. I wait for him to say the words we speak so often.

'. . . you smell *deliciously* of urine.'

He giggles gleefully. I thump him with a pillow, and he tickles me. We must look like giddy, smitten teenagers cavorting on the sofa. As he pulls me closer, I inhale that warm scent of home and allow my body to melt into his. I feel briefly reassured.

Oscar, Charlotte and Mickey – newly initiated racehorses – charge across the rug on hands and knees, to whoops and cheers from the remaining Gallaghers. Steve shakes his head, watching them with tender bafflement.

'They're all nuts.'

'I was going to go with "different".'

'But they're lovable nuts. You'll get used to them. I promise.'

He kisses me on the lips. I can feel his heart beating against my chest. My shoulders drop. Then—

'Uncle Oscar keeps tickling me! Uncle Stevie, I need you! You're more fasterer!'

He grins and rolls his eyes.

'You lucky girl. You're dating the fastest racehorse on the track.'

He kisses me lightly on the nose and dives into the fold, whinnying and tossing his mane. Ruby Mae clambers delightedly onto his back and I am left alone.

And he's right . . .

'Come on, Stevie! Put your back into it!' Frank cries, empty cola bottle in lieu of microphone.

. . . I am a lucky girl.

'And he's neck and neck with our Oscar.'

But I want to be *the* girl.

'Wait, though. What's this? Here's our Shiv coming up on the inside track . . .'

I want to be the front-runner.

'. . . but Stevie pulls it back!'

I want to be *our* Pippa.

'And would you believe it, it's a win for our Stevie!'

Will I ever be?

2 March 2019

06:39

'Sorry it's taken us a while to get here. Been a hectic night out there.'

The taller of the two policewomen lisps slightly and repeatedly chews at her dry lips. The shorter one blinks a lot, her eyes darting round the room like they're giving chase to a fly. They both appear ill at ease, backs flat against the wall as if awaiting mugshots.

Finally the tall one steps forward holding out a large see-through plastic bag. She reminds Steve of a Quentin Blake pencil drawing, all limbs and angles.

'We thought we should get them back to you as soon as possible.'

Their too-clean uniforms look uncomfortably stiff, as if they've been dressed in the next size up, to grow into.

'Your wife's effects, recovered at the scene.' The shorter one speaks with a gentle Geordie accent.

Steve slowly takes the bag, unsure what he is meant to do with it. Thank her? Have a look inside to confirm the contents? He does neither; just holds the zip-locked seam tight between his fingers.

There's something of the awkward cocktail party about the scene. Three guests loitering in a hallway, desperate for a top-up to lubricate proceedings. Uncomfortable smiles and ponderous silences that no one is quite sure how to break.

'Her handbag is in there,' tall cop continues. 'Her mobile phone and a pair of shoes. High heels. They were removed from her feet at the scene. If you have any questions . . .'

Questions? Does he have questions?

The shorter policewoman takes up the baton. 'There was an eyewitness, and we've gathered as many details as we could from him. He drove past just before the accident, but was able to make out what appeared to take place.'

Steve is suddenly wide awake, desperate for answers but also terrified of what he's going to hear.

'Apparently your wife was, er, distracted, at the time of impact.'

'Distracted?'

'Yes. According to the eyewitness, she appeared to be typing on her phone.'

'Texting? While she was driving? No. No way. Pippa would never do that.'

Geordie cop bristles, not used to being challenged.

'I assure you the gentleman was quite certain, Mr Gallagher, and we have no reason to doubt him.'

'Well I assure *you* there must be some mistake.'

A vein on her right temple pops out and begins to pulse. An unfortunate tell. She stares at him, her mouth pursed in a tight circle. Steve holds the side of the chair, a feeling close to rage stirring in his belly.

'The gentleman has given a clear statement laying out exactly what he witnessed.' She reaches into her back pocket, pulls out a small black notebook and flicks to the middle. 'He states that your wife was "clearly distracted by her mobile telephone, and then appeared to drop it into the footwell". He states that he didn't see what happened next as he had overtaken her vehicle by this point. A moment later, he heard the sound of the collision.'

Steve struggles for air. He feels an intense pressure on his ribcage.

The sound of the collision.

Suddenly the room is filled with exploding glass, screeching tyres, crunching metal. Pippa's screams. For a moment Steve is in the passenger seat, watching the action play out: her body flung forward like a rag doll, her head hitting the windscreen, while he sits paralysed, blinded by the oncoming lights.

Tall cop takes over, her tone gentle. 'It appears she must have drifted across to the wrong side of the road, and then collided with an oncoming car. I'm so sorry.'

Steve can see the words floating around his head, from the 'Giving Difficult News to Grieving Spouses' chapter of the Good Policing Guide, as they tilt their heads in concerned unison, hands clasped as though in humble prayer.

'The other driver was treated for minor injuries but has been discharged, virtually unharmed.' Tall cop finally looks over at Pippa. 'Which is one good thing.'

Steve notices the Geordie cop glance at her watch. As she looks up, she sees that his eyes are on her and flushes, mortified, tired.

'There is one more thing we need to ask you, Mr Gallagher,' she says, sounding defensive and boorish again. 'Now, this is always difficult and I'm afraid you may find it distressing.'

More distressing than the love of my life being in a coma?

'We need to ask you if your wife was depressed or in a disturbed frame of mind recently.'

'What do you mean?' Steve is incredulous.

'Can you think of any reason why she might have been distracted last night? Were there problems at home, in the marriage? Any triggering incidents?'

'It's hard to think about,' the tall cop, the good cop, chimes in. 'Most likely it was simply an unfortunate accident, but we do have to rule out, erm, you know . . .'

'Self-harm,' says Geordie cop.

For some reason, Steve feels a potential burble of laughter rise from his stomach.

'Are you asking me if she did this on purpose?'

'As I said, we simply need to rule out that line of enquiry, sir.'

Steve looks over at Pippa. The bandages. The drips. The bruising.

'No. Not self-harm.'

Quentin Blake turns to Geordie and they seem satisfied.

'Well, unless you have any questions . . .' says Geordie. 'We don't like to intrude at a time like this.'

A time like this.

'We will of course stay in contact with the hospital regarding your wife's statement,' says tall cop. 'When she's up to it,' and they both turn towards Pippa one final time. 'For now, we just wish you, you know, the best. You and your wife.'

As Steve stands alone, blinking in the new emptiness of the room, he hears a weary bleep from the plastic bag in his hand. He opens it and pulls out Pippa's mobile. The battery is flashing red. Without thinking, he finds a charger in his own bag and plugs the phone into a wall socket, as he has done so many times before.

'Can't have you without it when you wake up, can we? Who knows what's been going down in your six hundred group chats, eh?'

Whir, beep, click, breath.

But he cannot sustain the bonhomie, not even for her sake.

'What the hell were you doing, Pip? You'd never drive in high heels! And *texting*? That's not you.'

He grabs hold of the bed sheet.

'*Were* you depressed, my darling? Is this my fault? My God, did I do this to you?'

An invisible pair of hands slides around Steve's neck, but he forces himself to speak.

'I've been distant with you. I've drifted. I know I have. And you needed more from me. But somewhere along the line, I ran out of patience, Pip. I saw it happen. I hated myself. But I never stopped loving you. You know that, don't you? Oh God, Pippa, tell me you didn't do this to yourself.'

Hot tears fall now, clouding his vision.

'Wake up, darling. Wake up and tell me what was going through your head. I need to understand! Talk to me, Pippa! I can't do this on my own.'

Whir, beep, click, breath.
Whir, beep, click, breath.

June 2010

Steve

Having laid out the fly sheet, I performed a neat Boy Scout's trick and lightly malleted four corner pegs.

'Make sure to secure the fly straight away, or you'll be singing *let's go fly a tent*!' I told Pippa. She loved *Mary Poppins*, could recite every line, so I was chuffed at my ability to weave that into my tent TED talk. 'Then you're ready to enact phase two: feeding the poles.'

'Sounds like a deleted scene from the Bible,' she said drily.

'Ignore the instructions,' I continued, 'and always take double the pegs you need. You can never have too many pegs.'

I fed the poles through the sleeves with skilled ease. They travelled silkily, like a hot knife through butter. It was incredibly satisfying. Next I crouched down to unfurl the inner shell, then clipped it onto the corresponding hooks so I was able to crawl inside.

'Hope I'm not boring you,' I said from within, anticipating that the answer would be a kind but resolute negative. But there was no answer at all. 'Pip? Pippa?'

'Who wants a vodka tonic?' I heard her ask, and a cheer went up from more happy campers than we'd surely arrived with.

'I'm still going with this beer, thanks!' I called out, subtly reminding her that I was also still going with our tent.

I tied up our essentials – loo roll, bread, bacon, ketchup, wet wipes, painkillers – in a plait of plastic bags and arranged them on the ground sheet in our porch, a small distance from the edge of the fly, to keep them as dry as possible. Finally I rolled out the foam mats, then our sleeping bags, which I zipped together to create a double bed. If only I had a rose, or a luxury chocolate, like in a hotel, to finish it off . . .

I leaned back on my haunches, so my head was outside, and stroked my hand across a patch of grass. *There*, a tiny yellow flower bending towards the sun. It might have been a buttercup, I wasn't sure. I looked out at the campsite – bright domes of canvas, every colour of the rainbow, stretching to the horizon – and felt a bit sorry for the colonies of wild flowers and insects that would be decimated by the four hundred thousand feet that were about to blanket-bomb them. Then I yanked the little flower from its bed of weeds and laid it on Pippa's inflatable travel pillow.

While the idea of a massive festival like Glastonbury was daunting, I was excited about the camping element. I imagined me and Pippa waking snugly as the sun rose, before lighting the camping stove for a one-pan fry-up. A couple of weeks ago, when I'd brought round a variety pack of mini cereals to add to our supplies, she was beside herself and I was convinced that I'd found my backpacking buddy. But now that we were here, it seemed that setting up base was of secondary importance to getting the party started. The same went for the rest of our group, who were sitting in a circle among clumps of luggage, bundled sleeping bags and a bottomless chiller filled with booze. It seemed to have been unilaterally decided that it all needed to be polished off as soon as possible, and the gang were making short work of the spirits that had been smuggled in inside empty water bottles.

There was no doubting my talent for tent assembly, but it wasn't cool. And music festivals, it turned out, were all about being cool, carefree and a bit mental, rather than skilled at camping. I had dressed, I thought sensibly, for the outdoors, in fleece, wax and rubber. Pippa's friends had replaced their usual wardrobe with the Glasto look: variations on sequins, glitter and vests ripped to reveal an apparent love for the Ramones and Led Zeppelin. Even Gus had swapped his skinny blacks for an open Hawaiian shirt. They'd all also undergone slight character transformations, annual shades of personality that flowered every June. Festival Tania had swapped telling us about all the men she'd been seeing for listing all the bands and DJs she'd already seen, which seemed to be every act on the line-up.

'I hope they're going to play some B sides,' she'd said, about a band I'd never heard of. 'Not just the poppy shit.'

As for Jen, her metamorphosis had taken place over the last few months, when she'd quit acting, quit London and moved back home. Reconnecting with her Bristolian friends had helped her to flourish, and she was now able to keep pace with the competitively loud drama gang. As if to remind us that she was a different creature from the shy, skittish girl I'd met three years ago, she'd turned up dressed as a stegosaurus.

Pippa wasn't pretending to be anyone else, or to know any more about the music than I did. Her only concern was that everyone should get on, get drunk and get glittered. She was applying glitter to each of her friends' faces in turn, very seriously, like she had found her true calling.

'All done,' I said, tentatively joining the circle.

Pippa threw her arms around me as though we'd been apart for weeks.

'You're the best! How did I get so lucky? My clever boyfriend.'

I loved it when she called me that, especially to other

people. I'd swell with pride, feeling lucky, sexy, cool – and now, clever.

I sat down between Pippa and a new acquaintance: a dishevelled hippie called Jacob, who might have been a friend of Jen's or a randomer who'd infiltrated our base camp. He had a ukulele under his arm and looked a few years older than the rest of us.

'Nice one, man,' he said.

'Wow, Steve,' said Tania from behind a huge pair of sunglasses. 'You did that so fast!'

'That's because I've bagged a camping genius,' Pippa said, squeezing my hand.

'You sure have. I'm impressed.'

A compliment from Tania was usually followed by a request.

'Can you do mine? I tried once, but it was impossible.'

I could feel Pippa's eyes flickering towards me. I knew that ordinarily she would tell Tania to 'Do your own bloody tent!' But that wouldn't sit well with the current mood.

'Sure,' I said.

'Have one of these.' Jen pulled a tin of Red Stripe out of the cooler. 'They're still quite cold.' She cracked it open for me; unnecessarily, but I was grateful.

I rolled the contents of Tania's large duffel bag onto the grass. It didn't take me long to realise why she'd never managed to put the tent up herself, and it wasn't just because she thought the world was in her debt: it wasn't a tent, it was a yurt.

The instructions stated that it was a job for a minimum of two people, and illustrated this with three line-drawn characters, faces blank with concentration. The sort of line-drawn people who got shit like this done with ease. I looked over at my fellow campers – actors, stoners, a stegosaurus – and decided it would be better to attempt it alone.

It took a while, but I managed to get the frame up by stretching my body into shapes I'd only ever made in a game of Twister.

'Let me help you, Steve,' said Pippa, putting down one glitter stick before pulling another from her wash bag and very much not moving from where she was sitting. 'You'll benefit from dual shading, Jen. It'll bring out the hazel flecks in your eyes.'

Thankfully, I love a solitary outdoor assignment you can perform with a beer in hand. It was something I saw my dad do often in the summer holidays. He'd wash the car, water the garden, fiddle about with the gutters. If there were odd jobs that needed doing, he had the perfect excuse to get a bit drunk.

A can of lager later, and Tania's yurt was up. I tied back the entrance flaps with a flourish, pumped with endorphins from the workout. There was a small round of applause.

'Sort-it-out-Steve!' Gus exclaimed, with a hint of scathing.

'Sort-it-out-Steve!' echoed the chorus, and the nickname stuck.

'Can you do mine?' Jen asked.

It had soon become accepted that Sort-it-out-Steve was going to pitch everyone's tents.

'Are you sure I can't help you?' Pippa said between make-overs. 'I don't want you feeling like you're here to work. I want you to enjoy yourself.' But I was on a roll. Lay it out, light peg, thread the poles, stand it up, heavy peg, inner tent in, clip it all together, final check, repeat.

My last job was an old-school tent, the kind with thick, cold poles that stood upright in the middle. It was a patchy, faded army green, and might have seen a lot of wars. There were no instructions, but I didn't need any – the task had become intuitive. Once it was up, I crawled in. The walls were morbidly fascinating, covered in ancient stains like a sordid cave painting. It smelled like something had died in there. Something *had*; several things, in fact. It was like a mortuary for insects. I swept the mummified remains of countless ants, spiders and a bee into my hand, then poked my head out.

'Whose tent is this?' I asked, hoping it might be Gus's. I would embarrass him by showing everyone my handful of sun-dried arthropods.

There were a couple of 'dunnos', then Jacob said: 'It might be mine.'

The fact that he didn't know whether it was his tent or not said everything about him. I was sure he wouldn't care about the bugs or the stains or the smell, so I didn't say anything, apart from 'It's up now.'

Jacob held out his arms as if praising the Lord. 'Thank you, brother.' It was at once heartfelt, disingenuous and supremely irritating. Ash spilled from the end of the spliff between his lips as he spoke.

'Sort-it-out-Steve!' Gus exclaimed once again, mimicking Jacob's stoner's drawl.

I could feel that tingle of another person's muck on me, their odours mingling with my own. The beers and my motorway Scotch egg brunch were already leaching from my pores, as if we'd spent three nights here. Was an hour after arrival too soon to shower? There would be no queues yet, and no verrucas – and I'd heard that the drains got blocked up with all conceivable human matter by the end of the weekend.

'Here, you deserve this.' Jen handed me another lager. It was warm from the late-afternoon sun, but I drained half like it was water, until it started to taste foul.

Pippa was picking through a bag containing wigs, and she pulled out a neon orange afro.

'For you, Steve.'

'Oh no, I don't need one,' I said, as my hands covered my head defensively.

'Of course you don't *need* one,' she said, batting away my helpless arms and pulling the nylon 'fro over my eyes. 'But you do need this . . .'

She took something small from the bag, I couldn't see what, and pushed it onto my face. From the way it tickled at the corners of my mouth, I figured I had now sprouted a handlebar moustache.

'There! Perfect!' She leaned in to kiss me, but thought better of it, squeezing my cheeks instead. 'You're my hero, Steven Gallagher. You do know that, right?'

Despite all the excitement, the drinks and the drugs, it was strangely peaceful here on our patch of grass. This was the calm before the storm. Apart from an occasional whoop or a frisbee whistling overhead, we were encased in a womb of sound; a dull cacophony made up of thousands of murmuring voices and the muted throb of bass from distant speakers. From our pitch, you could just make out the silver peak of the main stage – the mother ship of tents – and the steady stream of bodies trickling uphill towards it, like troops being sent into battle in wellies and parka jackets. There was an occasional gap in the ranks, where a tiny figure would break off from the march into a cartwheel or to wildly embrace someone they knew.

'Glasto, man,' Jacob said, following my gaze. 'It's a state of mind.' He got up and withdrew to his tent.

When he returned, his state was altered. He didn't sit back down, but began dancing restlessly on the spot, pneumatic knees pumping to the campsite soundscape, strumming his ukulele to a tribal beat to which my ears were uninitiated. The wind changed, and carried with it a new noise: the reverberate jangle of electric guitars being sound-checked. The call of the festival. In silent agreement, we finished our drinks, brushed the dusty grass from our bottoms and joined the pilgrimage to the main stage.

Our country stroll tipped us gently downhill into a valley, where our pace slowed as the crowd ahead was funnelled through a densely wooded area. Either side of us, lush banks of green sloped up to clear blue skies. The sun had shone all day, and the soil beneath our feet had dried just enough that you could sit without a rug or coat. As we waited for some movement in the mass of hats, caps, wigs and flags in front of us, I felt my wellies stick in unexpectedly churned-up mud. The land was being ploughed by all the footfall.

There was a hum of excitement in the dappled wood as the once distant music cranked up. The smell of fried onions floated in the air. We were squeezed closer together as we reached the front. Music was blaring from speakers hidden in the trees, but no one was dancing, not even Jacob, who looked tense.

'Who's playing?' I asked Tania, thinking we must have reached one of the secret woodland dance stages she had been raving about at the campsite.

'What?'

I nodded towards the musical trees, where I presumed the DJ might be hiding behind some leaves.

'This is security,' Pippa said.

No wonder Jacob looked edgy. He patted nervously at the pockets of his denim jacket, then pulled out two fistfuls of baggies, podgy with powder. With the sleight of hand of an uncertified magician in ski gloves, he stuffed them down the front of his pants. He saw me looking, and winked.

At the security gates, tired Glastonbury locals stood in attendance, wearing high-vis jackets and forced smiles. They were trying to be patient and appear welcoming whilst retaining an air of authority over the revellers filing past, some of whom were attempting to high-five them, even stroke their faces, as they felt the effect of whatever they'd imbibed on the walk over.

I was frisked briefly then waved through. Jacob was next in line. I put a few metres' distance between us before turning to see how he would fare.

'All right, geez?' he said to the man on the gate. Then he set his sandals in a wide stance, thrust his arms out and linked his hands behind his head like he was being arrested – which perhaps he soon would be. As he was given a light perfunctory pat around the pockets of his shorts, I was astonished to hear him say: 'Lower. Left a bit. Warmer. Warmer . . .' He was giving the guy directions, showing him the county lines that converged around his crotch!

Remarkably, he elicited merely a grin from security, and was unleashed to join the rest of us.

'Shall we get something to eat?' I asked. The fried onion smell was making me salivate.

'Eating's cheating!' Tania shouted.

'It's *way* too late to eat now,' said Gus.

I looked at my phone: it was 7.15 p.m.

'Pip?'

'I'm not hungry.' She smiled at me, a little guilty. 'You get something, though.'

A huge cheer went up from the next field, and our pace quickened in step with the hordes entering the arena. As we were carried through a passage lined with food trucks – a veritable food festival – we heard the first chords being struck by the opening act. It was clear we weren't going to be stopping. Burgers, burritos, pizza, noodles, churros, chips all faded into the distance as the great Pyramid Stage rose up in front of us.

None of us – not even Tania – knew the band playing onstage, but that made it even better. We weren't waiting for a tune we knew from the radio, just enjoying each song for the first time. It was nothing like the few gigs I'd been to over the years. This was more communal: a sea of people, moving as one, emptying their thoughts and not worrying about looking cool. Well, Tania and Gus might have been concerned about how they appeared, but we were so densely packed that I didn't have to look at them.

All I could see was the back of Pippa's head, and I was happy there. I buried my face in her hair, breathing in her shampoo. For a moment, there was no multitude, just me and her. I could give my weight to the shoulders surrounding us. We swayed like that for a while, reeds kept afloat by the undulating crowd. Pippa's head lolled back onto my chest. She was smiling dreamily. I kissed her, and a tiny shard of glitter flickered from her cheek to mine, catching the light from the dying sun. This could work for me after all, this festival thing, I thought. No drink, no drugs could make this moment any more perfect. I didn't need anything else.

All the undulating did start to make me need the loo, though. I desperately didn't want to break the spell, but it wasn't like I could simply pop off to the lavatory then resume this pose.

'Pip?'

'Mm, nice music, isn't it?'

'I need to go for a wee.'

'You can go here.'

I laughed, but she was serious.

'Where?'

'In the bottle.'

'Our water bottle?'

'I guess.'

'But it's got our water in it.'

'On the floor, then. You're a boy, it's easy.'

She disentangled herself from me and edged forward slightly, as if to give me room.

'Okay. Here goes.'

I thought about how this would work: I'd slyly undo my flies, drop into a slight squat and aim down. But would I be able to go? As I was rehearsing this in my head, the band upped the tempo, the crowd upped their response, and I was nudged sideways by a wave of eager dancing on my right, bumping into a girl dressed in dungarees on my left.

'Sorry!'

'No worries, mate,' she said, though I doubted she'd be so forgiving if she saw that I had my todger in my hand.

The anxiety was making me need the loo even more.

'I'll go,' I told Pippa. 'You stay here.'

'No way! We can't split up, I'll never find you.'

The gang heard this, and suddenly my bladder was a source of great interest.

'Steve's off for a wee, guys.'

'You gotta piss, huh, Steve?'

'Are you going to the bar?'

'No, the loo.'

'The loos are by the bar.'

'It'll be rammed.'

'Can I give you cash for some cider?'

'Will you find your way back okay?'

'If we get lost, we can ring you,' I said, keen to get a move on. If I'd known it would cause so much discussion, I would have snuck off without saying anything.

'Unlikely,' said Jen, showing us her phone screen. 'This is a signal dead zone.'

'We should work out a meeting place if anyone gets lost,'

Pippa suggested. She scanned the horizon, apparently working out our latitude and longitude. 'Where are we now?'

'Dead zone!' Jacob said, unhelpfully.

'There,' said Pippa, pointing to a tall pole a few feet away. A flag with a smiley-faced yellow skull and crossbones waved from the top of it. 'We're in line with that flag, that emergency exit sign and the big speaker to the right of the stage.'

I was impressed with her orienteering skills. She would still turn the wrong way out of East Acton Tube when going to our new flat, but she was now confidently pinpointing our location in a field the size of Berkshire.

She took my hand and we walked in single file through the brawl, mouthing apologies as we went. As the band finished their next song, the last of the set, there was a turn in the tide. We were no longer pushing our way upstream, but were swept along by a current of people, all destined for the loos.

Eight minutes into a queue of men that snaked its way round a maze of hessian-lined fencing, I started to understand what Jacob was on about, this Glasto state of mind. I tried to breathe as little as possible – short breaths in through my mouth – but I could still taste the cocktail of ammonia and sharp, acrid vinegar from the troughs that passed for toilets. I tried not to look down as I peed through a seatless circle, a porthole onto the horrors of a deep blue chemical sea.

'Bet that was a relief,' said Pippa, who was waiting for me expertly holding about six plastic pints.

I breathed a deep sigh, relieved in every sense of the word, and felt the oxygen returning to my blood. 'It was an experience,' I said. 'Next time I'm going on the ground.'

We re-entered the Pyramid's orbit, which was even busier now that the next act was up. With the happy skull and crossbones in our sight, I copied Pippa, who was leading the charge by thrusting the pints out in front of her as a kind of snowplough, finding gaps in the crowd.

'Still behind me, Steve?'

'Just about,' I called back. 'Spilling most of it.'

'Me too.'

I was doubtful that we would find our friends again, but as we closed in on the flag, there they were – in line with the pole, the exit sign and the speaker. The stegosaurus head-dress a spiky landmark.

'Hey, you made it!'

'Sort-it-out-Steve strikes again!'

Our wrists were sticky with spilt cider, but the gang were only too pleased to have their three-quarter-pints delivered to them. In fact, they were inordinately pleased to see us; almost ecstatic. Jacob playfully sparred with me, boxing out a beat on the top of my arm; Tania gave us both a hug that seemed genuinely warm; even Gus looked not unhappy at my presence.

'Thank you, Stee-vie,' said Jen, beaming. Her eyes were all pupil, a bit like the stretched black ovals of the smiley-faced cap'n fluttering above us.

We were also welcomed back by a new friend, who had come as a sequinned mermaid. Another of Jen's pals?

'Hi!' she said, very brightly.

'I love your outfit!' Pippa shouted back above the music.

They hugged and the mermaid woman sort of danced at us, so I sort of danced back. A plastic bottle containing a bright orange drink was being passed round. The mermaid offered it to me.

'Punch?' I asked, to which she more or less nodded.

I took a sip without letting the bottle touch my lips. It was tangy, like an effervescent vitamin drink. Not quite a substitute for dinner, but a good idea to get some electrolytes down me, so I poured a little more into my open mouth. Quite a lot more.

'Whoa, that's enough!' The mermaid snatched it back from me.

'Sorry.' I hoped someone hadn't peed in it, like Pippa had suggested to me earlier, then passed it round as a prank. 'Er, what is it?'

She thought about this for a second. 'Fanta.'

'Oh. Thank you,' I said. 'I haven't had Fanta for ages.'

'Mostly Fanta,' she said, and sauntered off.

'Who was that?' I asked Pippa.

'I don't know! Didn't she look amazing?' Pippa had drunk some 'mostly' Fanta too, and now her whole face had changed.

What's going to happen to me? I thought. Am I about to get high on illegal street drugs?

I looked up at the smiling skull and crossbones. It might have been a ripple of the flag in the breeze, but I was sure he winked at me.

'Are you okay?' asked Pippa. 'You having fun?'

I didn't want to show my alarm at having drunk the stranger's cocktail, so I tried to sound relaxed. 'What do you think was in that bottle?'

'Maybe Mandy?' said Jen.

'And you drank some too?' I checked with Pippa.

'Yes. Don't worry. She was a good mermaid.'

'Do you think I'm high?'

Pippa laughed, then stroked my face. 'Maybe from the sugar.'

I had no reference for these feelings. My legs felt a bit hollow, but that could have been my hunger. I could see spangled light at the edge of my vision, but that might have been the lights, which were spangly and strobey and growing more visible as the sunlight faded, trapping clouds of smoke in their beams.

I was hoping we were staying put for the night. We'd found

a spot with a good view of the stage, and Muse were up later, a band I'd actually heard of. But the gang wanted to dance, and Tania was spearheading a move to a dance tent. As we walked, she listed the DJs she'd learned would be playing. There were several called Dave and 'too many DJs', she concluded.

'Too Many DJs? Mint!' shouted Jen.

'Can you have too many?' I asked.

'Steve, you did a joke!' Pippa said, giggling.

'Did I?'

One of the many DJs had a residency in a bar, the next in a tuk-tuk; further on, a dreadlocked man who looked like he had just crawled out of his woodland home was beating a bongo, drumming passers-by into a frenzy.

We were soon swept into a whirlpool of people, all chanting: 'There's only one Jerry Baskets.' At first I presumed Jerry was a DJ, because our group began to chant along, but it looked like he might have been a boy celebrating his birthday in the middle of a group of teenage friends. The chant soon became a conga, which I was forcibly dragged into. Pippa, a couple of bodies in front of me, glanced over her shoulder to check I was still with them.

When the conga line broke up, I looked around for her. She wasn't ahead of me. I looked behind, but she wasn't there either. I spun round again, my eyes straining to pick her out, but the fairy lights strung between the surrounding trees only served to illuminate everyone in a speckled twilight.

'Pippa?'

I checked my phone: no missed calls, no signal.

I raised my voice: 'Pippa?'

'*Pippa?*' a couple of boys, probably friends of Jerry Baskets, called back at me. They were laughing, and suddenly I saw a reflection of myself from the way they imitated me: a child who'd lost his parents in the middle of a supermarket.

I decided my best bet was to head in the same direction as the boys, though I followed them at a slight distance so they didn't think I was looking for a fight after their piss-taking. The faces I was passing had begun to take on the appearance of gargoyles: some gurning, others giggling madly, lip-glossed mouths widening into cruel Cheshire Cat smiles. Sensible coats and sensible heads had long since been pulled off, left to be trodden into the mud along with countless empty baggies. I had grown irritable. The hunger, the beer, the abandonment – it all made for an unhealthy mix. Why had I agreed to come? To be with Pippa, of course, to experience all this with her; but it was obvious right from the start that I would end up being left out. I imagined that she'd already given up trying to find me. She would be on another level now with her drug-taking friends, glad to leave me behind, free now to get out of her tree along with everyone else without having to chaperone her sad-sack boyfriend.

Caught up in my reverie of self loathing, I stumbled into one of the fabled dance tents, which wasn't really a tent at all, just a swarm of writhing bodies. We could have been inside or outside, I couldn't tell, couldn't see the sky for the green lasers that were beating stripes overhead. I pressed into the scrum, hoping to get to the long bar on the far side. Perhaps Pippa would be waiting for me there.

By the time I'd wriggled through, I was sopping with the sweat of a thousand strangers. It was deeply unpleasant. Even my cagoule couldn't keep me dry. I looked down the line, which was six deep along the length of the busy bar. On tiptoe, I leaned right to left, my eyes straining to find Pippa's hair among the crush. I was never going to find her here. I felt like I was burning up, so I slipped off my jacket. Immediately it was snatched from my hands.

'Hey!' I shouted, as it sailed across the tops of people's

heads like it had come to life. I tried to follow its flight, but it was out of reach, then out of sight, and was soon followed by more clothing – a flip-flop, a bikini top – then an England flag and a beach ball. A crowd-surfing exodus of inanimate objects.

The nearest exit spat me out onto a rubber path, which appeared to be winding its way to a sign that read: *CARAVANS EMERGENCY EXIT*. Probably the wrong way, but I'd take my chances. I'd sooner walk the perimeter of the festival than put myself through another spin and rinse in the car wash that was the dance tent.

As I turned the corner, my way was blocked by a couple in full frot, oblivious – or unconcerned – that I was now inches away from them. They continued to bash up against some fencing as I gave them a wide berth, trying not to look. I couldn't help noticing the boy's ruched boxer shorts, however, which had been pulled below a bare arse. They weren't *doing it*, were they? A calf-length welly made its way around the back of the boy's legs, where it dangled for a moment. As it caught the light, it shone the same deep blue as Pippa's. Now I was fully watching them, and a painful chill ran through me as a wavy lock of colourless hair turned auburn as it swung round into the faint light. A million impossible thoughts ran through my head, from the hysterical to the murderous, and I felt sick and dizzy. I snapped my head forward and walked on as fast as I could, reeling, ashamed. All of a sudden, I was fearful of where Pippa might end up tonight, of who she might end up with. I trusted her, but it didn't feel like we were in the real world any more, where normal rules applied. These kids made me feel old and, though it would sound pathetic to them, a bit scared. The child who was lost in the supermarket had just wandered into a dark funfair where the rides were all ghost trains and nightmarish crazy houses and there wasn't a responsible adult in sight.

Find an older person, I thought. Someone reliable. Someone like this . . .

'Excuse me,' I asked a woman who was filling up a canteen of water. 'How do I get to the Pyramid Stage?'

'The Pyramid?' She thought about it a moment. 'Hmm. Philip?'

A man came out from behind the Portaloos to join us. I presumed the two of them were about to retire to one of the caravans. They must have been about the same age as my parents (who at this moment would be fast asleep after a Friday-night fish supper).

'Which way's the Pyramid?' she asked him.

'Ah. I do know that. We've come from there. But I've just done a load of acid.'

'Philip!' she exclaimed, before thrusting out her hand. 'Give me some.' She disappeared behind the loos.

Philip stayed where he was, looking through me, or into me. I didn't know what to say, so I said nothing, and backed away until he receded into the darkness.

The Pyramid, when I eventually found it, was even busier than before, and more raucous. I strained to look for our meeting place, but the air was thick with smoke. Even if I did manage to press through the crowd and find the smiley face flag, would Pippa be waiting at the bottom of it? No. She was lost to the night and I had to let her go. It was a sign, I decided, a warning from the Ghost of Festivals Yet to Come that I just didn't belong here.

'I'll go find the tent, have a nice freshen-up with some baby wipes, and a little cry,' I said out loud. 'That'll sort me out.' The thought of crying myself to sleep while from not-so-afar the festival pumped out music into the wee hours gave me a sort of masochistic comfort, but I didn't have much else to cling onto.

Up ahead, the path opened onto a clearing. A few people were clustered in small groups, or staggering around alone, in a smoky area where the music was more relaxed, more recognisable. The smoke was meaty, and I was surprised to smell something wonderful and inviting in it. The food trucks were going strong.

'You're still open?' I asked a guy who was sipping coffee behind the grille of a gourmet burger van.

He looked at me as if to say, 'No shit, Sherlock.'

Of course they were; they would soon be welcoming an onslaught of drunken rockers and ravers, belatedly lining their stomachs with burgers and chips and kebabs. My nose picked out the sour, spicy smell of Thai food, and I was drawn irresistibly to a van advertising pad thai. I felt a pang of regret that Pippa wasn't there; food tasted better when I could enjoy it with her.

'Steve?' The voice was small and muffled by a mouthful of food. Pippa was sitting on a low hay bale, her knees nearly level with her shoulders, holding a wooden fork that was dug into a paper box of noodles. In an instant she was on her feet, and then on mine as we hit each other at high speed.

'I've been looking for you everywhere,' she said, dropping a chewed piece of peanut down my T-shirt.

'Me too,' I said, and felt a tear fall a short distance from my cheek, mingling with the sweat on her neck. I managed to suppress a sniff, but she pulled back and fixed her gaze on me.

'Are you okay?'

I shook my head, unable to express how happy I was to see her, and how guilty I felt for doubting her. 'I'm sorry,' I managed.

'Oh my darling,' she said, tears adding a sheen to the glitter splashed across her cheeks. 'What have you got to be sorry about?'

'For being boring. And uncool.'

'Are you kidding?' She pushed the box of noodles into my hands so she could gesticulate sufficiently (this was never insincere – her hands were as much a part of her speech as her larynx or her lips) and tapped at her temples as if to show me where her thoughts were being articulated. 'There isn't *anyone* I'd rather be here with than you. When you were doing the tents I just felt so proud to be yours. You're not like anyone else, you're – you're—'

I could feel noodles slipping through my fingers, but I didn't care. I wanted her to find her words.

'Inspirational.'

I smiled and she smiled back at me. I could never tire of looking at the geography of her face.

'I'd given up trying to find you,' I said.

She threw her arms around my neck and rested her forehead against mine.

'Never give up. I'll *always* find my way back to you, Steven.'

2 March 2019

07:39

Steve stands by the window, shaken by the call. He knew it was coming, but nothing could prepare him for the distress that poured from the speaker, the pure pain of her guttural cry, still ringing in his ears. He looks out on the world, seeking comfort in the pavements that swell with Saturday-morning footfall: hospital staff arriving with flasks of coffee; families visiting loved ones; lycra-clad joggers and welly-booted dog walkers.

'Ding-dong. Room service.'

Nurse Craig is holding the door open with one leg while clutching a plastic breakfast tray.

'Now, it may not be cordon bleu, but I know from experience that the cornflakes are edible. So . . .'

He knocks the door wide with his hip and enters with a flourish.

'Hm,' he says, casting his eye around the room. 'Where shall you dine this morning, sir?'

It's clear that the only suitable space is the table by the bed, but Craig glides about in a figure of eight, making a show of seeking out the very best surface.

'Et voilà.'

He places the tray down on the over-bed table, wheeling it away from Pippa and pulls the chair up to it. Steve doesn't move.

'Come on, buddy.' Craig's voice softens. 'Few mouthfuls. You won't know yourself.'

He walks over and gently takes Steve's arm, leading him to the chair as if he were blind.

'I'll be back to check you've had some. Just eat what you can.'

Suddenly he is crouched down in front of Steve.

'You're doing really well,' he says, looking him directly in the eyes. 'I mean it. Keep going. This isn't easy, but she needs you.'

Steve gulps, caught off guard by the man's sincerity. He nods, eyes wide to stave off another onslaught of tears. And with that, Craig is gone, the door wafting closed behind him.

Steve reluctantly picks up the mini cereal box and rips along the perforated cardboard. He opens the tiny plastic bag within and forces himself to attempt a few flakes. His mouth is far too dry, swallowing is impossible. He spits them out into a paper napkin and screws it up. He pokes at the anaemic scrambled egg with his fork. It has solidified into the shape of Italy, a dribble of clear fluid leaking from the tip of the boot. He pushes it absent-mindedly around the scratched plastic plate. No. That's not going to do it. He moves on to the toast, which is cold and flaccid and bends in his hand like a shatterproof ruler. Determined not to let the side down, he takes a bite, chews slowly, swallows and repeats, each mouthful a fresh ordeal. Next he peels back the foil from the teensy pot of orange juice. This should help. Can't go wrong with fruit juice, surely. But he is wrong. The liquid burns his mouth, so acidic it could have leaked from a battery.

He realises his jaw is aching, not from the cardboard toast but from the hours of monologuing. His body is telling him to crawl into the bed beside Pippa and sleep for eternity, but he can't, he mustn't. Like a Depression-era dance marathon, where couples would go on and on until they dropped, choosing to die of exhaustion rather than let their feet stop moving, he cannot give up. He must find yet more words to wrap around her like a blanket, to rejuvenate her, to heal her. Words that may be falling on deaf ears.

But now Diana is on her way. Another voice to fill the room with expressions of love.

When he saw her name finally flash up on his phone screen, Steve had to move away from Pippa, instinctively shielding her from her mother's animal howls. There followed a frenzied blast of questions and unintelligible interjections before she abruptly hung up, swearing to be there within the hour.

Please drive safely, Steve texted her immediately after.

'I shaved yesterday, for the job,' he tells Pippa, stroking her wrist with his finger, careful to avoid the clear plaster sticking down the IV drip. 'You know what that means? Your mum's going to tell me I look like a child without a chin. Yep, I'd give it about eleven minutes.'

Whir, beep, click, breath.

'She's gonna love it. I'm a sitting target. It'll be Christmas all over again.'

He holds up a beige toast crust, turning it around in the light like a jeweller examining a rare diamond.

'Well, Craig was right. Absolutely definitely one hundred per cent *not* cordon bleu.'

He puts it in his mouth, chews twice and swallows quickly. Then he raises the fluorescent plastic pot.

'To you, my love. And all the breakfasts of our future.' He takes a sip, wincing as he swallows.

There is a commotion from the hall. He looks over his shoulder to find a woman weeping outside the door. She looks just like the man who arrived with his mother, Mr Redmond, but for the make-up tracing wet stripes across her cheeks. She gasps, doubling over, before a consoling arm comes around her, keeping her from collapsing. Steve cannot look away from the rectangle of glass – a window into her grief. He watches as Redmond puts his other arm around her, pulling her into a tight embrace.

Redmond glances up and catches Steve's eye. His expression is calm, stoic, until his focus shifts to Pippa, lying helpless amid the multitude of electronics and cabling keeping her alive. Suddenly a look of concern, of sorrow animates his face. His eyes flicker back to Steve. As the weeping woman breaks away from him, he puts a balled fist to his chest. Steve returns the gesture through the glass, then watches the grieving siblings walk away.

He turns back to Pippa, to the cold breakfast and the empty cup of concentrated orange juice. Like a marathon runner entering the last stages of the race, muscles burning, legs ready to buckle, but cheered on towards the finish by the support of strangers in the crowd, he finds he is lifted by Redmond's act of solidarity – and by Craig's. He necks the juice, then shoots the cup straight into the bin: a three-pointer.

'And to us getting the hell out of here.'

October 2011

Steve

Somewhere between check-in and boarding, I'd decided that this would be the trip where I'd pop the question. It wouldn't be easy, because I'd have to get him on his own, and alone time with my old headmaster was something I was still irrationally afraid of.

It was a question of permission. Of propriety. A rather old-fashioned one that made me question my feminist credentials. Nevertheless, it was a question that I knew Mr Lyons would expect – and that Pippa would find romantic. I might ask Diana too, but I knew her answer would be yes, and she'd be keen to get things under way immediately. With Mr Lyons, however, it would not be such a formality. I wasn't at all sure what his answer would be. He was fond of me, I could tell, but I got the sense that he was humouring me, indulging our relationship for a little longer, but fully expecting it to fizzle out by the end of our twenties.

One day it might become easier to hang out mano a mano with Mr Lyons, though I didn't quite know what that would look like. A drink down the pub? A trip to the hardware store? It all seemed so unlikely. No, it would have to be here, in the land of opportunity, where we'd be drunk as raisins from the Californian sunshine.

The trip was the latest offering from a multipack of madcap ideas that Mr Lyons had been feasting on over the last couple of months, since he unexpectedly announced his retirement halfway through the summer holidays, sending the school that had depended on his unwavering commitment for a quarter of a century into meltdown.

Diana dismissed his change of behaviour as a midlife crisis, but it was obvious that she was as upset as the apple cart, fearing that her ex-husband might start behaving like an ex-husband and open himself up to new romances – as she had done – despite continuing their non-platonic platonic non-marriage. ('All the sin of divorce, none of the guilt,' as my mum described it.)

Pippa, though, loved the sea change in her dad. I always presumed that her wild side came from Diana, but now that this rebel without a cause had emerged from his dusty cocoon, we were all keeping our eyes on him, out of fascination or concern, to see what his next flight of fancy would be.

What came next, he told us on another spontaneous visit to our flat, where he presided over a KFC bucket (his first since the eighties), was an 'all-expenses-paid long-haul rite-of-passage adventure. Without your mother, who won't get on a plane.'

'Where are we going?!' cried Pippa.

'The US of A,' he said in a Deep South accent via Windsor. 'San Fran, to be precise.'

'Who's paying all the expenses?' I asked, presuming he'd won a competition from the back pages of his *Reader's Digest*.

He took a bite out of a drumstick, looking extremely satisfied with himself, like he was playing the Colonel in an advert.

'*I* am.'

'If you're going to San Francisco . . .'

Usually I was the one making up song lyrics, but when Mr Lyons started singing during our first in-flight meal (rubber eggs, boiled mushrooms, chicken sausage and beans), Pippa came up with her own refrain. *'You're gonna eat a better breakfast there.'*

She and her dad were delighted by this, and the game of the trip was born.

I'd have been happy with 'I spy', which was quieter and attracted less of an audience, but Pippa and her dad played it with commitment from passport control to arrivals and across the Bay Area.

They sang as we left the plane, passing an American couple who needed to be winched out of their seats by the stewards.

'If you're going to San Francisco, make sure your bum can fit into your chair.'

Then, jostling to pick out our suitcases from the baggage carousel:

'If you're going to San Francisco, don't push in front of the man with the evil stare.'

'You two should have an impro show,' I said, celebrating their double act but also trying to communicate that they were getting a bit loud.

'A one-act impro troupe!' said Pippa.

'A one-act wonder!' Mr Lyons replied.

'Pippa and Papa!' Pippa shouted.

'Yes.' Mr Lyons laughed hard. 'For one night only!'

'Pippa and Papa Pippa!' I joined in, failing my audition, and not for the first time.

I'd brought a film camera with me, to take photos with that old-fashioned holiday vibe to them, but also so we didn't spend half the time reviewing the shots – me fiddling about with the settings as if I were at a job, Pippa going through them and insisting I delete the ones she didn't like the look of herself in.

I'd bought three rolls of film, not cheap these days, which I thought should suffice. I'd only use it to capture special moments, like dinners, cable car rides or our walk over the Golden Gate Bridge to Sausalito – special moments that I'd already planned out on a blank page of my *Lonely Planet*.

Using my notes, I tried to pitch the first draft of an itinerary in the taxi from the airport, hoping to get to a well-reviewed restaurant on Fisherman's Wharf (where you could get oysters for a dollar) in time for lunch, but Pippa and Mr Spontaneous were having none of it. We dumped our bags at the hotel, quickly changing from English autumn wear into short sleeves and sandals, and wandered along the Embarcadero, stopping off at each pier to sample whatever hot dog stand, ice cream truck or crab shack we passed.

'So, is this lunch?' It was midday, and I was getting confused. 'Or are we sort of snacking before lunch?'

'Whatever,' said Mr Lyons, already picking up the West Coast lingo.

'Yeah. Whatever,' Pippa echoed, looking at him admiringly.

When we were accosted by anyone pushing a leaflet for a boat trip to Alcatraz or a walking tour through Chinatown, I kept my eyes down and strode ahead with purpose – I'd done my research, I knew where the deals were. Then I'd turn round to see Pippa and Papa asking about prices and times, laughing and shaking hands, delighting everyone they met.

We hit Pier 39 and joined a group gathered at the water's edge to see what they were looking at.

'Seeeals!' Pippa cried, almost knocking a backpacker into the sea to get a closer look.

'They're actually sea *lions*,' I said, but she wasn't interested.

'I love them!' She clapped her hands, channelling her inner seal (or sea lion).

As we moved down the pier, we found more and more of them – a whole flubbering gang flopped lazily on the sprawling jetty. Pippa let out a shriek, scaring off a few more tourists, and her colony wailed back at her.

'Give me your camera,' she said.

She snapped away, on a sea safari. As she documented the animals, she gave them all names – Trevor, Brian, Mavis, Maud. It sounded like the register at an old folks' home. I tried to keep up.

'Look at Trevor, he's getting randy!' I said, pointing to one that was trying to instigate a pile-on.

'That's not Trevor,' Pippa corrected me. 'That's Winifred.'

'Oh.'

'She's dominating Brenda so she knows to keep her hands off Sid.'

'Aha,' I said. 'And which one's Steve again?'

'He's there, bobbing in the water,' said Mr Lyons from a bench. He had no trouble learning their names.

'How can you tell?' I asked him.

'He has sad eyes.'

We watched the sea lion blink salt water from wet lashes.

'Poor Steve,' said Pippa.

'I have sad eyes?'

'No!' said Pippa. 'Steve the Seal.'

'I thought you named him after me.'

'Don't be so self-centred.'

Pippa's commitment to watching the colony didn't waver, but after a while, her glee turned to concern.

'Don't you think they should be at sea? I mean, further out at sea? They *look* happy—'

'Except Steve.'

'Except Steve. But would they be happier away from all these bloody . . . human tourists?'

I supposed she didn't count herself as either human or a tourist, being a native to the colony.

'Just look at those kids waving at Maud,' she tutted.

'They're just waving.'

'No, they're *taunting* her. You can see she doesn't like it.'

I tried to find something in Maud's expression, but all I could read from her face was 'sea lion'.

'I wish they'd stop. She's not a . . . a . . .'

'Performing seal?' I said.

'Exactly.' She leaned over the wooden balustrade so far I was impelled to hold onto her hips so she wouldn't fall in. 'Here, Maud! Here, Maudy!'

'Pip, *you're* waving now.'

'I'm different.'

We spent the rest of the afternoon there, Pippa communing with her spirit animals, Mr Lyons sitting on his bench, watching her watching them. By the time we left, she had used up a whole roll of film.

I could have joined Mr Lyons on his bench, but Pippa was in earshot the whole time; it was too risky. A night into the vacation, and the question was still burning.

The following day, we took a boat to Alcatraz.

'If you're going to Alcatraz, don't bring in water if it's in a glass.'

During our guided tour of the prison, Pippa struck up a conversation with a couple of Australian girls, which presented me with an opportunity. While she was distracted, I'd get Mr Lyons into a cell and ask him. It would have to be quick, too quick perhaps, but it would make an amusing story at least – a freebie for his father-of-the-bride speech. He could say that I'd locked him in a prison cell 'and demanded he marry my daughter'.

My moment came when Pippa and her new girlfriends were lagging at the back.

'Look,' I said, stepping into an empty cell. 'I think Al Capone wrote on the wall in here.'

But Mr Lyons didn't follow me, just a group of women in very white trainers and matching fanny packs, who listened, intrigued, as I made up a story about Al Capone writing poetry dedicated to his lover.

When Pippa and the girls caught up, Mr Lyons was with them, charming the backpacks off the Australians.

I racked my brains for a subtle way to get him alone, but short of following him into the toilet every time he had to go, I was running out of ideas. If I suggested to Pippa that me and Daddy were off for some lad time, she'd see straight through it.

I was about to give up, thinking it was surely impossible whilst holidaying as a threesome, when I picked up a brochure for the hotel spa. It was right up Pippa's street, and the perfect way to get rid of her for an hour. Or just half an hour, I thought, clocking the prices of the treatments on offer.

While Pippa was in the shower, I pressed 0 and asked to be put through to the spa.

'Can I book three of your shortest massages, please?'

'Certainly sir, shall I charge it to the room?'

'No, I'd better get this. Can I ask, are the sauna and steam room unisex?'

'They're not, I'm sorry sir. Do you still want to book the treatments?'

'Yes, that's perfect!'

'Okay. You have a great day now.'

Over lunch, I announced that I'd be treating everyone to an early-evening pampering, to a muted reception.

'It's a weird thing to book when it's so warm out,' Pippa said.

Weird or not, at 6 p.m. we all met in our robes by a water

feature with a stone Buddha sitting peacefully under a burbling mini fountain, before being led off to separate booths for our treatments. After about five minutes of being massaged, I fell fast asleep, woken half an hour later by the sound of my own snoring, which had drowned out the gentle whale song. I came round in a daze, having quite forgotten why I was there.

'Shall we meet here in twenty minutes?' I heard Pippa say on the other side of the bamboo drapes.

'Where's Steven?' Mr Lyons asked.

'Probably nodded off.'

'Nodded off!' I called out, falling off the bed in a tangle of white towels.

'Steve, I'm going to have a steam then meet you by the burbling Buddha,' Pippa called back.

Mr Lyons and I sat at a polite distance from each other on either side of the marbled chamber. It would have been strange enough, but my nervous energy was making it all the more uncomfortable. There were nineteen minutes left on the clock. It was now or never.

I had just about readied myself to speak when a supersized hotel guest joined us. He smiled, whipped off his towel so he was dressed in nothing but blonde fur, and settled himself between us.

'*Guten Tag*,' said Mr Lyons, making a snap judgement as only a man of his self-confidence could.

'Y'all from Germany?' replied the man, unexpectedly Midwestern.

'England,' Mr Lyons said.

'London, England?'

'Near there, yes.'

'How about y'all?' The man turned to me with a squelch.

'Same,' I said. 'We're here together.'

He looked back at Mr Lyons on his left, then me on his right, making a judgement of his own. 'Oh I get it,' he said. Then he picked up his towel, opened the door and left in a puff of steam.

'What a nice man,' said Mr Lyons, glad to see the furry back of the homophobic hick.

'Lovely,' I said.

We leaned against the damp walls, waiting for the vapours to return. Ten minutes on the clock. When the room became thick enough with steam that I couldn't tell if his eyes were open or closed, I knew it was now or never. Again.

'Sir?'

'Hmm?'

'Can I ask you something?'

'Fire away.'

'Well . . .' I realised then that after the lengths I'd gone to in coordinating this moment, I hadn't actually thought about what I was going to say. I reached for the words and found they came from a Jane Austen phrasebook. 'I'm going to ask your daughter for her hand in marriage, with your consent.'

Mr Lyons fell quiet. I waited for a reply, but nothing came. His expression was hidden behind an opaque fog of eucalyptus oil and supreme awkwardness. My fears were realised.

'I mean, not yet, of course,' I said, back-pedalling.

I could only see his silhouette now. He was completely still.

'Just wanted, you know, to run it past you.' I was gabbling now. 'While I had you alone – in the semi-nude!'

He didn't laugh, but seemed to raise a hand, wiping sweat from his face. I did the same, nervously mirroring him.

'Maybe I should have chosen less of a hot spot to—'

'It's a wonderful thing, Steve, really.'

He'd never called me Steve before, only Steven. Perhaps the steam was obscuring our syllables as well as our faces.

'Yeah?' I said, expecting to hear a 'but'. Instead, silence, which I started to fill again. 'I'll wait a while, until I can afford a proper ring. Another couple of years maybe.'

'Ask her soon,' he said. His voice sounded different, distant.

'Oh yes, soon. Maybe in . . . a year?'

I heard him speak again, but what he said didn't make sense. The sounds belonged to his voice, but the words hung in the air, suspended, heavy.

'I may not be around that long.'

I wanted to stay in that moment in time, right before he spoke. But then the words were formed and fell into place, and everything had changed.

He told me it was cancer. He said it had spread, that they'd caught it late, that they feared it was advanced. I had so many questions, but we were aware that Pippa might be waiting for us, and didn't want to worry her. The thought of seeing her outside, rested and happy, wrapped up in towelling, filled me with dreadful love. She was the first and last person I wanted to see.

As we made to leave, Mr Lyons put a warm hand on my arm. There was something more he had to say while we were still safely cloaked in steam.

'I wasn't going to tell her here,' he said. 'I wasn't going to tell either of you, not yet. But here we are.'

'It's okay,' I said.

'I want this trip to be . . . an untainted memory. So please, don't say anything.'

'Of course,' I agreed automatically, as I always did.

*

Even though he'd resisted my itinerary, Mr Lyons did have a shortlist of specific San Fran jaunts that we were ticking off day by day. Top of that list was a streetcar ride across town to the Golden Gate Bridge. Pippa and Papa were in great spirits, yelling 'Stellaaa!' from the back seat of the tram like the rebellious, too-cool-for-school crew that Mr Lyons would have put into Friday detention not so long ago.

His behaviour over the last couple of months was falling into place – what before had seemed like the whims of a middle-aged madman I now realised was a sudden determined effort to fulfil a bucket list of life experiences. It dawned on me, thinking of how he'd absconded from his post at the school, just how long he'd been keeping the news from us.

Did anyone else know, beyond his doctor and me? Diana certainly didn't. And how long would I have to keep this secret? We were on day four of a week-long vacation. If my future father-in-law had been able to hold onto it for three months, surely I could manage three days?

'What's up, Steve?' Pippa asked me during a hiatus in Brando impersonations. I caught Mr Lyons' reflection in the glass. He was pretending to look out the window, but his eyes were fixed on me.

'Nothing,' I said, which was always going to be an insufficient answer. 'Just that I'm pretty sure *A Streetcar Named Desire* wasn't set in San Francisco.'

'Oh don't be such a killjoy.'

She'd been asking me 'What's up?' or 'Why are you so quiet?' since we'd emerged from the steam room the previous evening.

'Dad, you're so red!' she'd said. 'You look like you've been crying.'

Mr Lyons, the actress's father, had managed to laugh this off convincingly. He'd been able to carry the lie with more ease than me. In fact, he seemed to be having even more fun now – if that were possible – as if revealing his painful truth to me had made him lighter.

In my corner, the effect was quite the opposite. I regretted my vow of silence, a promise made in haste that I would struggle to keep without rousing Pippa's suspicions or becoming such a killjoy that I'd ruin the holiday for all of us.

'*If you're going to Sausalito . . .*'

As we walked across the bridge, I wondered what would cause Pippa more pain: telling her the truth while we were here, miles from home, miles from her mum and her friends; or keeping the truth from her – *lying* to her – something I should never do. It wasn't like it was a little white lie, either. It was a huge lie: a lie wrapped in a proposal wrapped in a holiday.

'*Our Steamy Steve will take you for a steam . . .*'

If I didn't tell her now, would I have to admit that I already knew when, in the end, she *was* told? How would she feel if she knew that I knew and hadn't told her? What kind of start to a life of honour and trust was that? The lie wasn't protecting her; it was only protecting the enjoyment of the holiday, which felt disrespectful.

'*His name is Steamy Steve from Sausalito . . .*'

But I also wanted to respect Mr Lyons, who, I had almost forgotten, had agreed to be my father-in-law – agreed whole-heartedly. As soon as I'd started to resent the position he'd put me in, I felt the early pangs of grief. How could I not sympathise with him wanting to preserve this trip as a happy memory?

'*Oh Steamy Stevie, Steamy Stevie Steam.*'

We were sitting outside a café when Pippa went inside to use the bathroom, leaving me and Mr Lyons alone together for the first time that day. I looked up from my iced coffee, exhausted from trying to pretend, exhausted from trying to figure it all out, and pleaded with him to tell her.

On our walk back across the bridge, we stopped to watch the sun setting. The water, the hazy clouds and the sky were perfect strips of Rothko blue, purple and orange. Pippa began to hum along to the distant strains of a saxophone, happy and unselfconscious. 'Sittin' on the Dock of the Bay'. She leaned forward, taking in a breath of the breeze that was blowing up from the water, and I glanced across at Chris. His blue eyes, normally so calm and glinting with humour, seemed to reflect a rampaging sea. He caught sight of me, held me in his gaze, then nodded.

True to her word, Diana crashes in within the hour. She looks like she's been spun out, mid cycle, from a tumble dryer – a grey cashmere jumper stretches away from her body, her lank wet hair sticks around her cheeks. On her feet, a pair of navy espadrilles dusty from the garden. Her breath is ragged as she catches a first glimpse of Pippa, all fluids, tubes and pumps. Here lies her flesh and blood. Her baby girl. Broken. And no way to fix her. Her hands are clenched into tight fists, fingernails digging into the palm of her hands.

Steve stands behind her, head bowed, trying to give her space whilst at the same time ready to catch her should her legs give way. He knows there is no preparation for this sight, no shield. Even after eight hours by her bedside, the paleness of Pippa's cheeks set against the black bruising and dried crimson on her forehead still makes his heart flip and his mouth turn dry.

'I was going to stop and pick up some breakfast,' Diana says. 'But then I thought it was better just to get here.'

Steve says nothing. He is no stranger to Diana's coping mechanism, having seen it throughout Chris's illness, then at his death in the hospice, at the funeral, at the wake. Pippa couldn't stand it, perhaps because it was so similar to her own, but at this moment Steve feels only gratitude. Let her speak now about anything. Anything at all.

'There was a shop – a kiosk – at the roundabout that did waffles, but I thought maybe that would make a mess in the ward. Later, perhaps. I think she likes a waffle. From her time in America. Are you hungry, Steven?'

Steve shakes his head.

'I went to bed at a quarter to midnight. Bit late for me, but I got tied in to a new Netflix. *Back to Reality*. Have you seen it?'

He shakes his head again.

'It's about a man who was training for the Barcelona marathon, but they found he had a congenital heart defect in a routine check-up for hay fever or something. Not my usual cup of tea, but it actually was very engaging. Also good to test my Spanish. I've been on that app every day, did I tell you? Anyway, people can achieve remarkable things when they put their minds to it. I think you'd both enjoy it.'

A momentary pause for breath before the second wave, but Steve knows there will be no stopping her now. If she stops talking, even for a second, she could fall apart. On a trip to a country pub, when Chris was doing well in the midst of his treatment, they played a game of giant Jenga in the garden. Diana went first, selected the wrong block, and the tower wobbled, immune to her cries of protest, before crashing down around her feet. The family were unified in tears of laughter.

He senses that she is about to pull out the wrong piece again.

'Let me go and get you a cup of tea, Diana.'

'No!' The word escapes before she has a chance to squash it. A squawk from a trapped bird who has just realised it is caged.

She looks at Steve, haunted and desperately frightened, her complexion a chalky white.

'Oh damn!' she says suddenly, moving towards the door. 'I didn't leave the cash on the table for Maria. I must go and send her a message.'

'No.' Steve is firm. 'You should stay here. Talk to her.'

Diana's eyes widen. The idea of being alone with Pippa terrifies her, but she nods weakly.

'I honestly think she's listening,' Steve says, trying to smile. 'She'll be so glad you're here.'

An expression of naïve hope crosses Diana's face.

'Do you really think so, Steven?'

Her voice is thinner than he has ever heard it, like the volume has been turned down within her soul.

'I do,' he says. 'Tell her you love her. Tell her stories of little Pippa. You know how much she loves hearing about her misspent youth.'

'She does, doesn't she?'

Diana moves closer to her daughter and takes her hand, her eyes glistening. She runs a shaking finger down Pippa's cheek.

'Well hello, my darlingest angel. It's Mummy here.' She sniffs. 'This is a pickle you've got into, isn't it?'

Steve waits by the door, not to eavesdrop, but because a small part of him hopes that Pippa might hear her mother and wake up.

'I came as soon as I could, my darling,' says Diana, sitting down beside her daughter. 'As soon as I heard Steven's message. Such a shock. You should have seen me, half undressed with tea spilled down my nightie. I may have cracked my ceramic mug, the one from the potter – but I'm not blaming you, don't think that. I put on what I could find and then . . . You know what? I should probably tell your auntie Suz. You'll have to show me how. Is it very late there? She berated me last time for disturbing her in the middle of the night . . .'

'I'll be back soon,' Steve says, creeping from the room, but Diana doesn't notice him leave. She has eyes only for her baby.

May 2012

Steve

The organ piped up with the first bars of the Bridal Chorus, cutting off the excited chatter, and the whole congregation craned their necks towards the arched entrance.

'I thought the royal wedding was last year,' I whispered to Diana, but she didn't hear. She was too busy fiddling with her phone, trying to work the camera.

Then Pippa appeared at the end of the aisle, in a sky-blue dress, her hair tied back with a garland of flowers. If she'd sprouted wings and glided towards us in mid-air, no one would have batted an eyelid, she looked so enchanting.

'Such a shame that Chris can't be here,' Diana said.

It *was* a shame, a terrible shame, but I hoped she wouldn't say the same to Pippa. I hoped today might prove a welcome distraction, after an agonising six months spent caring for her father. Chris had been invited, but had made an executive decision that morning, saying he felt a little too 'under the weather' to attend.

Pippa gave me a wink as she passed, then slid onto the bench in front of us.

'You look incredible,' I whispered, leaning towards her, causing the faintest pink blush to spread across the nape of her neck.

'I was just thinking, it's such a shame Chris can't be here.'

'Mum, *don't*,' Pippa hissed.

I reached for her hand over the back of her pew as we all

turned to watch the bride. Tania entered on her father's arm, looking ice cool under her veil, as if the aisle were a fashion show runway. She was towing an embroidered train so long that the miniature bridesmaids holding the other end were somewhere in the churchyard when she began her super-slow procession. I was thinking about doing my royal wedding joke again when I felt Pippa's hand grab hold of mine. It was the sight of Tania's father, who looked so chuffed to be giving her away; he was doing all the smiling and the blushing for her. As Pippa's grip tightened, I knew she was trying not to think of her own father, but unable to think of anything else.

When Chris had finally told Pippa about his diagnosis, our lives short-circuited; everything would now be coloured in Jackson Pollock splashes of emotion and counter-emotion. At first, she was distraught, but quite soon the tears dried up. The same thing happened with Diana, each of them managing to convert their pain into an active and unerring positivity. They formed a crack team, taking the fight to the Big C assault after assault.

Pippa would arrive at the family home full of can-do energy, like a motivational speaker, and spend hours finding obscure French films on DVD, planning long weekends, or securing tables at booked-up restaurants. Diana sourced homeopathic remedies, bought three blenders and emptied the house of booze. (I was too slow to stop her from impetuously pouring a bottle of expensive single malt down the sink, though the vintage wine may have found its way into her handbag.)

They wouldn't countenance hearing anything negative – not from me, not from the doctors, and not from Chris. When asked how he was responding to treatment, they would inform family and friends that he was looking fitter than ever, and I had to go along with it.

In truth, I was shocked at how quickly the first cycle of chemotherapy had weakened him. While it was true that his spirit and good humour were still intact, he looked like a different person. The head of the family, the head of the school, once so strong and exuberant, had thinned and hollowed. When he could no longer greet us at the door, he would welcome us in from an armchair, with Hardy at his feet, the dog's creaking tail straining to wag. However fatigued, he took the effort to dress for our arrival, usually in one of his tweed blazers, which he still succeeded in wearing with panache, though they now hung from his gaunt frame.

'Steven, how do I make them bigger?'

Diana was struggling to capture Tania as she kissed her newly pronounced husband on the altar steps.

'You mean zoom in?' I said. 'You have to pinch the screen.'

She looked at me blankly, then began to peck at her phone's screen with her thumb and forefinger.

'No,' I said. 'Pinch out.'

'What do you mean, *pinch out*?'

'Like this,' I said, trying to demonstrate.

Her focus suddenly shifted across the aisle, where a string quartet had begun playing to accompany the signing of the register. The familiar strains of a piece, Bach maybe, that Chris often put on at home. 'Oh, your father would love this,' she said, before returning her attention to the phone.

I shuffled to the edge of my seat and attempted to hold Pippa by the waist, but she recoiled from me.

'Pip?'

I leaned forward, and could see from her profile that she was staring straight ahead, her eyes glassy.

'Are you okay?'

She nodded vaguely. She didn't like it when I asked if she was okay, a question I was asking her a lot recently. I knew that she wasn't okay, and that anyway 'okay' was a woefully inadequate way to describe how she was doing, but I still felt the need to keep checking in on her and 'Are you okay?' was all I had.

As the music swelled, she let out a whimper, then a gentle tear fell, followed by a steady drizzle that was long overdue.

'You're doing so much for him, Pip,' I said, putting an arm around her trembling shoulders.

She began to speak, but whatever she was going to say was swallowed whole by a sob. She clutched a ragged piece of toilet roll to her mouth. I patted my pockets for a pack of tissues, but I'd brought none – I hadn't thought we'd need any.

'He's so proud of you,' I said. This made her howl. '*I'm* proud of you,' I added. But the nicer I was, the more heart-rending Pippa's cries became. She was now bent double and juddering.

Soon the whole church would be watching. I had to say something to bring her back.

'You know, when we were in San Francisco, I asked him for your hand in marriage.'

She stopped crying immediately, with a few sharp sniffs, then drew herself up and wiped the tears away with the back of her wrist.

'How 'bout that, huh?' I said, relieved. It felt like I'd managed to shut off a burst pipe that had been spraying me with water.

'Yes,' said Pippa.

'Yes?'

'Of course I will!'

She spun round to face me, then buried her face in my chest.

'Yes, yes, yes, yes, *yes*!'

*

On the back row of a vintage Routemaster bus, Pippa curled up beside me like a cat, her head resting in my lap, gurgling with joy. I was speechless, didn't know what to say. What *do* you say when you've accidentally proposed?

Other guests soon joined us, filling up the top deck.

'You two look like you're having fun back here,' smiled an aunt of Tania's as she and her husband settled nearby.

'We're engaged.' Pippa sprang up in her seat. 'Engaged to be man and wife!'

'Congratulations,' said Auntie.

'Well then,' said the uncle, 'when Tania tosses the bouquet, you can put your feet up!'

Pippa howled again, but this time with laughter, as if it was the most insanely funny thing she had ever heard. The uncle chuckled along, pleased as Punch with the success of his banter.

Pippa looked at me so sweetly. 'Say it,' she whispered.

'What?'

'*We're engaged.*'

I didn't know what my face was doing, but I was sure my expression was bleak.

'Aren't we?'

Pippa crashed into the golf club ahead of me, startling the staff who were putting the finishing touches to the tables, stopping only to pick up an empty glass and an unopened bottle of champagne from the bar.

'Pippa, wait!' I called after her.

'That must be the shortest-lived betrothal in history,' she spat, before storming through a side door.

'What's going on, Steven?'

Diana stood behind me, looking forbidding despite her peacock fascinator.

'I think I just proposed to Pippa.'

'You *think* you did?'

'Yes. By accident.'

'I see. Well I hope she turned you down.'

'I guess she did.' I wanted the laminate floor to swallow me up. 'Have I blown it?'

She thought about this for a second, then said: 'Do you know how Chris proposed to me?'

'In Paris.'

'No.'

'I thought—'

'We were engaged when we arrived in Paris, and had the most romantic time there, but he proposed in Dover.' She looked deep into her glass as the bubbles lifted memories to the surface. 'We'd driven down first thing to get the early ferry. Well, *he* drove, I slept the whole way. I was so nervous the night before, you see, tossing and turning, because I knew he was going to ask. Why else would we be going to Paris?'

She picked up a napkin ring and began to turn it over in her hands.

'But when I woke,' she continued, 'he'd parked up at the end of a little lane overlooking the white cliffs. So white, I thought I was in a dream. Chris poured me some tea from a flask and began rummaging in the glove compartment. Then he pulled out a little velvet box. What's he doing? I thought. He's got it all the wrong way round.

'He said: "We *are* going to Paris, but I wanted to say this here. Because it's on this island that we met, and on this island that I want to spend the rest of my life with you. You've brought a *joie de vivre* to my shores, which, like these cliffs, will remain solid, dependable and true, if a little pasty." Then he pushed the driver's seat back so he could kneel in the footwell, which made me laugh so much . . .'

She trailed off, unable to finish. I was rooted to the spot. The tinkle of stainless steel on glass startled her from the memory, and she shook it off like she'd been doused in cold water, and straightened herself back into the pillar of stoicism she'd become for her former husband.

'All I'm saying,' she said brusquely, 'is that the bar has been set high – maybe too high for you after this. Just don't make such a hash of it next time.' She turned to go, leaving me feeling like an absolute lemon, before adding: 'Assuming there will be a next time.'

It took a few days for the dust to settle, during which I orbited Pippa silently, watching her to see when she might be ready. When it felt safe to talk, I showered her with apologies, promising that I would do it right next time.

'Please stop talking about it,' she said, an instruction I duly obeyed.

Then, one Sunday morning, a day on which we would ordinarily visit Chris to help cook a roast dinner (or a puréed smoothie dinner, which we'd all eat with him if he couldn't manage a roast), there was an opening. Chris had a friend staying over, visiting from New Zealand – 'A *girlfriend*,' Diana reminded us several times, her eyebrows arching athletically – so we had the day off.

I took it as a sign, and woke early so I could surprise Pippa with breakfast in bed. Scrambled eggs, smoked salmon, toasted bagel and a cafetière of coffee. You could hardly call it cooking, but it was a dish I'd been able to reproduce to such a standard lately that I no longer required supervision. I stroked the edges of the pan to find the softest, yellowest scram for her plate, then arranged the salmon, which I'd sliced into long strips, to spell out *Marry me?*

'What's this in aid of?' she said as I entered the bedroom.

'Just a bit of light breakfast reading,' I replied.

When she saw the message, she let out a delighted gasp, which pleased me no end.

'So?' I said, but she was too involved in the plate to answer, forking away the salmon, then digging through the eggs as if trying to excavate some buried Roman treasure. It was then that I remembered how she'd described Jen's engagement surprise: her fiancé, Jacob (the hapless dopehead from Glastonbury turned hopeless romantic), had wrapped the ring in foil and hidden it inside her favourite dish of macaroni cheese.

'Did you forget to put it in, Steve?' Pippa said, only gently chastising me. She must have presumed I had left the ring on the kitchen counter.

'There isn't a ring,' I said carefully. 'There will be one, but I don't have it yet.'

'You can't do this without a ring!'

'No?'

'What am I supposed to do? Wear this,' she prodded the bagel, 'on my finger?'

'I didn't think it would matter,' I protested.

'None of it matters, does it?' She covered her face with her hands. 'It's only the rest of our lives.'

'The rest of our lives . . . *together*?' I said, holding up the bagel. I hoped I'd brought forth a smile under her fingers, so I tried again: 'Is that a yes?'

'No!' She jumped out of bed, and the cafetière tipped over, spilling coffee everywhere.

'Where are you going?'

'I'm *disengaging*,' said Pippa. 'When you're really ready to ask me, ask me.'

The weeks that followed were fraught. Chris started another round of chemo, which meant we were up and down –

emotionally and geographically – desperately trying to help raise his spirits and lighten the load on Diana, who had now moved in with him.

We were spending so much time on the train from London to Guildford that we got to know the guard, Mo, quite well. If Pippa was bubbly and energetic, Mo would stop to chat for the length of a stop or two. If she was low or, as was the case after particularly harrowing visits, asleep, he would walk by without even asking to inspect our tickets.

'Your dad's very lucky,' he said on one of the jollier journeys.

'Not *that* lucky,' joked Pippa darkly.

He laughed. 'But seriously, I wish I'd shown the same dedication to my old man when he came down with a spot of the . . . you know.'

'We know.' Pippa reached out to touch his elbow. Unlike me, she had no fear of contact with strangers.

'Keep going as you are,' he said.

When Chris was home, Pippa would drink shakes in the garden with him, or read James Bond novels to him in the living room. When he was at the hospital receiving treatment, she and Diana fought constantly. Even if it had been a relatively easy day they'd find something to argue over. They needed to be unpleasant to each other as much as they needed to be kind to Chris.

Any surplus bad temper was brought home and dumped on me. I couldn't get anything right, and the thing I'd got most wrong, *twice*, followed me round like a spectre. I'd made as many proposals as I'd had driving tests, but was yet to pass.

I was offered a job shooting polo parties, which, selfishly, was a great excuse to get out of the way for a bit. The polo club was near Mum and Dad's, so I stayed over one Saturday night. When Charlotte heard I was there, she appeared within the hour. Then the twins turned up – all three sisters only

too glad to leave the kids behind with their respective fathers –
and soon it became a big family sleepover. I arrived back from
the job on Sunday evening to find Mum pulling out the table
extensions and Dad thrusting two legs of lamb in and out of
the oven like they were the end of a meaty wheelbarrow.

'Stay all week, I don't care,' Pippa said, when I asked how
she felt about me staying another night. I ended up staying
for three.

It didn't take long for them to sniff out exactly what was
going on in my head.

'You treat that girl right, Steven,' said Mum.

'She's out of your league, Stevie,' said Siobhan.

'You should put a ring on it,' said June. 'Before she
scarpers.'

'What does that mean?'

'It means *propose*, Dad. Like Beyoncé sang.'

'Oh yes,' said my dad. 'Beyoncé.'

'I thought you'd end up with Lola,' June went on.

'So did Lola!' Siobhan shrieked.

'How is Lola?' asked Mum.

'No idea.'

'You should put Nana's ring on it!' cried Charlotte.

'That's a wonderful idea,' said Mum, welling up all of a
sudden. 'Frank?'

Dad was already on his feet. He returned moments later
with an old cigar box that must have belonged to Grandpa.
It was a rare sight to see my dad display more than the pri-
mary colours of emotion, but he was unable to control his
quivering cheeks, which danced about his face as he opened
the box, inhaling the memory of his father. He took out a
small bundle of tissue paper and unwrapped it, his cheeks
contorting once again as he showed us Nana's engagement
ring. The silver had discoloured, the three small set diamonds

had faded from years of hibernation, but it was beautiful, it was personal, and it was about to be given a new lease of life.

I had the ring polished, insured, then housed in a new walnut box. I kept it close, carrying it around with me wherever I went. It was beginning to feel as if there would never be a perfect moment to do it, but I'd be prepared if the time came.

One morning I walked into the kitchen to find Pippa standing listening to the radio. As 'It Must Be Love' started playing, she turned to me and smiled. I went over to give her a hug. Then she climbed onto my slippers with bare feet, and for the first time in many months, we started to dance.

'I love you,' she said quietly into the collar of my dressing gown.

'I love you, too.'

'This would be a good time.'

Did she know about the ring?

I stepped away from her and reached into my pocket. As I knelt on the lino and took hold of her left hand, I could tell from her face that she had no idea. I could see that she was about to roll her eyes and say, 'Not this again, Steve.'

And as I lifted the ring towards her, I knew I had finally got it right.

May 2013

Pippa

'You okay in there, Pip? I'm just outside if you need me.'

His voice sounds muffled through the rusty tin wall.

'Yep.'

Ten days ago I was a princess dressed in vintage white lace, coiffed and buffed to perfection, waxed, polished and moisturised like never before.

Ten days ago I was revered and loved by all I surveyed.

Ten days ago I was being served soft salmon blinis and watching the bubbles dance gleefully through my pink champagne.

Today I am a bra-less, sunburnt, peely-nosed tourist peasant, squatting inelegantly over a muddy hole in the ground, my yellow Havaianas positioned either side on the near-fossilised imprints where thousands of flip-flops have stood before me, trying desperately to avoid urinating on my own feet. The shack door is held shut with a frayed piece of fluorescent fishing twine, which looks about as much use as a sauna in the desert. My skin feels salty with sweat, my hair is begging for a wash and I can still feel the low murmur of last night's street noodles, deliberating whether to come up or go down.

But on the plus side, my pubes are finally growing back. Tania's inspired idea that I surprise Steve with a full (and I mean FULL) Brazilian on our wedding night (*I swear, Pip. Drives them wild. You'll see. Did it for Danny. He couldn't get enough of me, babe!*) backfired tremendously when on the fourteen-hour plane journey over, I was rendered so obscenely itchy by several days of stubble growth that I could barely sit still. Steve found it hilarious, tears streaming down his cheeks, as I writhed and wriggled in my seat, trying to scratch the offending area without attracting attention.

Beneath me, the sprawling tribe of red ants tunnelling through the dried clay are disgruntled by this unscheduled downpour. They rush this way and that, like a pack of hyper-active children scattering from the school gates. My toilet is encircled by ad hoc pieces of corrugated metal that seem to slot together like rusty stickle bricks. The stench of sewers is stagnant in the air, making my eyes water. I can feel the gravelly sand creaking underfoot. Determined not to lose my balance, I engage all of my (embarrassingly minimal) core strength in order to remain vertical. Lactic acid is burning in my thighs. I wobble, and put out a hand against the wall to keep me upright.

Jesus Christ!

I yelp in pain. The metal has heated up like a griddle pan. I don't know what I expected given the fact that I am essentially squatting inside a baked bean can in the midday sun.

'You sure you're all right? You've been a while?'

'Tickety-boo.'

I examine my scalded fingertips, aware that the stinging sensation is heightening. For some reason the throbbing feels profound. A baptism of fire. The blisters on my thumb and forefinger are already beginning to swell like bubble wrap. It's not pretty. In fact the sight has temporarily halted my wee in its flow, so I flip my hand over. Ah that's better. My immaculately manicured shellac nails in Vintage Dusk. Shiny, sleek and not a chip in sight. My perfect ten-day-old manicure from my perfect ten-day-old marriage.

Marriage!

The word sends a tingle through the base of my spine, and for a moment I fear I may lose my footing.

I'm married.

I. Am. Married!

Ten days ago I became someone's wife. Pippa Lyons has cast off the frivolity of her youth. New Pippa is going to drink less, work harder, exercise more, spend less, praise more, argue less, be more patient, watch fewer box sets, read *proper* books, write more, BE more.

Pippa *Gallagher* is going to be everything Pippa *Lyons* dreamed of being. And more.

Okay, it reads like every New Year's resolution list I ever made, but this time it *will* be different! After all, it's not every day you make a vow of eternity to one person.

When I told Steve my wifely aspirations on the plane, he smiled slightly wistfully and kissed my nose.

'Maybe don't go changing *too* much. I kind of like Pippa Lyons as she is.'

'Yeah, but she'll be the same! The same but better! D'you see. Like an upgraded mobile.'

He laughed. 'But I'm happy with my current model. I've only just figured out how to make the most of my add-ons. I don't want an upgrade any time soon.'

I rolled my eyes, pretending to be frustrated, but secretly his response delighted me. I nudged his arm with my head until he put it around me and I nestled into his chest.

I want to climb inside him sometimes.

Yuck. What have we become? That gross couple who only need each other to feel complete. That saccharine couple who leave love notes for one another around the house. That besotted couple who make cards for their seven-day wedding anniversary because *One week is a big one, baby.*

That soppy, sappy, smoochie, coochie, loved-up couple who stare in awe at their wedding rings when no one is watching, reeling at just how lucky they got.

'And will you please all be upstanding for the bride and groom!'

The thunderous applause resonated from behind the wooden door.

Steve turned to me, offering his hand.

'You ready, Mrs G?'

The noise level surged as the stamping of feet and the chinking of glasses became more insistent.

'Ready, Mr G.'

As we glided in, fingers entwined, I thought my face might break I was smiling so much. All those people exuding love. Snapshots from the photo album of our lives.

And then time became elastic. The night spun in a merry-go-round of food, laughter, tears, embraces and speeches. Oh, the speeches. The spoken words that will warm me like a blanket of love for the rest of my life.

Dad telling tales of my childhood, remembering every detail like it was yesterday. His illness evident to the world now – no way of hiding those stick thin legs, those veiny hands, those swollen ankles, those cracked lips – but, as ever, standing with the posture of a true gentleman. Proud and gallant.

Oscar, nervous for the first time ever, regaling us with bromance stories of how he and Steve fell in love. He had the room in the palm of his shaking hand.

And then came Steve.

Steve who hates public speaking.

Steve who would rather eat coal than be the centre of attention.

Steve who reduced a hundred and fifty people, to snotty, emotional wrecks.

You could have heard a pin drop as he sailed through his speech. Seamless. His hazel eyes fixed on me as he spoke. A speech that, as his mum told me afterwards, he was born to make.

And then the room erupting like a football stadium when he finally said the two words everyone was waiting for: *My wife.*

As I watched him that night, I knew without a shadow of doubt that right now, in the championships of love, we would win, hands down.

Because we were invincible.

It was us against the world.

And nobody, but nobody, would *ever* love like we did.

Then came the honeymoon.

Well this, like any great adventure, began with great adversity . . .

Arriving at Phnom Penh airport, wending our jet-lagged arses through a passport queue as long as Primark's during Boxing Day sale, tracking down the correct rickety bus to take us into the hills, realising we were in fact on the *wrong* rickety bus to take us into the hills, hitching a lift in the opposite direction with three red-eyed surf bums in a fluorescent green Mini who were clearly as high as Kilimanjaro, being forced to evacuate said Mini when it veered straight into a tree during a fit of marijuana-induced hysteria, and finally staggering under the crushing weight of our brand-new, wildly overloaded backpacks along dusty pavementless streets with not a signpost in sight until at last, with fraying tempers and aching limbs, we finally stumbled upon our lodgings.

Finally. Clean sheets, a shower, a cup of tea.

We announced ourselves at reception. The concierge was a thin, ferocious whippet of a creature, her dark shiny hair cropped aggressively in a chin-length bob, her flawlessly smooth skin rendering her ageless. She could have been anything from twenty-five to eighty. It was disconcerting.

'Hi. We're here to check in.'

'Name. Address. Date of your births.'

'It's Steven Gallagher and Pi—'

Before Steve could finish, the words had erupted from my mouth, bubbles spewing from a ring pull.

'Mr and Mrs Gallagher.'

He looked at me, his cheeks flushing. We twinkled at each other.

A rush of adrenaline. What a kick! *We're bloody married!*

'Yeah. She's right. Sorry. We're Mr and Mrs Gallagher.'

And with those words, the last few gruelling hours dissipated in a puff of smoke.

'We've booked till Monday night.'

'Passports, please.'

We handed over our passports. She gave them a cursory glance before placing them at the far end of her desk. Then she flicked slowly through an enormous notebook, running a bony finger over each of the names. God. It was torturous. Just let us in, gatekeeper! My eyes were stinging and my stomach felt as if it was eating itself. But more than that, I felt twitchy with anticipation, waiting for our honeymoon to begin – like someone was holding onto the back of my bicycle when I had a wonderful, empty, freewheeling downhill ride in front of me.

Finally she stopped, finger hovering in mid-air, and stood stock still like a mannequin. The silence was deafening.

'Is, er, everything okay? I've got the card I booked it on. I can show you—'

'No, sir.'

Her dark eyes snapped up, like black pools of disgust, her skin appearing even more stretched against her taut blank-canvas face.

'No, Mr Galangear, everything is most *not* okay.'

She whipped round to the young boy sitting on a small stool at the far side of the office. He couldn't be more than fourteen, and with his perfect skin and diminutive stature, it was clear he was her son. She jerked her head ferociously towards the entrance, and he got up, shuffled silently to the door and locked it.

She whipped back to us.

'You have made broken law.'

'What?'

'You are the criminals.'

'What are you talking about? We have a reservation! A booking! Unlock the door immediately.'

But the woman simply shook her head, unruffled.

'You are guilty. You make a crime.'

'That's ridiculous! We've paid. Here! I have the email from Mr Luang.' Steve pulled a printout from his back pocket. 'Seven nights, half-board. You can ask Airbnb. They—'

She suddenly exploded, spitting words like lashings of molten lava.

'Airbb offers are not LEGAL here! I tell you!' Her voice had taken on a strangled tone, like someone was sitting on her voice box. 'No!! He will not make sublet! The police will make charge! No sublet in my block!'

She was drawn up to her full height now, body rigid with rage. She suddenly reminded me of the woman in *The Incredibles* with the austere bob. Edna Mode. I made a mental note to tell Steve later.

But Steve was clearly not thinking of Edna. Nor was he

seeing the funny side. The ragged lightning vein across his left temple, the vein that only appeared in moments of extreme stress, had jutted out, and his jaw was clenched as if he was sucking a sour sweet.

Sensing imminent disaster, I tried a different tack.

'Listen . . .' I smiled sweetly, woman to woman. Charm offensive. 'I *totally* understand your predicament, but there's clearly been a misunderstanding. We can sort this out without the police. We're on our honeymoon. If you let us stay tonight, we will come down and discuss it in the morning. We're very tired, you see. We really need to sleep. I'm sure it can all be resolved.'

She stared at me, steely-eyed. This lady was not for turning.

'No, Mrs Galangear. You help me to make arrest of Mr Luang, you can leave with bags. If you not help, you can be for the arrest and jail. And I keep *these*.'

She snatched up our passports and, quick as a flash, slung them into a small metal safe next to her. Before we had a chance to react, the dial was turned and the safe was locked.

A moment of stunned silence . . . then all hell broke loose.

Steve began yelling, insisting he would call his lawyer.

The young boy sank even lower on his stool, willing the ground to swallow him up.

The woman picked up her phone and simply screamed over and over, 'Police! Police! Police!'

And I, overcome with exhaustion, hunger and disappointment, began howling into my T-shirt. I know, I thought I was made of sterner stuff too.

Looking back, I reckon Steve was under the impression that it was his manly assertiveness that resolved the stand-off, but I know better. I saw her face when I got going. I heard the windows being thrown open around the complex. I saw the faces of concerned tenants as they peered out.

What was that infernal racket? Was someone being attacked in reception?

Mrs Incredible looked in turn stunned, then enraged, then petrified as I simply wailed, louder and louder, thumping my palm up and down on her desk.

'No! It's not fair! This is our honeymoon! Don't you understand! Our honeymoon! We've planned it for months! You're spoiling everything!!'

My voice kept rising and rising.

'How can you be so cruel! We're good people! We've done nothing wrong! NOTHING!'

The witch clearly had no comprehension of just how vocal a Brit in distress can be. To say nothing of a Brit with a keen sense of injustice and an acting diploma under her belt. Even Steve looked stunned as my voice rose like an opera singer's, notes of anguish reverberating around her cramped office.

'Can't you see? You are *ruining* our lives!'

Bit dramatic, granted, but I could see something was shifting in her. As I took a final gulp of air, threatening to shift this outburst up a gear to its ultimate decibels, I saw her gesture to her son to unlock the door. He didn't need to be asked twice.

With pursed lips and puce face, she began slinging first our bags, then us and finally our passports out of her office, accompanied by a torrent of Cambodian expletives that crashed like a wave against our backs as she slammed the door behind us.

And that was how, tired, humiliated, starving and jet-lagged, we ended up checking into the most expensive, decadent, luxurious, romantic hotel either of us had ever experienced.

Because after all, that's what credit cards are for, right?

Seven days of unparalleled pampering that would render

real life impossible to return to. Sunglasses polished, fresh fruit drinks delivered poolside in case madam was thirsty, baths strewn with essential oils and rose petals, towels twisted into elaborate origami swans and dragons, guided trips to the most spectacular food markets we had ever seen. Seven nights of feeding each other strawberries dipped in Swiss chocolate as we lay tangled in the sheets after the sweatiest, craziest, wildest sex of our lives.

And it was there, at the 'Fuck-It' Hotel, that my period, clockwork for fifteen years, simply thought, *Fuck it*.

There. That should do it. I attempt to straighten up, my head hitting the roof of the metal shack, my joints creaking like a stiff old woman after an aerobics class.

Mission accomplished.

Granted, I've got more wee on my hand than on the stick, but hey, given that I have been balancing precariously in a roadside shack that looks as if the merest breath of wind would bring it down, I'm pretty impressed with myself. Besides, urine can be used as a moisturiser, right? I'm sure I read that in *Grazia*. More to the point, I know Steve will be at the ready with his bumper bottle of hand sanitiser. Steve's an avid sanitiser at the best of times – after touching bus rails, free newspapers, gym equipment, copper coins, even sometimes after shaking hands (though I've finally trained him to do this in private) – so the slack day-to-day hygiene of Cambodia has really challenged him.

I glance down at the stick in my hand. It seems to be doing something. The urine is visibly seeping up the central strip. It's strangely satisfying. I recap the sample end as the instructions decreed and slip it into my pocket. Then I unhook the entirely futile string lock and bump the metal door open with my hip (not gonna make that rookie error again), and as it swings shut behind me, I feel like a victorious cowboy exiting a saloon.

'All done?'

I am momentarily blinded by the glare of the midday sun. I blink several times, and finally Steve's concerned face emerges from the glaring light spots in front of me.

'How did you get on? Success?'

I pull the stick out of my pocket and hold it up with a flourish.

'Ta-da. I'm the aqua-jet ninja.' No idea where that came from.

'Okay. Good. I mean, that's good. Well done.'

I nod my head.

'Maybe don't wave it around, though. I mean, I don't know, but maybe . . .'

He peters off, and for the first time since our honeymoon began, neither of us know what to say.

He reaches for my hand. I jerk it away sharply.

'Erm. I wouldn't. Bit of collateral damage. You got any sanitiser?'

He grins. 'Is the Pope Argentinian?'

'Er, no?'

'Actually he is. The new one.'

'Oh.'

'Never mind. Bad joke.'

I smile. Finally, an element of normality in this oh-so-abnormal chain of events.

He rummages in his shoulder bag and pulls out the fat bottle. He flips off the cap and squeezes a pea-sized amount into my palm, and I rub my hands together, relishing the feeling of the stinging cleanliness between my interlocked fingers.

'Better?'

'Better.'

He reaches for my hand once more. This time I give it to him.

'Shall we?'

We walk a little distance along the sun-baked roadside, to where we abandoned our backpacks. The warm air is dangling between noon and dusk, as the Cambodian sun shivers and crackles off everything it touches. We sit side by side, using the backpacks as bean bags.

Nothing to do now but wait.

One little minute that might change our lives forever.

I was outside the entrance, gripping my father's frail arm as if it were a lifebuoy on the open sea. Through the glass panels I could see friends and family, laughing and embracing as they took their seats. The sunflowers I had collected that morning from the market lent the room a warm golden glow, just as I had imagined. Little pockets of canary-yellow happiness.

Meanwhile, I stood here waiting, a girl balancing on a precipice, suspended on a dangling cord between past and future. And suddenly, it all spilled out.

'Dad. What if I'm not enough? What if he gets bored of me? What if I get bored of him?'

'Pippa—'

'What if he dies? What if he's run over? What if I'm—'

'Pippa.'

His voice, that velvet voice that had been the balm to countless 'Pippa panics' since I first found words, was speaking to me now. A voice that had changed in texture, become more breathless, but was familiar nonetheless.

'Darling, look at me.'

I looked into his face. His painfully thin face that the

rampaging cancer was doing its damnedest to destroy. But it couldn't take his eyes. Those eyes that were twinkling at me now. Seeing me. Loving me.

'The past is a foreign land, Pippa. The future an unknown quantity. All we have is now. This.'

He took my hands in his and kissed them.

I nodded slowly, aware of my thighs shaking under my sheer tights.

'He loves you.'

I nodded again, more emphatically this time.

'And Mum and I love you. More than anything in the world.'

I looked up at him, the veins twitching beneath his watery blue eyes. His once thick hair now sprouted in tiny clumps, like patches of newly sown grass, the brutal chemo having claimed most of it.

'My strong, difficult, brilliant daughter. Be brave. I'm so, so proud of you.' His voice caught, like a scooter on gravel.

'Don't make me smudge my make-up, Dad.'

'Don't make me smudge *mine*.'

I smiled. It was working. That magic touch. I could feel myself growing under his gaze. Stronger. Straighter. Like the stalks of the sunflowers in my hands.

'Be present. One foot in front of the other. That's all we can do. Look. He's waiting for you.'

I inhaled deeply and blew out to the count of eight as Mum had told me to.

As I did so, the music started. The notes we had selected to accompany the beginning of our new life together. It soared up to the rafters, swelling through my veins.

'You ready, my darling?'

I wiped away a tear with my fingertip, adjusted my bouquet and nodded once more.

'I'm ready.'

The usher opened the door. And holding tightly to my father's arm, I leapt into the unknown.

'I reckon that's over a minute, Pip.'

I check my watch. He's right.

'Do you want to look, or shall I?'

I think about it, my stomach knotted.

'Let's look together.'

'On the count of three?'

I pull the stick from my pocket, keeping it closed in my fist. Our eyes are fixed on each other. He is pale beneath his tan.

Okay. One, two . . .

Three.

We both look down as I flick the stick over.

And there, without a hint of indecision, are two bold blue lines.

October 2013

Pippa

A ludicrously attractive waitress meets us on the seafront with a glass of champagne. The waves are crashing onto the shale beach, and the sky, though school-skirt grey, frames a determined sun reflecting off the ocean.

There is something chapel-like about the high vaulted dining room. Other-worldly. I feel it as soon as we enter, with the sun's frosty rays flickering onto the highly polished wooden floorboards and bouncing off the posh-looking cutlery. Surely it's obvious we're interlopers? Two overdressed muppets who look as though they have won their visit on the back of a cornflakes packet, out of place amongst the perilously cool, the supremely wealthy and the those in the know.

As we approach our table, we pass a couple about our own age. The girl is quizzing the waiter anxiously. 'So just to check, does the dressing have blue cheese in it? If so, I'll just have oil. And I mentioned I can't have oysters, and I need my steak really well done. No blood. Sorry to be a pain, it's just . . .' She pats her tummy shyly. Her husband smiles, looking as though he might explode with pride. I feel my womb physically contract, reminding me that three months ago, it would have been me checking every ingredient. The room starts to feel unbearably hot. I feel Steve's hand in the small of my back, guiding me gently forward, moving me away from the danger zone. I swallow hard. Don't think. Just keep walking.

Lunch at the Oyster Pearl is number nine on Dad's

so-called 'Kicking the Bucket List'. People sell their eyes, souls and aunties to bag a table here. And even then, you may be waiting three years for the privilege. With bombastic, orgiastic, ecclesiastic reviews from even the thorniest of culinary critics, and the floor-to-ceiling windows making guests feel they are actually dining *in* the North Sea, it is easy to understand why. After several begging letters, relentless emails, endless pushy phone calls and a series of shamelessly desperate shout-outs on Facebook, I finally succeeded in securing a coveted table for the three of us.

And here we are. Well, two out of three anyway.

'Are you warm enough, sir, or would you like to keep your coat on?'

It's our stunning waitress back again. Steve is wearing his best (only) smart shirt and is therefore very keen to get it out on display as soon as possible. As we hand over our jackets, she tells us what an absolute honour it is to welcome us to the restaurant. Would we like an extra cushion for our chairs? Are we affected at all by the window draught? Will we be taking still, sparkling or naturally carbonated water with our meal? (Naturally carbonated? A sudden childish image of the chef crouching over a water vat and farting into it.) But seriously. No wonder this place has a waiting list.

Oh Dad, you should be here. Why did you have to pick this morning to be so very sick? Why couldn't you have simply soldiered on as you always do? Dad, like me, never admits defeat. It was Mum who finally put the kibosh on his coming with us. She watched as he attempted to run a comb through what was left of his blonde hair to make him presentable for his 'lunch date'. But it was when she caught him struggling to tie his polished shoes whilst simultaneously vomiting quietly into a bucket that she finally vetoed this outing. A lump rises in my throat as I think of his words as we said goodbye on the doorstep.

'Go tick number nine off for me, Squeak. You and Steve are my team reps. Send updates and I'll be bushy-tailed for the next one.'

I hugged him to me – gently, because he was so painfully thin – and for just a second, I prayed for time to stop. I felt safe there, like I could protect him and he could protect me. In that moment, he was my rock and I was his. Interchangeable. The child and the protector.

I stood on tiptoe and whispered in his ear, 'Don't you dare go doing anything drastic while we're out. Okay?'

He looked at me and laughed. 'I wouldn't dare.'

But I didn't return his smile. Instead I squeezed that hand I knew so well. 'Promise me, Dad.'

He raised three fingers and made the Boy Scouts salute. 'Cubs' honour.'

Steve takes some bread from the basket and dunks it into the 'truffle whipped and cracked local sea salt butter'. I watch as he takes a bite, his eyes widening as he does so. 'Bloody hell, Pip. That's EPIC. Here' – he holds out a chunk – 'roll it around in your fingers! It's so soft!' As always when it comes to gastronomic delights, his enthusiasm is infectious, and before I know it, we are both making snowballs out of dough balls and rolling them in the best (only) whipped butter I've ever tasted.

Steve raises his glass. 'To Chris Lyons. You make the best daughters. And the best bucket lists. We love you and wish you were here.'

I lift mine – 'To Dad' – and as our glasses clink together, a rogue tear makes an unscheduled break for the border. Damn it. Don't let me cry. Not here. Not in front of all these unfeasibly cool Oyster Pearl-ites. No, no, no. I keep my eyes wide open and refuse to blink in an attempt to dissipate the gathering liquid. It is only a partial success. Steve leans across the table and brushes his thumb over my wet cheekbone.

'Why don't we text him?' he says gently. 'Tell him all about this squishy-squashy bread.'

I smile. He's right. He's always right. I grab my phone from my bag and begin composing a text.

Pops Daddykins! We've made it. Wow. It's mental here. 'Lunch by the sea, in the sea', as it says on the tin. Here is the first photo of many. The squish-squash bread. It's like clouds with crusts. I'm bringing some home in my handbag. Heaven. More pix to come!

I leave my phone out on the table beside me, and for once Steve doesn't tell me to put it away. He knows I won't relax until I see that the message has been received and that Dad is typing back to me. As my eyes remain fixed on the screen, I play with my necklace distractedly, twiddling the two silver sea lion charms between thumb and forefinger. There is something strangely calming about its cold smoothness between my fingertips. I close my eyes and try and steady my breathing. Focus on the memory.

Our final morning in San Francisco. Dad fastened the clasp around my neck over a pancake breakfast, the pair of charms landing with a gentle thud on my collarbone.

'There you go, Squeak. Now you get to see your sea lions every day.'

It was the best souvenir he could have given me. A tangible memory of that carefree, laughter-filled escape that feels now as if it belonged in another lifetime. We were the Three Stooges. The Three Amigos. The Triumvirate – *I'm the father, Steve's the son and Pip, that makes you the holy goat*. We ate, drank, swam and rode trams around that pulsing city, *grabbing that Golden Gate by its golden gonads*, as Dad put it. But best of all, I saw the sea lions. Real-life, right-before-my-eyes sea lions.

We followed the barks, growls and grunts to the legendary Pier 39, and on turning the corner were met by one of the most ecstatic sights imaginable. Dozens of beautiful doe-eyed pups, rolling and lolling on the slippery stones. Piles of playful, thwacking, tumbling sea lions spread across the wooden pallets and looking up at me as though they had been expecting me. Some were coupled up, stroking their mates' beards affectionately. Others dreamily tickled their own bellies. The young ones appeared to be giggling as they dived and wrestled each other like toddlers heading into nursery, while the larger ones (I ordained them the grandparents of the pack) just blinked into the sunlight, content, tummies stretched to bursting point from their excess of indulgent fishy dinners. It took my breath away, like one of those epiphanies people speak of. There they all were, right in front of my eyes. I was overcome. Steve tells me I hopped from foot to foot like a maniac, clapping my hands and whooping like a hyena. He *claims* I then promptly burst into tears. But I'm sure I was a lot cooler than that . . .

'Would you guys like a photo together?' She's back, our super-hot waitress, flashing her million-dollar smile.

We look at each other. Steve is not one for couply photos – safe to say he loathes them – but for Dad . . .

'Sure, why not.'

He passes her his phone and gets up from his chair to come over to my side of the table.

A gasp from our waitress. 'No no! *You* must stay seated, sir.'

Steve looks slightly startled but does as he's told. She turns to me and gestures, and I move round to his side instead, draping my arms around his shoulders. Pressing my mouth against his ear, I whisper, 'Silly me, what was I thinking! One must *never* ask a man to move from his seat!'

Steve snorts with laughter and attempts to turn it into a cough.

The waitress looks up, eyes wide with alarm.

'Are you all right, sir? Can I get you anything? Water?'

'No, I'm fine. Sorry. Bit of bread got stuck.'

She looks relieved and begins lining up the shot.

'Hmm. Not quite right. Hang on . . .'

She pulls out a neighbouring chair, clambers up and elongates herself to her maximum height to capture our best angle. What the . . .

I wait for Steve to spontaneously combust. This level of attention is his idea of walking into hell's burning inferno. But no one seems to notice that we have a towering waitress standing on a chair beside us. She extends her arms above her and snaps several pictures. Finally she climbs down to review them.

'Fabulous. There are lots here. I have to say, you look terrific, sir. Glowing. This light really brings out your eyes. Here.'

Steve brushes off the compliment nonchalantly, but I can tell that he's pumped. She leans in to show him the images and scrolls through the entire collection. Truth is, I can't even see his eyes in half the photos, as her shadow is covering his whole face. But I say nothing. I wait for her to mention my radiant skin or glossy hair or attractive dimples, but she simply passes Steve back his phone, her hand lingering on his as she does so. She lowers her voice and leans in a little more.

'A photo is such a joy, isn't it? Something to cherish. *Always.*'

Wait. Was that a quiver in her voice? And with a meaningful pat of his hand, she's gone.

We both watch in silence as she glides away through the other diners.

'Well. Someone's got an admirer.'

Steve fumbles for his handkerchief and blows his nose uncomfortably – an engrained habit that I've learned is exacerbated by any exposure to physical scrutiny. He proceeds to snatch up the chic newspaper-style menu from under his plate and point out random words and phrases.

'Pan-fried scallops! Sea trout with pickled fennel. Interesting.

265

Ooh! Russet apple soufflé! Bring it on. That bread has made me so hungry.'

Bread does that to Steve. Bread, nuts, crisps, beer – anything that for most normal people would fill a hole and tide them over till dinner. Instead, he gets more hungry, as though an invisible compartment has opened up in his belly as his digestive juices are set to work. It makes me laugh. I love his appetite. I will always love his appetite.

I flick through the waitress's selection of snaps and select the least dreadful to send Dad. As I do so, I check to see if he has replied to my first message, but nothing. A momentary compression in my stomach, like air being forced into a balloon, as I see him as he looked on the front steps this morning – a listless black and white sketch of his former vibrantly painted self. But despite being thin, fragile and exhausted, he was still smiling with face-breaking love as he waved us off.

Stop panicking, I tell myself. He's fine. He gave you his word. Nothing drastic over lunch, right? He's not going anywhere. Dad *always* keeps his promises.

I type quickly.

Miss you, Dad. Steve has pulled. He may come home with a new girlfriend. Scallops next. Will bring doggy bag. Love the (temporarily) Two Amigos.

I press send. The envelope sign flashes at the top of the screen as it attempts to force my message across the tech wilderness and drop it safely into Dad's phone.

But the message isn't going anywhere. It just keeps sending, on and on and on – always sending but never delivered. I suddenly think of Narnia, where it's always winter but never Christmas. Ah, that must be why he hasn't replied – there's obviously bad reception in the restaurant. I check my outbox and there it is, my last message, still dangling somewhere along the A25 between Whitstable and Surrey. I wave my phone around trying to find an invisible pocket of Wi-Fi, but to no avail.

I look back at my phone.

Message pending.

A tightening around my heart, like cold bony fingers clutching at its chambers; the dull thump of rising panic. I need to send this. Must maintain contact. If I loosen the belt between us, even a notch, anything could happen. Anything could—

No. Breathe.

Not gonna happen. He promised. Remember?

Maybe the reception is better out front.

'Messages aren't going through. Gonna nip outside and see if the car park's any better. Won't be long. Sorry.'

Steve smiles.

'Don't be silly. Take your time.'

As I get up to go, Steve's new girlfriend arrives at our table, a tiny egg smoking on an oversized platter.

'A little amuse-bouche. Hay-smoked quail's egg with dill aioli. Compliments of the chef.'

She places it down in front of Steve.

I mean, there's attentive and then there's stalking.

'And how are things?'

So close to saying, 'Hmm, pretty much identical to how they were when you asked us three minutes ago,' but I bite my tongue.

Her attention is focused solely on Steve. Come on, I think. At least pretend to acknowledge me.

'The manager wondered if you would like to have a kitchen tour with head chef Ricky Warner before your first course comes out. We don't usually invite the public in during service, but we'd be honoured if you wanted to join us, Mr Lyons.'

Erm. Hello?

'It's a very special, once-in-a-lifetime experience.'

Steve throws a look at me. I throw a look at the waitress. She throws a look at Steve.

This could go on for some time. Like some kind of weird focus-shifting drama school game.

I finally break the chain.

'I actually just need to send an urgent message. Where would I get the best reception?'

'The reception is a lot better in the kitchen. So you could kill two birds with one stone!'

She suddenly looks a little uncomfortable.

'As it were. So – would you like to follow me?'

She smiles and heads back towards the kitchen, stopping near the swing doors and looking at us expectantly. You could hear a pin drop. I glance around the room. The other diners are staring shamelessly, wide-eyed. It's clear we are the entertainment. Keen to avoid further exposure, we follow her swiftly across the dining room, through the saloon-style doors and into the buzzing kitchen.

Our waitress announces us with a slightly self-conscious cough.

'They're here, Ricky.'

A strange hush descends. We huddle behind her, like children on a school trip, as a petite man in a black beanie and round tortoiseshell glasses looks up from a towering soufflé. There is a manic glint in his dark eyes, as if he has just heard the best joke imaginable.

'Aha! My guests *d'honneur*! Come in, come in!'

He pulls off his apron and bounds towards us, a puppy on its first walk.

'Welcome to my kitchen! The best place on God's tiny earth.'

As he talks, his expressive hands dance through the air, cutting it into pieces with a whoosh.

'Now you have seen my secrets, I shall have to kill you!' He giggles wildly. The waitress's eyes widen in horror as she glances from Steve to the floor. Why does she look so mortified?

Finally he offers Steve his hand and his expression changes to a sombre one.

'I'm so very glad you felt you could join us, sir.'

They stand shaking hands for a long, long time.

'It is an honour to know we can be of service.'

Steve looks down at his hand, clearly unsure how to terminate this greeting without offending.

'That my food can bring you joy during this difficult time. Well, it is why we do what we do.'

I look at Ricky and then back at Steve.

'We all admire you. Such fight. Such – how do you say – *pluck*.'

The chefs all stop chopping and observe Steve, pained expressions of respect and sympathy on their faces.

Oh, wait.

I look at the waitress as she gestures to a sous chef to fetch a chair in case Steve needs to sit down. And suddenly it all makes sense.

Horrible, ludicrous, absurd, hilarious sense.

They think *Steve* has cancer! They think *Steve* is the guest of honour.

I need to say something. I need to put them straight.

But then that laughter, that terrible, infamous, blissful laughter that descends like fog in the most inopportune of places, is upon me. A snort, turning into a chuckle, turning into a giggle, turning into a steamroller of hysteria that brings tears streaming down my cheeks.

It's not that it's funny. Indeed, this whole earth-shattering situation is the most un-funny thing that has ever happened to me. But for some reason, in this moment, as a bemused Steve stands awkwardly shaking hands with a celebrity chef, being stroked and mollycoddled and pitied, I feel like my cheeks will break. Our waitress is watching me in disdain. What kind of girlfriend laughs at a time like this? I try and speak, but the rolling hysteria renders me mute.

Okay. Deep breaths. In and out. I need to get it together. I look like a lunatic. In and out. In and out. Steve is looking at me. Everyone is looking at me.

'Ms Lyons?'

A voice from behind me. I whip around, and it's the maître d'. What's she doing in the kitchen? She looks tense.

'I'm sorry to disturb you, but we have a phone call for you at reception. I believe it's your mother. She sounds—'

But I can no longer hear her as I stagger away, slamming through the swing doors with Steve behind me, skidding through the packed dining room, knocking into chairs, oblivious to the tuts of the clientele as I hurl myself against the reception desk.

If I get to that phone quickly enough, maybe I will circumvent time. Maybe I can stop the call happening at all. Maybe . . .

I am back in the car. I have no idea how I got here, but I have.

I'm staring straight ahead, willing the journey to be over and yet to never end. My reflection in the window. My eyes. Or are they his eyes?

Please, Dad. Please. I need you. This can't happen. This can't be happening. You promised. You never break your word. Stay with me. Stay with me, Dad. Stay . . .

Steve reaches over and places his hand over mine. His eyes

may be fixed on the road in front of him, but his heart is fixed on the passenger sitting next to him.

'We're gonna get there, darling. We're only an hour away. He'll wait for you, I promise. Your dad is a fighter.'

Wait. Get there. Fighter.

I can see Steve's words floating in front of my face. Not speech bubbles, but physical, tangible entities. Drifting and popping. The odd one loiters beside my ear. I can see it out of the corner of my eye. Refusing to move. Willing itself heard. But none of them actually mean anything. They are abstract. Random. Disconnected.

I think Steve is still talking.

It sounds like he is underwater. Is he underwater?

Or am I?

The road markings dissolve beneath us.

Faster and faster. We are getting somewhere. Somewhere I cannot bear to be and yet never want to leave.

Hurtling towards somewhere. Into something. Something that could leave me with nothing.

A future without a past. A tree that will never again make a sound when it falls.

No. No. No, Dad. No.

Stay with me.

I'm dizzy. My brain feels hot. I reach under the seat. A plastic bag. And I am sicker than I've ever been before.

On and on and on until there is nothing left.

And yet still I retch.

My body making space for the pain that will consume every inch of me.

With each minute, we are getting closer.

I close my eyes against the darkness and prepare to leap into the abyss.

2 March 2019

09:39

Steve stands at the end of a bright passageway connecting the ICU to the rest of the hospital. It looks out onto a paved garden, damp green with moss, with neglected borders from which shoots of hardy daffodils have begun to appear through the mulch. He has discovered that if he waves his arm, the motion causes the sliding doors to open, bringing in fresher, less sterile air that doesn't smell of disinfectant.

He rests his forehead against the window, the glass warmed by a shaft of morning sunlight, and breathes deeply. He is unable to move closer to the source of the breeze, still tethered to his wife by an umbilical cord that's stretching through the corridors, but the cord has slackened since Diana arrived. It feels good to know that Pippa has another protector with her now. For the first time since hearing the news, he's allowed someone else to do the carrying.

As the doors he entered through eight hours ago slide open again, the draught carries with it fresh voices. He moves closer to them, through the gap and into a wide waiting area.

'Mum, tell him to stop pinching me!'

'Why are you lying? I didn't touch you.'

He stops abruptly and shakes his head. Surely he is imagining things?

'Mum, tell him!'

'Sammy, leave your sister alone. I won't tell you again.'

No mistaking that voice. He pushes open the door.

'Uncle Stevie!'

And as if by magic, there they all are. His life. His supporters. His whole world crammed into one tiny room. Charlotte, Siobhan, June, the kids, Mickey, Pat, Tania, Gus. He half expects someone to shout 'Surprise!' and detonate a party popper in his face.

Ruby Mae hurtles towards him, wrapping her arms around his waist like a chimpanzee. Not to be left out, Sammy sidles up and joins the hug.

'They insisted on coming,' says June.

Another face steps through the throng. Oscar. He looks almost sheepish, his hair unbrushed, his creased T-shirt back to front.

'Hey, Stevie.'

'Oscar, I said don't—'

'I know, mate. But word got around. Everyone wanted to be here. For you. For her. We're family.'

Slowly, silently, his universe encircles him. His collection of lighthouses, gathered to guide him through his darkest night. He didn't realise how desperately he needed them. Now they are squeezing him tight, into a rugby scrum of mismatched heights, an unbreakable unit, in the middle of a hospital waiting room.

'Okay,' Steve says finally. 'Love you all, but can't breathe.'

With some badly concealed tear wipes, the crew finally disband and return to their posts around the room. Steve looks at them and realises there are a couple of noticeable absentees.

'Mum and Dad?' he says.

'Staying down in Auntie Niamh's caravan,' says Mickey.

'No reception.' The twins speak together, the first time they've done so in years.

'That was weird,' says Siobhan.

273

'That was funny!' says Ruby Mae.

'When Pippa's all better,' June says, and it's unclear whether she's addressing her brother or her children, 'Granny and Grandpa can come visit.'

'How is she?' Tania speaks next, barely recognisable, her eyes so puffy from crying she might have just had her own surgery. 'Can I see her? I really need to see her.'

'Diana's in with her now. But you can go in after.'

Tania swallows. She is gripping her right hand with her left in a failed attempt to stop them knocking together. In fact, her whole body is shaking, her knees, her thighs, her belly. She looks as though she is standing on a vibration plate at the gym.

'And is she . . . will she . . .'

But the words won't come.

'She's stable, Tan. That's all we know at the moment.'

She nods meekly, desperate to say more, to be of more comfort, but instead tears pour down her cheeks in rivulets.

'She's gonna be fine, babe. I just know it,' says Gus, as he puts a long arm around her waist. 'Our girl has more fight in her than Mike Tyson. You'll see.'

Steve cannot bear to watch Tania's desperation to believe. He turns away to find Charlotte sitting by the door. She smiles and taps the chair beside her. She is wearing the poker-faced expression of a medical professional, which he finds instantly reassuring. He realises he has no strength for other people's anxiety right now. He can barely manage his own.

'Have they told you how they think she's recovering from surgery?' She wastes no time. 'I know they removed a blood clot earlier, but the surgeon said the pressure was still—'

'Wait. How do you know that?'

'I collared him in the corridor.' She grins, that slightly lopsided Gallagher smile. 'Poor bloke. Not sure he knew what had hit him. They say doctors make the worst patients – I'd say they make even worse visitors.'

Steve stares at the floor.

'I just don't know,' he says. 'He's not giving much away. He told me to talk to her, so I have been. For all the good it's done. I'm so scared, Char.'

Charlotte takes his face in her hands and rests her forehead against his. It's a gesture inherited from their mother, and the familiarity threatens to floor him.

'Listen, Stevie. I'm not going to tell you it's all going to be okay, 'cos I love you too much to bullshit you. But I truly believe that she's in good hands. Even if he is too old to be wearing an earring.'

Steve makes a strange sound, but refuses to accept that it might have been a laugh.

'You guys have been through a lot these last few years,' Charlotte goes on. 'And you'll come through this. I'm sure of it.'

He can only nod.

'Come on, Steve. She's a Gallagher!'

'Yeah.' He smiles. 'Yeah, she is.'

Ruby Mae steps forward shyly. She is holding her hands behind her back.

'I made something for Auntie Pippa.'

Steve leans forward to his niece. The teenager hands him a piece of folded card.

'Oh Rubes, that's so thoughtful.'

'It's a drawing. I had to do it in the car, so it's not very good or anything.'

'No, it isn't.' Sammy chimes in. Ruby Mae rolls her eyes.

Steve opens the card. A colourful, Manga-style Pippa looks back at him. She has huge almond eyes, funky make-up and an electric blue jumpsuit.

'That's brilliant, Rubes. She'll love it.'

'It would have been neater but Mum's driving was really bumpy.'

'No. It's perfect.'

'Ruby chews her check. 'Can I take it to her?'

'Not right now. I'll show her first, then as soon as she's up, you can talk her through it.'

'Promise?'

'Cross my heart.'

'Stevie?' It's Oscar, holding out a small bundle. 'I thought you might want some stuff from home, so I popped over to your gaff. Still got that spare key.'

He offers up the items one by one, like a wise man in a nativity play, presenting Joseph with gold, frankincense and myrrh.

'Pyjamas. His and hers. Dug them out from under your pillows, sorry. Apples – just because I saw them and thought, you know, vitamin C and all that. And your toothbrushes. I know how much you love a good brush. And when Pippa wakes up, she won't want her breath to ming.'

Steve takes Oscar's eclectic gifts in one hand, keeping Ruby's drawing in the other. He looks around at the family and friends who are watching him, waiting on him. Suddenly their kindness, their love, their support is stifling. Without a word, he gets up and runs from the room.

He speeds along the corridor, breath billowing through overworked lungs.

'I'm coming back, Pip. I'm coming.'

July 2015

Steve

Our nervous wait was finally broken by the arrival of a white-tailed rescuer, who floated down the corridor like a superhero.

'Dr Cole,' we greeted him, rising in unison.

Pippa and I were putting all the faith we could muster in this smart, slightly aloof man, who could have had no idea how much we revered him. For weeks his word had become gospel in our house:

'Dr Cole said one glass of wine is totally okay.'

'Cole said non-organic milk might actually be better.'

'What did the doctor say about yoga?'

'I don't think he mentioned yoga.'

'I wonder what he *would* say . . .'

He wasn't much older than me or Pippa, at the other end of his thirties perhaps – in fact, we might well have been among his very first IVF patients – yet we saw him as a kind of wizard.

He swept towards us flanked by two nurses. We'd been through quite a journey with him already: consultations, letters, scans. He'd become a friend, a pen pal, a confidant – and was more intimately acquainted with Pippa's private parts than I cared for him to be. Despite his omniscience and our burgeoning relationship, however, he did have to give his notes a cursory look to remind himself of our names.

'Good morning, Pippa, Steven,' he said. 'Do you want to follow me?'

We gathered our things, and I looked across to the couple

sitting opposite us, who I'd been avoiding engaging with since we arrived. I don't know why we'd kept ourselves shut off from each other – we were all there for the same reason, and it might have been comforting to chat – but we were steadfast in our Britishness.

'Good luck,' they said now, smiling warmly.

As we followed Dr Cole down the short corridor, I whispered to Pippa: 'I thought it was bad luck to say, you know . . .'

'What, *good luck*?' said Pippa.

'Now you've said it too!'

'Before a play, yeah,' she sighed. 'Anyway, it's better than saying *break a leg* when you're in a hospital.'

'True,' I said. 'Different sort of theatre.'

We were let into a quiet room at the end of the hall. Another windowless off-white box, same yellow pedal bin in the corner, same holes in the wall that piped oxygen – a reminder that the room could be repurposed at a moment's notice. It was reassuring to see Dr Cole's sporty backpack and bicycle helmet hanging from the back of the door.

'Take a seat,' he said. 'I'm just going to bring up your notes.'

'This your office?' I asked, looking around for some more clues to his life as a civilian.

'Um, yes. For today.'

'What are you riding these days?' I asked, in a voice quite unlike my own.

'Just a bike,' he said. He tapped at his keyboard, then launched into a familiar routine: recapping our complete fertility history to date. 'So I first saw you a year and a half ago, when your periods stopped.'

'We thought we might be pregnant again,' I said.

'But we weren't,' said Pippa, 'and they stopped for three months.'

'Then we tested your hormone levels and, let me see . . .'

He raised a pointed finger so it was an inch away from the screen. 'Your FSH was—'

'Really high,' said Pippa.

'Sixty-five,' I said.

'Which I thought was a good thing.'

'But then it did get lower. I think twelve?'

'No, higher,' Pippa corrected me. 'And my AMH – which we wanted to be high – was really low, like nothing.'

'Nought point three,' Dr Cole said, trying to keep up with us while reading from the monitor.

'Wow, that is low.'

'But then that got higher.'

'Higher, lower,' said Pippa. 'It's like *The Price is Right*.'

Dr Cole cleared his throat. 'So two years ago you got pregnant naturally?'

'On our honeymoon,' said Pippa.

'Then again six months ago,' I added.

At this point in our fertility story, the listener would usually respond with a small, sad gasp, but clearly Dr Cole wasn't one for polite displays of emotion.

'And both pregnancies ended in miscarriage,' he concluded. 'Is that correct?'

He knew the answer, but looked to us for confirmation.

'Yes,' I said.

'We've been having sex every two days, 'cos that's how long they said sperm can live inside me for,' Pippa said, filling the silence. 'Is that too graphic?'

'Not at all.' Dr Cole almost smiled. 'That's what we recommend.'

'Of course it sometimes gets a bit "whack it up there, get the job done, back to *Line of Duty*". Sorry, that really is—'

'Yes maybe a little bit.' He cleared his throat again. 'You've been injecting with Menopur, is that right?'

'Steve's been injecting me.'

I'd got it down to a fine art. Load up the needle, flick out the air bubbles, pinch Pippa's belly, and when she'd stopped laughing at the absurdity or crying at the injustice of the situation, I'd inject, dab, then dispose.

Dr Cole continued to read from our notes. 'And after three weeks of stimulation, your ovaries have produced one potential follicle.'

'*One*,' Pippa said, bemoaning yet another unhelpful number that had been dealt to us in this cruel game of blackjack. 'Most people have about ten, right?'

Dr Cole looked at us, unsure how to reply.

'Our chances are very slim,' she went on. 'We know that.'

'Everyone's different, Pippa,' he said, going off script. He managed to sound realistic but not discouraging, and looked at Pippa paternally.

I wondered if he had children of his own – he wore a wedding ring – and cast around the room for evidence: a framed photo perhaps.

'So. The nurses will have been through all this with you, but just to clarify, we will be passing a scan probe with a fine needle attached to it . . .'

My eyes landed on the giggling face of a child, a baby, but it wasn't the progeny of Dr Cole. It was a photo stuck onto a greetings card, sitting on a shelf next to a box of surgical gloves. I could just make out the words *Thank you for everything* written inside.

'. . . before extracting fluid from the follicle.'

I was wondering whether we should send a home-made effort like the one on the shelf, or a custom card from a website when I heard my name being mentioned.

'Then Steve will take the box to King's?' Pippa was saying.

'Me? What?'

She nudged my knee with her own. 'You need to listen to this, Steve!'

'After egg collection,' Dr Cole said, swivelling his chair so he was square on to me, 'the follicular fluid will be stored in a portable incubator, which you will need to take to the assisted conception unit at King's. We advise that you take the train. Quickest journey this time of day. There you'll produce a sperm sample before returning to collect Pippa.'

'Sure. I know.'

I did. I'd read the booklet given to us at our first consultation several times. But it didn't feel like something that was actually going to happen, even now that we were finally here.

'So unless you have any more questions . . .?' We didn't. 'Steven, you can wait in reception or go straight to the ward, up to you.'

'Oh, is it happening now?' I asked.

'Why don't I give you a moment,' he said. On his way out, he dropped a folded blue-green gown on the desk. 'Just remove underwear, socks and any jewellery.'

The door shut behind him, and Pippa started to undress.

'Can you unzip the top bit?' she asked me. 'I can't reach it.'

It was hot out, the middle of a July heatwave. Pippa had chosen to wear a bright sunset-orange dress.

'Do you think this is okay?' she'd asked, deliberating in front of the mirror that morning.

'You look lovely.'

'I know, but is it acceptable for a hospital?'

'There's no dress code, is there?'

'That's true.'

'It is bright, though.'

'I know. But it makes me feel happy.'

'Then you should wear it.'

I'd put on a happy short-sleeved shirt in solidarity, with

small blue and yellow flowers printed on it, and we'd arrived at the hospital in sunglasses and sandals, which felt completely inappropriate, as if we were off to the Med rather than a medical centre.

Pippa's hospital gown was almost the same length as her summer dress, but she didn't look happy in it.

'You okay?' I asked.

'I'm fine. Do me up.'

I tied the cord behind her back, just tight enough so it would definitely cover her bum.

'How do I look?'

'Sexy.'

'Floor's cold.' She padded on the spot. 'I forgot my slippers.'

'Slipper socks in here,' I unzipped her overnight bag, which I'd sneakily topped up before we left, knowing that she would have packed too light (she had – just a gossip mag and some wholly unnecessary make-up).

'You're my angel,' she said, looking inside. 'Is that a sandwich? What's in it?'

'A surprise. In case you don't want the hospital food.'

It was then, for the first time that day, that Pippa welled up.

'I love you,' she managed to say, just as there was a gentle knock at the door.

Dr Cole entered the room with the two nurses and a porter, who offered Pippa a seat in his wheelchair. She gave me a nervous *here we go* smile as she tentatively lowered herself into it, before being wheeled away looking helpless but hopeful.

Pippa

A couple of junior doctors, they said. Would I mind a couple of junior doctors sitting in on the procedure?

Now call me ignorant, but last time I checked, a couple meant two. Three tops.

A couple of hundred, more like!

The operating theatre is swarming with them. Fresh-faced boys and wide-eyed girls, earnest, eager, attentive, scribbling notes like they are fast approaching a deadline.

They don't look old enough to even *play* doctors and nurses, let alone *be* them.

Well, *voilà*. This is me. Take it all in, boys and girls. Let me be your guinea pig.

What's that I hear you ask? Do I feel exposed? No! Not at all. Why should I? I've only got my legs strapped wide open and a paper gown barely covering my vagina. Standard Friday morning.

'Right,' says Dr Cole. 'That's the cannula in now. Notice the angle we discussed.'

Noddings and murmurings of accord. More dutiful scribbling. I look down at my left hand, barely recognising it without my rings on. I trace the indentations they have left on my wedding finger.

'And I'm right in thinking you've had a general anaesthetic before, Pippa? You know what to expect?'

Dr Cole has the disarming ability to make me feel like I'm back at school. The baritone voice, the rock-steady hands . . . everything about him screams competence, experience, focus. So why am I so terrified?

'Yep!'

My voice is too high. I clear my throat and try again, like a teenage boy trying to conceal his warbles.

'Yes. I've had a couple, actually. Miscarriage, fibroids removed, Barbie's plastic trainer stuck up my left nostril . . .'

Why do I always try and make him laugh?

'Not in that order, of course!'

I am rewarded with a smile. Result.

'And no adverse reactions? No sickness? Palpitations?'

'Nope, fine. Hard as nails, me! Not allergic to anything.'

'Lucky old you.'

He hands a piece of paper to the student nurse next to him, who swiftly clips it to the board above my bed.

'Oh, apart from chickpeas. But it could just be that I don't like the smell. Anyway, they make me gag.'

Dr Cole nods gravely. 'Olives do that to me.'

'Really? Green or black?

'Both. But my wife loves them, so more for her.'

Why for the love of God are we discussing olives?

'Okay . . .'

He is holding up what looks like a disproportionately large needle. Bloody hell. Where did that come from? And more to the point, where's it going? Good job Steve's not here. Needles make him dizzy.

'I know we discussed this earlier, but just to clarify, we will be passing a scan probe with a fine needle attached to it into your right ovary and extracting fluid from the follicle. While we will generally find an egg seventy per cent of the time, in your case that chance could be slightly lower. It's a very straightforward procedure and you will only be under for about twenty minutes. Does that all make sense?'

I nod. Wow. Dr Cole has seamlessly slipped into another costume. No more chickpea chit-chat. No more patient smiles. No more twinkle. Just quiet resolve and focus.

'Sats on, please. Oxygen ready?'

I suddenly miss Steve. I glance around at my audience, aware of the pulse that is thumping in my wrist and thighs and skull.

Wait. Is Junior at the back checking his phone? Come on, mate, bit of respect. Surely Instagram can wait. I've got my vagina on display here. Or maybe I'm being unfair. Maybe it's an urgent message about a terminal patient in another ward. But then he catches my eye, flushes scarlet and swiftly pockets the phone. Right. Less terminal patient update, more dating app match, I would say.

The needle is now attached to the cannula in my hand, and Dr Cole is looking at me.

'Right, the anaesthetic is going in now, Pippa. If you could count backwards from ten – it's going to be like a lovely strong G and T.'

Gin and tonic, you say? Now *that* I could handle.

Ten. Nope, can't feel anything. Nine. This is definitely a single. Eight. Mostly tonic. Seven. Better tell them it's not wor . . .

Steve

'All right there, Miranda? How are you feeling?'

A matronly nurse, who sounded even more Irish than my mother, was tending to a woman coming round from her procedure. The patient mumbled back in a low groan; she didn't sound great to me, but it didn't seem to worry Nursey.

'Your colour has come back now. When you're feeling up to it, I'll get you a nice cup of tea and a biscuit.'

I had found my way to the ACU recovery ward, where I now stood in the doorway, very aware of being the only male presence.

'Excuse me?' I said. 'Is this where I should wait for my wife?'

'Egg collection?'

'Yes.'

'Pop your things down there,' the nurse said, pointing to a gap in the row of beds, a bay into which Pippa's bed would presumably be reverse-parked. Then a murmur turned her attention back to the waking woman's bedside. 'You just say the word, lovey. I've got a Hobnob with your name on it.'

It wouldn't be long before Pippa would be lying here, coming round from her anaesthetic, confused and in pain. 'Pippa' and 'pain' were words that should never be spoken together. I wanted to do anything I could to help make this easier for her, so I left her bag on the chair, open, the magazine visible. Then I placed the foil-wrapped sandwich next to it, to serve as a message that I'd been there, that she was safe.

Maybe I should put her phone on charge somewhere she could see it?

'Excuse me?' I stage-whispered. 'Sorry.'

'Yes, young man, what can I do for you?'

'Is it safe to leave my wife's phone out?'

'Well I'm not going to look at it, darling. And there's no one coming onto my ward that will.'

She said *my ward* like a Mafia don saying *my patch*, but with a Dublin accent.

'Sorry,' I said. 'When she wakes up, can you tell her that her phone's charging on the cabinet and there's a magazine in the bag? Oh, and a sandwich and some fizzy water.'

'Why don't you put up some pictures while you're at it?'

Hadn't thought of that. I looked through the bag for some paper and a pen. I could draw a quick cartoon of us, to lift her spirits . . .

'I was joking,' the nurse said.

'Oh yeah, I know. I was just—'

'Don't worry, I'll look after her.' The nurse was a mob boss again. 'You'll be off soon, so get yourself together now.'

I got myself together and waited, perched on the edge of the chair, where the blue padding gave way to grey plastic. The ward was silent but for the nurse, who was chattily dissecting her lunch.

'This is without doubt the best one. Broccoli and cauli-flower.' She slurped from a pink mug, sounding like a toddler pretending to drink. 'Delicious. You'd never believe it was from a packet.'

There was a squeak of wheels from the hall as a bed was rolled in, Dr Cole and the nurses in pursuit. It was Pippa.

'How did it go?' I said, jumping up from the seat so fast I was halfway across the ward before I was able to stand still. 'Is she all right?'

'It all went as expected.'

As expected? Now is not the time to be mysterious, Doc.

I followed the bed as it was wheeled to a stop. Pippa looked pale and lifeless, her lips slack and falling apart in an upturned U.

'Are you sure? She looks a bit . . . weird.'

'She's absolutely fine,' he said. 'Now it's your turn. This is the incubator.'

Only then did I notice what else had been wheeled in alongside my wife: an insulated cube, encased in metal, which Dr Cole had opened up like a boxy briefcase. It was about the size of the TV I would watch as a boy in Charlotte's room when she was out snogging, the one with integrated VHS.

'As you can see, it contains three vials,' he continued.

'Three? Is that good?'

'It's normal. We've taken as much follicular fluid as possi-ble to help support the egg during its incubation.'

I stared in awe at the three precious vials. Beyond them, hiding in the blackness of the dense insulation, were ten to twenty empty vial-shaped holes.

'I'm going to close the incubator now,' Dr Cole continued. 'It has to stay at an ambient temperature, so do not open it again or touch these clasps. Okay?'

'Okay,' I said, as he clamped it shut.

'It should remain upright and as still as possible. If you lose it – please don't lose it – or it's compromised, there's an emergency number on the side.'

'I won't lose it!' I said with a silly smile. When people take a serious tone with me I get nervous, and when I get nervous, I get chirpy. And Dr Cole's tone was stern. He'd been extracting follicular fluid all morning. He must have needed a sit-down and a piece of cake.

'But if I *did* lose it,' I blurted out, 'how would I find—'

'Put the number into your phone now,' he said, wise from countless briefings with endless nervous men like me.

Pippa let out a groan from the bed. I forgot my task for a moment and leapt to her side.

'She's fine. Off you go.'

I stroked some wisps of hair from her frown and kissed her forehead goodbye. She smacked her lips together, then settled back to sleep. She looked like she'd passed out after a night in Soho.

'Right. I'm off,' I said, though it felt wrong to leave her.

'Steven?' Dr Cole said as I walked past him. 'Aren't you forgetting something?'

I turned round.

'Oh, the box.'

He almost smiled as I returned to the bedside to pick it up, the almost-smile disappearing as my fingers slipped through the handle as if it wasn't there. I tried again, readjusting my grip now I'd felt the weight of it.

'Heavier than it looks, isn't it?'

'No, it's fine. Not heavy at all.'

It *was* heavy. I was expecting to lift my sister's telly, which was easy enough even for my eleven-year-old self, but this was the weight of a beefcake's kettlebell, the kind that could anchor a ship.

'Any other packages need delivering?' I said.

'Off you go.'

'Yep. Definitely off now.'

Pippa

'Hello there, Pippa, dear. I'm Nurse Kierly.'

Where am I? Mouth is dry. I can hear crying. Is this a hangover?

'You're all right. You're back in the ward. Your retrieval went smoothly. Would you like a sip of water?'

I murmur, vaguely aware that I'm in a bed and something has just happened. Something important. My pelvis aches. I think I could be bleeding. Is that a pad between my legs? My womb feels hollow.

'Let's sit you up a bit, shall we, love.'

I'm gently lifted and some drops of water are poured into my parched mouth. I swallow gratefully.

'There now. Well done. That's better.'

Are my cheeks wet? Are they tears? Am I crying?

Yes.

I think I'm crying. I try to speak. It's more of a croak.

'Where's Steve?'

I want Steve. I need to see him.

'He'll be on his way to King's now. Try and rest.'

My mobile pings near my ear.

'There we go again! Your lovely husband plugged in your telephone before he left. It's been buzzing and beeping away!'

'Sorry.'

'Don't be daft, I don't mind! I'll put it here beside your bed so you can reach it.'

As she places the phone on my side table, I notice her face

for the first time. Kind. Lived in. The long working hours etched across her brow like fault lines.

'Popular lady, aren't we?'

And suddenly I have to ask. I have to know.

'Do you know how it went?'

She looks at me, her eyes creased with sympathy.

I feel weak, vulnerable. Stupid for putting her in an impossible position. I know she can't answer, but I'm desperate for reassurance.

'All I know is that your lovely man went off with a couple of vials in a case. I'm sure he won't be too long.'

Couple. There's that word again. What does it mean? One? Two? She bowls on like a well-meaning steamroller.

'Anything you need, I'm sitting in that chair in the corner. And when you're ready, there's a lovely Hobnob with your name on it.'

She winks. I try to smile as she walks away, show gratitude for her kindness. But nausea is rising in my throat. Salty saliva filling my mouth like a tap has been left on in my cheeks. Think I'd have more chance of running a marathon than stomaching a Hobnob right now.

I rub my lips together. Cracked. My mouth tastes bitter. Metallic. Stinging.

Where's Steve? I wish he was here. I really don't like hospitals.

Steve

The literature didn't say it was going to be this heavy. I should have got one of those Ubers. Should have warmed up, at least. Tennis stretches.

The electric crackle in the rails told me a train was approaching, and my right shoulder dropped ever so slightly in relief.

Soon I'd be able to put the thing down and rest my arm, which had started to twang from its own electrical pulses.

Don't be busy, don't be busy, don't be busy, I prayed as the train thundered into the platform.

It was half empty, thank God. There was even space for my little metal friend to sit next to me.

Now don't you move. Don't switch yourself off. And don't fall over.

Out of nowhere, a guy landed in the carriage on one foot, having cleared the platform edge with a long jumper's hop as the doors hissed shut. It was hardly an abnormal event, but I was startled, and when I looked down at the incubator, I found that I'd wrapped a protective arm around it.

Wonder if there's anything going on inside, I thought. Hang on in there, egg, that's a good boy. Or girl.

A couple boarded at the next stop eating bagels, and I regretted not making myself a sandwich. It was lunchtime, and I'd only had a biscuit for breakfast, so as not to rub Pippa's nose in the fact that she wasn't able to eat before the anaesthetic. The girl whose bagel I was ogling whispered something to her fella, tipping her head towards the box. He levelled me with a four-letter stare before they got up and moved further down the carriage.

What? I shouted to them, in a parallel life. *Never seen a man travelling with his incubator before?*

I sat back in my seat, watching suburbia flashing past me once again. Then a worrying thought made me sit up straight. *Hope they didn't think it's a bomb.* I considered my little metal friend warily. *I mean . . . it does look like a bomb.* Suddenly every passenger was eyeing me with suspicion, edging away slowly and thumbing 999 into their phones.

Why didn't they give it to you in a bag for life? I wondered. Actually, that would be very appropriate.

'If you see anyone acting suspiciously, please inform a

member of staff or call the British Transport Police,' came the announcement, timed just to taunt me.

I'd be screwed if a policeman got on.

'We'll take the box from here, sir.'

'But it's just an incubator, officer. Look, it has an NHS sticker on it.'

'Can you step away from the box, sir? We won't ask you again.'

'I can't do that, officer. It has to remain upright and at an ambient temperature at all times. If you destroy this in a controlled explosion, Pippa will never forgive me.'

Pippa.

I took out my phone. No calls or texts.

Are you awake? I typed. *Let me know you're okay? Text me when you wake up.* I pressed send.

'The next station is Earlsfield.'

Just one more stop, my little friend, then we change onto the Overground. And no one gets on at Earlsfield.

The brakes whined as we came to a halt on a crowded platform. The train opposite was completely empty. *Must have a fault. Just my bloody luck.*

As the seats filled up, one of the newly arrived passengers stood over me. I ignored him until he said: ''Scuse me. Can you move your, er . . .?'

'Incubator,' I snapped back, hoping that would deter him. It didn't. 'Fine, I'll just . . .'

I lifted it off the seat with great care – and a passive-aggressive show of effort – then lowered it between my legs with a dull thud. He didn't even thank me, the seat stealer, just sat his lazy arse on the square print that had been nicely warmed by the incubator.

Some people.

I gave the box the once-over. *Let's just check you're all present and correct. Clasps? Still fastened. No cuts or bulges. Wait a minute – is that red light meant to be on? I don't remember seeing a light before. I'd have remembered a red light. A red light is never good. I'm going to call that number – where is it?*

'Ladies and gentlemen, this train is being taken out of service due to a signal failure at Clapham Junction. Tickets will be accepted on buses.'

Oh shit off, no.

I joined the stampede onto the platform, shielding the incubator as best I could from the multitude of pushy passengers. The crowd was pressing towards a narrow escalator, at the top of which I saw the couple with the bagels. They stepped off, but didn't head for the exit with everyone else; instead they made to cross over to another platform, stopping on a bridge to speak to a couple of police officers.

Snitches! I couldn't believe it. Perhaps they were just asking directions, but I couldn't take the risk. *I can't get arrested. I haven't got time. Even if they don't arrest me, they're going to want to look inside. But they can't open it, because if they do . . .*

I took a punt and headed past the congested stairway and along the platform, looking for an alternative route out. And lo! Salvation! Like a mirage, the grubby glass doors of a lift materialised from the bricks. They slid open, enfolding me and my little friend in the portal of escape, one machine looking out for another.

'Level one,' came the sonorous voice of the lift.

'Level one: complete,' I replied. I'd defeated the big bad bagel boss and was ready for the next stage of the game.

My phone vibrated in my pocket with a message from Pippa. *Awake. How you doing?*

I had sworn not to put the incubator down again unless it was on the soft seat of a taxi, so I typed back with one thumb.

All good here. V easy journey.

Pippa

Ping!

I reach slowly for my mobile, every movement perilously hard work. It's as though I've gone to sleep and woken up as an old lady.

I blink my eyes to adjust to the light radiating from the screen. Bloody hell! So many messages. Four are from Steve.

Are you awake?

Let me know you're okay.

Text me when you wake up.

I love you.

They're interspersed with a smattering of choice Mum specials.

Jut a thought r.e. Steve's speed. Does he eat enoUg vegetarians?

What?

Not speed, SPERM.

Oh well, that's much better then. Glad of the emphatic capitals too.

BEETROOT meant to boost mobility. Or is it motility? Either way, BEETROOT!

More sage advice from the expert. Thanks, Mum.

How was Opera station?

I mean Opera STATION.

Nope. Still nothing.

Operation!

Not an all-singing public transport intersection then. Shame. Finally it's Tania.

How's the fanny Pips? Love ya rock chick

I scroll back and start a slow reply to Steve. It's a struggle.

Awake. How you doing?

I can see he is online, and he responds almost immediately. The blue bubbles ripple under his name and I can see his furrowed brow as he is typing.

All good here. V easy journey.

There's a ripple of polite laughter in the ward. Nurse Kierly seems to be starring in her own stand-up show, the recovering women providing her with a captive audience.

'Listen to this, ladies!'

No choice really, have we?

She begins reading aloud from a well-thumbed schlocky gossip magazine.

'*Linda Broadwick, thirty-four, created life-sized cake versions of her twin daughters to celebrate their birthday!*'

She looks around the room, inviting a response. Nothing.

'A cake!!!'

Nope. Still no takers.

'But how could you ever eat it?' She erupts into a peal of laughter.

Ow, that noise hurts. No, no, please stop. It's rattling in my head, cutting through me like fingernails scraping down a blackboard.

'And where would you cut it!'

Her laughter rises, and I feel a punchline is imminent. Please let it be so.

'"Here you go, Mrs Clarke. Who wants a slice of my daughter's forearm?"'

Her guffaws are reaching fever pitch, a mottled flush rising over her cheeks and her wispy hair spiralling free from her bun as if it too is elated by the story.

'"LITTLE SLIVER OF BUTTOCKS, ANYONE?!"'

And that's it. She's gone. Tears rolling down her cheeks, hands clapping together like a sea lion. So overcome with glee, she is forced to sit down to gather her breath. Her delight is visceral, bouncing off the faded blue walls and into the fragile ears of her mute, entirely horizontal audience.

I turn to face the wall, pulling my pillow over my head to muffle the sound.

Steve

'Sixth floor,' said another plummy voiceover artist in another lift, informing me that I'd nearly completed the game. I'd reached the hospital level without having lost any of my lives or, more importantly, the incubator.

'Hi,' I said, introducing myself to the nurse on reception. 'Steven Gallagher?' She looked back at me, clearly expecting a little more information, so I lifted the box onto the countertop. 'I've come with this.'

'I see. You can leave it there. We'll look after it.'

'Thanks. Give my arm a rest before—' I stopped my inner monologue from spilling out just in time. 'What happens to it now?'

'We'll send it to the lab, who will assess the eggs then select the best one. In the meantime, you'll need to produce some sperm. Take this.' She handed me a plastic sleeve, the kind I keep paperwork in for my taxes. 'Your name is already on the sample pot. You also need to fill in these forms and bring them back to us.'

'Fill in the forms, fill the pot. Got it.'

'You don't have to *fill* it,' she said.

'What?'

'The pot.'

I couldn't tell if she was making a joke or trying to put me at ease. I felt neither amused nor reassured.

'There's actually someone in the sample room at the

moment,' she said, quickly moving on. 'I'll call you as soon as he comes out.'

I took a seat and tried to block out the thought that another man was giving his sample right before me. *Wish he'd hurry up. If more guys start arriving, they'll all be waiting on me.* With a shudder, I imagined them lining up outside the room.

My phone vibrated with a text from Pippa.

How goes? Just had Mum attack. She had several thoughts on our sex life. Wanna hear?

Maybe later, I replied. *Might kill the mood.*

How is mood?

I heard a door open and shut, and a man emerged with his forms, looking sheepish. Hope he washed his hands, I thought.

My turn now, I typed. *Will let you know.*

The sample room was behind a grey door, which led to a pleated curtain. Whether the curtain was for soundproofing or to add some strip-club glamour, I wasn't sure. Probably it was there to provide an extra layer of privacy, to allay any concerns that someone could burst in uninvited. Either way, it was another surface that I had to touch.

A shiny leather armchair dominated the room, the bright halogen light that bounced off it giving it the feel of a thoughtfully furnished interrogation cell. *How many guys have sat in that today?* It was best not to think about it. I opened a drawer to find a stack of very well-thumbed magazines, the dog-eared corners flapping over to reveal pictures of, well, flaps.

Looks like it's been in the bath, I thought. No thanks, you can go back in there.

I turned to the flat-screen TV on the wall, and picked up the remote. A menu of pre-loaded films popped up, accompanied by some jazzy muzak – the kind that plays when

Michael Douglas is being seduced against his will. Tempted by a promising thumbnail, I clicked 'play' and sank reluctantly into the armchair.

Well! This is . . . distinctly nineties.

As I thought about seeing what else was on offer, I caught sight of the remote in my hand. Like all remotes I'd known before, it had a build-up of unspeakable, unknowable grey matter between the buttons.

Can't believe I just touched it. Maybe I should give it a clean. But where? Not in the sink . . .

I explored all the surfaces, looking under the chair and through every drawer, for something to clean it with.

Seriously? All the hand sanitiser pumps in this building. All those sterilised bags and tubes. I cannot believe they didn't leave out some Flash wipes!

My phone buzzed against my thigh. I washed my hands, then took it out of my pocket.

Are you in? What's it like? Must be so strange.

Is strange. Will tell all later. Should get on with it now.

Shall I take a sexy photo? Will that help?

What, from your bed? Aren't you still in ward? With eight other women?

Oh yeah. Good point. I leave you to it.

I closed my eyes, took a breath.

Come on then, Steven. Let's get this done.

Pippa

I must have drifted off, because I am jolted awake by my phone ringing. I grab it clumsily and put it to my ear.

'That was quick, babe. Good porn?'

'I beg your—'

'Shit. Hi, Mum.'

'Hello, love. Are you awake?'

Usually I would argue that this was a moribund question, but I don't have the energy.

'Just about.'

'And how was it?'

'Yeah, went okay. The nurse told me they took a couple of vials of liquid.'

'A *couple*? What does that mean exactly?'

Maybe we are related after all.

'I mean, a couple could be anything, Pippa. Did they specify? It could mean two eggs, could mean five.'

'No, Mum. I told you. There was only one follicle, so only one egg. At best.'

A long pause as Mum calibrates her thoughts.

'I see. Well, never mind. Did you get my textual message about beetroot?'

'I did, Mum. Thanks.'

'Very good for motility.'

'So you said.'

'For Steve's you-know-what.'

'I know what.'

I lean my head back against the pillow and close my eyes. There is an ache behind my lids.

'I'm making some Polish beetroot soup – or it could be Ukrainian, I'm not sure. Same ballpark, anyway. I thought Steve should have some before he does . . . it.'

'Well he's there now, so . . .'

'Oh! I thought he did the deed in a day or two?'

'No, he's doing the deed as we speak.'

How did we get here? In what universe did we get to a place where my mother is thinking about my husband masturbating?

'Shame. I made it specially. I would run it over to him, but it hasn't softened yet.'

'Don't worry. It was a nice thought.'

A moment's silence. I can hear her brain whirring, weighing up whether to offer whatever she was going to say next.

'There was one other thing.'

Here we go.

'After you two make love . . .'

Help me.

'. . . does Steve stay inside you long enough?'

Speechless.

'You know, after he's—'

'Mum!'

'Because it really is *crucial*, Pippa, so I've read. Can make all the difference. Also, climaxing together . . .'

Jesus God.

'. . . increases the blood flow to the uterus. There, I've said my piece!'

I look around the ward. Despite speaking in a whisper, I feel utterly exposed – as though I've left the curtains open after a shower and have found myself naked, dripping wet, flailing to cover my modesty with a too-small hand towel in front of gawping neighbours.

'Look, Mum. Even if I wanted to discuss this with you, which I don't, this really isn't helpful today.'

'All I'm saying is that your father and I conceived you off the back of an almighty—'

'Mum! Please! Stop! I'm in hospital. I've had a needle in my ovary! Steve is carrying our hopes across town and you're—'

'Oh love. I'm so sorry.'

She takes a deep breath. When she speaks again, her voice is gentle, almost childlike.

'I'm a bit all over the place. I just want this for you. So much. For all of us. And if it doesn't happen today—'

'Mum.'

'I'm sorry, darling. You're right, we can talk another time. I love you.'

'I know. Love you too.'

We hang up. I rest my head against the thin hospital pillow and try to breathe.

Perversely, Mum's incessant messaging is something of a relief. Anything is better than the resounding, painful silence of her absence after Dad's death. She simply withdrew. From family, from friends, from herself. I would message every day, I would call, I would pop round; I even started sending weekly postcards to make her smile, but to no avail. She blocked my efforts like a jilted lover. Dad's absence was too much for her to compute and she shut down like an overheated laptop. Finally Steve and I staged an intervention – Operation Diana Retrieval. We let ourselves into the house, armed with a care package of her favourite things: Marilyn Monroe movies, Italian white wine, *Good Housekeeping* magazines and liqueur-filled chocolates. The house was cold and dark, like it had been locked up for a vacation, and there she sat, thin as a pin, unmade-up, wrapped tightly in Dad's university jumper, sipping whisky from his favourite tumbler and listening to the Test match on full volume. A tragic twenty-first-century Miss Havisham. My heart ached. She barely noticed us as we set to work opening curtains, dusting surfaces, emptying vases of dried-up funeral flowers and depositing out-of-date food into bin liners.

It was a winding road, but slowly, delicately over the next few months, Mum and I learned to laugh again. We realised we hadn't allowed ourselves to have fun together for such a long time. Naturally, life had revolved around Dad and his illness and tending to his every need. We would have girls' nights in on the sofa with diabolically sexist rom coms and throw popcorn at the screen. Steve acted as butler when the Prosecco dried up. I set up 'Pippa's Beauty Emporium' in the spare room and issued Mum with vouchers drawn on the back of old receipts that she could reclaim at her leisure. Despite the tears, the grief, the gaping hole in our lives, we giggled like never before. I was grumpy Polish beautician Magda and Mum loved her. 'Do it again! Do it again!' she would exclaim as I stroppily slapped cold cream onto her face and announced, 'New hair sprouted on top lip! I must rip out. Keep still!'

It was strangely beautiful. The three of us. A little commune.

And gradually, as the months passed, Mum slowly began to shine again. A touch of blusher. A comb through her hair. Her eyes got brighter and she started to accept the meals that I prepared and Steve so lovingly reheated. I never felt closer to her than I did during this time. I could sense Dad everywhere – delighted that his favourite humans on earth were realising how much they loved each other. I felt his arms around the two of us, guiding, leading, supporting.

My chest feels tight and my breathing constricted, like something is sitting on my ribs, weighing me down. The dull ache in my womb is deepening, a constant reminder of what's at stake. The rhythmic symphony of trolleys clanks through the distant corridors like Marley's chains, and the heady scents of disinfectant and fear drift into my nostrils.

I sense movement in the bed next to me. The rustle of a sheet, the clearing of a throat. The girl on my left is awake. I glance over. Her long shiny, plait is swung over her shoulder and reaches almost to her waist. It's immaculate, not a strand out of place. My heart aches as I recognise the look of anxious, tearful hope across her brow – her eyes glued to her phone screen. I try to look away, give her some space and focus on my own life, but something forces me to engage.

'This is like the world's worst hen party, isn't it?'

She looks round at me, startled. Indeed, she looks so intensely shocked you would think I had just been speaking in tongues whilst floating six inches off the bed dressed as David Bowie. I have clearly just trampled on law one of recovery room etiquette: no one makes conversation except on a strict need-to-know basis. The first rule of Recovery Ward Club is that no one talks at Recovery Ward Club.

'Sorry?'

I should back off. Leave her alone. Sit quietly in my own head, and let her sit in hers.

But I can't. Something tells me that talking, communicating is the only thing that might keep us both from going under right now. I am struck with how vital it is to build bridges, in this room and beyond; to find a way to connect during the terrifying journey ahead.

'This. Right here. A room full of women thrust together against their will, doing a lame activity that no one wants to be doing. Aka a hen do.'

The girl still looks baffled, and for a second I fear she may call security. (Or at the very least the Hobnob nurse – same difference really.)

'I don't really . . .'

'No. Sorry. Terrible analogy. I'm babbling.'

It's my chance to give up. Pretend this blip never happened. Bury myself in my phone, the easy way out.

But something about her makes me continue.

'I'm Pippa, by the way.'

'Reema.'

'Hi, Reema. I would shake your hand, but when I lean to the right, I feel as though my vagina may drop out.'

An embarrassed smile. Something is softening in her, I'm sure of it. I persevere.

'So. Is this your first round?'

Silence. She's clammed up like an oyster. Damn. Too personal.

'Sorry, absolutely none of my business. You don't have to—'

'Yes, it is.'

Her voice is barely audible, like it's coming from deep underground, a bulb pushing through heavy soil, attempting to reach the warmth of the sunlight.

'And last. You?'

'Yeah, first time.'

Reema lifts her eyes and finally looks at me. A hesitant smile. Then, suddenly, from across the ward:

'There now, lovey. You're in recovery, and when you feel better, I've got a Hobnob with your name on it.'

I lower my voice. 'Do you reckon she has a packet of Hobnobs under that chair with every possible girl's name stamped on it?'

That's when it happens. Reema's eyes suddenly crease at the corners like unironed sheets, a warm sound bubbles from her mouth, and I hear the first hiccup of genuine laughter. I feel a thud of satisfaction, like I've just stumbled upon that elusive final answer in a pub quiz. A mixture of triumph, relief and pride. Then . . .

'I know you, actually.'

I'm bewildered.

'Well I feel like I know you. My husband and I watched that series you were in last year. *Quantum*? You were a scientist. We loved it.'

I blush. Being recognised is always strange, but never more so than in a gynae ward.

'Thank you. Yes. It was a riot to film. Great cast.'

'You were brilliant. Truly. I'm not just saying that.'

'That means a lot. Thanks. It's weird, isn't it. When careers are at their best, hearts can be at their worst. And vice versa. I just can't quite seem to strike that work/life balance. Maybe one day, eh?'

We watch Nurse Kierly as she travels the room on her stand-up tour. Each bedside her new arena, as she reels off the same set of jokes and banter. It's quite something. Irritating, possibly. Repetitive, certainly, but impressive nonetheless.

'So. How's your husband doing? Is he there yet?'

'Steve? Yes. He's there. Yours?'

Reema shifts uncomfortably, twisting the end of her long plait around her forefinger.

'Well, he got there over an hour ago and I've heard nothing since.'

'That's okay. No news is good news. I'm sure it all takes a while.'

'Hmm, maybe.' Her voice has become thin, fragile as tissue paper. 'I just hate this waiting.'

'Me too. It's like purgatory, isn't it? Are we going up to heaven or down to hell?'

Reema looks at me sharply.

'Sorry. Bit dramatic.'

We fall into silence, lost in our own thoughts. Finally . . .

'If this fails, we have no other chance.'

'Don't say that, Reema. It only takes one egg, remember.'

'It's not that. I have lots of follicles. They think there were seven or eight eggs. It's Vinay. He . . .' She trails off, unable or unwilling to continue.

I study her face, determined not to let her lose herself in the doubt we're all drowning in.

'There's a problem with his sperm? But that's good! I mean, not *good* good. But good, better than being a problem on *your* side, good. Sperm can be improved. There are supplements and all sorts. And if you've got eggs . . .'

But Reema simply shakes her head.

'They have told us it's very unlikely to work. And that means we may never be able . . .'

Those words.

Those three little words that cannot be uttered.

Never. Be. Able.

I want to hug her. Reassure her. Tell her that everything will be okay. But I can't. No one can.

'Could you try again privately? If it doesn't . . . you know.'

She stares at the floor, pensive.

'We could. I mean, it's not the money. Vinay's parents have plenty of that.'

'All right for some! Maybe you could ask them to cough up some cash this end!'

But this time I cannot make her laugh. She turns to me, her dark eyes filling with tears.

'They don't know we are here. They don't know anything about this part of our lives. And they never will.'

I can hear the tightness in her throat as her words become staccato.

'We felt like we failed them when it didn't happen naturally.'

'But that's not true! You haven't failed. No one can predict this.'

'Yeah, maybe. But that's the way it is.'

We both fall silent, the endless fluctuating vibrations of hope and disappointment ringing in our ears.

'I'm sorry.'

She smiles, brushing a tear from the corner of her eye. She doesn't want to cry here.

I admire her.

'Thanks. So enough about me. What's your story?'

'Oh God, not a very jolly one. Won't be reading it to any small children at bedtime. Would give them nightmares.'

I take a deep breath, suddenly feeling like I'm standing naked in school assembly.

'You don't have to, Pippa.'

'No. it's okay. Basically I got pregnant on our honeymoon. It was crazy, unexpected. But wonderful. They don't know what happened. It was all fine. It was alive. Until it wasn't.'

Breathe, Pippa, just breathe.

'Then after that – well, my periods just seemed to stop. I was only young, but my hormone levels were all over the shop. They still don't know why. Maybe the shock of the miscarriage caused my ovaries to freak out. Anyway, they said we had no chance.'

'I'm so sorry.'

'Yeah. It was pretty grim. Then miraculously we fell pregnant again last year. But it only got to seven weeks. Anyway. The NHS have handed us a free hit with this, so we've given it a go.'

I realise I have been pulling at the skin around my thumb. There's a drop of blood on the sheet.

Reema leans over. 'Well they must think there's a chance then?'

I shrug, not meeting her gaze.

'There's only one follicle. So who knows if there will be an egg – and if there is an egg, who knows if it will be good quality, and if it is good quality who knows if it will . . . blastoplast or whatever it's called . . .'

'Blastocyst.'

'And if it does blastocyst, will it get to three months this time? And if it does get to three months . . .'

'Then there's no reason to believe you won't have a beautiful baby in nine months' time.'

I gulp. Tears are streaming down my cheeks. Shit. Where did they come from? I brush them away but they just keep falling. More and more.

'I'm sorry. I was fine. I don't know why . . .'

'Don't be sorry. Here, I've got a spare packet of tissues. Catch.'

Reema tosses me the tissues. I catch them with one hand. Impressive, as I can't see a bloody thing.

'Cheers.'

I blow my nose, aware of how loud it sounds in the whispering ward.

'Any word from your husband?'

Reema shakes her head. 'Maybe I should call him. I just don't want to pressure him. He's been so anxious lately.'

After a moment, she continues.

'I'm really struggling, 'cos he just shuts down. And I want to talk to him about it all. Share it. Because he's a good man.'

Ah, those darn good men.

'I keep thinking of Steve carting his box around. It's tragic, isn't it? Farcical.'

I try out a laugh, but with little success. Reema says nothing.

'And I just feel so guilty.'

'Don't, Pippa! This is life. It's no one's fault..'

My nose has started to run again. I wipe it furiously with the tissue, hoping brusqueness will stem the threatening tears.

'That's what Steve says. And it makes my heart hurt. I mean, most days we're fine. More than fine. It's like when we first met. Not a care in the world. And we're really, really happy. But then it just creeps up, doesn't it? Drags you under.'

'I know, but you have to try and stay hopeful.'

'But it's hope that's the killer. They give you all these statistics about your chances, or lack of them – how your levels are crazy low, how you should consider other options. And then they tell you that you have to stay positive, that stress is the main enemy on this journey. Basically it feels like you're being told your house is burning down, but whatever you do, don't be stressed. Sit tight. Relax. Make yourself a nice raspberry leaf tea and watch it burn.'

Reema laughs. 'I'm drinking that stuff too.'

'And all these stories of happy endings don't help. Women accidentally falling pregnant after being told their ovaries are kaput. Makes me think maybe we'll get another miracle. Are you allowed two miracles?'

'I think two's allowed.'

A trolley squeaks into the ward. The new patient looks pale, drowsy, confused. Like the rest of us.

'You know what, Pippa. I think the time may have come for a Hobnob. Can I tempt you?'

I smile at my new friend. Women are wonderful things.

'Go on then. Let's go wild.'

Reema is asleep, her hand dangling over the side of her bed. The large clock on the wall is perilously loud. How can it only be seventeen minutes since last I checked? Nurse Kierly, meanwhile, is keeping us updated on every stage of her new crossword.

'Hmm, a yellow light bulb? What could that be?'

I unfurl a corner of the foil and attempt a nibble of my sandwich. Oh God, he's taken the crusts off – why does that make me cry? I attempt to chew, but my mouth doesn't work.

I don't think I can eat this. I never can't eat. This is so weird. I don't know what I'm feeling. I don't know if I'm scared or happy or sad or frightened. I feel kind of suspended. Out of body. Like I could look down from the ceiling and see Pippa Gallagher trying to eat this lovely crustless sandwich her lovely husband made her.

I attempt another nibble.

I kind of want to tell Bed Pippa Gallagher down there that it's going to be okay, that he is going to ring and tell her it's all worked out. That it was all worth it. But Ceiling Pippa Gallagher can't say that. And Bed Pippa Gallagher wouldn't accept it. So here we all are. Hanging. No-man's-land.

My phone pings. Mum.

Thinking of toy.

And another.

Toy

And again.

YOU

I try again with the sandwich. He makes the best sandwiches. *Could we adopt?* The right amount of filling to bread. *I just don't know where I am with it all.* He only butters one side. *But I want him to be a dad. More than anything in the world.* A slick of mayonnaise stops the bread being too dry. *How has this happened to us?*

The phone rings again. This time I see it. *Steve Mob.* I grab it.

'Tell me. Just tell me. Quickly.'

I can hear his breath like he is right beside me. I can almost feel it on my face.

'I've just been in and . . . I've spoken to them and . . . I'm sorry. I'm so sorry.'

'What? What's happened?'

'They couldn't find an egg. I'm sorry, darling.'

A silence. The sound of my heart beating in my temples. I

can hear the nurse, still talking. A car roars past on the main road. The sound of drilling. The scream of a seagull. Is someone laughing?

'Pip? Pip, are you still there?'

I look at the women. How can they not see? How can none of them see? A bomb has just exploded underneath my bed. My blood is spattered around the walls like fresh paint. That's bits of my pulsing heart over your sheets. The flesh, the gristle, the bones of me. Tell me you heard the bomb?

'Pippa? Talk to me. Talk to me. Try and breathe.'

I do as he says. The noises clear slightly. I begin to exhale.

'It's okay. I'm okay, love.'

We sit and listen to each other's breath. Finally . . .

'Are you okay, Steve?'

A pause. I need to touch him.

'I really thought it would work, Pip. I felt it.' A sniff.

'Are you crying?'

'Yes. Yep, I'm crying. People are watching me.'

How can he always make me smile?

'Oh darling. It isn't over. It isn't. We'll be okay. We can try again. Somehow.'

'I know. I'm sorry.'

'Don't be sorry! Never be sorry. You need a good cry. You've been so strong the last couple of years. Now we have to be strong for each other.'

'And we will. We will.'

He is sniffing and stumbling to try and contain the emotion that needs to be freed. I can't remember the last time I heard him cry. It breaks my heart.

A moment passes. Then . . .

'Right,' I say. 'Do something for me?'

'Anything.'

'Go and get yourself a pint of Guinness – actually maybe a half, I don't want to be here that much longer.'

'No, I want to come and get you. I'm not leaving you.'

'It's an order.'

I can hear a smile in his voice. 'Okay. A half could be good. I love you.'

We hang up. I hug the phone like a security blanket, like a bit of Steve's soul is hiding in the SIM card.

Suddenly, from across the room, Nurse Kierly offers up another crossword clue.

'Walks beside you. Hmm. Six letters. So not *dog*.'

I whisper to myself:

'Friend.'

Mr Bramin clicks off his pen torch and slides it back into his top pocket.

'Pupil response is the same,' he says to the nurse, but the whole room hangs on his every word. 'Though that's to be expected with the current level of sedation.'

The nurse's pen squeaks as she rewrites a line of Pippa's story onto a whiteboard hanging over the bed. Steve has spent several hours trying to decipher the scribbles and symbols, but they look like letters from the Greek alphabet.

Bramin addresses Steve and Diana. 'We can begin to ease off the sedative, to see how she responds on a lower dosage. This will be a relatively slow process – we don't want to risk an adverse reaction – but she cannot remain on these drugs indefinitely. Best-case scenario, she may begin to acknowledge or respond to what's going on in the room.'

'Okay,' says Steve. He looks to Diana, expecting her to begin questioning the doctor, but finds she has started to busy herself with the bed sheets – unfurling then refolding the hospital corners as if she were tucking her daughter in for the night, oblivious to the other people in the room.

'It's funny really,' she blurts out. 'When she was younger, Pippa was forever playing at being unconscious.'

Mr Bramin watches but says nothing, as Diana fills the space with forced chatter.

'She was notorious for it!' She laughs a little too loudly. 'The number of times we got messages on the machine from school. *Mrs Lyons, we thought she had fainted. We thought she was really ill! We thought she was unconscious*, et cetera. She just couldn't resist! If we were having a dinner party, we'd find her at the bottom of the stairs, spread-eagled, like the Lady of Shalott. Christopher would play along, of course. *What have we here, then? She must have been sleepwalking, Di. Well I never. We'll have to carry her up to bed, I suppose. Only thing for it. You mustn't wake a sleepwalker.* He'd pick her up like a rag doll, and off they'd go upstairs. You could see one little eye opening as he carried her out, to check on her audience. She loved the reaction she got. It shouldn't have been funny. People worried. But her father loved it. And I suppose I did too, in a way. Our Little Lady Fauntleroy.'

Mr Bramin smiles at her, but she is wholly unaware, caught in the safety net of the past.

'Sometimes you would just lie there for ages, wouldn't you? Playing dead.'

The room suddenly feels crowded.

'Any changes you observe in her level of consciousness, call me,' says Mr Bramin, patting himself down unnecessarily. 'The nurses will be checking her regularly. You know where the buzzer is, don't you?' Steve nods. 'Very well. I won't be far away.'

With that, he heads swiftly out of the door. Diana begins to tremble, as though his exit has invited an icy blast. Her voice softens to a whisper.

'But you *always* got up in the end, didn't you, my love? Eh?'

A tear falls onto Pippa's swollen cheek.

'And you're going to get up this time.'

Steve holds his breath, aware that the floodgates might be creaking under the weight of her suppressed angst.

'I wouldn't have made it through these last few years without her, Steve.'

'I know.'

'She saved me after Christopher died. She picked me up and brushed me off and taught me how to walk again. And I don't know if I've told her enough. That she's the reason I keep going. My greatest achievement, my finest hour. I'm scared she doesn't know.'

Diana looks at her son-in-law, burning pain building behind her eyes.

This is the invitation Steve has been waiting for. He walks towards her with open arms. She crumples into them.

'It's okay. It's going to be okay.'

'I don't know.' She shakes her head. 'I'm so scared, Steven. What if she doesn't—'

'She *will*.'

They are still for a few moments, until Diana breaks away, brusquely tearing a paper towel from a dispenser on the wall. She dabs at her tears, embarrassed by the uncharacteristic display of vulnerability.

'So. Tell me, Steven . . .'

He bristles at her change in tone.

'. . . while I've got you here – my prisoner – how *are* things with you two?'

'Erm . . .'

'I don't mean to pry, but you know what she's like with me. Never tells me a thing.'

She screws up the green towel and looks around for somewhere to put it. Steve gently takes it from her clenched fist and walks over to the bin, grateful for the opportunity to escape her gaze.

'Well,' he begins, 'we're all right. I think. It's been a tough year for us both, you know. The baby thing has been really hard, but yeah, we're doing all right.'

Diana tilts her head with a wry smile, encouraging him to go on.

'I've been quite busy with work and everything, and maybe we haven't talked as much as we usually do – you know, like, properly. But she knows I'm always there for her.'

He looks at Pippa, and a strange prickling begins to spread from his thighs up to his belly.

'At least I hope she does. She does, doesn't she?' He looks at Diana, imploring her for support.

'Everyone knows you love her, Steve.'

Whir, click, beep, breath.

'But I have found it hard,' he says, surprised how much he wants to open up to Diana. 'I thought things would be perfect for us. Easy, you know? Because we deserved it.'

'Life doesn't work like that, love.'

'I know, but it *should*.'

He's aware of how childish this sounds, but he doesn't care. These words, which have barely existed as private thoughts before, feel fully formed, and desperate for oxygen.

'We're the strongest couple I know. We worked at it. And we just . . . fit. And yet life keeps throwing shit at us. Sorry.'

'Swear away.'

'It's just not fair,' he says. 'I planned to give her everything. She's all I have ever wanted. But the last year, I think I've pulled back. I've been scared.' He taps his thumbnail against his front tooth, as if his hand is considering a move to muffle the rest of his speech. 'Scared of losing the most important thing in my life, because I can't seem to make her understand that she is enough for me. More than enough. I have never needed anything except Pippa. Never.'

Diana smiles, her eyes filled with tears.

'That makes two of us.'

Whir, click, beep, breath.

'Tell her, Steven. If she can hear us at all, then tell her. You're the only one she ever listens to, after all. The only one, other than her father, who can get through to her. Get through to my baby now, please.'

She covers her face and retreats to the window.

Whir, beep, click, breath. Sniff.

Whir, beep, click, breath. Sniff.

Steve turns the chair around and sits facing the wall behind Pippa. He opens his mouth to speak, but finds himself barren – he has said too much and nowhere near enough. Leaning towards his prostrate wife, he inhales the smell of her neck. That familiar scent of safety. He takes her left hand in his. Their wedding bands touch with a clink, as if speaking to each other in a hushed, private language.

'Tell me what you're thinking,' he manages to whisper. 'Where are you, Pip? Tell me.'

May 2017

Pippa

'Swear to God, first time I'd even *seen* his penis since KK was born, and bang – twins.'

Tania is leaning against the table, inhaling her fourth cupcake, judiciously balanced for fibre intake with intermittent handfuls of pretzels. The burden of her relentless fertility hangs heavy on her brow. Her vast belly protrudes like a conical beach ball, whilst fifteen-month-old daughter Kay is sitting up in her buggy, making an ants' nest out of raisins.

'No more sex. *Ever.* Danny can go elsewhere. I'm absolutely fine with that. Hookers. Masseurs. No problem. But if he thinks he is *ever* putting that inside me again, he's got another think coming. No siree.'

Tania jolts, her hand instinctively grabbing her womb.

'Man alive! They kick me like motherfuckers. Why did I give up smoking?'

I laugh. Thank God for Tan. Never one to toe the party line. She's always made it known that for all the gummy smiles and cute babygros, motherhood is fundamentally exhausting, sexless and tedious as hell. 'Oh, and you will never have control over your flatulence again.'

My God, I treasure her for it.

'Look at me, Pip. Where did I go wrong? Why can't I be more like *her*?'

I follow her gaze. And there, like a slow-mo hair-flicking

Wonder Woman, is Nisha. She is, as ever, doing two things at once, her focus split between a small Motorola in one hand and a sleek iPhone in the other. No one would know she had given birth less than five weeks ago. Her hair is shiny and blow-dried, her make-up flawless, her suit pressed, and her petite figure has pinged back into shape like an elastic band, not a telltale bulge in sight.

'I mean, where the fuck is the puke down her back? And that's *make-up*, Pippa! Bloody *make-up*! I can't even remember the last time I brushed my hair. You do know she's got two nannies?'

I didn't.

'*Two!* Two Norlands! Do you know how much that costs, for fuck's sake? One for while she's at work and another for the night-time stint. Apparently it was non-negotiable.'

Two Norlands. Two mobile phones. We watch in silence as Nisha conducts a virtual business meeting at a baby shower, ferociously texting with one hand whilst fielding endless calls with the other. It's mesmerising. I'm trying not to judge her. I mean, let's face it, it's kind of extraordinary that a person can spend nine months creating a perfect little human inside their belly and then, when it arrives, view it as dispassionately as a new handbag.

Tania lowers her voice. 'I'm guessing Freya gets a ten-minute cuddle during Mummy's morning espresso and then it's *s'long, little soldier*.'

This sounds about right. Nisha is currently oblivious to the child nestling in her uber-efficient nanny's arms.

'I'm just jealous. I mean, Nish hasn't let a little thing like a needy baby get in the way of her life. Whereas this blanc-mange before you no longer has a life to be got in the way of.'

Tania sighs, a deep, dramatic sigh. Baby Kay, as if on cue, throws a handful of raisins at her mum's belly with a dribbling cackle of delight. I bite my cheek in an attempt not to smile. Tania's melodrama is one of her finest qualities.

'Earthly greetings, sex kittens!'

And there he is. Unchanged. Untapped. Unfiltered. Our Gus. Six foot three of pleasure you can't measure. Legs longer than Naomi Campbell's, floppy hair the chaps swoon over, and a cosmic twinkle in his eye that lights up a room. Little Sidney is dangling face forwards like a dejected rag doll from the fluorescent harness on his chest.

'Finally got the hobbit to sleep. Now it's time for Daddy to party!'

I stroke the baby's lolling head, his golden curls feeling like feathers under my palm.

'So where's the husband?' Tania asks, scanning the guests.

'God knows; he did a Freddie flounce. We had a tiff on the train down. Something tedious.' He looks fleetingly downcast, then . . . 'But who needs a husband when a boy has wives!'

He drapes his long, tanned arms around Tan and me. I get a waft of his Fahrenheit aftershave. Strangely dated, but I love it. He has worn it since drama school. I feel a comforting rush of nostalgia.

Tania gestures at her empty glass.

'Well me and the beach ball need another bloody drink. Gustav?'

'Thought you'd never ask.'

She turns to me. 'Pips? You're looking a bit dry there. How about Gus and I grab two bottles and a bowl of Twiglets and we set up camp in the downstairs bathroom?'

Gus high-fives her.

'Yeee-ha. Bring it on, bitches!'

They turn to me, eyebrows raised expectantly.

'No. You guys go for it. I've gotta go and do my stint with Lady Godiva over there.'

Gus sticks out his bottom lip like a petulant child.

'Oh come on, Pip. Pleeeeease. A bender with you two was my sole motivation for getting my arse all the way down here. I mean, who's even heard of *Hartcliffe*?'

I laugh. Gus has always been so scathing of anywhere that isn't his beloved London. But I hold my ground, tempting as the offer is.

'Well you know where to find us.' He blows me a kiss and sets off.

Tania calls over her shoulder. 'And watch out for those low-flying knockers of hers. Could take an eye out.'

Jen is topless, sitting astride a small hand-carved nursing stool swaying to the music, a beatific smile playing across her lips. The left side of her nursing bra is flapping open, revealing a pendulous bosom. A large naked baby with an overwhelming mop of red hair is clamped onto her gargantuan exposed nipple. 'Life partner' Jacob, draped in baby muslins and a patchwork blanket made out of Tibetan prayer flags, is kneeling beside her, plucking his ukulele and humming to the tune of their joy. A sea of blankets and candles surrounds the three of them. I watch as chubby Wren ('first bird we saw after his birth') finally releases her nipple, eyes drooping shut and soft downy head sinking against her. I can almost feel it. Those tiny fingers kneading my chest. The slumped body a hot-water bottle over my heart.

Suddenly four-year-old Scout, dressed only in gold tights and sequinned cowboy boots, pirouettes into view like a whirling dervish, leaving a Hansel and Gretel trail of cake crumbs in her wake. She screeches to a halt beside Jen, demanding 'milky'. Jen happily agrees, releasing her other breast. Scout grabs it and sucks hard.

Steve chooses this precise moment to return from the

bathroom. I can see him by the door, trying desperately not to look at the milking festival under way. I watch as he turns to the nearest bookshelf, stroking his chin – the universal sign for 'I'm engrossed over here' – and lets out a loud, unconvincing hum to convey his oh-so-casual jauntiness.

Jen takes a deep Mother Earth breath, eyes trained on me.

'So. How are *things*, Pip?'

Here we go.

'Fine! Yeah, things are great.'

I must sound as unconvincing as I feel, because Jen raises an eyebrow. She pats the blanket beside her.

'Come. Sit.'

I glance at Steve, willing him to feign a heart attack, but alas, he is now nose-deep in *Crystal Healing for a Tormented Generation*. Trapped, I do as I'm told. It feels like I'm attending a meet-and-greet with the Dalai Lama.

'I know it's been a tough year for you guys. It has been a year, hasn't it? Or is it longer?'

'Yeah, er, more like two.'

'*Two* years! God, that's awful! Such a long time. And still nothing?'

As if on cue, a rivulet of milk spouts from her unoccupied nipple and trickles down her bare torso, as if to say, *here is womanhood, getting it right*.

I try to focus.

'Oh Lord. Can you sling me a muslin, Pips? Think you're sitting on one.'

I shift my weight and pull an already milk-soaked muslin from beneath me.

'Thanks. Just an absolute milk machine at the moment. It's insane. I mean, look at the size of these!'

She thrusts her naked chest forward, cupping a weighty

breast in each hand. She doesn't need to. I can see nothing else. They eclipse the sun.

'Sometimes I worry the little one's going to choke on my own milk supply!' She laughs proudly. I have no idea how to respond.

Scout decides she has had enough of her after-school snack and spits Jen's nipple out, wiping her mouth with her sleeve, then darts off to seek out her next course – Smarties.

'But listen, Pip, you need to stay positive. It's happened once, right, and that means it can happen again. So you guys mustn't give up.'

Twice actually, but who's counting?

She smiles down with a look of excruciating sympathy. I feel a wave of nausea hit my belly.

'Jacob and I have been thinking about you both so much. Haven't we, my love?'

But Jacob, eyes closed, is lost in the music.

'And we wanted to say, you guys should go visit Michaela at the Turmeric Wellness Clinic. She worked with some friends of ours who had . . .'

She is struggling to find the right word.

'Who couldn't . . .'

I tilt my head. Yes?

'Who were . . .'

I let her suffer. It's cruel, but somehow satisfying.

'. . . experiencing unforeseen delays.'

Christ, she makes our relationship sound like a rail announcement.

'Basically it's about unblocking those chakras and breaking down boundaries. Somewhere inside . . .' she reaches out and touches my chest, 'albeit subconsciously,' she touches my belly, '*you* are the one stopping this from happening.'

Oh wow. Did she just say that?

323

'You're tense. You're rejecting. Your body's saying no to that fertilisation!'

She pauses for effect, then shifts Wren onto her other breast, patting her nipple dry with the muslin.

'Michaela's work will help optimise your fluidity and juices.'

Juices! Is she really talking to me about juices? Save me, Steve. I glance over, willing him to suddenly remember we've left the oven on, but he is glued to his chosen read, head bowed.

'Let that egg move, Pippa! Let it dance along those beautiful tubes of yours!'

My fingers tighten around the hessian blanket. I know Jen means well, but I'm scared that if this goes on much longer, I may break something. She has begun to sway her hips on her stool as if demonstrating the motion of her free-flowing ovulation.

'It's all within. D'you see?'

I realise she is looking at me, expecting some response to her fertility monologue.

'Maybe. I mean, yes. I do. Thank you.'

'Trust me, you should call her. Michaela's amazing. She helps so many people create their safe body space.'

'I'm sure she does. We'll definitely look into it.'

Is she finished? There's been a few seconds' pause in the speech. Maybe it's safe to go now.

'Well I think Steve and I had better—'

But suddenly Jen reaches out and grabs my hand, her eyes filling with hormonal tears.

'I just so want you to experience the freedom of sexual relations, Pippa. Like Jacob and me. You deserve it all. It should be effortless.'

Jesus Christ.

She looks over at Steve, who is flicking the pages more

and more ferociously. How much of this can he hear? Her voice drops.

'And I can see he's blocked too. It's clear as day. He's all dried up. If you want, he can talk to Jacob. There'll be simple ways for him to increase the volume of his semen. Yellow maca can—'

And that is it. A red mist descends and suddenly I'm on my feet. She can pick me apart, I can take it. She can dissect my juices, my eggs, my tubes, my womanhood. But she does not get to bring my husband into this.

'You know what, Jen, I'm only listening to your bullshit because you've just given birth and I'm presuming you are chemically imbalanced right now.'

I kick off the blanket that has become inopportunely twisted around my foot. Take that, power stance!

'Also, much as you like to pretend that pushing something the size of a watermelon out of something the size of a lemon is an orgasmic, life-enhancing experience, I know you will have ripped and shat and screamed like everyone else.'

My voice is rising. The room is shrinking. Faces turn towards me in abject horror. Drinks are suspended between hand and mouth. Aha. Now I have Steve's attention. He is staring, willing me to stop. But it's too late. A floodgate has been opened. My waters have broken.

'You're not helping me, Jen. You're not even trying to help. I swear to God, in any other circumstances I would have been out of that door an hour ago. You're arrogant. You don't know anything about our lives. And I don't want to know any more about yours. Steve, get our coats. We're leaving.'

I begin to walk away, but shit, there's more.

'And put your tits away. There's no need to have them both out and you know it.'

*

The traffic is excruciating. Gridlock. Stasis. Blockage. Every-where. It's suffocating.

Our bus hasn't moved for twenty minutes, and that's twenty minutes we've been stuck at the scene of my crime. So close I am convinced I can still hear Jacob's bloody ukulele.

Steve is waiting for me to talk. I am waiting for a spontan-eous nuclear explosion to come along and obliterate all traces of me.

It would be for the best.

I'm staring out of the smeared window at the people pass-ing by.

Happy people. Normal people. Laughing people. No one who reflects this madwoman I can see splintered back at me through the glass. Sane, rational people who don't scream obscenities at a friend who has just undergone the miracle of new life. What is happening? When did I become the person who storms out of a friend's baby shower?

Yes, Jen can be galling; yes, we're having a rough time right now; yes, we are tired and losing faith and sick to the back teeth of this endless unfair battle, but we are stronger than this. Even that first brutal round of IVF didn't break us. We are the couple who can weather any storm. Aren't we?

I look over at Steve, his face pinched with concern, and turn back to the smudged window pane.

'I'm so sorry, Pippa. We can't find the heartbeat.'

The nurse's pretty face had gone pale.

'It's stopped.'

What?

'No. It can't have. It's grown. I can see. It's . . . it's bigger.'

'I know. I'm sorry. It must have happened a day or two ago.'

'Look again. Look again. It's alive, I know it is.'

Steve's hand squeezing mine. His colour drained. A panic behind his eyes and pain seeping through his shirt.

'It's definitely stopped, Pippa. I'm so sorry.'

Silence. And then a noise that came from beyond my being. Animal. Primal.

'You're wrong. You're wrong! You're wrong. You're . . .'

I can't breathe. My throat seems to be swelling up. It's like a boulder pinning me down, forcing the breath from my lungs.

'You said it was alive! We saw it. We saw it.'

I could tell I was scaring her, my body flailing this way and that, but there was nothing I could do. A lightning current of electricity was running down my spine.

'This is a mistake. Our baby is alive. Look again. Look again! LOOK AGAIN!'

I was retching now, the sickness of the last two months still bubbling within me. Bile on the sheet.

Time was a broken glass, shattered segments of reality skittering across the hospital floor as I unhooked my legs from the stirrups, the gel still wet on my thighs. The noise kept frothing from between my lips, a groaning sound from deep underground – unasked for, unending, unparalleled.

I was led from the ward. I think it was Steve. Or maybe a nurse. Maybe someone else. Escorted away like an injured animal.

Men and women, couples old and young, averted their gaze, trying not to look this face of human agony in the eye, in case it was catching. This poor, broken, destroyed woman who had lost any sense of dignity.

The next few months thudded by in a dream. Friends, family, colleagues – everyone had something to say. Some reassurance.

It will happen again, Pippa . . . This is a good sign. You've been

pregnant once now, so . . . Don't give up, guys. This is so common –
statistically one in three . . . I bet you, this time next month you'll
be . . . My friend, she was told it would never happen and then . . .

But our grief was paint-stripper for our souls. It was like
wading through treacle. We had fallen down a steep precipice, and no matter how loudly we shouted, how high we
jumped, how frantically we waved our flag, no one was coming down to save us.

The pregnancy had been a shock, both of us anticipating
a few years of frivolous newly-wed fun before real life kicked
in. But two indisputable blue lines on that dusty Cambodian
roadside had decreed that wasn't to be, and by the time our
honeymoon rucksacks were unpacked, panic had given way
to wonder and delight. The crackle of excitement was ignited
in us, and just like that, everything about it felt right. Random,
yes. Surprising, maybe. Unexpected, for sure.

But right.

We were ready. We were so ready. Like everything with
Steve and me, the universe was on our side. We were born to
be parents. And little baby Gallagher was going to be the
most loved child in the solar system.

Before the conception, I had never had cause to formally
introduce myself to my hormones. They were just things that
happened to me. Like a slick stage-management team, un-
seen, unthanked, unacknowledged, working tirelessly behind
the scenes to ensure daily life went off smoothly. They were
the mechanics bit of me that I never gave much thought to.

But Dame Pregnancy would teach me to take nothing for
granted.

Overnight, these oh-so-straightforward hormones became
desperate to make themselves known. This was their
moment! Their chance to shine! Day and night they partied
inside me, taking it in turns to hog the limelight, grabbing the

microphone, determined to make themselves known in a host of extreme and excruciating ways.

My small (but according to Steve 'bloody perfect') breasts were swelling by the day. My nipples grew and darkened like plum stones and were insanely sensitive; I couldn't let Steve go near them. I was weeping at adverts and falling asleep at bus stops. I was forgetting things, and losing things, and breaking things, and dropping things. Any sense of spatial awareness seemed to have been left on that roadside in Cambodia. The strangest things would turn my stomach. Oranges had to evacuate the building. Completely. Even the colour brought me out in hives. Strawberry yoghurt, a previous firm favourite, made me throw up if I so much as saw the pot.

An early scan revealed that there was indeed a little Gallagher growing inside me – hardly a surprise when my body was behaving like it had been invaded by an alien – and as we watched the seven-week baby dancing around on the screen like an animated musical note, we clung to each other in wonder.

The bus lurches forward.

'You okay, Pip? Can I do anything?'

Steve is watching me, clearly concerned. The glass has steamed up beneath my forehead. I haven't said a word during the long journey home.

I shake my head.

He continues, more tentatively, 'It's just, I was wondering – and no pressure, just an idea – but maybe you should talk to someone?'

I look at him.

'I mean, it's been a shitty time, and maybe some professional help would . . . well, help. Maybe for both of us.'

That sweet, innocent, well-meaning face. Reaching out to

me. Desperate to make things better. But my belly is still roaring with grief, my heart pumping the tears of the last couple of years. I whip around on him like a wild animal.

'You know what would help, Steve? If you just stopped trying to make everything better. You can't make this better. This is just shit! We are in the fucking shit!'

A collective inhalation from the top deck at this flurry of expletives. Steve flushes, but says nothing.

I feel sick, like I've just hit a puppy. I try to think of words that can make this better. Any of it. All of it.

But none come.

I feel like maybe I have broken something precious that can never be repaired. And then, when things can get no worse, it happens. Steve's phone rings on the seat beside him. I look down at the screen.

'Why the hell is Lola ringing you?'

Silence.

'Steve. Please tell me why your ex-girlfriend is calling you.'

He looks at me, pleading.

'Look, you know I hate to keep anything from you, Pip.'

The world seems to be slowing around me. I can hear the thud of my pulse beating in my temples. Those are not words a wife wants to hear.

'She just asked me to do a bit of work for her. A few months back.'

A pain in my temples.

'I wanted to tell you straight away, but you were – *we* were – struggling a bit and I just . . . well, I couldn't bear to worry you.'

I am staring at him.

'Not that there is anything to worry about! Nothing. Christ, Pip! I swear. She offered me some photographic work for her magazine, and with everything we've got coming up – I mean the treatment and all – I just wasn't in a position, financially, to say no.'

My breathing is ragged now. I have to get off the bus. Steve and Lola. Lola and Steve.

'I was going to tell you, Pip. I was. I just thought I would wait till you were feeling a bit stronger. You have to believe me.'

I feel like I'm drowning. Steve has lied to me. My Steve. My best friend.

'I've only done two sessions. And she wasn't even there, I swear. She just needed someone to shoot a gallery opening, and thought of me. I was going to tell you, but it was the week you had that late period and you thought . . . we thought, maybe . . .'

He trails off.

I know what we thought.

I remember that night like it was yesterday. Weeping uncontrollably as I sat on the toilet, pyjamas round my ankles. The bright streak of unwelcome blood on the toilet paper like crimson tears.

Steve came in and put his arms around me, reassured me and told me we were just beginning. That there was nothing to fear. That our baby would come when the time was right. He carried me to bed and kissed me tenderly and stroked my hair until I finally stopped crying and fell asleep.

Yes. I remember that night.

I grab my bag and ring the buzzer. Once, twice, three times.

He hates it when people ring the bus bell more than once.

I ring it a fourth time, eyeballing him as I do so.

'What are you doing, Pip? This isn't us. Come on. Let's talk. Please.'

A fifth time, just for effect.

'I'll see you at home.'

I get up quickly and swing down the steep stairs. I almost lose my balance.

'Pip, wait. I'll come with—'

But the double doors squeak open and I'm off, running down the street away from him.

I never run away from him. Only towards him.

And yet right now, I have to be alone.

2 March 2019

11:39

'Hang on, Suz, I'm losing you.'

Diana is speaking to her sister in Perth, talking loudly into her iPad, mouth flat against the screen as if its microphone were buried deep inside.

'The Wi-Fi here is erratic. It's NHS, not really meant for this, I guess. Are you on a beach?'

The tinny voice coming from the other end is burying a splinter in Steve's head.

'Just a minute, Suz. I'm moving outside, but the battery might go any minute.' Diana bustles from the room, her voice fading as she turns the corner. 'Any better?'

He breathes out, grateful for the momentary respite.

Whir, beep, click, breath.

He looks to Pippa's phone, which has been charging on the bedside table. He gets to his feet and stretches. His joints feel knotted and old. Without thinking, he unplugs her phone and switches it on, and the home screen lights up in front of him.

There she is. A moment of pure happiness. An invite to a friend's parents' house to visit a litter of puppies. Pippa delirious as she lay flat on the kitchen floor, her head as close as possible to the jumble of tiny scruff-balls. A soft pile of wagging tails, wet noses and scrabbly oversized paws. As they chewed on her ponytail, scrambling over her head, she looked up at him, euphoric. Steve took a photo that captured the moment perfectly. He presses the phone to his chest with a desire to absorb this version of her into his heart. Then, in a flurry of bleeps and vibrations, the phone burst back to life like a firework.

He knows her passcode, it's the same for everything, so he unlocks the screen just to see what's there.

3 missed calls.

425 unread emails.

Notifications from group chats rising in number like a malfunctioning stock market ticker.

Then his heart lurches as he spots an unfinished text message. To him.

How could you

As he stares at the three words, panic gnaws his belly with piranha teeth.

'How could I *what*, Pip?'

He grabs the large plastic pouch left by the police, frantic for clues, and tips the contents onto the floor, then crouches down, manically sifting through them. Hairbrush, magazine, door keys, water bottle. Standard. But then . . . perfume, high heels, lacy bra and a pair of knickers he hasn't seen before? Stockings and her wedding negligee? *Massage oil?* Numb, he looks up from the items on the floor towards his wife in the bed and back again.

'Oh Pippa. Tell me this isn't what it looks like.'

Visions of his wife flicker in front of his eyes. Pippa dressed in the underwear, a seductive smile on her lips. The curve of her waist, her breasts clinging to the silk negligee, her finger pressed to her lips. The images flash faster, an old-fashioned flip book. An unknown person enters. A man. He walks towards her and takes her in his arms. She looks up, her mascaraed eyelashes fluttering shut, and—

Steve jumps to his feet.

Whir, beep, click, breath.

He swallows down on the metallic bile rising in his throat.

'I won't believe it. I won't. *Where were you going?*'

The door swings open behind him. Tania's pale face peeks round the door. Steve realises he was shouting.

'I . . . I saw Diana leave,' she says timidly. 'I can come back.'

'No, it's fine,' Steve says, turning away to compose himself. 'Come in, come in.'

Tania inches into the room.

'Actually, Tan, I could use some air. Can you stay with her for a minute?'

Tania looks at him, eyes widening. For once, she is utterly lost for words.

'It's okay. Just talk to her. About anything.' And he bolts from the room, Pippa's phone in hand.

Tania shuffles forward nervously. As she reaches the bed, she grips the railing, her bloodless knuckles as white as the sheets. She barely blinks as she takes in her best friend. Pippa, whose hair shines like autumn conkers. Pippa, whose smile lights up the darkest night. Pippa, who has been there through every heartache, fury and joy. Pippa, godmother to her children.

'Oh God, Pip.'

Her head snaps away, her eyes screw up. She has to steel herself before turning back.

'Sorry. Hey there. Got rid of the hubby for a minute. Just you and me, missus. Old school.'

She takes a deep breath and raises her arm in their BFFFE salute.

'Come on, mate. Don't leave me hanging.'

Whir, beep, click, breath.

She lowers her arm and finally allows herself to look properly. A sharp needle scratches its way down her chest as she surveys the damage.

'Well, this is a new look for you. I must say the purple eye-shadow really works. I would never have thought it was your colour, but it really brings out the freckles. And I'm loving the tubes. Very cyberpunk.'

Whir, beep, click, breath.

'KK loves the unicorn onesie you got her. Literally won't take it off. Bathtime is interesting. Danny caved the other night – I went in and found him bathing her in it. Yep, we're smashing the parenting this end.'

Whir, click, beep, breath.

Perhaps it is the pools of shadow in Pippa's sunken cheeks. Perhaps it is the stillness of her ever-moving hands. Perhaps it is the chapped lips sucking for air, but Tania suddenly begins to shake uncontrollably.

'Jesus, Pips. This is my fault. This is all my fault.'

She tries to breathe through her nose to steady herself.

'I knew something was wrong last night. I just felt it. And now you're here. I could have done something. I could.'

She gently touches her best friend's fingers.

'I told you to go. It was my idea. You wouldn't have been driving anywhere if it wasn't for me. I got your message and I tried to get back to you – I *swear* I did – but the kids were just impossible. KK wouldn't let me out of her sight and the twins were chaos and Danny was at a work thing and . . .'

She stops, running out of road.

'But I should have been there. You're always there for me. Always. And the one time you really needed me, I let you down.'

She feels like she's swallowing a piece of stale bread, and reaches for the plastic cup of water, which she drinks shakily.

'I don't know what to do,' she says in a rasping whisper. 'What to say to you. How to be.'

She looks beyond the door, but Steve has yet to return.

'You have to be okay, Pips. I have no idea what I would do if you weren't here.'

A gulp. Her voice drops so low, it is barely a whisper.

'You're irreplaceable.'

February 2019

Pippa

It's a supremely fine line. I mean, look, of course I want it to be *accurate* – it's called 'life drawing' after all – but I don't want to cause offence. I'm going for *just accurate enough*. If that's a thing. Poor pasty Patrick seems a rather shy guy, eyes to the ground, shoulders hunched, posture apologetic. Even the way he dropped his white towel to the floor at the get-go was less 'Look at me!' and more 'Sorry, everyone, this is all I've got.'

Strange career choice for an introvert.

But then again, maybe not.

Perhaps by taking off all your clothes, by ridding yourself of your daily armour, your commonplace camouflage, you are laying yourself bare. People can no longer try to dig and delve and work you out. There is no point in strangers probing for hidden truths or unspoken answers, because you've got there first.

You've stood there and shown them all that you are and all that you ever will be.

Wow.

Actually it's kind of clever.

Maybe it's the perfect job for someone wanting to hide in plain sight. No one asks you any questions.

I take it back. Hats and Y-fronts off to you, Patrick.

Back to the task in hand. (Well, fortunately not *in* hand – that would be discombobulating. More *of* hand.) I am holding my pencil out in front of me, with one eye shut in the way

I've seen real artists do in books or on the telly. Something to do with achieving perspective, I think. I, however, have no idea what perspective I'm hoping to achieve, and therefore I just remain fixed in that position for a moment or two, looking resolutely thoughtful. Beside me Tania is perched on a high wooden stool, her demeanour as serious as her commitment. She is dressed in a floaty boho kaftan and yellow silk turban, every inch the artist.

Never knowingly undersold, our Tan. Jumps in with both feet, dressed for the part no matter what it entails. Head to toe lycra for summer sports camps, castanets and flamenco skirt for Spanish lessons. It's one of the many things I adore in her.

One eye glued shut, she too is consulting her pencil with expert ignorance, wafting it around in front of her face like a conductor's baton. All attention is focused on pasty Patrick's penis. By my calculation, it appears to come to about a quarter of the way up my pencil. I mark the spot with my thumbnail and then carefully lay the chewed pencil against my easel.

Holy smoke! That can't be right. Proportionally it looks like an arm! Or maybe I've drawn his arms to look proportionally like penises.

Truth is, I'm no expert when it comes to penis size. It's not something I've thought about with any real dedication. It always annoys me that women's magazines would have you believe we talk of little else, but in my experience (which, granted, is far from extensive), I reckon it's kind of irrelevant. Surely it's more about teamwork? How people's bodies react to each other in any given moment, not who has what or the bigger the better. I mean, I know I got lucky with Steve. We just seemed to fit, right from the start. There were never any awkward moments, no niggles or pain or embarrassment. It was as though our bodies knew they were destined to hang out together for a long, long time, so they decided they may as well be friends.

Good God, the studio is sweltering. I roll up my sleeves, aware that sweat is forming on my brow and gathering behind my knees. The ponytailed man on my left has taken off his personalised plimsolls and pop socks and is blowing out his cheeks like an impatient racehorse. I try not to look at the state of his feet, which are cracked and flaking and letting off a pungent waft of stagnant pond water. I don't want to make a fuss, but I am positioned *directly* in the line of fire. The stench is being circulated by the fan heaters installed for the model's comfort, making it more Bikram yoga studio than art class.

Creative Retreats at the Crafty Hen House. That was what it said. An innocuous-enough-looking flyer that Tania jauntily handed over with our post-jog glass of wine, casual as you like. I skimmed it and was about to do the requisite piss-taking (*Which losers actually go to these things? Wow! Let's organise a* massive *party there. Looks a blast*) when I glanced up and saw that her expression was deadly serious.

'We're going.'

'We're . . .'

'Last weekend of Feb. You're all mine. You need a change of tempo, Pips. And don't start pretending to look in your diary and saying you're busy, because we both know that would be bollocks. Your social life is as dry as your sex life right now.'

I open my mouth to indignantly refute this claim, but swiftly shut it again realising I can't.

It *is* dry. We have sex twice a month, and only when the ovulation sticks decree it.

'I've done a ton of research, and apparently art and creativity are good for anxiety. Count yourself lucky – we were one click away from a week in a holistic spiritual centre in Newton Abbot run by the Hari Krishnas. So there.'

And that's how we ended up here, sharing creaky bunk beds in a wisteria-strewn pile in Northamptonshire, along with an eclectic gaggle of fine-haired menopausal women and beardy plimsolled men, measuring poor Patrick's penis with stubby HBs and counting down the hours till we can go home.

I mean, Tania wasn't wrong. It has been a shit few months, and she's probably right to be worried about me. I'm exhausted. I haven't been sleeping. Not really. Not that proper invigorating sleep where you wake up and feel anything is possible. Each night has felt like my sheet and duvet are in cahoots, intent on entangling me, dragging me down, pinning me to the mattress. I'm too hot, too cold, too crampy, too awake. As I toss from side to side, the sheets just strengthen their grip. It's like I'm flailing in quicksand and I should lie still because everyone knows fighting it just makes it worse, but it's impossible. I can't go down without a fight. It's instinct.

'Psst, Pip!' I turn to Tania, who is now gesturing to her sketchpad, a gleeful grin flickering at the corners of her mouth. I follow her twinkling eyes to the source of her delight.

Patrick has been awarded an insanely long phallus. I snort and hold my nose in an attempt to suppress the wave of childish hysteria that is threatening to engulf me. Tania sees this and, as always, relishes pushing me closer to the precipice of no return. She leans closer, whispering, 'Working title – *Patrick the Human Tripod*!'

We are back at school, the giggles rising up from our unpolished shoes, under our laddered tights, through our eternally hungry bellies, over our futile sports bras, into our tangled ponytails, threatening to take us down and render us broken on the classroom floor. The more focus that goes into suppressing the wave, the more graphic the thoughts of decapitated family members, starving children in Africa, beloved pets being flattened by lorries, the more the laughter multiplies and bubbles within us.

As this childish euphoria washes through my veins, I become acutely aware that I haven't felt this sensation for ages. The rippling abandon that frees your mind and unchains your heart. That sense of floating inches above the ground, untouchable. Like you are existing inside a child's bubble blown from a bendy plastic wand. Free as the air. In fact, I can't remember the last time I laughed until my cheeks hurt.

I look up and see the beautiful Ghanaian woman opposite me waving her hand at the tutor, trying to get her attention. She stands up slowly, and it's not until she emerges from behind her canvas that I see it. A perfectly swollen belly pressing against the thin fabric of her cotton dress. A mystical dome holding the untold tale of a new life. She looks calm and powerful and womanly.

The bubble pops.

The euphoric tide subsides.

I stop laughing.

Maybe it's the heat of the room, or the lack of sleep, but I am finding it hard to breathe. Gold spots gather behind my eyelids, each breath becoming shallower, like I am being slowly submerged in hot oil. My pencil falls from my fingers and I'm scared I might topple off my stool. I turn to Tania for help, but she is already there. Without a word, she has one arm wrapped around my waist and the other hooked under my armpit and is leading me out of the room.

'You're okay, my love. Just breathe for me. In and out. In and out.'

I can feel the other class members trying not to look at us.

No one wants to be a rubbernecker, slowing their vehicle to witness all the gory details of a car crash.

'Come on. Let's get you outside.'

She guides me down the hallway. Gently. Slowly. As though I'm an ailing patient in a nursing home.

'Too bloody hot in there, wasn't it? Miracle we weren't all dropping like flies! I'm getting you a Fanta.'

There are certain moments that define a friendship, and this feels like one of them. She knew. She knew exactly what was happening inside me just then, and how much I loathe myself right now.

I'm fearful of the irrational person I've become. A person having a panic attack at the sight of a pregnant woman.

But Tania shows no judgement, no criticism. Only care.

We sip our canned drinks on the courtyard bench in silence, relishing the cold fizzy liquid as the bubbles pop against the roof of our mouths, making our eyes water. Signs of spring budding on the bushes and trees. A shard of sunlight piercing the clouds. I can feel Tania's concerned gaze on me, but she remains silent. The only sound is the rustling of trees and the hammering of a lone woodpecker on the other side of the valley. The tightness in my chest eases a little as I am struck by the miraculous peace of the English countryside.

All of a sudden, a lone princely stag emerges from the car park. He swaggers past, bold as brass, tilting his antlers towards us like he's doffing his cap. So close we could almost reach out and touch him. We watch in awed silence, enchanted, as he saunters off into the forest.

'Ooh. Wait!'

Tania suddenly reaches into her handbag and pulls something out, dangling it between her thumb and forefinger.

'You're welcome.'

I look over.

Bootlaces. Fizzy strawberry bootlaces.

For as long as I can remember, these have been our thing. No birthday present complete, no cinema outing satisfactory, no apology accepted without a bag of strawberry bootlaces marching alongside. I smile as she counts out seven laces each onto our laps.

'*Five is too few, ten too greedy.* Thought these might come in handy with all that vegan muck they're serving us.'

She sucks on one end of a lace, deftly wrapping the other around her thumb like the dexterous pro she is.

'Mmm. Sheer unadulterated E numbers. What more could a girl want?'

A gentle breeze lifts some early blossom from the branch of the cherry tree. It floats down, landing by my shoe as an offering. I pick up the petals and rub them through my palm like confetti. Tania waits, knowing words will come when I'm ready.

Finally . . .

'It's just not getting easier, Tan. I think I'm feeling stronger, and then boom – I'm back to square one. And it's not just the baby thing. Though that's massive, of course. All-consuming sometimes.'

She places her hand over mine but says nothing, and all at once, like a floodgate smashing open, the words begin to spew from my mouth, tripping over each other in a frantic bid to reach the light.

'Sometimes the sadness feels like a silent tumour, pervading every inch of my being. Like I've let an angry homeless man into my house and now I can't get him out. Like he's claimed the place as his own.'

Tania swallows. I can feel how much she wants to make me laugh, make me forget. It's palpable. But she holds back.

Deep down she knows I need this – have needed it for months. I need to talk, to be listened to. To be heard. It's almost as though I am in a trance. I know she's there. I know we are together, but for once the words are bigger than me. This is their time. Not mine.

'Because it's my fault, Tan. I invited him in. And now he's boarded up the doors. He knows a good deal when he sees it and has no plans to check out any time soon.'

She's watching me, eyes wide. I think I'm scaring her. I'm kind of scaring myself. I attempt to smile.

'Shit. Scrap this. Sorry. Let's go back in. Patrick's penis waits for no man!'

I start to stand up.

'Sit down, Pippa.'

Whoa. Whole name. We never call each other by our whole names. Whole names are saved for deaths and break-ups.

'Keep going. Eat your laces,' she lifts up a strand of strawberry, 'and keep going.'

I do as I'm told, letting my gaze drift to a branch swaying in the breeze.

'I always believed I was destined to act. But it's all gone wrong.'

'What do you mean?'

'I mean, look at you. You make money. You have a family. You've achieved. You got out in time and found another path.' (With typical Tania decisiveness, when acting stopped giving back she had jacked it in and promptly became an interior designer as if it was the easiest transition in the world.) 'But I was stubborn, I refused to budge, and now everything has ground to a halt.'

'That's not true, Pip. You had that commercial campaign last year.'

I raise my eyebrows.

'What? You were great in it! You were the best!'

One farcical series of online ads for laxatives. Even the unconditional support of my best friend can't buff this expenses-only job to a campaign.

'Come on, Tan. There's resting and then there's being in a coma.'

She laughs, relieved that I'm still capable of humour.

'Sure, *Quantum* was great but it's not getting another series. I have the odd audition, but it's always the same old story. "You were *so* close, Pippa", "they *really* liked you", "they've gone in another direction", "it's just so competitive at the moment", "something will come up soon". I feel like I'm in the slipstream of someone else's adventure, someone else's success. Does that make sense?'

Tania thinks, and then nods slowly.

'I mean, did we *really* practise tongue-twisters before breakfast every morning?'

She smiles, then chants: '*What a to-do to die today at a minute or two to two. A thing distinctly hard to say but harder still to do. For they'll beat a tattoo at a minute to two, a—*'

I cut her off.

'Was there actually a time when we scoured casting magazines for opportunities? Who was that girl who travelled miles across England on a bumpy coach to do an unpaid short that would never see the light of day? Where is she?'

'She's still in there.' She lays her hand on my chest. 'We've just got to seek her out, haven't we?'

I shake my head. I can feel the tears gathering behind my eyes.

'No, she's not! I can't find her, Tan. I can't. And believe me, I've looked.'

She puts an arm around me, and for a moment I let myself be comforted. I rest my head on her shoulder. I can feel my salty tears dripping on her kaftan and am aware that my nose is running like a tap. But Tania doesn't care.

Slowly I pull away and wipe my eyes on my sleeve.

'And Steve's doing so well. One up, one down, eh? And my God, I want him to succeed. More than that – I want him to fly! He deserves to. Honestly, he has become one of the best photographers out there. I mean, in the beginning he just had a good eye. But now he has real skill. Some of his photos take my breath away. They are simple. Elegant. Perfect.'

I pause and take a breath.

'I just wish he wasn't working with *her*.'

Tania raises an eyebrow.

'What, with Lola? Oh, Pip. You can't think that he would ever—'

'I know, I know, I know. It was years ago. And I accept that it was never right between them. Apparently he barely even sees her at work. It was just he was the only photographer she could think of at such short notice. He can't help it if he was so good they wanted to keep him on permanently.'

'It's a good thing. He's making proper money and proper contacts. You've got nothing to worry about.'

I let out an involuntary sigh.

'She's just so sweet and easy and accommodating. And I'm irritating and hormonal and stubborn. They have history and his family loved her. What if he wants to go back there, Tan? What if he realises what he's missed out on? I mean, why would he want a grumpy, insecure frump when he could have a successful, attractive gym bunny?'

Tania reaches out and holds her finger against my lips, silencing me.

'Enough.'

'I know, I know. I'm spiralling. I trust him. Completely. If

Steve says there's nothing to worry about, then there's nothing to worry about. He's never let me down. Not ever.'

'A-men to that.'

We suck on our bootlaces and I notice that the woodpecker has stopped hammering. For a moment there is total stillness, the constant chatter in my head temporarily quieted too. I squint into the sunlight, letting the rays warm my face.

'And I fucking miss Dad. I miss him with every fibre of my being.'

'I know you do, darling, I know.'

'And it's so shit, 'cos when I have one moment, one second when I am swept up in something – when miraculously I'm *not* missing him – I miss missing him. Sounds ridiculous, but it's true.'

'It doesn't sound ridiculous. Your dad was the best.'

'Because by missing him, he's still with me. Carried in my pocket, in my heart. He once said cancer wasn't cruel. It was brutal, it was tough, it was unfair, but it wasn't cruel. He said cruelty was deliberate, intentional. He said cancer was neither of those things. I try to cling on to him saying that when I begin drowning in how much I want to see his face or hear his laugh. Because the grief doesn't go anywhere, does it? Not really. It just hangs around like a groupie. It runs its fingers through my hair on the bus. It sits on my lap at the cinema. It squeezes into the furthest corners of my wardrobe, invades my sleep . . .'

I take a deep breath, closing my eyes.

Finally Tania blows out her cheeks and ceremoniously hands me another bootlace – despite knowing full well we have already exceeded our daily quota. But I barely notice, suddenly aware of what I've been trying to say all along.

'Because when he was alive, I had a *witness* to my existence. And now I just feel so alone.'

'But you're not alone!'

Tania leaps to her feet and crouches in front of me, staring intently into my eyes.

'I'm your witness, Pippa! I've always been your witness! See! Look at me! I see everything! Everything!'

She looms closer until the landscape is blotted out by her face. We are neither of us sure if we're crying or laughing.

'I know. And I'm yours. But somehow Dad made sense of me being me, and every little thing I did felt more real when he was beside me. And now he's gone.'

As if on cue, my phone vibrates.

Tania raises an eyebrow.

'Could that be another witness right there, m'lady?'

Missing you, darling. I'm hoping for the world's classiest embroidered key ring. Just putting that out there. Love you.

I smile.

'You've got *him*, Pip. Most people search their whole lives to find a love like you guys have got.'

I stare at the message. She's right. He is the best, the best of all things, but that in turn can make me feel like the worst. And I'm lashing out, hurting someone who is only good.

'We're arguing all the time, Tan. He suggests something, I disagree, we row. That's pretty much the state of play.'

'Sounds a barrel of laughs. Lucky Steve.'

But I can't crack a smile.

'You need to be feeling good about yourself to take advice, don't you? To feel *worthy* of help. If you're feeling pointless, then any advice feels like a dig, a judgement. Do you know what I mean?'

Tania nods.

'And he never asks me for anything. He just says he wants us to find a way through – a new path. He says he believes in us and always will. But the truth is, Tan . . .'

I pause. I have never said these words out loud.

'Part of me thinks I have to let him go. That he is too special. That he deserves more. He'll say he doesn't, that I am enough, but I'm not. I want him to have the world. Family. Kids. The lot. And someone else could give him that.'

My throat feels tight. My eyes blinded by tears.

Tania pauses for a long time before she finally speaks. She chews her lip. I know it's costing her.

'Do you still love him, Pip?'

'Fuck! Christ! I mean, God, I don't doubt my love for him! No way! *Not ever*. That's never been in question and never will be.'

She looks relieved.

'I think we can take that as a yes.'

I stare at my hand, twisting my wedding ring with my thumb and forefinger.

'It's just every conversation at the moment is a potential spark. Will it ignite? Will it spread? Our words can turn into an inferno in a heartbeat.'

'Everyone argues, Pip. Danny and I row all the time. It's normal.'

'Not with me and Steve. Not really. It's new and it's bloody exhausting. I don't think I know what a reasonable response is any more.'

Suddenly Tania's eyes widen and she screams in my face.

'YOU'RE A MAD WITCH AND I HATE YOU AND I'M NEVER GOING TO SPEAK TO YOU AGAIN!'

I jump away from her.

'Jesus, Tania!'

She sits back calmly and grins.

'If it helps, *that* would be considered an unreasonable response.'

And finally, I smile.

'You're a nutjob.'

'Thanks, old girl.'

She sips the last dregs of her Fanta. For a moment I feel like I'm done, empty, all the words flown. But then . . .

'And those hormones I've injected. I feel like an ugly fat pincushion. I mean, look at me, Tan.'

I squeeze the fat on my belly. Tania looks confused.

'Look at what? You're one of the hottest chicks I've ever met. What are you on about?'

'I don't feel it. All the poking. The prodding. The pills. The probes. I just . . . I feel old.'

I look at the floor, suddenly ashamed.

'*Old?* You're thirty-seven! You're a whippersnapper!'

'I don't know. It's like . . . it's like I've got a puncture somewhere. My body has given up on me. I fed it right, I exercised it. I tried to give it love and confidence, and yet it's rejecting me, flicking me the V sign like a moody teenager being asked to tidy her room. *What? Make a baby? Fuck off. No way. I'm not doing that.* And I feel so angry with it. With myself.'

'Right.' Tania is suddenly on her feet.

'What are you doing?'

'Up!' She's standing in front of me, hands on hips like an army sergeant.

'Tan . . .'

'*Get up!*'

I slowly do as I'm told. Tania reaches out and grabs my shoulders. 'These!' She wiggles them from side to side like an eighties dance move. 'Beautiful. Powerful. Sexy.'

'Stop it.'

She grabs my breasts. 'These!'

'Get off!'

'Perfect. No sag. Best tits out there.'

Two women emerge from the house. They must be intrigued by the borderline assault occurring in front of them, but in true English style, they simply will themselves invisible.

Tania places both hands on my hips. 'These bad boys!' She shakes me from side to side. 'Hot. Feminine. Highly shaggable.'

She spins me round, grabbing my buttocks from behind. 'And as for this masterpiece! Finest arse around, and everyone knows it. Excuse me . . .' She calls out to the women, who look up, pretending they have only just noticed us. 'One word to describe these buttocks.'

'For God's sake!'

'Come on. First word. No conferring.'

The first woman smiles. 'Enviable.'

The second ponders, closely studying my behind. Finally . . . 'Ripe.'

Tania applauds. 'Couldn't have said it better myself.'

The women give her a thumbs-up and head towards the lake.

'See?' She turns me around slowly and places a hand on either side of my head. 'It's all up *here*, darling. You can make this better, I promise you. You need to remember how wonderful you are. 'Cos I can see it. *He* can see it. Hell – even *they* can see it!'

She gestures to the women, who are disappearing down the lane.

'You're the only one that can't.'

Suddenly Tania's eyes fill with tears. She truly believes it. I can see it in her face.

'Do you know what you're gonna do, Pippa Lyons?'

I shake my head, fully aware that she is about to tell me.

'You're gonna spice things up. You're gonna get out there and remind young Stevie lad what he's got. And more importantly, you're gonna remember what *you've* got. Dr Tania is prescribing some serious unscheduled sex. A hot-diddy booty call is in order, and I've got *just* the shoes.'

2 March 2019

12:39

Tania sits next to Pippa, gently clasping her cold fingers. The silence between them is glaring, alien.

'I've been going through her phone,' comes a voice from the doorway.

She whips round to see Steve holding Pippa's mobile.

'I just wanted to see if there was anything there, anything I'd missed,' he says, looking fleetingly ashamed. 'I know I shouldn't have, but I read her messages.'

Tania gasps, the panic in her eyes palpable.

'I need to understand,' he says. 'Help me.'

'She didn't mean it, Steve!' She jumps to her feet. 'You know that, don't you?'

He is taken aback by her fervent reaction, but says nothing.

'She's been emotional, stressed,' Tania barrels on, stumbling over her words. 'You've . . . you've seen it, haven't you? She's been pushing us all away. But she loves you. She would never, *ever* do that. I'd never let her.'

Steve is confused, but something in him senses he should let her speak.

'She wrote me that message because it's been on her mind lately. The whole baby thing. She got it into her head that you could never have a family if you stayed with her. The family she so wants you to have. But she wouldn't have left you. She couldn't. You're her everything.'

She pauses for breath, focusing properly on Steve for the first time.

'*Left* me? Wait. Was she thinking of—'

'Shit.'

'She was going to leave me? Did she honestly say that?'

'I shouldn't have . . .' Tania flushes, mortified. 'You said you'd read—'

'I need to know, Tan,' Steve says, taking her by the shoulders. 'What exactly was she thinking?'

Tania looks from Steve to Pippa, racked with guilt at inadvertently betraying her friend.

'We talked a lot on our weekend away and I thought I'd got through to her. But then she messaged me last night. All it said was: *I was right. I'm not enough.* Or something like that. I messaged back straight back saying: *Call me. We will sort this.* But then KK couldn't sleep because she had a cold, and then . . .' She starts to cry. 'Then *this* happened. I thought I could calm her down, Steve, but I guess she never read it.'

Steve's legs buckle under a wave of exhaustion, and he flops down to the floor among Pippa's spilt effects. He picks up a small glass bottle.

'She has massage oil. Underwear . . .' His voice is tiny. 'Is there someone else?'

'Someone else?' Tania splutters.

'Just tell me. Where was she going?'

She crouches down slowly and looks him dead in the eye.

'She was coming to see *you*, you pillock. She had it all planned out. This was all for *you*.'

1 March 2019

Pippa

Pointing my painted toes like a femme fatale, I roll the first stocking carefully over my foot. *The First Stocking.* Sounds like a Sherlock Holmes novel. I can't believe I've got to the ripe old age of thirty-seven without owning a pair of stockings. Christ, without even *wearing* a pair. My drawers are crammed with pairs of practical tights, but something about the purely aesthetic sensual nature of stockings has always eluded me. And more to the point, wouldn't they be insanely uncomfortable? I mean, what's to stop them sliding down and bagging around your calves? Would 'hold-ups' *really* hold up? I'm highly doubtful. And suspenders. No can do. Even the word makes me come out in hives. But perhaps most significantly, at £25 a pair (daylight robbery), they are not conducive to an actor's bank balance.

No, I shan't be buying any more in a hurry. Tonight and tonight only.

With my tongue between my teeth in concentration, I proceed with supreme caution, determined not to ladder them. Toe, then heel, as Tania showed me. Wow. They do feel different. The new sensation of silky nylon as it clings around my feet, my ankles, my calves, my thighs. When was the last time I wore something with the sole intention of pleasing him? No, more than pleasing – of *thrilling* him. It feels like another lifetime. Back in the heady, beddy, garment-sheddy days of courtship.

The rising anticipation of surprising him dressed like a siren feels foreign, dangerous, nerve-racking and intensely sexy. I spray my perfume into the air and walk through it twice, as Mum taught me all those years ago: *Never directly onto the skin, Pippa. Waft and walk. Perfume heralds a woman's arrival, and prolongs her departure, so it's vital we get the balance right.* Steve loves this scent. It always drove him wild when we sat together on long car journeys with friends, his face buried in my neck, our limbs entwined like tangled seaweed; or huddled up on public transport, one headphone each, oblivious to anything but each other.

We would look at one another with that smile. We knew the secret. We knew what was waiting for us. We held the keys to the universe. Me and him. Him and me.

He would whisper in my ear, 'Christ, I need to get you home,' and I would feel the blood rush to my crotch. 'Your smell, your hair . . . you.' It must have been nauseating. I mean, who wants to witness that? But we didn't care. We didn't notice. There was nothing else. I loved watching his beautiful eyes change colour, like a spreading ink drop through oil. They would take on the cloudy, intense look of the sky deepening for an approaching storm.

The shrinking universe. Just us.

I remember it would take all of our willpower not to devour each other there and then. Sometimes I would have to physically move away from him. Sit on the other side of the bus. Try and think about something else. Anything but the feeling. The urge to undress each other and lose track of time and space.

Must. Distract.

Flick through a free newspaper.

Attempt a cryptic crossword.

Engage in small talk with a lonely old man opposite.

Look for something *incredibly* important in my handbag. Anything to get us safely home and into bed.

I slip my stockinged feet into the shiny black stilettos. I borrowed them off Tania. Who else? *Mate, there's no such thing as a booty call without stilettos, stockings and a mac. Entry-level seduction.* She's always been more au fait with this kind of thing than me, so I was a willing student. The surprise booty call idea, a mere kernel at last weekend's craft retreat, took shape rapidly, and now here I am, dressing to impress. Steve was working an event in a swanky hotel out of town, and was staying the night as it was set to wrap up late. Tania's idea was that I would be his surprise 'room service'.

I think Steve will be pleased. God, I hope he will.

The narrow shoes are pinching my toes already, and I know I will have horrible blisters tomorrow, but for now, they're doing their job. Suffer for your art, as they say. Well these shoes are the ultimate suffering. Even I can tell my legs look the part. Toned, smooth, long.

Yeah, okay. I guess I look sexy.

I run my hands over my wedding negligee, remembering the twitch of ecstatic pride as he handed me the crêpe paper package, a burgundy ribbon tied loosely around it.

'Something for our first night, my soon-to-be wife.'

That slightly nonchalant wrapping of a shop so confident that you would love the contents of your package, that they barely needed to tie it. And they were right. I had never seen, felt or worn anything like it. Simple yet elegant. Sexy yet classy. Maybe it sounds clichéd, but I think it was the first time I had felt like a woman.

I shake out my tousled hair and pull the belt of the mac tightly around my waist. Okay, there is a hint of female flasher. But I think (hope) in a good way.

One final layer of lip gloss, one bonus spray of scent and that's me.

As ready as I'll ever be.

Still can't quite believe I'm doing this. Am I going crazy? What if he laughs? What if he's asleep? What if he doesn't find me—

No. STOP. Just STOP, Pippa. For once, don't think, just do.

Tonight we will turn back the clock.

Tonight he will see me and be overcome with desire.

Tonight he will push me into the hotel lift and wrap his arms around my waist.

Tonight will be the beginning of our new tomorrow.

I grab my handbag, flick the light switch off and slam the flat door behind me.

2 March 2019

12:45

'Is that right, Pip? Was all this for me?'

Whir, beep, click, breath.

'Were you coming to see me, my darling?'

Whir, beep, click, breath.

'Pippa, talk to me. Please. I need you to tell me.'

He stands over the bed, her phone still clasped in his hand. Tania's words ricocheting round his brain.

She was coming to see you, you pillock. She had it all planned out. This was all for you.

If Tania is right, then all this is his fault. He reads and rereads Pippa's unfinished message, frantically searching between the words for an answer.

How could you

How could you

How could—

And suddenly, as clear as day, it hits him. Why didn't he see it before? The answer hiding in plain sight.

'Oh fucking hell, Pippa. You were *there*. You came to the hotel. You saw me with Lola, didn't you? You saw me with her and you thought I was . . . Oh Christ, baby, no. No, no, no. I told you, it's just work. I would never betray you. Ever. You have my heart. I couldn't—'

Beeeeeeeeeeeeeeeeeeeeeeeeeeeeeeeeeeeeeeep.

A piercing noise fills the room. Steve jolts backwards. Smoke alarm?

Beeeeeeeeeeeeeeeeeeeeeeeeeeeeeeeeeeeeeeep.

He looks around wildly for any sign of fire. Nothing. The corridor outside is empty.

Beeeeeeeeeeeeeeeeeeeeeeeeeeeeeeeeeeeeeeeeeep.

The screen behind Pippa's head flashes furiously. It is as though every gauge has been awakened, every button pressed, in a frenzied switchboard of activity. His attention is yanked back to Pippa herself as her back arches off the bed like a fortune-teller fish. She convulses, froth gathering at the sides of her mouth, eyelids forced open, revealing the whites of her eyes. He tries to hold her arms down, terrified she will throw herself from the bed, but is unsure how forceful he can be.

'Pippa? Pippa?'

He slams his hand on the emergency buzzer that Bramin showed him, and yells towards the door.

'Hello! Somebody! Help! We need help in here!'

1 March 2019

Pippa

Beeeeeeeeep. Our battered Corsa bleeps and flashes twice to tell me it's definitely locked. Well, that's the company line anyway. I'm pretty sure today it's just laughing at me – 'No going back now, Pippa! You're officially a half-naked lunatic in the middle of nowhere. *Bonne chance, mon amie.*'

It's not too late to bail. I could just hop back in the car, kick off the stupid torture shoes, turn Magic on full blast and drive away in a cloud of exhaust fumes. No one would be any the wiser. There's leftover macaroni cheese in the fridge and the new series of *Queer Eye* on catch-up. No. Be brave, Pippa. I ignore the delighted tauntings of my automobile and slip the fob back into my mac pocket. I realise I'm shivering. It's so much colder here. Baltic. Okay, I know I'm only inches off the M25, but I swear it's dropped ten degrees. I can see my breath streaming out in tiny puffs of crystal heat. My thin silk negligee that seemed such an inspired choice of attire in my cosy centrally heated flat now seems as ludicrous as a bikini in the Arctic.

Maybe it's Tania's chafing high heels, but as I look up, the distance between me and the hotel foyer seems to stretch out like chewing gum. And why is this bloody car park so dimly lit? I mean, don't get me wrong, in this particular instance I'm grateful for it. The fewer people subjected to me dressed as a Soho hooker the better. But for your average middle-aged, middle-income, middle-visioned punter, this would be a treacherous journey. Like crossing the Atlantic on a raft.

Not to mention the potholes that I have just discovered first hand, hitting the tarmac like a drunken student after one too many tequila slammers. Shit. Terrified that I've laddered my mortgage-crippling stockings, I fumble for my phone. I swipe the torch icon and it lights up obediently. Holding the beam over each leg, I survey them up and down, up and down – a weird nocturnal MRI. Miraculously they have escaped without injury. Not a stitch out of place. No holes. No ladders. No catches. Phew.

That's got to be a sign, right? That I'm doing the right thing by being here. For me. For us. For our marriage. Surely that's the gods saying: we saved your expensive hosiery, and in return you must now go forth and ravish your devoted sex-starved husband.

Right. Onward. Come on, Pip. Nothing ventured and all that.

I stand up, brush myself down and hold the phone out in front of me like I'm fending off an attacker. The beam pools around me, illuminating the surrounding area. That's better. A far higher chance of reaching my destination when I can actually see where I'm going.

So. Only this car park between me and a new beginning.

As I set off once more, I realise that any attempt at grace, sensuality or – let's face it – dignity is utterly pointless. Just getting to the hotel entrance in one piece will be a personal triumph. Any vestiges of self-respect were left behind in my now locked car. As I teeter along, part fledgling foal, part inebriated stripper, determined to remain vertical on my skyscraper heels, all I can see is Steve's face when he spots me for the first time.

It drives me forward.

Raising my face to the night sky, I feel the moonbeams kissing my brow. I smile, the stirrings of excitement flickering in my belly.

2 March 2019

12:47

'Please, she needs help!' Steve's calls echo through the long corridor.

Within seconds, three nurses have appeared. They rush to Pippa's bedside, closely followed by Diana, her face bloodless. She grabs his sleeve.

'What happened, Steven? What happened?' Her voice rises to a falsetto. 'Tell me! I don't understand. What's happening to my baby?'

But Steve can no longer speak. He's watching a scene from a film: a young woman fights for her life, surrounded by her petrified loved ones.

'Excuse me, we need you both to move to one side, please.'

A nurse ushers them towards the window.

'Pippa. I'm Nurse Parker.' There is calm authority in her voice, intended for Diana and Steve as much as Pippa. 'The doctor is on his way. We're going to move you now.'

1 March 2019

Pippa

'Good evening, madam. How may I help you?'

Bloody good question. And one I'm pretty certain there is no answer to. Who am I trying to kid? I'm not a temptress. I'm a wife. An out-of-work-actress. And right now, that's as far as it goes. I suddenly have absolutely no idea what I am doing here. Why do I always listen to the hare-brained schemes of my spontaneous best friend? Oh to be able to disappear, evaporate into a puff of smoke and slip down between the perfectly gleaming floorboards unnoticed.

Instead . . .

'Yes. Hi. I'm here to see . . . erm, well actually, it's complicated.'

I must just say, this place *reeks* of money. Expansive bouquets of orchids, scented candles the size of plant pots, the delicate tinkling of water features, the clink of heavy crystal coming from the bar.

'I mean . . . erm, I'm . . . erm . . .'

The concierge blinks slowly. His smile is unwavering. Any opinions are concealed behind an impeccably trained veneer of professionalism. If he is the gliding swan on top of the lake, I'm the flailing legs beneath the surface.

'Are you here to *meet* someone, madam?'

A slight lift of the eyebrow. A minute tilt of the head. That emphasis on *meet*. Oh good Christ. He thinks I'm a hostess, I'm sure of it. I change my strategy.

'No! I'm here for a beer!'

I realise I am shouting. And rhyming. Neither tactic lends me the credibility of a bona fide guest, but I plough on.

'Which way is the bar, please? For my *beer*.'

'We have two, madam. And a restaurant. The Hemingway Bar is at the end of the hallway, second door on the right. And the Savoy cocktail lounge is just beyond the spiral staircase, behind the velvet curtains. We have a concert pianist in there tonight. Which one is it to be? For your . . . *beer*?'

I can feel the colour rushing to my chest. I know there will be perfect blotches gathering around my clavicle, beneath my cheekbones, under my chin. Think, Pippa, think.

'The cocktail lounge, please.'

Shit. Should have said the bar. Bet the cocktails will cost a fortune here. But hey, right now I could do with something strong. Bit of Dutch courage.

'Very well. And may I take your coat for you, madam?'

'God, NO!'

The concierge's other eyebrow raises to meet its partner. We both know what is going on under this mac.

I smile sweetly. 'I mean no, thanks all the same. I'm gonna keep it on. Bit nippy out there. Need to warm up. Getting over a cold.'

Always too much detail.

'Thanks for your help.'

'You're welcome, madam. Enjoy your . . . *drink* with us.' He smiles at me.

Wait. Did he just . . .

Leave it, Pippa.

I head off towards the bar, trying to walk like a business-woman. I attempt a meditative chant as I have been advised in times of stress. These shoes are mere extensions of my feet. They are like slippers. I can walk with grace and poise. I am welcome here. Beneath my mac, I'm fully dressed. These shoes are mere extensions of my feet. They are like slippers. I can walk with grace and poise. I am welcome here. Beneath my mac, I'm fully dressed . . .

2 March 2019

12:49

'Windpipe is swelling. We need to increase oxygen.'

Bramin delivers instructions to the supporting nurses at a pitch somewhere between talking and shouting, like a sports commentator. An air of adrenalised calm. His eyes flick rapidly between Pippa's face and the frenzied monitors behind her head.

'I'm going to give her an epinephrine injection, please hold her steady.'

As they handle his wife more roughly than he could have anticipated, Steve has to remind himself that they have seen this all before. There are protocols they can follow, to bring her back from the brink. And yet every case is unique. The doctor will have to gamble here, using past successes or failures as paradigms. Gamble with Pippa's life.

Bramin has prepared a large needle with two vials of clear liquid. A nurse rips open Pippa's flimsy gown. As the needle approaches her daughter's exposed flesh, Diana gasps and turns away. She cannot bear to watch, pressing her head hard against the window frame.

1 March 2019

Pippa

I hear the cocktail bar before I see it. The low rumble of expensive conversation and the dulcet tones of piano jazz filter out. Right. Maybe I will get us two whisky sours to take to his room. He loves whisky and I could use something to warm me up. Literally and metaphorically. The lighting is muted, romantic. Candles on tables and a roaring log fire in the corner. Heavy curtains and decadent rugs.

Once more, I am grateful for the dim lighting. Everyone looks about seventy per cent more attractive than normal. I catch a glimpse of myself in a huge gilt-framed mirror. Not bad. Hair shiny. Legs longer than I remembered them. I clock the free platters of nuts, olives and Twiglets on the tables and make a mental note to grab a handful of each on the way out. The mac has big pockets and I was too nervous to eat supper earlier, so my stomach is growling and tying itself in knots.

There is a polite non-queue at the bar – regulars propping it up casually, making small talk with their 'friends' on the staff.

'Another of your usual, Mr Lloyd?'

'So glad you approve of the new mezzanine, Mrs Treadaway.'

Ah, the shared geniality of the wealthy.

I pick up the heavy leather-bound menu and flick nonchalantly to the whisky cocktails.

Whoa! What the . . .? £24 for a whisky sour! That's almost as much as the stockings! Maybe we'll be sharing.

I smile at the barman. 'Hi there. Can I please get . . .'

And then I hear it. That hiccuping laugh. That sound that nourishes my heart. Unmistakable. Unmissable. Unforgettable.

Steve.

But he mustn't see me yet! It would ruin everything! I glance over my shoulder, shifting my weight towards the group of large men next to me for cover.

This is exciting. Like a hot foreign thriller. I am finally the Russian spy in my own erotic novel. I scan the dimly lit room. Where the hell is he?

There it is again. Another laugh. It's coming from the other side. I whip round to face the windows behind me.

Nope. That's not Steve. Too old. Too fat. Too female.

Then suddenly I see him.

Half of him, anyway. He's seated in a snug near the fireside. His hair swept off his face. He looks younger somehow, dashing. My heart lurches with joy. I want to run to him, throw my arms around his neck, giddy with his scent. Sod the surprise. He's there! He's looking so happy. He's looking so handsome. He's looking . . . up at someone else.

Wait. What?

As the crowd between us parts further, I suddenly see it all. There is a woman seated next to him. Cosy. Familiar.

My shoulder blades begin to shake. An earthquake is rumbling beneath my feet but I cannot move.

She says something and Steve throws his head back in laughter. Proper belly laughter. The flickering firelight casts his face in shadow, but it's clear that he looks truly happy. Radiant. Free of the weight of pain and disappointments. The persistent furrow of his brow has gone, smoothed by her company. I watch as he gently removes something from the collar of her jacket. She glances down, giggling. And as she does so, I get a proper look at her face.

I retch, but my stomach is empty.

'Are you all right, madam? Would you like some water?'

I feel like I am choking, like the air is being sucked from the room. The menu falls in slow motion, landing with a thud.

Get out. Get out. Get out.

I stagger blindly out of the bar and across the foyer, and collapse against the marble pillar by the exit. I pull out my phone and begin to type.

I was right, Tan. I'm not enough.

2 March 2019

12:52

Pippa's convulsions subside, her body finally still. The kinetic energy coursing through her limbs just moments before has all but evaporated.

Another doctor has joined Bramin. They are speaking too quietly, too hurriedly for Steve to hear. Diana moves away from the window and takes her son-in-law's hand. They stand side by side, a pair of frightened children, lost in the woods, completely dependent on the surgeons on the other side of the bed.

1 March 2019

Pippa

The rain is sheeting down, barely dispersing over the windscreen before the next layer descends. It's like unconvincing film rain. That rain that you don't believe exists until it happens to you.

I'm struggling to breathe. Remember what Mum told you, before Dad's funeral: 'In for four. Hold for eight. Out for four. In for four. Hold for eight. Out for four.'

Or is it the other way round? Numbers are making no sense.

Nothing is making any sense.

What has just happened?

Is it over? Are we over?

He lied to me. Steve lied to me.

A sudden flash of Lola's beatific face as she gazed at him in the firelight. Devoted. Besotted. Perfectly matched.

His gallant smile as he spotted the speck of dust on her jacket.

The casual intimacy as he brushed it off, returning her to her customary state of sublime perfection.

What was I thinking? I'm a fool.

My outfit is crass. He would have laughed at me. The hormones have made me fat. I shouldn't be dressing up in negligees.

Has it always been her?

Even when it wasn't her, maybe it was?

I can't give him what she can. I can't give him anything. Why am I trapping him?

The tears are making it hard to see. They are dripping off my chin and onto the steering wheel.

And suddenly I can see a baby. Their baby. Oh Christ. No. Anything but that.

A dark-eyed, rosy-cheeked cherub cooing up at her parents from a bright green picnic rug. Lola is tickling her chubby feet, whilst Steve lovingly brushes some pollen from Lola's sundress.

I screw my eyes up.

Get out. Get out. Get out.

Try and breathe. In and out. In and out.

Maybe I'm wrong. Maybe it was nothing. Maybe I misread . . .

But I know that look. I'm sure of it.

It was not nothing. It was everything.

Perhaps I should have known.

Our Lola.

She is perfect.

Our Lola.

She fits into their lives.

Our Lola.

She always loved him. Maybe it only took me unravelling for him to realise that it was all a big mistake. He should never have left her all those years ago.

But when was he going to tell me?

What am I going to do now?

With one hand on the wheel, I fumble in my mac pocket. It's deceptively deep, and I have to raise myself off the seat. Finally I find my phone and toss it out onto my lap. Without slowing down, I slot it between the wheel and my left hand and begin to type.

BEEEEEEEEEEEEEEEEEEEEEEEEEP!

Shit shit shit.

I slam the wheel hard to the left. A furious driver sails past me, hand clamped against the horn, gesticulating, swearing, flashing.

I drifted into the outside lane and missed him by a whisper.

I immediately drop the phone and it lands in the passenger footwell. I wave my hand in apology, but he is no longer looking at me.

What the fuck was I doing? I could have died. I could have killed someone. Only idiots text and drive.

I glance up into my rear-view mirror. Jesus, I am a mortifying sight. Rivulets of mascara dripping down my cheeks like a tragic heroine in a French silent movie.

The hammering rain is showing no sign of abating. My windscreen wipers are on full tilt, but nothing is clearing my vision.

Suddenly a song begins playing on the radio. I hadn't even noticed it was still on.

Fuck.

No. Please. Anything but this.

Our song.

Barefoot. Standing on the tops of his feet like I was feather light. Swaying from side to side. One body. Not a sliver of air between us. Our bodies pressed. Our lips connected.

Smiling, whispering, laughing.

The tears begin falling again, dense as the persistent rain. I can't see. Frantically fumbling to switch the radio off, I only succeed in turning it up.

It must be love, love, love . . .

No!

My head might burst. Must turn it off. I look down, and my shaking fingers make contact with the dial. I push it off.

Better. For a split second I can breathe again.

But then there's a light so bright, I am blinded.

And then silence.

2 March 2019

13:12

Mr Bramin shines his torch into Pippa's eyes, raising the left lid, then the right to check for any response. Diana and Steve are still holding hands, the only energy they have left spent in the battle to keep each other upright.

The other surgeons and nurses have gone, and the room is calm, as if the cacophony of shuffled feet and whining equipment and raised voices belongs in another lifetime.

'As we feared, Pippa has suffered a seizure – a reaction to the easing-off of the sedation drugs, but her ICP is now stable. It's very hard to say how this might have affected her brain function, and we won't be able to assess that without another CT scan until – or indeed *if* – she regains consciousness. It's still a waiting game, I'm afraid.'

Diana sways on the spot, but it is the doctor who supports her this time. Steve watches as Bramin leads her out of the room.

'What's happening?' Diana's voice doesn't sound like her own, but then nothing sounds right any more.

'You've become faint,' Mr Bramin says. 'Let me get you something sweet to drink.'

Steve and Pippa are alone. He sits down on the bed and buries himself into the sheets with her, oblivious to the wires and the hygiene and the rules. Nothing matters except having her in his arms.

'Come back to me, Pippa. If you can hear me, angel, come back. I can't carry on without you. We're a family. Complete. We always have been. You're all I've ever needed.'

June 2012

Pippa

'You're all I've ever needed.'

His voice is muffled, distant, like he is whispering through a wall. I smile, my head nestled into his chest, enjoying the soft warmth of his slippers beneath my bare feet. We rock from side to side, like a metronome.

Tick tock. Tick tock.

I am at peace, suspended in a dreamland between wake and sleep.

Tick tock. Tick tock. Whir, beep, click, breath.

'Will you be my wife?'

Tick tock. Tick – what?

What did he just say?

He has gently stepped me off his feet. I feel cold without his body pressed to mine. Now he is on the floor, kneeling. He reaches for something in his pocket. A box. He flicks it open and there is the ring. My perfect ring. The room is shrinking. It's just me and him. Me and him forever. I nod, tears streaming down my cheeks. As he pulls it from the padding and slips it onto my finger, we both know it will remain there until the day I die.

Tick, whir, tock, beep, tick, click, tock, breath.

2 March 2019

14:39

Steve is fast asleep, wrapped around his wife. A deep, dream-less slumber. The tears, the hope, the grief, the talk has exhausted him. He has nothing left.

Diana stands by the window, chewing her fingernails. On the window ledge, a skin forms on a cup of untouched hot chocolate. She watches a group of wiry teenage boys below, football boots muddy after training, eating greasy chicken wings and brazenly tossing the bones onto the pavement. Young, carefree, their whole future stretching ahead of them.

The clock ticks.

Pippa lies motionless but for the continual undulation of supported breaths.

Whir, beep, click, breath.

Whir, beep, click, breath.

Whir, beep, click . . .

Her lips seem to part, infinitesimally.

Breath.

A young nurse enters discreetly on her rounds. She looks from the woman at the window to the man by the bed, remembering him from the night before. They are oblivious to her presence. She's glad he has someone with him. No one should be alone at a time like this.

She moves closer to the patient and is startled by what she sees. A bruised eyelid quivers open, then blinks itself shut again. Without saying a word, she slips from the room and runs to fetch the doctor.

2 March 2019

14:41

Pippa

Light. Shards.
Weight. Chest pressed.
Breathe.
Fingers. Locked?
Eyelid. Stuck.
Breathe.
Underwater. Bubbles burst. Engine sounds.
A car.
Dark, fuzzy head.
A man?
Head rises. Eyes widen.
Can you see me?
Mouth moving. Words distorted.
A woman approaches.
Scent. Lavender?
Her lips. What is she . . .
Buttons pressed. Room explodes.
The man.
Smiling tears.
I don't know him.
And yet . . .
There's something. A feeling. Just out of reach.
His smile. Warm. Like sunlight on my cheek.

I cannot name him.
And yet.
He feels like . . .

Home.

Acknowledgements

Thank you to our siblings, Fia and Jamie, who we would scale mountains for.

To our precious brother and sister in law, John and Cat.

To our superhero nephews and niece, Max, William, Oskar, Amber and Harry.

To beautiful Stella, who we will read this to.

To Jacqueline and Edward for their love and support.

To Charlotte Mills and Grant Gillespie for their early reads and encouragement.

To Katie Haines, the best literary agent, who makes you want to do more than you had deemed yourself capable of. And to Gina Andrews for her stellar assistance.

To Michael Wharley for photography guidance.

To Joe Lansley for the gift of his time and his invaluable second opinion.

To Mel Harris and Susannah Tresilian for helping us find Pippa and Steve.

To Jane Selley for giving the book a fetching trim.

To Bea Grabowska for her generous editorial help.

To Alara Delfosse, for her tireless and peerless work promoting the novel.

To Nathaniel Alcaraz-Stapleton, for his voyage round the world, and Flora McMichael.

To our beloved friends, our daily life support machines. You know who you all are.

To Sally Cockburn, oh captain my captain, for being the world's best English teacher.

A special thank you to Sherise Hobbs for hearing us,

championing us, then taking us by the hand and leading us gently into the strange and wonderful world of novel-writing, ready to leap.

And, of course, to Stanley, who all of this was for.

An Interview with Olivia Poulet and Laurence Dobiesz

Q: How did the novel come about, and how would you describe the story?

Olivia:
Larry and I wrote a radio play together, and then an editor heard it and approached us and asked if we would be interested in writing a novel based on the characters in the radio play.

Laurence:
It's a love story told from two perspectives – the characters, Steve and Pippa . . .

Olivia:
. . . and then an omniscient narrator in the middle chapters.

Laurence:
Steve has rushed to Pippa, his wife's, bedside. She's been in an accident. He's told to talk to her because she might be listening. And so he begins to try and find some words. He struggles at first, but then he's told to just say anything, say why you love her. The doctor also adds that the next twelve hours could be crucial in bringing her back.

Olivia:
And from there begins his dialogue as to how they met, and the journey through the beginnings of their relationship, and the heady, giddy courtship, into marriage, into the more complicated and difficult elements of a relationship, through

to where they are now, by her bedside, frantic for her to come back to him. Because through talking, he realises that . . .

Laurence:
He might reach her.

Olivia:
. . . and there really is nothing except her. And so it's a love story in its truest, messiest, most raw form because it isn't just roses and petals . . .

Laurence:
And bubbles . . .

Olivia:
. . . it's more real and it's the ups and downs. But hopefully along with a lot of humour as well, because life is awful and funny, I think.

Q: How important was it for you to tell the story from the perspective of both Pippa and Steve?

Olivia:
I think that, by telling it through two characters's perspectives, we're able to look at the tiny day-to-day aspects of relationships that make it very relatable. But in amongst that there are little moments of magic that make it a love story and make it unique. I think that it's quite tragic as well . . .

Laurence:
Yes, Steve's in a high stakes situation. Circumstances are fraught and desperate, but he just needs to reach Pippa.

And so he digs into his memories. And they're things that everyone goes through. As teenagers . . .

Olivia:

. . . fear of rejection, and hopes, and dreams, and wanting a family, and wanting to be part of someone else's family, and wanting to fit in, and not fitting in, and school days. And I think that's the unique element of the book is that we're looking at a full gamut of a relationship, well, up to age thirty-eight.

Laurence:

When we hear Pippa's side of the story, it's in the first person. So you have a sense of immediacy that she's almost . . . Wherever she is, however present she is, she's going through it. In the moment.

Olivia:

The idea is that Pippa is potentially going through that memory. She's in it, in the coma, whereas Steve is talking her through these memories. So his sections are in the past tense, which is quite a nice thing, I think, that shows the difference between them as well.

Q: What are the themes you think readers will find in the novel?

Laurence:

We've explored the big dramatic themes, but hopefully there'll be a lot of relatable instances for people of whatever stage of marriage, or relationship, they are in in their lives.

It's all those little moments, little mishaps that make up the whole tapestry of a relationship.

Olivia:
From that first time you tell someone you love them. First time you go to bed with someone. First time . . .

Laurence:
First time you board a London bus . . .

Olivia:
Yes . . . First argument. First holiday. And combined with the fact that things do go wrong in a long-term relationship, and things . . . well, life is tricky. And it's the people you surround yourself with that helps you get through these things. And I think that's what's quite beautiful about Pippa and Steve is that they are a team and they are a family. Whether or not they end up with children, or don't end up with children, or whatever. However their marriage pans out, they are a team and they've got each other's backs.

Q: What was the process of writing as a couple?

Olivia:
One of us would take a chapter and write it, then the other one would do a pass over it. And then with the middle chapters, we very much wrote them together, actually with two computers. Then with dialogue, we would play it out between us like we were writing a script and listen to it and work out what worked. And because we're both actors as well, that's something that really helped us.

Laurence:

Yes, we mapped out the story, the arc, and more or less the character arcs, the beats of the whole piece. And then I think we thought, 'What do we want to write today, which chapter in their lives?'

Olivia:

We would both go and sit and do our own writing, but it wasn't like I took Pippa and he took Steve. I mean, often it would be that one of us would do the first pass.

Laurence:

We'd start off with whoever had . . .

Olivia:

. . . the impetus.

Laurence:

. . . yes, the impetus and the inspiration. We'd go off separately, start, then ask each other how that was going, sometimes swap, rewrite, and edit, and then finesse. And actually, it mostly worked.

Olivia:

We had our moments, but fundamentally it was great. And we've got quite different skills, which helps a lot. I go away and come back with 600 pages and he goes and comes back with one brilliant one. And that worked really well, that we would be able to polish each other's. We're both good at dialogue, but he's very good at editing and saying, 'That's not necessary,' and I'm quite good at encouraging him to just risk it and write more. So I think it's quite a good . . . . . .

Laurence:

. . . process.

Olivia:
Well, hopefully it's a good process and a good partnership.

Q: Were there ever any disagreements on anything you'd written?

Laurence:
I think there were disagreements, but I think where there was a disagreement over a decision, or a line, or a direction you're taking in the story, there was usually a reason why. There was a decision.

Olivia:
Yes. So someone usually ended up sort of being right, because it couldn't go any other way.

Laurence:
I think it flagged up maybe a little bump where the story wasn't moving as smoothly or . . .

Olivia:
. . . or we were getting stuck in one bit.

Laurence:
. . . where we needed to reconsider another way through. So those moments are important and useful and . . .

Olivia:
And we wanted to make it kind of truthful. I was aware that there's been times where people have said, 'Oh, but Steve's so lovable and he's so wonderful, and Pippa's more . . . It's just, she's not unlikable, but she's a bit swept up in herself.' And I think that we were just really aware of trying to draw

a very real relationship. And in a relationship, it isn't always entirely equal and it isn't always that both sides are universally good and kind and easy with each other. And I think that we were both wanting to create quite real characters that had their flaws and their insecurities.

Q: Did you draw on your own personal experiences in writing the book?

Laurence:
Well, it's our first novel and I think it was probably a good idea to write close enough to what we know because it would be a bit mad not doing that. There's obviously some crossover.

Olivia:
There are things we've called upon in our lives, of course. In terms of their sort of love story, there's obviously bits of us and bits of our family . . .

Laurence:
. . . bits of our friends and our families.

Olivia:
But there's also an awful lot that we created and kind of padded out and changed and adapted because it wouldn't be the greatest story if it was just our biography . . .

Laurence:
. . . our biographies.

Olivia:
But things with grief, for example, it's something we've both been through, both understood and it was hard to

write about but it was a good thing to write about and that we could call upon. Same thing with best friendships and sometimes having some wonderful people around us who help us and pick up our pieces. And we used bits and pieces of our friends, only little bits.

Laurence:
There are moments and events, which some friends will hopefully enjoy seeing reflected by.

Olivia:
But mostly we wanted to create a love story that was Pippa and Steve's.